# A Place of Acceptance

# A Place of Acceptance

Gail Warren

Plane
Tree
Press

Published in the United States of America
Plane Tree Press
Bellingham, Washington

Photos, cover design & layout by good eye design.
julie@goodeyedesign.net | 360.714.8608

First Printing: June 2003
10  9  8  7  6  5  4  3  2  1

ISBN     0–9727618–0–2
Library of Congress Control Number:
2002096853

*To Chuck, Mary and Julie*

*and*

*in Memory of*

*Georgia Ruth Byers*

*This book happened because of many people who have touched my life. A few contributed in tangible ways to the completion of this novel. I express my gratitude to these individuals: Micki Gilliland, my editor; Joesephine Davidson and Urban Waite, for proof reading; and Lisa Lincoln, for her enthusiasm.*

*Chuck, my husband and unique friend, for his loving support, buoyant energy, and his prods during the writing process that kept me going. Our daughters, Mary and Julie, for their encouragement, but most of all, for their love and acceptance.*

# Chapter 1

Todd Keeley felt nervous about bringing Trevor with him to the service. He read the memorial bulletin and fidgeted with his cuff. Trevor hadn't known Nathan Woods who was dead at forty-five. But that wasn't the problem. Todd's apprehension centered with his family. Was he ready for Trevor to meet them, especially his father? "A wretched way to die," he whispered to Trevor. "I heard Nathan got the bends when he surfaced too fast." He wondered what had persuaded Nathan to try scuba diving.

"Sad," Trevor said. "You know him well?"

"Not too well. I was sixteen when he moved in across the street. He had his problems, but yeah, he was amiable with me. His mom liked me and she was always interested in my life and me. Haven't seen her in five years, but I came for her."

Todd folded his hands and sat silently against the pew for a few minutes. He'd seen his father and mother, seated at the rear of the church, as he and Trevor entered. How would they respond to Trevor? Todd glanced down the aisle, then leaned against Trevor. "That's my sister Kate and her husband at the end of this aisle. You want to meet them?"

Shifting his weight, Trevor looked down a row of people to a sandy blond head. "I think it's time. It's either that or head home."

"You think I've kept you hidden too long?"

"Long enough. What's the point?" Trevor steadied his pale blue eyes on Todd.

"No point, I guess. It's just easier, but I know we can't conceal our relationship forever."

"Right. Some day they'll determine we're a couple. Tell them we work together, I share the rent." Trevor tugged the cuff of his sports coat over his thick wrist. "It's true."

At the end of Todd's aisle, Kate sat with her husband, Dave, reading the bulletin. Feeling Dave's eyes on her, she turned to him as he spoke. "It took enormous courage for Nathan to try scuba diving," he said.

Kate nodded. "I feel sad for Florence. She'll feel lost without him." She scanned the front of the sanctuary and tilted her head to see Florence, Nathan's mother, who sat hunched in the front pew next to her daughter.

Giving a side–glance down the pew, she noticed her brother. Who is the handsome man next to him? she wondered. Is he with Todd?

Todd's mother breathed in the fragrance of roses that spilled out of vases near the altar, fresh from her yard. Her eyes sought the front where she'd seen Todd and his friend seated. His roommate? She thought she'd seen him with Todd before but wasn't sure. With the strain between Todd and his father, how would the reception go? she wondered. She watched the minister walk to the pulpit. Then she focused on the pastor's words, a grieving mother, a dead son whom she had loved as he had loved her.

When the service ended, the pastor said, "You are all invited to the home of Kevin and Charlotte Keeley, neighbors of Florence here in Portland, for refreshments and fellowship." Charlotte glanced at Kevin who sat next to her; they watched Florence stand and shuffle down the center aisle clinging to her daughter's arm. Charlotte felt her throat tightening; her eyes moistening with shared grief. When Florence passed, Charlotte stood with Kevin, felt his hand on her elbow as they left to ready the food.

Kate caught up with them in the parking lot. "Dave's going to pay the sitter and get the kids. Let me ride with you and I'll help at the house." Once inside the house, Charlotte set out salads. "You're good to do this, Mom." Kate's blue eyes smiled.

"The least I could do. Nathan was Florence's joy because he had time for her despite the setbacks of his illness."

"Is Todd coming to the house?" Kate set down the punch bowl.

"I noticed he had someone with him at the church."

"I imagine after his thirty mile drive, he'll want to see Florence." Charlotte brushed a blond curl from her cheek.

"I'll get it," Kate said when the doorbell rang. "Todd, hello." She put her arm around her brother's neck.

"Good to see you, Kate, despite the circumstances."

"Sad, isn't it." Kate gave Trevor the once over, noticing how arresting his pale blue eyes seemed with his thick black hair.

"This is Trevor Johnson, my housemate," Todd said, turning his smile to Trevor. "My sister, Kate."

"Oh, uh, hello Trevor, glad to meet you." Todd watched her eyebrows rise into the hair on her forehead as Trevor's huge hand grasped hers.

"My pleasure, Kate," Trevor said. With a side–glance to the living room, Todd saw his father pivot and go into the kitchen. He felt his stomach tighten at the same moment his mother appeared, smiling.

"Come in and find a seat. We have plenty of food." She touched Todd's arm, nodded at Trevor, then the doorbell diverted her attention and she greeted Dave and her grandchildren. Seeing Jonas, his brown hair with comb lines and Amanda in a yellow dress with puff sleeves, she smiled. She hugged them, but felt Jonas break free when he saw Todd.

"Hi, Uncle Todd." Jonas grabbed Todd's waist in a hug.

"Leave Todd alone and come with me," Kate said. She hauled Jonas off with his sister toward the buffet counter. Dave considered Trevor, then turned to his brother–in–law.

"How are you?"

"Doing okay. I'd like you to meet Trevor."

"Dave Winston, pleased to meet you." Dave grasped Trevor's hand.

Charlotte extended her hand next. "I'm Charlotte. You're Todd's friend?"

"I share the rent," Trevor said. Charlotte felt a nauseating stab of fear. A knock on the door interrupted and she welcomed more guests, including Florence, into the entryway. With her were her daughter and a few of the women from the garden club. Dave greeted Florence and helped her to a chair. Her daughter Debbie walked past the group and found Kate in the kitchen.

When Todd and Trevor entered the living room, Florence looked up. Todd walked to where she sat and bent over her ear. "Remember me? Todd Keeley. I'm so sorry. . ."

"Oh dear boy—how good of you to come," Florence said.

"I don't know what to say."

"Nothin' you can say." Florence clutched her handkerchief and dabbed her blood–shot eyes. She lifted her face and studied Trevor a moment. "Who's that with you?"

"This is Trevor," Todd said pulling Trevor's arm to bring him closer.

"Your partner?" Florence smiled. Candid as ever, Todd thought.

"Right, he lives with me."

Charlotte overheard as she passed to the kitchen. Partner? She took a teapot, telling herself she was imagining things. What was the matter with her? She knew Todd lived with Trevor. They shared the rent, nothing more. When she walked with the tea back to the living room, she looked at Kevin. He stood at the kitchen entrance, his deep–set eyes staring at Florence and the men. She wondered if he and Todd would ever be friends.

Trevor was releasing Florence's wrinkled hand. "I'm sorry about your son's death."

Florence's lips trembled. "Thanks." She wiped fresh tears from her eyes.

Charlotte poured tea in china cups, then returned to the kitchen feeling Kevin's unease when he stepped close to her. "As you can see the man has charmed Florence," he said.

"She'd love any friend of Todd's. You know she's fond of him. Take it easy dear," she said touching his arm.

When Trevor straightened from greeting Florence, he brushed his hand against Todd's elbow and mumbled, "Let's meet your dad."

Todd nodded and looked at Florence. "Please excuse us." He felt Trevor's hand usher him into the kitchen.

"Hello Dad," Todd said.

"Hello."

Todd tossed his head, ran his slender fingers through his hair exposing his high forehead. "I want to introduce you to Trevor."

"Don't bother. You disgust me." Kevin stepped aside and into the living room. Charlotte felt anger surge, burning her cheeks. She cringed when Trevor backed up against the sink. Kate studied the raspberries she stirred in the punch. Todd took a breath, filled a plate with food and sat down in the kitchen. He set his plate on the counter, and before he could spread a napkin, Jonas darted from his chair and plopped on Todd's knee, giving his uncle an enthusiastic hug. Charlotte handed a plate to Trevor, which he silently filled.

"Ready for second grade, sport?" Todd thumped his nephew's arm.

"Yeah, but I wish we could have more summer."

Kate raised her eyes, glanced at Charlotte when she saw Kevin's eyes turn toward the kitchen. "Jonas, get off Uncle Todd's lap," Kate said. "Let him eat."

Before the boy could move, Kevin stepped into the room. "Take your hands off Jonas."

Todd stood, slid Jonas to his feet. He thrust his plate against the counter shattering fragments of porcelain, strewing pasta and dip across the room. "Hell with you," Todd yelled. He bolted out the back door, which he slammed behind him, leaving the guests in stunned silence. Florence's hands flew to her face at the raucous disturbance. That dear boy, she thought. Trevor dared a glimpse at Charlotte who blinked back at him before he averted his eyes and walked out.

Todd stomped ahead of him toward the car. When Trevor caught up, he grasped Todd's shoulder. "I'm not riding with you. I'll drive."

"So drive, Trevor. Don't stop anytime soon as far as I'm concerned. I'm out of here. I don't have to take this garbage." His green eyes flashed.

Trevor reached into his coat pocket, found his keys and started the car. "Your temper didn't help."

"He started it, the jerk. He has no right . . . implying I'm a pervert. He makes me sick."

"It was ugly."

"I mean it. I'm looking at rental ads. Alaska has jobs for marine biologists."

# Chapter 2

Charlotte squinted in the light that glared off the sand. She wiggled her toes, felt the gritty grains sift through them. Six weeks had passed, and as far as she knew none of the family had heard from Todd. Nor had they talked about the incident with each other. She had not even talked with Kate, who had poured her energies into nursing. Rather, they'd engaged Jonas, keeping the conversation focused on school when he'd entered second grade. What had triggered Kevin's outburst? He was out of character, contemptible. Todd's behavior . . . she shook her head. She raised her eyes to look at the seagulls that hovered and squawked overhead. She held her hand against the sun, shielded her eyes and scanned the waves. This stretch of Oregon beach was delightful. The weekend was supposed to be for unwinding, she thought.

Her limbs felt leaden, but she threw out her arms, ran toward the tide, pushing hard one foot, then the other into the packed wetness, then glanced back at the molded footprints she had made. The memory of the reception still felt like a wedge driven through her heart, her family's heart. She couldn't persuade Kevin to talk about it. I'm part of the problem. I didn't interfere the moment it happened. I was a coward, she thought. I hate confrontations. Charlotte sighed.

She stooped, pulled her Reeboks from her pack, slipped her feet into them and continued toward the rocky shore exposed by a low tide. Todd's fondness for Jonas had been apparent since Jonas' infancy. Kevin had no right. She'd tried to contact Todd but the proprietor told her he'd moved, and handed her a changed telephone number. The one time she called him, no one had answered.

The gulls soared; the sandpipers skittered back and forth with the waves. Carefully she stepped to a pool. She bent over, peered into the water. Bright sea anemones, those weird and wonderful creatures clung to the rocks. She saw her heart shaped face reflected in the water and remembered past years when she and Kevin had brought Kate and Todd here when they were kids. They had reveled in their kids' delight at seeing the wonders of the beach: the crabs and clams, the mussels that moved in mass if you poked one with your finger, the sand dollars, the purple and orange starfish. These funny sea anemones. Now I'm a grandmother twice. She smiled at no one. Sunrise, sunset.

She stepped farther out on the rocks where she found the flattest one, eased down on it, set her pack beside her. The fall sun felt warm against her skin, though her body felt out of sync. When Mom was alive, my health was excellent, Charlotte thought. She felt a tear trickle down her cheek. You've been gone ten months. I could use you now, Mom. The beach isn't working its magic. I'm not relaxing. Stuck in the middle between Todd and Kevin is enough. Now this lump.

She brushed her breast. She'd felt a slight lump under her left breast nipple last night when she showered. My breasts are lumpy anyway, she thought, normal for me. Or used to be. No surgeries ever. No hospitalizations either, except for two pregnancies. "What if I have breast cancer?" she spoke aloud. Can't be. Our family has no history of cancer. I dealt with Mom's death, Dad's too, but this? Why haven't I told Kevin? Too personal, too scary. I tell him everything. Too angry?

She retrieved a tuna sandwich, bit into it and swallowed with a sip of diet Coke. I know what Kevin will say. Get to my doctor. Well. I'll call on Monday. I want to know, but my stomach doesn't. Kevin will accept me cancer or not, until I'm dead. I'll tell him at dinner tonight. He has the right to know. The gulls swooped, snatched crumbs from her sandwich.

She stepped off the rock, moved toward the sandier beach and began looking for sand dollars. Maybe my lump's benign. Anyway, it's premature to think otherwise. A happy thought. Everything seemed vivid today, aching in her heart. She looked across the white–capped surf to the horizon where a red kite rippled and dipped. In the distance, someone attempted to keep that kite up against intermittent gusts. She watched how the birds flew in flocks, how the sun glistened off their white wings, how they landed with a whoosh, pecked the sand for food, then whooshed again. I can never remember their names, she thought. Ordinarily she felt exhilarated seeing their wings etched against the sky.

Kevin sat on the jetty where he watched the tide ebb and flow; the waves gnaw the beach. Charlotte won't be angry with me forever, he thought. Something came over me. He pushed the memory away. He stood, stretched his arms and jean–clad legs, and breathed in the salty air. His body was solid, lean from diet and exercise. A few extra pounds at the belt revealed his sixty–five years, yet younger men could envy his physique.

Charlotte, he thought. She seems preoccupied. Is she wondering if we've lost contact with Todd forever and blaming me. We haven't heard from him, he thought rubbing his broad, clean–shaven chin. I haven't heard from my brother either. When Charlotte's ready to tell me what's on her mind, I'll listen. They needed this weekend reprieve. Earlier Saturday morning, they'd agreed on some time together, some apart. Despite being Charlotte's idea, it was okay with him.

With the sleeve of his sweatshirt, Kevin wiped the spray from his bronze wire framed glasses. The warmth of the sun on his back rekindled his memories of other excursions alone with his wife at the beach: the walks, the intoxicating roar of the surf, the crackling fires, the popcorn and love making with Charlotte. He remembered the family beach trips when the kids were young and so were they. Thirty years ago they had shared the exhilaration of winter storms during beach walks against gusty winds and biting rains. The elements had stung their faces and hands, soaked their clothing until it clung to their bodies.

The wind rumpled his short auburn–gray hair, threw his thermos against the rocks. Kevin laughed aloud as he grabbed it, along with his sack lunch. He imagined the dinner he would share with Charlotte at some romantic restaurant. He took an apple from his sack and watched the waves approach the jetty.

The smell of clam chowder filled the restaurant. "This place okay?" Kevin shut the door behind him, adjusting his eyes to the dim light. Charlotte looked at the candles on the tables, and saw a plate of halibut pass by in a server's hand. "The fish looks good. This is fine." They sat at a table for two and ordered fish for Charlotte and chicken for Kevin. Charlotte unzipped her windbreaker and hung it on the back of the chair. Their salads and bread arrived at once. She took a sip of water, passed the bread to Kevin. Dribbling olive oil and vinegar over her lettuce, Charlotte picked up her fork and took a bite. She watched Kevin tear his bread.

"I need to talk to you," Charlotte said.

"I know."

"No you don't. This isn't about you. It's about me."

"Okay, tell me about you."

"I found a lump in my breast."

"A lump? When?"

"Last night when I showered."

"You've got to get to the doctor right away."

"I know. I knew that's what you'd say."

"Of course that's what I'd say." Kevin leaned toward Charlotte. "How big?"

"About the size of a marble, small marble. You can check it out when we get back to the hotel."

"Why'd you keep to yourself for a whole day?"

"I needed time for myself. I'll call Dr. Morgan on Monday. He'll work me in."

Monday afternoon Charlotte walked through Dr. Morgan's waiting room that teemed with women and a few children. She signed in at the receptionist's counter, glad her gynecologist had squeezed her in the day she called. Was it so urgent?

She felt anxious and stared at the aquarium of colorful fish that swam through the tunneled caves, oblivious to the perils that patients faced. She looked out the window at the hospital campus where Dr. Morgan also practiced. Her mind whirled with thoughts. Todd had moved. Kate and Kevin weren't talking about him, and she hadn't dared to change the status quo. The garden women had kept Florence busy and Florence's daughter, Debbie, stayed with her at night. Oddly, Charlotte missed her spontaneous gossip. At least Kevin seemed alive again in a way she hadn't seen him in months. Somehow, the threat posed by a breast lump had brought them together in a situation they couldn't ignore.

*My knowledgeable gynecologist will examine me in a few minutes. I'll know whether my life will make a drastic change, if I have cancer, if I have long to live.* She felt a knot in her stomach and dried her moist palms on her jeans. The thought occurred that the ominous lump might be normal. The lab will test it . . .

She picked up a magazine. A sixty–eight year old man in a photo with his wife and their St. Bernard was recovering from prostrate cancer. Glad you're not Kevin, she thought, picturing him with their dog, Spike, fetching a thrown stick.

"Mrs. Keeley?" A nurse spoke her name. Charlotte jumped to her feet, followed the woman who turned her head around toward Charlotte. "Second room on the right. Dr. Morgan will be with you soon. Undress from the waist up. Here's a gown. Tie it in the back." I'm sixty–two, Miss Nurse, whoever you are. I haven't seen you before, but I know what to do, Charlotte thought. I've done this a million times.

"Okay," she said to the nurse and watched the door close. She peeled off her blouse and bra, tied the skimpy cloth around her neck. Then she stepped up and sat on the examination table.

She heard a tap on the door. "Hello Charlotte," Dr. Morgan greeted her with his deep voice.

"Hi." Charlotte looked up.

"A lump in the breast?" he said and closed the door behind him. His eyes studied her file. He was fifty-something with large features and gentle brown eyes. Charlotte felt no consolation today in his familiar face, his comfortable manner. Dr. Morgan's eyes met hers. "Show me where, and tell me when and how you discovered it."

"Right below the nipple. Uh, I found it when I was showering Friday night."

"I'll examine you. When were you last in to see me?" Who cares, she thought.

"I guess about a year ago I had my last annual check up." Why does he think my memory is more accurate than the file in his hand? Charlotte wondered with irritation. She waited briefly until the nurse appeared. Charlotte laid back and Dr. Morgan examined her left breast where she had indicated. She noticed his hands; his nails were manicured, clean and white.

"Yes, I feel it, Charlotte. The size of a small grape, about three fourths of an inch. I don't have enough information yet to tell you anything for certain." He flipped through her file. "You're right, your last mammogram which was normal was a year ago. I'd like another one for a comparison to help determine the nature of the lump, its size and texture. It feels solid, which means I'll order a biopsy to be sure." *He's so matter-of-fact, so same as usual,* Charlotte thought, biting her lip. He put down the file. "You may dress, then we'll talk." Dr. Morgan left and shut the door. Charlotte dressed and sat down. When the doctor returned, she strained forward.

"Do you think I have cancer?"

"Charlotte, I can't answer that yet. I understand you feel apprehensive. A solid lump doesn't mean it's malignant. Could be a benign tumor or cyst. We need to check it out, so we'll know. The nurse will take you to imaging in a few minutes for a mammogram."

"What happens if it's solid?"

"If the mass is solid, we'll numb the breast with lidocaine, an anesthetic, and do a fine needle aspiration."

Charlotte's nod changed into a frown. "What's that?"

"In your case, a small needle used to remove some cells from the tumor, which are put on slides and sent to the pathologist. A technician will take four pictures. The radiologist will examine your breast by ultrasound."

"All this today?"

Charlotte felt dizzy. "mammogram today" she heard. "—have the results by—I will call you."

"When did you say?"

"By late afternoon today or tomorrow I'll have your mammogram report. You may need to come in for more tests tomorrow. If this is a cyst, there's no problem."

Charlotte's heart pounded, she frowned. "What if it's not a cyst?"

"It could be malignant." Dr. Morgan nodded. "In that event, I will refer you to Dr. Cumberland, an excellent breast surgeon who can remove the lump along with any necessary lymph nodes. He'll decide whether he wants to remove some of the tissue or the entire breast."

Entire breast? Dr. Morgan looked blurry. Charlotte took a deep breath and let it go. She felt his hand on her shoulder. "I've thrown a lot at you. I'm sorry you have to deal with this troublesome situation." She swallowed. He came back into focus. What must she look like? "I want you to get the mammogram. We'll go one step at a time from there. I'll call you."

"All right," Charlotte said with a bleak look. She gave Dr. Morgan a tight smile.

"Valerie will take you to imaging and I'll talk with you soon." Dr. Morgan disappeared and moments later reappeared with his unknown nurse.

"I don't think you've met Valerie."

"Nope." She saw the woman's hazel eyes and pug nose.

"She's been with me for . . . what . . . three months?"

Valerie smiled. "Hi Charlotte, I'm glad to meet you."

Young, they're all so young, Charlotte thought. "Hi," she said.

"Follow me," Valerie said. Charlotte followed the woman, staring at her brown hair, which she had secured in a barrette at the nape of her neck. She slipped into another gown, which she tied in front this time and found an outdated magazine in her cubicle.

When a slender red-haired woman called her for her mammogram, Charlotte said, "I found a lump for you to check out." She prayed to hear something reassuring.

"I hope it's nothing serious, but you're smart to come in." The woman adjusted Charlotte's breast on the machine. Charlotte held her breath as instructed for a moment.

"Ouch," she winced when the plates of the x–ray machine came together and flattened her breast.

"Please wait in the room while I look at the x–ray," said the young woman. While others finished and left, Charlotte waited, flipping magazine pages in her cubicle.

"Mrs. Keeley?"

"Yes." Charlotte opened the door.

"You can go home," the slender woman said. "Your doctor will contact you if there is any problem."

Charlotte stepped into the elevator and out at the lobby level. She strode through the main entrance engrossed in her thoughts. Outside, she glimpsed the feathery foliage of a Japanese maple; its red leaves, brilliant in the sun, focused her senses. Will I see this again next year? The thought stung her. Fall was her favorite season. Its beauty had especially affected her, even as a child. She'd walked to grade school, but in the fall, she'd skipped. She couldn't resist the crisp, pungent air, and the riotous colors. Today their redness reminded her only that the leaves were dead.

The car seemed to drive itself the few miles to their brick home. Charlotte's preoccupation of mind was the kind that makes one wonder how no accident or wrong turn occurred. When she pulled into the driveway, she passed Florence, who had one arm in her mailbox. She waved with her free arm, smiled and then removed her mail and started toward Charlotte. "How are you, Florence?" Charlotte managed as she stepped from her silver Toyota.

"Doin' okay for an old lady. I still have Debbie. She treats me good." Debbie had kept her mother occupied so well that Florence hadn't quizzed Charlotte since the reception. "Haven't seen Todd around. He okay?" Florence shuffled the ads in her wrinkled hands.

Charlotte inspected the concrete walk, kicked at a maple leaf. "He's just busy, Florence, real busy."

"Was wonderin' cause he seemed mad when he left your house after Nathan's service." That's an understatement, Charlotte thought. She looked at Florence's frail face, at the wisps of hair that played against her sunken cheeks.

"I'm glad that Debbie could stay with you."

"She's gone now, back at her house," Florence said, loneliness in her eyes.

Charlotte felt her face flush, realizing she'd neglected Florence, due to pride and embarrassment over her husband and son's behavior at the reception. She didn't feel like talking about her medical fears either. "This is a bad day, but I'll have you over for tea soon." She put her arm around Florence's back.

"That'd be nice," Florence said and turned in the direction of her own house.

Charlotte opened her mailbox to the same pile of ads, walked into her kitchen and tossed her sweater across a chair. Turning on the faucet, she filled the teakettle and when it whistled, poured the boiling water into a mug with a black tea bag. The rich color seeped from the leaves, releasing its orange spice aroma. Charlotte opened her refrigerator and took out a yogurt, then checked her messages. "Just me. Wondered how your appointment went. I'll be home early." She felt a bit comforted at the smooth sound of Kevin's voice.

She walked into the living room, pulled the drapes against the twilight. The comfortable room wasn't cold enough to turn on the gas fireplace, so she sank into her beige recliner, let her loafers drop to the carpet. What had the garden club members said about Todd's blowup? I've missed the last few meetings, she thought. Did Florence understand more than I imagined? Charlotte ran her hand through her blond curls. Well. Maybe those in the living room hadn't heard Kevin or Todd's exact words. She felt her breast lump again, sipped the tea, and closed her eyes. Enough of this. Her thoughts drifted. She calmed her mind. I did the right thing. Nothing to do now but wait.

When she stirred to fix dinner, the phone rang. "Yes, Dr. Morgan. Does that mean cancer? More tests. Nine in the morning. I'll be there." She held the phone and leaned against the kitchen counter as the door opened.

Kevin closed it behind him, pitched the newspaper through the kitchen entrance onto his living room chair. "Who was that?"

"Dr. Morgan. I need more tests." Kevin laid his sports coat across a dining room chair. He walked to Charlotte turning her around to face him.

"More tests? Something show up on the mammogram?" Kevin's deep-set brown eyes searched hers.

"Yes. He said he'd discuss it with me at nine. Nothing conclusive until I have a biopsy." Charlotte buried her face in Kevin's chest. "Something's wrong. I probably have . . ."

"Cancer? You don't know that." He brushed her forehead with his chin. "Wait till tomorrow."

The next morning Kevin stirred raisins into boiling water and sprinkled in some oatmeal. "You better eat breakfast," he called into the bathroom. "I'll go with you to the clinic."

"You don't need to go." Charlotte walked out in a well-fitted pair of black jeans and a blue sweater that emphasized her full bosom. "I'm not going to know much until the tests are back anyway." She smiled at Kevin, and despite her effort, he saw the apprehension in her blue eyes. She invariably looked good on the outside, no matter how she felt.

"Here's your coffee." Kevin pulled her to him. "You're beautiful." He kissed her. "Call me when you've talked to Dr. Morgan. If you feel like it after your tests, I'll meet you for lunch. I want to hear how things went right away. Promise?"

"Promise," Charlotte said.

Later in the morning Dr. Morgan sat opposite Charlotte making full eye contact, a manner of his that had established her trust in him over the years. Her distress overshadowed the confidence she usually felt with him. "This is not what we ever want," he said. "I'm afraid your mammogram indicates possible malignancy in your tumor. A white blotch is evident under your nipple where you felt the lump. This suggests some cancerous cells have broken out of the ducts and caused a tumor to develop in the surrounding tissue."

Charlotte studied her hands, caught her breath, and then jerked her head up. "How . . . bad is it?"

"It isn't conclusive. We'll get an ultrasound first, then a biopsy if the lump is solid. Your breast tissue is dense, so an ultrasound will show if the tumor is solid. If so, I recommend you see Dr. Cumberland." Charlotte wanted to be brave, but felt her heart pounding. "He'll want to do his own breast biopsy. He's noted for his technique that removes only the cancerous tissue and the necessary lymph nodes."

Charlotte watched Dr. Morgan's face blur a second, and then she realized he'd stopped talking. She looked again and he smiled; she felt his compassion. "I'm sure you feel overwhelmed. You came in immediately, which is advantageous. We caught this in an early stage and I can assure you, Charlotte, that your chances of whipping it are excellent." Charlotte pursed her lips and shook her head up and down. Just a shadow maybe, she thought, not cancer. The doctor folded his manicured hands and leaned forward. He rose and again Charlotte felt the warmth of his hand on her shoulder. "Valerie will take you to imaging. Call the office tomorrow morning and I'll discuss the next step with you by phone after we see the ultrasound. Carry on," he said and left.

Charlotte let out a long breath. While she waited, she thought of Kate who kept at her about self-exams. Thanks to Kate, she'd examined her breasts like a good girl, discovered the lump. "You're the age, Mom, when the average woman is diagnosed with cancer. And three of every four diagnosed are fifty or older," Kate had said. Why me, why now? I'm retired.

Valerie directed Charlotte toward the lab. The slender red–haired woman from imaging spoke her name. "I bet you're not thrilled to see me again, but I wish you the best. My name's Jenny."

"Hi," Charlotte said.

"I need to take four pictures of your breast. Grab your belongings." Jenny led Charlotte to another x–ray room. She placed a metallic marker on the lump and looked efficient doing her tasks, familiar with matters foreign to Charlotte. "In a few minutes a radiologist will do an ultrasound."

"What's the difference between a solid and a cyst?" Had the doctor told her?

"A cyst is a harmless sac of fluid that can be collapsed by removing the fluid. A solid lump," Jenny turned so her green eyes looked straight into Charlotte's, "could be more serious."

"Meaning?"

"Meaning, you could have cancer." Jenny glanced down as she spoke to give Charlotte privacy. "I don't know. Your doctor will explain everything to you. I'm not qualified to tell you anything, sorry." Charlotte bit her lip. Then Jenny squeezed her forearm. "I know this is scary."

Before she left, Jenny said, "You can wait here for the radiologist. You're welcome to use the phone." She pointed toward one that was hidden among an array of papers piled on a desk. "I wish you well, Mrs. Keeley." Jenny put out her hand, which Charlotte grasped as she raised her eyes to meet Jenny's gaze in an unspoken bond before the technician left the room.

Lapsing into her own thoughts, Charlotte thought of her mother, her stroke, and her death. After her stroke, Charlotte had resigned her college teaching position in the English department to help her mom cope. Mom needed me more, she thought. Back to Kate. She's a good nurse and Dave shows promise as an architect. Kevin plans to retire within the next year. Would they travel? She had reason to whip this. Besides, Mom had a stroke, not cancer; it's not in this family.

Charlotte reached for the phone visible beneath the clutter and dialed Kevin's office. Before he answered, a plain looking young man with wide–set brown eyes came into the room. "Are you Mrs. Keeley?"

"Yes." Charlotte cancelled the call. She noticed the man's disarrayed hair and baggy clothes.

"I'm Dr. Samuel Larson, a radiologist."

"Yes."

"Your doctor has ordered an ultrasound of your breast."

"Right."

"I intruded on your phone call. Do you need a minute before we begin?"

Charlotte would have loved to talk with Kevin right then, but deep inside she knew she was beginning a journey she would face alone anyway. She looked up. "No, go ahead." She watched the awkward, yet sensitive man buzz for a nurse who appeared at once.

When Dr. Larson finished, he said, "I don't think you have a cyst Mrs. Keeley. You're Dr. Morgan's patient, right?"

"Right." A shiver ran up her spine.

The doctor paused, as if in search of the right words. "Mrs. Keeley, I admire your courage in alerting your doctor right away. This lump is solid and your surgeon will be doing a biopsy." Dr. Larson's wide–set eyes smiled. "You are free to dress and leave." When the doctor shut the door behind him, Charlotte did what she needed to do. She picked up the phone and connected with Kevin's engineering firm. "Hi, it's me."

"At last. How'd it go?"

"Whew . . . the radiologist doesn't think it's a cyst."

"Not a cyst?"

"Not a cyst, so it's cancer, Kevin, I know it."

"Do you see Dr. Morgan tomorrow?"

"No, I'm supposed to call. We need to talk."

"Let's have lunch, so I can see you."

"Okay. Meet me at Toni's Deli near the clinic."

"I know where it is."

"Can you be there by twelve-thirty?"

"Yep, see you then. Watch the road."

"I will. Bye."

When she parked the car, Charlotte saw Kevin seated at a window table. He waved and when she entered, he pulled out her chair. "I ordered you chamomile tea to calm you down, plus a half veggie on rye. Hope that's okay. Tell me what you found out."

"Oh, I don't know, Kevin." Something about a white blotch that looks like cancer cells have broken out of the ducts." Charlotte glanced at him, stopped talking and waited until the chatty server placed their order on the table and left. "He mentioned a breast surgeon," she said in a low voice, "Dr. Cumberland, who'll do a biopsy—the needle thing where they take out sample tissue—and decide if he should remove the lump or my breast." Charlotte winced, not looking at Kevin.

"I know about him."

"Well, good, because I don't."

"Yeah, I read that he removes the cancer, but keeps the breast. He takes the diseased tissue and leaves the skin. Then he takes a 'tummy tuck,' right? Fills in the empty pocket with stomach tissue, and puts the skin back, which saves the breast." The slightest grin came to the corners of Kevin's mouth.

Charlotte clunked the table with her teacup. Was this funny? She felt her tension rumble around inside her (was he teasing her?) until it escaped in a tearful laugh. She wiped her eyes, looked at Kevin. "The tummy tuck amuses you. You'd like me to have a tummy tuck, wouldn't you?" She curled her lips into a smirk.

"No, but I like to hear you laugh."

"Cancer's not funny."

"I agree. Just get your diagnosis before you write your obituary. Even with a malignancy, your chances are good these days." Logical Kevin.

"How was your morning?"

"Okay, but we can talk about that later. Keep busy until tomorrow, and then call Dr. Morgan when you've decided about Dr. Cumberland. He sounds like a good choice."

"I guess."

"Pay attention, then when you get home, start a good book. It will pass the time. You haven't attended your book club lately."

"I know." Charlotte took a last swallow of tea, swung her coat over her shoulders, then felt Kevin's arm firm around her shoulder.

"See you tonight," he said.

"Bye, Kevin. Thanks for lunch."

Charlotte drove the car into the garage. Eventually, she thought, I have to talk with Kate about this. Still, I don't know anything. Then there's Todd. Stepping into the kitchen, she took the teakettle and walked into the extra bedroom where she watered the African violet, which sat on the old sewing machine her mother had given her. She'd make a cup of tea, she thought. Returning to the kitchen, she put the teakettle on the burner. Then she'd call Kate.

Charlotte took her cup into her sewing room and sat in her wicker chair. Kevin is here for me, supports me, makes me laugh. When will he feel comfortable again with Todd? she wondered. I'm contacting Todd if I have surgery. I'm his mother and he'll want to know. Why did he bring Trevor to the reception after Nathan's service? Todd's appearance was appropriate, since he'd been sensitive to Nathan's struggle and a favorite of Florence, but why Trevor? She shook her head.

When Charlotte called his office the next day, Dr. Morgan advised her that her tumor showed up in the ultrasound. He recommended she call Dr. Cumberland for an appointment. She pulled a magnet off the refrigerator, took the card it held and traced her finger across the raised lettering of Dr. Cumberland's name and number. She started to call Kevin first, than dialed Dr. Cumberland's office instead.

Thankful, Charlotte discovered the doctor could see her Friday. When she hung up, she called Kevin. His secretary said he had left the office for a meeting.

# Chapter 3

"Mom, Amanda's messing with my dinosaurs again," Jonas shouted out of his bedroom door. He glared at his sister. "Get outta here."

Amanda stuck her tongue between her teeth, wrinkling her nose. With her eyes intent on her brother, she opened her mouth and in her sassiest tone said, "Wasn't hurtin' anything." Jonas, flushed with anger, reached for Amanda, but she escaped his grasp, ran to her room and slammed the door.

Heading down the hall, hands dripping from wet lettuce, Kate intercepted. "Why do you always fight when I'm getting dinner? Don't you like dinner?"

"She's messing with my stuff. She shouldn't be in my room." Jonas' brown eyes sparked and his wiry body was set to fight.

"No, she shouldn't, but she's still little and you're almost eight. Did she hurt anything, Jonas?"

"No, but she could." He jetted his chin. "You won't let me punch her like she deserves. I have to be good all the time and she can do whatever she wants."

"No she can't. It's time for dinner, if I can finish it. Go to your room and calm down. I'll talk to Amanda." Kate found Amanda sitting bright-eyed on the bed. Her dimpled hands held a toy phone to her ear, the receiver concealed by cascading blond curls. She lifted her chin and eyed her mother when she approached. Amanda's possible innocence, captured in her blue eyes, was enchanting, but Kate wasn't deceived. "Stay right here until I call you for dinner. Don't go into Jonas' room."

"What's going on?" Dave gave a quick glance from the computer desk as Kate passed on her return to the kitchen. "Same old struggle. Can't you put a lock on Jonas' cupboard?" Kate rolled her eyes. "His precious dinosaurs."

"I see." Dave fingered his mustache.

"I don't want his room padlocked, but a cupboard lock for his toys might be a good idea."

"So Amanda doesn't have to mind us and her own business?"

"Dave, she's *four*. I'm fixing dinner. I didn't see you race in there to discipline her."

"No, you didn't." Dave followed Kate into the kitchen.

"Since you're here you can set the table."

"Okay, okay." He grabbed four forks with one hand, Kate's waist with the other and kissed the nape of her neck. Her soft smooth skin, slightly moist, excited him deeply, even when she was upset. Her head bent down, her sandy blond hair fell forward covering her fair cheeks. Kate felt Dave's full lips, his beard brush her neck as he squeezed her slender waist and patted her hip.

"Oh Dave." Kate sighed with fatigue. "If you rub my back tonight—" She came to an abrupt stop. Strained beyond the usual, her round eyes looked pale in her face.

"What happened today?" Dave said.

"Mrs. Baxter died." Kate bit her lip to keep back the tears. "Her family seems to blame me, but can we please discuss this later? The broccoli smells scorched." She frowned and struggled to bring herself under control as she lifted the pan off the burner.

"Sure." Dave placed the silver and some plates on the kitchen table. "Shall I go get 'em?"

"Dinner's ready by the time they wash."

"Yes, Nurse Kate."

Kate placed the last dish in the cupboard and snapped off the light. Dave returned from the bedtime rituals. "I didn't mention the lock suggestion," he said, "but I promise you we'll deal with it. They're awaiting your good night kiss."

"Okay, my turn. Be right back, but not before I change into my sweats." She climbed the stairs and found her son in his bed, looking like he wanted assurance from her that she wasn't angry about his outburst. "Good night, Jonas." Kate leaned over to kiss him. "We'll talk about keeping your dinosaurs safe from Amanda. She needs to learn and we need to be patient."

"She makes me mad. I wish I had a brother."

"Well, you have a sister. I know she makes you angry." She trailed her finger through his straight hair. "Brothers aren't easy either. Amanda gets mad at you too."

Jonas rolled over. "Sometimes she screams at me. Night, Mom."

When she walked into Amanda's room, Kate kissed her daughter's cheek and tiptoed out without waking her.

Dave had relaxed into an armchair. He ran his hand through his matted brown hair while he wondered what discussion might follow. Kate appeared in the room in sweats and slippers. She let out a sigh as she stretched out in the comfortable recliner across from Dave. She looked at him when she felt his eyes on her.

"What went wrong today? Wasn't Mrs. Baxter eighty–three years old and expected to die anytime?"

"No Dave, that's Mrs. Beaumont, an older lady. Mrs. Baxter came in about ten days ago with a kidney infection. She had a heart attack and died on my shift with an angry son and remorseful husband arriving too late. It shouldn't get to me, but it does." Kate's words raced out.

"Slow down. Why was her son angry?"

"I'm getting to that. Mrs. Baxter went into cardiac arrest this afternoon after her husband had spent the morning with her. He fed her lunch. He expected his son to come about seven tonight. At four, they called Jim, that's his name, but when he arrived with his father, she was dead. Jim said he didn't get along well with his mom and he wanted to talk with her. He started crying. His dad might have been empathetic, but he just stood there watching his son shake and . . ."

"And?" Dave waited.

"Jim shouted . . . if there'd been a decent medical staff we could have saved her. Which was impossible, Dave. The staff was there in a flash, worked on her an hour. I'm glad her husband and son weren't there while they battled for her life. Not fun to watch." Dave listened as she relived her experience.

"Then Jim burst out, `I'm gay you know. I wanted to tell Mom tonight so she would know who I really am. Now she's dead and she'll never know.' "

Dave gaped at Kate, "What did you say?"

"I said I was sorry. Mrs. Baxter's doctor who was with another patient, heard the commotion and stopped to console Jim. Told him that unfinished business made grief painful. Jim and his dad stood there not saying anything."

"So you felt it was your fault?"

"That's how they made me feel," Kate blurted, throwing her hand across her chest. She paused and took a breath. "He had to hide his life from his mom at least ten years, maybe longer. He didn't tell me his personal history."

"He didn't?" Dave feigned surprise. Kate gave a half smile.

"Then I shook their hands and they thanked me for the days I spent with Mrs. Baxter. Her husband said he knew I did my best." When she paused for reassurance, Dave nodded at her. "I hope they can resolve their differences. Tomorrow will be a new day for me with someone else in Mrs. Baxter's bed. I won't see those men again. I need time to deal with it too."

"I know you do, Kate." Dave stood, took her in his arms. "You're a remarkable woman. I love you for who you are and what you give. You 're tough skinned and vulnerable. Not an easy assignment." He brushed his thumb against her cheek, over the faded summer freckles that sprinkled across her nose. "I wonder if the circumstances, I mean Jim's being gay, upset you."

"Of course. I felt terrible, as if I should have prevented her death, so he could fix their relationship. I know it's irrational, but he might spread rumors that our hospital is negligent."

"Maybe the whole thing stirred up family matters."

Kate leaned forward. "Fixing relationships, you mean. Maybe, but don't play analyst." Despite her irritation with Dave, (was he making inferences about her relatives?) Kate put her arms around his neck, wiped tears on his shirt. "I hope our family gets a handle on our communication problems. I suppose this incident has made me see a possible future down the road, if we don't deal with conflict. Why does it hurt so much?"

Dave lifted her chin and looked into her blue eyes, now bright with tears. "Because life is hard—and we're afraid of the unknown. Let's go to bed."

When the phone rang, Kate answered. "Hello Kate, this is Mom. Sorry I'm calling so late . . . I meant to tell you earlier, but—"

"Tell me what?" Are you and Dad not getting—"

"We're getting along. We don't talk about certain things—" Charlotte hesitated. "I discovered a lump in my breast last week and I'm seeing a breast surgeon Friday."

"What? Why didn't you call me sooner? Is it malignant?"

"Yes . . . well, I'm having a biopsy to confirm it, but my doctor thinks my chances are great. I didn't tell you because . . . well, I wasn't sure. I've been worried . . . I don't know."

"You having surgery?"

"Yes, removing just the tumor, I hope."

"Who's doing it?"

"Uh, my doctor recommended Cumberland. He's supposed to be an expert breast surgeon."

"A tall lanky man?"

"Don't know, Kate. Have you heard of him?"

"I've seen him at the hospital. I'm sorry, Mom." Kate's voice was soothing. "How's Dad taking this?"

"He's supportive, steady as a rock, like always."

"Call me right away when you know more."

"I will."

"And Mom?"

"Yes?"

"Um, good to hear your voice."

"Me too."

Kate slid into bed next to Dave. He wrapped his arms around her. "Your mom has cancer?"

"Yes," Kate sighed. "Breast tumor."

"At least you're talking again."

# Chapter 4

Friday morning, Charlotte parked her car in the parking garage of the medical building where Dr. Cumberland practiced. She stepped out, found the elevator and went to the fifth floor. She had insisted that Kevin go to work. She could deal with this. She took the new patient health forms, clipboard, and pen the receptionist gave her. No cancer history in the family. She didn't deserve this. She checked boxes beside more questions, returned it to the desk and sat down again.

"Mrs. Keeley?" A prompt, plump, middle–aged nurse spoke to her. As Charlotte stood, the woman smiled. "Is this your first visit with Dr. Cumberland?"

"Yes. I hope it's my last," Charlotte said with a firm look toward the woman whose silver hair folded softly into a round knot at the back of her neck.

Maintaining a pleasant expression, the nurse looked at Charlotte. "That's understandable, Mrs. Keeley. You should know that many of our patients' biopsies are benign, even with a lump."

"Good for them. I'm not on your list." Charlotte felt patronized, but astonished by her own curtness.

"Let's put you on the survivor's list," the nurse said without pollyannaism. "Dr. Cumberland will need to examine you. Come this way." The woman escorted Charlotte to a patient room, then left. She sat stiffly, her eyes focusing on the wall of body diagrams that illustrated cancerous cells in action. The nurse with the round knot entered the room. "Dr. Cumberland will be with you soon. You can get into this afterwards," she said handing Charlotte a gown. "Please remove your clothing above your waist." The door closed with a swish as the nurse left. Charlotte unbuttoned her coat and closed her eyes.

In five minutes, a tall lean man in his late fifties entered the room where Charlotte waited. He reached for her hand, firmly grasped it. "Mrs. Keeley, I'm Dr. Cumberland. Dr. Morgan informed me that you're his patient and I have your mammogram and ultrasound."

"Yes."

"I'll examine you after we have talked. You're no doubt wishing you could be elsewhere. Your mammogram and ultrasound do indicate some abnormal cells," he told Charlotte. "I'd like to examine you and take a tissue sample before we even talk about the next step." Charlotte held her purse to her chest, listened without speaking. "I'll do the biopsy today, send the tissue to the lab and by Monday afternoon we should have the results. Then I'll discuss specific treatment options with you and your husband."

Charlotte straightened a bit, gave Dr. Cumberland a quick glance. "Get it done."

"Some cells are benign, so I'll take tissue from several places. I'll numb your breast, then insert a probe that will suck out the cells. The cells go on a slide, then on to oncology. Waiting for the results is tough, but in twenty four hours you should know if the tumor is benign or cancerous." The doctor's voice was gentle, his eyes on Charlotte. She held his gaze, nodded her head. "Dr. Morgan will receive the complete report. Do you have any questions?"

"My mind feels like mush," Charlotte said. "How long will this take?"

"About twenty minutes max."

Charlotte shrugged. "Let's get started."

"I'll be right back, " Dr. Cumberland said. "My nurse will be with you soon."

Charlotte removed her coat, and started removing her blouse, when the nurse tapped the door and joined her in the room.

"Hello Mrs. Keeley, I'm Brianna. I'll be assisting Dr. Cumberland during your biopsy." Pleasant and matter-of-fact, she seemed kind, Charlotte thought. Questions rather than irritation now surged in Charlotte's mind.

"Is everyone as angry as me?" She searched the nurse's face.

"Well, I see every emotion: denial, anger, fears. You're a human being. Be assured the doctor will answer any questions he can, and expects you to be informed." She paused tucking a stray hair into her round knot. "It's your body, Mrs. Keeley. Go easy on yourself. You didn't expect this."

"No." Charlotte blew a breath past her lips.

"Go ahead and change," Brianna said and left. Charlotte removed her blouse and bra, slipped into the gown and heard a crinkle as she sat on the papered examination table. She looked around the room, her eyes stopping at a photo of a potted, pink geranium hanging on the wall. An attractive green and peach–striped couch sat beneath it. She noticed the end table with magazines on it. This room was for serious reflection and counsel. Life and death stuff.

As she left her perch to get a magazine, she heard a soft knock. "Ready?" Dr. Cumberland's voice sounded as smooth as velvet. Charlotte scrambled back onto the table.

"Yes," she said. Dr. Cumberland stepped into the room followed by Brianna. Charlotte noticed him for the first time. His hair was rusty, with white streaks, receding at his brow. He had wrinkles across his forehead and around his eyes and mouth. Before she was aware of it, she was engaged in small talk about her children and Kevin. All the while the lanky doctor examined her breasts.

"Do you have a cat?" Dr. Cumberland's blue eyes danced like light.

"A cat? Why do you ask?" Charlotte scrunched up her eyes.

"Just curious. Our cat gave birth to a litter of four kittens this morning." Dr. Cumberland's ruddy complexion accented the twinkle in his eyes. When he looked at Charlotte, she burst into laughter.

"No, we have a dog. You can keep your kittens," she shot back with obvious amusement. Brianna glanced at her and grinned.

"Now I think we're ready to begin," Dr. Cumberland said. When he'd finished the procedure, he looked at Charlotte. "I'll call you as soon as the report is in. I hope by Monday. I'll see you and your husband then. Anxiety is natural, just keep it positive and have a good weekend." Charlotte gazed at Brianna's clean nails as she placed a Band–Aid on her breast. She watched Brianna label and secure the slide, and flash her a thumbs-up before she left the room.

Saturday Charlotte vacuumed the house, scrubbed the kitchen and bathroom floors, and dusted each piece of furniture as if she expected guests for a week. In the evening, she had dinner with Kevin at their favorite Italian restaurant. Across the wooden candlelit table, Kevin studied his wife. Her face looked lovable framed in blond curls. He didn't notice the gray hairs at her scalp or the crow's feet in the corner of her eyes. He saw that they were incredibly blue. "You kept busy today," he said, his lips spreading in a broad smile.

"Don't know when I'll be cleaning again." Charlotte eyed her food, piercing a broccoli crown. "A lot of good eating this has done." She laid the fork on her plate instead of raising it to her mouth. Her eyes studied the tablecloth, which she smoothed with her palm.

"I know." Kevin swallowed hard, rotating his wineglass. When Charlotte met his gaze, he touched his goblet to hers. "To your good health."

Charlotte cut back Shasta daisies and snapped the yellowed geranium leaves. She noticed the golden brown pile of leaves that had fallen from the maple, scattered across the yard, and waited for the rake. This was a night for waffles, something comforting. She cleaned up and went inside to prepare supper. Soon Kevin walked into the kitchen, kissed Charlotte and set a book on the stool. "Waffles, right?"

"Right—you're home early."

The aroma of fresh coffee wafted into the bedroom where Kevin hung his sports coat and changed into Levi's and a pullover. He walked back to his wife. "I have good news and bad news. I can't miss an important meeting tomorrow if I want the contract for the new bridge. I got the call this afternoon. The bad news is I can't see the doctor with you if I go to the meeting. Why does everything happen at once?"

"I don't know." Charlotte fixed her eyes on the bowl of fruit in front of her. "Dr. Cumberland hasn't called, so I don't know when he will see me anyway." She tossed a banana peel in the garbage. "Go to your meeting."

"I'm sure you'll hear when he has the biopsy report." Kevin noticed Charlotte's cheeks and her hands as slices of banana fell from her fingers into a bowl. He stood behind her, slipped his hands under her sweatshirt enclosing her breasts in his fingers. "If the doctor schedules surgery, I promise I'll be with you to discuss it with him." He smelled her scent, felt her silken flesh, his hands caressing her as they had a million times before. "I love you," Kevin said.

"I know . . . I know you'll be there." She handed him the waffle iron, which he plugged in near the table. "Right now let's have some waffles and fruit—no more depressing thoughts."

When they finished dinner, Kevin lifted the book he'd put on the stool. "I stopped at the library. I knew you wouldn't start reading a classic."

Charlotte took the book. "Thanks—*Harry Potter* zap my worries away."

"Want your coffee now?" Kevin called into the bedroom Tuesday morning. Charlotte stepped into her jeans and pulled a peach sweatshirt over her head.

"Yeah, I'll be out in a minute." When she walked into the kitchen, Charlotte noticed the sun shining through the window illuminating the table, which held a plate with a piece of toast spread with marmalade and a cup of coffee. "Thanks," she said.

"My appointment with the perspective contractor is at eight. Call me if you hear from Dr. Cumberland. I'll see you tonight." Charlotte looked up at Kevin. How handsome he is, she thought, seeing his beige sports coat with a brown and blue paisley tie. He moved with long strides toward the door, his attaché case in his hand. Kevin glanced at the front lawn and frowned. "Don't work too hard raking leaves today. October sure brings them down, doesn't it?" Then Charlotte saw his wide smile, his even teeth.

"Go on," she said and waved him out. He vanished past the front window and she sat savoring her coffee and toast. She watched huge yellow leaves flutter from the maple tree, which dominated the front yard. When the phone rang, she was startled from her musings.

"Hi, Grams, it's me, Jonas."

"Hi yourself, Jonas. Ready for school?"

"Just about, but Mom said I could call you. I can't wait till we go to the zoo." Charlotte scanned the wall calendar. Saturday was the day all right. She'd forgotten it completely.

"Right. We're going to have a super time," she said, mentally juggling medical scenarios. If plans changed, she'd explain it later.

"We getting ice cream, Grams?" Jonas asked.

"Of course. Have fun reading at school."

"Okay, Grams. Bye."

"Bye, Jonas." Charlotte smiled. She enjoyed her bright grandson and his beautiful sister, but the zoo wasn't the first thing on her mind today. When would the doctor call? Jonas is leaving for school, Kate will be heading for the hospital, and Kevin has a meeting. Sitting here won't help me pass the time. Raking leaves might be a good idea.

She dumped the coffee grounds into a compost can under the counter, then placed her mug and a few dishes in the sink. In the living room she removed last weeks' newspapers to the garage, straightened the couch pillows and grabbed Kevin's slippers. In the bedroom, a bright ray of sunlight flooded across the unmade bed. Charlotte sprawled on it for a few moments soaking up the warmth of the sun. Then she took her coat and gloves, placed a phone on the porch and proceeded toward the maple tree, rake in hand.

The crisp air reddened her cheeks, as the raking sent her blood tingling through her veins. She heard the crackle of dry leaves underfoot and the smell of rotting leaves beneath them saturated the air. She breathed in their pungency. Her gloves dampened with the moldy muck as she scooped the leaves into bags. In forty-five minutes, she had filled several. While she leaned against her rake, brushing a strand of hair from her face, the phone rang. Her heart raced as she ran to the porch to answer. "Hello?"

"Mrs. Keeley?"

"Yes."

"This is Brianna from Dr. Cumberland's office. Your lab reports are back and the doctor would like to schedule an appointment with you."

"When?" Charlotte responded at once.

"He can see you at one today. Your husband is expected as well."

"Uh, yes, thank you. We'll be there." The added expectation of Kevin's presence unnerved her, although they had planned for him to go. Did they think she would need his support? She removed her gloves, placed the rake in the garage and went inside to call Kevin. He was out of his office. It was ten. His meeting would have been over by now, she had hoped.

She stripped her jeans, sweatshirt, panties and bra, threw them in the laundry, and walked into the bathroom to shower. She caught the image of her face in a full length mirror and studied the creases around her eyes, the crow's feet that no age defying cream could erase. Her eyes scanned her body in the reflection that didn't lie. She stood five feet, six inches, full breasted, with a slim midriff for her sixty-two years. Putting her hands on her waist, she turned sideways revealing her rounded hips, not as firm as once; a few varicose veins trickled down her thighs. Her breasts tilted down without her bra, but they still pushed out in front, completing the profile. The thought of losing one of them sent a tremor down her spine. How would Kevin feel? All the time telling me how he loves them, she sighed. I know Kevin loves me for myself, she thought, but I want to be complete.

Here I go again, she scolded herself and stepped into the shower. Not so much as a firm diagnosis yet. While the hot water splashed over her, Charlotte examined her breast again, feeling the lump. Still obvious, but unchanged. She finished her shower, then dried and brushed her hair. "I want to be blond forever," she murmured at the mirror, "at least till I'm frumpy and look like an old lady." She dressed in slacks and a sweater.

This time Kevin answered when she dialed. "Hi Kevin, it's me. Dr. Cumberland can see us at one today. Can you meet me at the medical center in a couple hours?"

"I promised I would. What's his office number again?"

"The fifth floor, 509. See you then."

"Charlotte, let's plan to grab dinner afterwards so you won't have to cook tonight. We'll get a latte and browse the shops."

"Browse the shops? It depends on the news. But dinner would be fine." She hung up, wondering why she felt so edgy. Shopping might be a welcome diversion, even with bad news.

She stepped to the street to get her mail. The screen door banged shut when she returned to her kitchen. She heard a voice. "Got a minute?"

Startled, Charlotte turned to see her neighbor, Florence, making her way up the sidewalk. "Hello," Charlotte said. "Yes. What's up?" I don't have too many minutes, she thought. She had to tell Florence about this cancer, but not now. While Florence gasped for breath, Charlotte invited, "Come in and sit down a minute." Florence walked into the kitchen, found a chair at the table and plopped down.

"I saw you gettin' your mail. Just wanted to catch you . . . only have a minute," she blurted. "Did you hear about Mrs. Baxter? She died a day or so ago. Heart attack. Couldn't save her. The nursery man told me . . . bought some pansies this morning."

"No, no, I didn't know." Charlotte shook her head. "In her fifties wasn't she?"

"Yep, fifty-six. Terrible shock to her husband. They have a boy, too. I mean a grown up son." Florence frowned. "Didn't your daughter tell you? Just thought she would've since she was there when she died."

"No, I've been busy." Charlotte fingered her hair. "I haven't talked with Kate much lately." Pam Baxter was in the garden club with her and Florence, but Charlotte had never mentioned Pam's name to Kate. Had she referred to a son? Charlotte regarded Florence. "I doubt Kate knew Mrs. Baxter except as a patient. We've never discussed my acquaintance with her. She had no reason to tell me."

"No, I guess not," Florence said, rubbing her spotted, arthritic hands. Her white hair, drawn back with a comb, thinly covered her crown; a few wisps fell across her forehead and over her ears. Her thin lips quivered as she wrapped her frayed brown sweater tightly around her frail body. "I met Mr. Baxter a few times—took me home from the garden meetin's. Ever meet him?" Florence's brown eyes gazed across the table at Charlotte who saw in them as much loneliness as curiosity.

"I met him once or twice." She studied Florence, wishing she had time to offer tea. "How did the nursery attendant know Kate was on duty when Pam Baxter died?"

"He didn't know. I called Mr. Baxter at home when I heard about it. His son was at the hospital with him. Said a nurse named Kate talked to them. I figured it was your Kate." Florence's face relaxed into a smile and she gave Charlotte an assuring nod.

Amused, Charlotte paused a moment to digest the news. "Well. I'm glad you told me. I'll ask Kate what happened."

"Yep, well hope it didn't upset her." Florence looked at the door. "Guess I best be about my chores. Gotta plant my winter pansies in pots, purple and yellow ones. Let me know what you hear. I best be goin' now." Florence put her palms on the table and pushed herself up. Her hand on the doorknob, she said, "Bye, bye," and shuffled down the walk. Charlotte snatched a yogurt, ate it and headed for the clinic.

She checked in with Dr. Cumberland's receptionist. Charlotte poured hot water over a teabag then sat in an upholstered chair, concentrating on its burgundy and navy diamond pattern repeats.

"Hello Mrs. Keeley," Brianna said. "We'll be right with you."

"Hi, my husband's coming too."

"I'm here," Kevin said, as he breezed in the door and sat next to Charlotte. Her tense face softened.

"Glad you made it."

"Am I late?"

"No, not late."

The nurse joined them in a few minutes and smiled at Kevin. "Mr. Keeley."

Kevin smiled back and nodded. "Yes, call me Kevin."

"I'm Brianna, Dr. Cumberland's nurse." She shook his hand before guiding them to Dr. Cumberland's personal office and left them to wait for him.

When the doctor arrived, he greeted Charlotte, then looked at Kevin. "I'm Brent Cumberland."

"Kevin Keeley, glad to meet you," Kevin said.

The doctor took a folder from his desk. Charlotte tensed. "Some cancerous cells detected in your left breast concern us," Dr. Cumberland began. "Your lymph nodes appear to be clear, which is important." He smiled, genuinely pleased. "You have some options. I can do a surgical procedure, a lumpectomy that will remove the diseased tissue and some healthy tissue surrounding it. I may remove one lymph node to be sure it is clear. Generally, a lumpectomy is successful followed by five or six weeks of radiation. That way you save your breast."

He noticed Kevin and Charlotte were leaning forward, intently listening. "Some doctors feel there is less risk of cancer spreading if the entire breast is removed, which would be your second option. I don't feel that's necessary. However, if you make that choice," he observed the furtive glances the couple exchanged, "I can remove the breast tissue leaving a pocket of skin that I implant with . . ." He stopped, seeing Charlotte and Kevin's smile.

"The tummy tuck," Kevin said. "We talked about it." He laughed first, then Charlotte.

"So you know your options." The doctor laughed too. "You'd lose breast tissue in the second option, but retain the skin. With the implanted tissue your breast will look and feel natural."

After a moment's silence, Charlotte's brows creased together. Her eyes locked on Kevin's face as Dr. Cumberland observed. "Talk it over," he said. "It isn't so urgent that you must decide immediately. Call me when you're ready." He steadied his eyes on Charlotte. "Your chances for complete recovery are high." Charlotte nodded her head. "Give yourself credit and continue to fight it with confidence."

"What do you recommend?" Kevin said when Charlotte remained silent.

"I recommend removing the cancerous tissue. We can follow up with a complete breast removal later if that becomes necessary, but it's improbable." The doctor turned his clear blue eyes on Charlotte. "You have input in this decision. I want your agreement and support before I proceed with any surgery." He paused. "I know your breasts are personal to you."

"And my stomach." Charlotte smirked. Kevin grinned at her playful banter.

"I'm sure you have questions. Think this over, then make a decision. Call me anytime and when you decide, we'll move ahead. Feel free to seek a second opinion."

Kevin extended his hand first. "Thank you. This is not what we wanted to hear, but it could be worse. I'm glad her lymph nodes seem unaffected."

"Yes, that's good news. It could be much worse."

Charlotte took a step forward to shake Dr. Cumberland's hand. "Thanks for seeing us. I do have one question."

"Anything."

"Did you find homes for those four kittens?"

"You remembered." Dr. Cumberland's eyes laughed again. "Yes, three down, one to go. My grandchildren helped us out with homes for them, but now they're making noises about the last one. Our kids won't talk to me if the little ones win." He chuckled.

"I bet," Charlotte said. "We'll be calling you soon."

"Take care. I'll be here. Good bye, Kevin."

Charlotte and Kevin walked from the clinic into a rainy afternoon. Leaves stuck to the sidewalk, though the wind whirled around them. "Let's go somewhere we can talk," Kevin suggested. "How about the Dutch Bakery if we can find a quiet corner?"

"Fine with me." Charlotte felt glad that Kevin chose her favorite place. The aroma of yeast and cinnamon permeated the room as they entered the shop. Charlotte loved the blue tiled floors and windmill wallpaper strip, which bordered the ceiling and set off the powder blue walls. Above the glass-cased baked goodies was a menu of sandwiches and soup.

"Want something to eat?" Kevin asked as they sat down on two wooden chairs at a round table.

"Let's eat later, well, I guess we could split a cookie, something good and fattening." As Kevin returned with two coffees and a peanut butter cookie, he noticed Charlotte's face, cupped in her hands, her eyes staring at the table.

"We have to make a decision," he said.

"We have the results," she said, groaning. "What do you think?"

"I wish I had a crystal ball. In my gut, I like Dr. Cumberland. You know that's important to me. Do you?"

"Yes, I like him. I'm not sure . . . how can we know his track record?"

"Have you reason to doubt?"

"No, but my health has spoiled me." Charlotte looked at her lap. "I feel weird having something abnormal in my body. I'm scared. I have to face this differently than you because it's part of me. I don't want to lose my breast." Her knuckles moved over her mouth.

"I don't want you to lose a breast either, but it's better than losing you." Obviously, she didn't want a tummy tissue breast. "We have to get the cancer."

She broke a piece of cookie. "Do you think we should just remove the lump?"

"He said you can go further, if necessary."

Charlotte glanced around the room. "How would you feel, the breast man, if I had only one?"

Kevin felt a piercing pain. "If you think I would feel—less love for you—because of surgery, then we have a bigger problem than I thought. I'll love you Charlotte with two, one, or no breasts."

When Charlotte saw the distress reflected in his eyes, tears brimmed in hers, then spilled down her face. "I know you will," she said, dabbing her cheeks. "I want to control everything and I can't. Tummy fat isn't the same as a real breast. Part of me would be gone, a part you appreciate."

"Stop it. I appreciate *you*." Charlotte let his words sink in for several minutes while they watched the raindrops drip down the window.

Finally she tasted the peanut butter cookie, discovered her coffee cup and warmed her hands around it. "I don't want another opinion."

"I think we can trust Dr. Cumberland." Kevin nodded.

"I want him to remove the lump. That should take care of it."

"That sounds more like you." Kevin smiled. "Then it's decided."

Charlotte wet a finger and lifted some cookie crumbs. "What if they don't get it all?"

"We'll deal with it."

"Aren't you afraid?"

"Yeah, I'm afraid." Kevin leaned toward her. "Remember what the pediatrician said when the kids got sick?"

"Courage." Charlotte looked into his brown eyes.

"Right. That applies now."

"Could we go home for dinner? I have some frozen spaghetti sauce."

"Of course," Kevin said before he took Charlotte's elbow and walked alongside her into the rainy evening.

# Chapter 5

The next morning Charlotte called Dr. Cumberland's office. "I've decided I want to schedule a lumpectomy as soon as possible."

"Yes, Charlotte," the receptionist said. "I will tell Dr. Cumberland you called. He'll get back with you soon, I'm sure. It's a matter of finding an available operating room. If you haven't heard from us by tomorrow afternoon, call again."

"Thank you, I will." Charlotte laid the phone on the counter. She walked to the sink window where she noticed an unfamiliar Mazda pulling into Florence's driveway. A tall graceful woman stepped out. Charlotte recognized Florence's daughter, Debbie. She had been thirty–something and married when Florence moved across the street. Charlotte thought she lived an hour's drive away.

The Keeleys knew Nathan better. Despite his illness, Nathan had for the most part supported himself and maintained his own apartment. He had never married. Cherished by his mother, they had kept each other going. When he'd felt increased confidence, he planned the fateful scuba diving trip. Thank God, Debbie has stepped in, Charlotte thought. I'll have more time for Florence when I get this lump out of the way.

She made a list of groceries and drove her Toyota to the store. She parked a distance from the entrance then walked briskly. Ahead, she saw Kate approaching her.

"Hi Mom, lunchtime," Kate said, lifting a container filled with pasta salad.

"Hello Kate. I suppose you're busy as ever at the hospital."

Kate neared her car and stopped. "Busy is right, always something. What's the scoop on your tumor?"

"Decided on a lumpectomy. I called to schedule surgery this morning."

"And?"

"They'll call back."

"A lumpectomy sounds like a wise choice." Kate set the salad on the hood of her car. "Uh . . . Mom, I'm sorry we haven't talked much lately. I don't feel too comfortable. . . with Dad. . . since Todd—"

"I understand." Charlotte gave a little shiver as raindrops starting falling. She hadn't called Todd.

"Jonas chatters about going to the zoo. I'll postpone the outing with him so you won't have to deal with it."

"You're a dear. Tell him we'll re–schedule."

Kate picked up the plastic container and opened her car door. "Call me when you know the date of surgery."

"I will," Charlotte said, then scurried through the rain into the supermarket. When she returned home, she waited for the doctor to call. He didn't.

Kevin walked into the kitchen at six, newspaper in hand. "Did you hear back from Dr. Cumberland?"

"Not yet. You sound as anxious as I do. I told Kate today."

"You called Kate?"

"No, I ran into her at the store." Charlotte stirred chicken strips in olive oil, added some broccoli. Remember we promised Jonas a trip to the zoo? He called a few days ago and reminded me it was supposed to be Saturday."

"Yes." Kevin pitched the newspaper to his chair.

"I told Kate we had to put it off and she volunteered to tell Jonas."

"That's good. He won't break. When you feel up to it we can go." Kevin headed into the bedroom, changed into Levi's and continued to the living room. He didn't want to know if Kate had asked any more questions about Charlotte's surgery or anything else. He sat down and opened the newspaper. In the end, Charlotte would make him explain those words he'd shouted at Todd, but could he? He didn't understand his own behavior. He knew it was inexcusable. The truth was too disturbing. He didn't want to know the truth about Todd, didn't want reminders about his missing brother. Not now, at least not until Charlotte had surgery. He wanted to protect her from stress. He read the news until Charlotte called him for dinner.

The moment they sat down, the phone rang. When Charlotte answered, a person in scheduling gave her a date. "Can you make that?" Charlotte felt tempted to say no, that she planned to wash her hair that hour. Of course, she could make it.

After listening, she said, "Yes, I understand. Thanks for calling." Kevin's deep–set eyes held hers. Charlotte sat down. "Lumpectomy

Monday at nine. I have to check in for prep at eight."

"That was fast." Kevin pushed his fork till it was even with the tip of his knife beside his plate.

"If all goes well, I can go home the same day. Of course someone should drive me."

"Oh, we'll find *someone*." Kevin began his slow grin. He looked past the table to the kitchen counter where *Harry Potter* still lay untouched. "You haven't read any magic."

"Nope." Charlotte grinned, leveling her hand beneath her nose. "I'm up to here in adventures of my own." While Kevin washed the dishes, she called Kate.

A woman came into the patient room Monday morning to prep Charlotte for her lumpectomy. Kevin kissed his wife and left her. He wandered until he located the waiting room. When he found it, he noticed the ordinariness of the room. A couch, two brown leather chairs, one occupied by a young man with an infant. The ordinary stuff seemed significant. He sunk into his own thoughts. He had one more meeting with a firm, which he hoped would wrap up a contract to build another bridge across the Columbia River near Portland, Oregon. Charlotte wasn't aware of this yet, hadn't recently asked about his work. Kevin understood her stress had preoccupied her. He liked his work, but he was getting older and this was his last effort before he retired.

The younger of two sons, Kevin had grown up in Vermont in the late forties and early fifties. Stephen, his older brother, had been his playmate and friend. Their parents owned a hardware store where they worked too hard with few days off. The experience persuaded Kevin he would obtain an education and do better when he was able. Despite the daily grind, each Sunday Ethel and Martin Keeley attended worship in the Baptist church with the boys wedged between them. Kevin remembered sitting with Steve, each of them dressed in slacks and a clean shirt. Every Sunday Steve held a wad of gum under his tongue, which he retrieved during prayer time and blew huge pink bubbles one after another daring Kevin to pop them.

Later during their scouting years, Kevin followed Steve to unmarked trails, leaving them lost, hungry, and at last reprimanded by the scout leader. Steve mastered scouting, even as a buffoon. Kevin was just a good scout. He embraced the blessings and responsibilities of faith in God, and was mindful of explicit rights and wrongs. He didn't like stepping over the lines drawn by his parents and the church, unlike Steve, who had thrived on bending those conventions as far as he could.

During his high school junior year, Kevin convinced his parents he could find work after school, besides their hardware shop. For Kevin's sake, the Keeleys encouraged his independence and his added income at a local grocery. Steve, eighteen at the time, stayed employed at the shop for another year until he graduated, and then joined the army.

Kevin took a deep breath, aware of his surroundings. The man and baby had left the waiting room. He sat alone. He turned his wrist, noting his watch read nine-fifteen. Charlotte should be in surgery now. Steve. He still missed Steve. After working for the National Parks for a summer repairing trails and assisting in visitor information centers, Kevin had enlisted in the army to take advantage of the GI bill for his education. His folks couldn't afford to help him. At nineteen, he joined Steve in Korea. He shook his head now, dismissing the reminders of that anguish in his life. A part of him still wished for simple, logical explanations, clear–cut answers. Why had Steve never contacted him again? Could he? The wound was ancient and kept in the past.

An image of Stephen then, reminded him of Todd now. They each possessed a streak of non–conformity, a quality Kevin's sense of tradition found odd. His brother's characteristic quick temper, his intensity, his infinite curiosity, were present in Todd. As a boy, Todd asked zillions of questions. Why do crabs walk sideways and how do starfish grow new legs? Why aren't spiders stuck in their webs? Why, why, why?

Now a vague chasm stretched between him and Todd. It widened from time to time, without explanation or examination. Does Todd know I feel—disappointed?—Kevin asked himself, his own feelings uncertain. Their relationship, tied by common interests in wildlife and the natural sciences, was superficial. Yet, he felt a pride in Todd, who had remained with scouting through high school and earned a degree in marine biology, an intelligent man.

Kevin remembered that before the births of their children, he and Charlotte had discussed priorities to spend time with them. They'd turned out fine with jobs and lives of their own. His grandchildren gave him pleasure beyond his imagination. Jonas loved to play catch in the backyard or chase on the beach with Spike, the Keeley's dog.

Todd had physically moved away, but he'd hidden his emotions since his teens. Who could blame him? "You could take more interest in his life," Charlotte once said. Though he hadn't met Todd's roommate until the reception, Kevin had heard Todd speak of Trevor's athletic muscle and skill. Todd had wit, but he was no jock. Trevor? A real hunk. Kevin had eyed the shoulders that filled out Trevor's sports coat. Why hadn't a woman grabbed him? he wondered. Unconsciously he furrowed his brows, moving his mouth into a grim line. What were Todd's intentions? Kevin felt the uneasy anxiety that plagued him whenever things didn't happen the way he expected. He longed for a blueprint to recapture a compatibility with his son. Grappling with the questions was more than he could do. He felt ashamed of his shallow thinking. Alaska, Todd must be there. The phone number that the proprietor had given Charlotte had an Alaska area code.

Kevin jerked up his head when the office door banged shut and a patient entered. He stretched his legs and arms, suddenly aware of his watch around his bronze wrist. An hour had elapsed since Charlotte went in for the lumpectomy. He stood and strolled across the room, inspected a large jade plant, dusting a petal with his finger. When two arms seized his thighs from behind in a bear hug, he stepped ahead to keep his balance. A familiar voice rang out. "Guess who?" Spinning around, Kevin raised a delighted child into the air, swung him around and touched his feet to the carpet.

"Hey, it's Jonas."

"Yep." Jonas giggled and his deep–set eyes were warm with affection. Unaware of his charm, Jonas elicited exchanged smiles from others amused by the commotion.

"Why aren't you in school?" Kevin frowned with suspicion.

"No school today."

Kate flashed a grin at her Dad, concealing her laughter from

Jonas, as she embraced him. "Teacher's workshop. How's Mom doing?"

"Exactly what I was wondering. You heard what time we'd be here?"

"Yes, an issue we need to discuss. Mom called me when the surgery was scheduled. I'm a bit mad at you."

"I left that to her, but I did remind her." He looked at Jonas. "About the zoo . . ." Kevin took Jonas' hand and led him to a chair.

"Mom told me. It's okay. Could we go when Grams is feeling better?"

"Sure we will, Jonas. This week won't work, but we'll definitely go."

"I wish I could see a brontosaurus at the zoo."

"They're ex—"

"Extinct, I know Gramps, they're all dead. I'm learning stuff about them in school. Still wish I could see one." His voice was wistful. "Dinosaurs are awesome. I love 'em."

Kate enjoyed this fond exchange between two of the four significant males in her life. She wondered if anyone had informed Todd about Mother's surgery. Not knowing, he would feel left out. She ached to talk to her parents about her brother, but now was not the time. Why hadn't she called Todd about this medical problem? She didn't know.

"I have fifteen, don't I Mom." Kate felt Jonas' fingers tug her arm and she stirred from her thoughts and faced his brown eyes. "Don't I have fifteen different dinosaurs."

"Yes, yes you do."

"One of 'em's glued together with three legs cause Amanda broke it." Jonas scowled, and narrowed his eyes.

"Did you get mad at her?" Kevin asked.

"Yeah, but she was only three then. The last time she got into my stuff, I got so mad that Dad got me a lock for my cupboard." His voice rose triumphant, bringing grins from patients.

"Well, let's see when Grams will be ready for visitors. She'll be so glad you came, but I don't think they'll let you into her room." Before Jonas responded, Kevin walked to the desk to ask when his wife might be finished with surgery.

A receptionist checked and returned to her desk. "Your wife should be through and in the recovery room in a few minutes. The nurse will notify you so you can go in to see her. She'll be drowsy at first, and one visitor at a time is best. Sorry, no children."

Jonas led them to the children's waiting area, where he searched and found a dinosaur book. Five minutes later the nurse walked toward them. "That's a huge one," she said looking at the dinosaur. Then she smiled and invited Kevin into recovery.

Charlotte lifted her head a bit and smiled groggily. "I think Dr. Cumberland told me everything is okay, but maybe I was dreaming."

"Great, that's wonderful." Had the doctor actually seen her? "How are you feeling?"

"I'm sore, but glad it's done."

Kevin leaned over his wife, lifted a damp curl from her cheek. "Someone in the waiting room wants to see you."

"Kate?"

"Yes, and Jonas."

"I want to see them too. Do you think they'll let Jonas in here?"

"Not in recovery, but I'm sure he wanted to come." Kevin kissed Charlotte's cheek. "I'll be back in a few minutes, but Kate will be in first." He proceeded to the waiting area, motioned his daughter into the room, and resumed his conversation with Jonas.

"Hi Mom. I'm so relieved you're okay. It's a good thing I saw you in the parking lot."

"I knew I could count on you," Charlotte said. Kate thought her mother's face looked pale and drawn. Not a surprise. She wanted to ask if Todd knew, but decided against it.

"Jonas is with me. He can't wait to see you and make a new date for the zoo trip. I swear that kid thinks animals are the most awesome creatures God created. Don't worry, though, you can have all the convalescent time you need. He's involved in school projects, particularly dinosaurs. He's been eating up books." Kate saw her mother's smile fade, her eyes close. She bent over and hugged her. "I think you need your rest now," she said and left the room while Charlotte drifted off.

Kate looked across the waiting room to the children's section. Jonas was sprawled across a chair facing Kevin who was intently reading something. As she approached the engrossed twosome, Jonas rushed to her. "Hey, Mom, they found a dinosaur that had wings."

"Wings?"

"In China," Kevin said, grinning. "They discovered fossils of a feathered creature, identified as a small dinosaur. His deep–set eyes twinkled as he laid aside the *Nature* journal.

"*Four* wings, right, Gramps?"

"That's what the journal says, and feathers on the tail."

"Two sets?" Kate's eyebrows went up.

"One on its forelimbs and the other on its legs," Kevin said.

"Amazing, sounds like lots of feathers. How big?"

"This long all the way to its tail." Jonas spread his arms out.

"Three feet," Kevin said. "With a body the size of a pigeon."

"They call it, Mi . . . how do you say it Gramps?"

"Microraptor gui," Kevin said, his face animated.

"Wow," Jonas said, "one hundred twenty five million years old."

"Whoa, I see," Kate said, placing her hands on her hips. "How am I going to break you away from here? It's time to go home."

"Can't I see Grams?"

"She's in a special room now where they don't allow children, but when she's home, you can see her."

Jonas scowled and stuck his hands in his pockets. "I wish I wasn't just a kid."

"I'm sorry, Son. If Gramps brings her home tonight, I'll take you to see her tomorrow."

"Glad you came," Kevin said to his daughter.

"Me too, Dad." Then using a quieter tone, "Was the surgery a success? Mom seems tired."

"She told me that Dr. Cumberland already spoke to her since the procedure, said things went fine, but I'm not leaving until I hear it from him. I'll call you as soon as I find out."

"You better."

"I will."

Kate paced a few steps toward the door. "Dad, does Todd know about Mom's cancer?" Kevin pressed his lips together and inspected the rug. Kate waited. He coughed, noticed Jonas across the room, absorbed in a book. "I haven't talked with him in two months."

"What about Mom?  Has she talked with Todd?" Stupid question, she thought.

"No." Kevin lowered his voice. "He moved, you know." He pointed his foot, stuck his fingers in his pockets. "You could call your brother and let him know what's going on with us. Have you?" He turned his eyes to the floor in search of lint.

"No, I haven't." Kate looked down, rubbing her palms across her thighs. "We need to talk." Kevin's dark eyes looked baffled when they glanced up then back to the floor.

Jonas scooted to them with a book. "Look at this one," he said, pushing the dinosaur picture in their faces. A welcome reprieve, father and daughter smiled at Jonas and the dino sketch.

"Now we have to go home. Call me, Dad." Kate looked at her father and watched Jonas return the book to a shelf.

"Bye, young man." He laid his hand on the boy's shoulder.

"Bye. Don't forget the zoo, Gramps."  His eyes begged a promise.

"No way. Tell your little sister I said hi." Taking Jonas' hand, Kate walked to her car.

In the hospital cafeteria, Kevin ate some lasagna, a roll, and coffee before returning to Charlotte's room.  When he entered the hall, he glanced down it and saw the back of a tall rusty haired man who looked like Dr. Cumberland. Charlotte seemed as beautiful as ever when she smiled at him. She was sipping tea and on the table beside her lay an empty plate. "So they did feed you." He set her cup on the plate. Kevin leaned over and kissed her cheek.

"That's all?" she said. He touched her neck with a tender hand, and then he stretched across her body sideways taking her in his arms.  He kissed her squarely on the lips, holding himself off her breasts. "Better?"

"Much."

A nurse waltzed in, put a blood pressure cuff on Charlotte's arm. "The doctor is coming this way. I'm sure you're eager to see him." She finished her job, then left.

"You look better since you woke up and got something in your stomach," Kevin said.

"I had a pain pill, too." Charlotte smoothed the sheet over her body. "Did you keep Jonas occupied while Kate talked with me?"

"With dinosaur books, yes. He's not letting us off the hook on the zoo trip either."

Charlotte smiled. "He'll keep us young. When were we last at the Portland zoo?"

"Sounds like fun, but I don't think the animals will be out sunning themselves this time of year." Dr. Cumberland had entered the room.

"Hello," Kevin said, extending his hand. "You have good ears." The doctor grasped Kevin's hand and touched Charlotte's shoulder.

"I have very encouraging news. I'm reasonably certain we removed all of the cancerous cells. The lymph node looked healthy. Now I recommend radiation five days a week for the next five to seven weeks." He looked at Charlotte. "You did everything right for early detection. I expect full recovery for you. Congratulations."

"Yes." Charlotte slapped Kevin's hand in a high–five.

Kate dreaded returning home, knowing she couldn't let more time elapse before she called Todd. She stopped at the day care to pick up Amanda, who, along with her brother, squealed with delight when Kate turned into Dairy Queen. She'd allow the children a hamburger and ice cream since she didn't feel like fixing lunch. After Jonas ate the hamburger, he grasped the cone, ran his tongue around the cool smooth ice cream. He licked off a drop that dribbled down his chin. "Is Grams gonna be okay?" he asked.

"I hope so, honey. I made Gramps promise to call me when he talks to her doctor. She will need lots of rest. If everything isn't okay, she might feel sad." Kate's voice broke, but as she bent to lick her cone, she smiled at Jonas. They finished their ice cream and when they arrived at home, Kate's neck had a kink in it and her back ached. She laundered some clothes and sat down to read. She had a quick dinner ready when Dave arrived.

"Macaroni and cheese. Not my favorite, but it'll sustain life," he mumbled on his way to the bedroom where he shed his sports coat and found his Levi's.

"It better," Kate said. She put a carrot raisin salad on the table and called the kids.

"What did you find out about your Mom?" Dave left the table at

Amanda's clamor for ketchup, which he dribbled over her macaroni.

"I haven't heard the doctor's report yet, but expect Dad to call soon. Mom felt tired, but was in good spirits." After Dave excused Jonas and Amanda from the table, he began clearing the dishes.

"I'll get 'em later," Kate said, rubbing her neck. "Let's sit in the living room for a few minutes while our offspring are still getting along."

"Oh, please, I want to do the dishes," Dave mimicked protest, but followed Charlotte to the couch. "You had time with your Mom?"

"A minute. She dosed off while I was talking." She stuck up her hand. "Don't say it. I need to call Todd. He doesn't know she had surgery. Last summer at Nathan's memorial, we all knew that Trevor was a real partner. Somehow, he wasn't just a friend anymore, if he ever was. None of us has talked to Todd since. What's wrong with this clan?"

"Wrong?" Dave silently held his own opinions, but was curious how Kate and her parents felt about her brother. He wanted to hear more. He and Kate had not spoken about the incident.

"Let's face it, Dave. Todd's gay." Kate's eyes penetrated his as he listened, smoothed his beard, and gazed back with his warm brown eyes. "It's not right. Something is wrong with Todd. We're losing him," Kate said. "He obviously doesn't want to be around us with Trevor."

"Would you, after that scene?"

"No, but what can we do about it? It's his problem." Kate wrinkled her brow. "Remember how Mom was scrutinizing Trevor in the kitchen? Did you see Dad clam up and turn stiff and awkward? Before he—" Kate stopped.

"Told Todd to keep his hands off Jonas?"

"Yes." Tears welled in Kate's eyes.

"Why is it a major crisis if Todd's gay?"

Kate's face turned white and incredulous. She turned away from Dave, then spun around and gaped at him. "Anything's okay with you, isn't it?" she burst out. Her face flushed. "This will destroy my parents. Do you understand that?"

He understood Kate was tired, her behavior irrational. She had empathized with Jim Baxter and now this. "Have you told your folks what you think about Todd?"

"No. I know how they feel about homosexuals."

A thunderous sound of footsteps in the hall and an angry voice ended their conversation. "Mom, Amanda's in my stuff again."

"It's bedtime for both of you," Dave called out, lurching from the room. He chose to help put the children in bed, but shortened the usual rituals.

When he returned, he found Kate in the kitchen, still perplexed, but calmer. "Honey," she began, "I'm so ambiguous about gays, but my feelings are real." She twisted a dishrag in her hands. "So why am I confessing them to you like I'm a bigot?" Dave listened and continued to put dishes in the cupboard without speaking. The phone rang and Kate answered it.

"Hi Dad. All of it? That's great. I'm so relieved. When is she coming home? Good, tell her I'll call her tomorrow." Kate paused before hanging up. "Radiation? How often? Me too. Thanks, I'll tell Dave. Bye."

# Chapter 6

Sitting at the Formica kitchen table, Trevor read *Sports Illustrated* and expected Todd's return home. It's colder in Kodiak than in Oregon, he thought, and walked to the furnace thermostat, flipped it higher. He could still feel the air whistling beneath the wooden back door and into the room. Since coming to Alaska, he and Todd had spent most of their time becoming acquainted with the jobs they had found with Alaska's Fish and Game Department, researching seals. Trevor ran his hand through his hair. Kevin Keeley's behavior last summer had shocked him. Surely, he had a clue before then that Todd and he were partners. Had the fact not registered with Kevin before last August? I can't believe he could be such a jerk, Trevor thought. It was a sore subject with Todd so they did their jobs and didn't discuss it.

Trevor remembered his own father tossing a football with him. How would Dad feel about me being gay, if he had—if he and Mom had—survived the accident? he wondered. He had fallen in love with Todd when they met on the job in Oregon. He wished Todd felt better about himself. As far as he was concerned, Todd had spent too much energy feeling guilty. He's still wearing himself out trying to be what he imagines others expect of him, especially his family, Trevor thought.

He stretched his muscular arms, stood up. He walked to the stove where he stirred the pan that simmered with dinner. A stunning man he was with his angular face and pale blue eyes in stark contrast to his thick, black as a crow, hair. Trevor stood on the faded spot of brick colored linoleum, stirred and pondered. Charlotte will have an easier time than Kevin, since she's open and can accept change. He thought about his own reluctance to show any overt affection to Todd, since Todd had cautioned him against it. He'd never met his folks until the memorial reception. Todd didn't want him to show affection around anyone. Trevor knew Todd must advance with tiny steps in his effort at authenticity with himself and his parents. How long would the risk be so scary and the pretence so necessary?

The cool fall air nipped Todd's back as he whipped along a trail near his house. His knees didn't like jogging so he'd settled for a quick stride. He wanted some time alone. To think. His breath left clouds before him in the crisp air. The pungent scent of spruce filled his nostrils. Should he call his sister? He hadn't heard from anyone since summer. Red sumac, and yellow maple leaves, wet with rain, covered the ground like a carpet. The drizzle had stopped. A protected dry twig crackled beneath his foot. He'd go three miles today.

As he moved along the route, he thought about Nathan's memorial. Maybe I shouldn't have taken Trevor. Nathan had never met Trevor, but he'd spent time talking with me, Todd thought, when he was between jobs and had time on his hands. Todd kicked the wet leaves. A memorial reception seemed like a safe place to bring Trevor. He wanted to show his family his situation with Trevor, not tell them. Then came the explosion. He showed them all right: his lover, his temper, and his vulnerability. Had his folks known? He knew they didn't approve of his relationship with Trevor. Hell, he knew deep down they wouldn't. Todd felt the tingling warmth in his leg muscles move through his torso and he rubbed his hands and unzipped his jacket. He stared at the spruce needles on the trail. How can I be the son of such a rigid man? What does Dad imagine about me? How can I tell him who I am with Trevor? What'll happen to our family? I can't live this lie anymore.

Trevor's head turned toward the entry, when he heard Todd's key click in the lock. When Todd opened the door, a smell of beef and onions wafted in the air. "Hey, smells like beef stew. I'm starved." Todd threw his coat across a chair and ambled into the kitchen.

"Been walking?" asked Trevor, still at the stove. "Your face is red."

"Yeah. I put in my three miles. How about some stew?"

The hot stew tasted good. Later Todd let a hot shower beat on his back, but it didn't wash away the thoughts churning in his mind. Was he losing his family? Had he ever had a real relationship with his parents and sister? He squeezed some shampoo into his hand and lathered it into his hair. Then he rinsed it and turned off the water, toweled dry his lean body. He'd pulled on some shorts, tied his white terrycloth robe, and was reaching for his comb when Trevor handed him the phone.

"Your sister." He nodded, then exited the room allowing Todd privacy.

"Hello?"

"Todd . . . this is Kate."

"Hi Kate. I, uh, have been wondering how all of you are."

"That's why I called. Mom had breast surgery this morning. A lumpectomy to be exact."

"Cancer? When did she find out?"

"She discovered a lump herself not long ago. I didn't know about it myself until the last minute. You know Mom hates to worry us."

"Is that it?" He tossed back his wet hair. "Well, I'm glad she's okay. You sure they got it all?"

"That's what the doctor told Dad. She'll need to follow up with radiation, but I think she's lucky it wasn't worse. She's doing fine, came home this afternoon. I thought you should know."

After a long pause, Kate, having given the message, wanted to end the conversation. Before she found the words, Todd broke the silence.

"Maybe . . . I might come and visit her. Do you think she'd like that? I've been thinking about a trip anyway."

"Sure, Todd. You know she'd love to see you."

Todd twisted the cord. "I haven't talked to her or Dad since last summer." He hadn't meant to jump into this. He yearned to have his life simplified, to be a regular guy, one his parents and sister would love. In the pit of his stomach, he felt a knot. This wasn't going to work by long distance. Pushing his hair behind his ears, he tried to sound casual.

"Anyway, we have some catching up to do,"

"Yes we do." Kate shifted on the couch.

Todd took a breath, realizing Kate sounded pleasant but not enthused at the prospect of seeing him. "Are you and Dave okay? How are the kids?"

"We're good." Kate's voice softened a little. "Really we are. Jonas and Amanda are growing so fast."

"I miss seeing them." Kate didn't respond, so Todd finished. "Well Kate, nice talking with you. Please give Mom my best."

"I will. Bye."

"Bye Kate." That's it, Todd thought. He moved to the living room. Trevor watched him over the edge of the newspaper.

"How'd it go? Something wrong?" Todd flipped his hair and flopped onto the couch.

"Mom had breast surgery this morning. Kate sounds as if it worked, but she'll still need radiation follow up."

"Nice of Kate to let you know."

Ignoring the comment, Todd said, "I told Kate I might go see Mom."

"You mean we might go?" Trevor put the paper aside.

"No, I just said I might. You . . . you weren't mentioned, Trev."

"Can't say I'm amazed."

"It wasn't the time. I can't deal with these emotions long distance. I didn't want to discuss us with Kate by phone, but I do want you to go with me. I think it's time to go back. I'm the one who stormed out."

"Todd, you know I agree you should get in touch with your folks, especially with this news of your mom. Your dad didn't bother to call you, so it's not going to be easy."

"I didn't say it would be easy. He didn't tell Kate either." Todd rose as color flooded his face. "Dad's going to have to take me as I am or not at all. I'm sick of walking on eggshells, and I'm not pretending anymore around my folks." His green eyes burned.

"We're not around them . . . now we live here. You've always walked on egg shells haven't you?"

"Yes . . . I have." Todd flinched, shrinking from the ache in his personal memories.

"A visit would be fine, Todd, but it sounds like you want to challenge their homophobia."

"Maybe I do."

"For God's sake, I've lived with you for more than two years. Your parents aren't clueless. Your dad was way out of line . . . his insinuation about Jonas." Trevor toed the worn spot in the carpet. "He was so hypersensitive, maybe they're in denial, but I can't believe they haven't figured it out. Your sister must know."

"Yes. And my parents must know, but Goddammit, they won't mention it." Todd put his head in his hands; his blond hair swept over his forehead and concealed the tears that stung his eyes. "Mom has never said a word, Dad's worse and Kate's unbelievable for a modern woman. But they all know," Todd suddenly sobbed. "They know." His partner got up from his chair, went to Todd, and sat next to him. Trevor's face softened with tenderness as he looked at Todd. His pale blue eyes caressed Todd's anguished face. In a moment Todd leaned sideways and fell into Trevor's arms. "I love you," he choked. "My life was unbearable before I met you." Feeling Todd's damp hair against his chest, Trevor held his shaking body, letting him sob until he was relaxed enough to sleep.

# Chapter 7

Florence gazed out her kitchen window admiring the yellow and purple pansies she had put into three clay pots. She pulled her sweater around her shoulders, filled a watering can. Her fingers ached when she closed them around the handle and walked onto the wooden porch with it. The yard boy had mowed the lawn for the last time before winter and the sweet grass smell lingered in the air.

She looked across the street to Charlotte's house. I haven't seen her around much, she thought. Todd neither. What made him so furious the day he stormed out of the house? she wondered. Charlotte didn't talk about it. They don't like him being gay, that's probably it. Don't want no one to know. Just like I didn't talk to no one about Nathan. She steadied the can with hands that quivered as the last drop of water poured into her flowers.

I think I'll go see Charlotte, Florence thought. She went into her bedroom and took the brush off her dresser, swept up the loose hairs around her ears securing them in a comb. She dabbed on pink lipstick and set out with careful steps.

When she looked up, Florence saw Charlotte wave from her kitchen window. When she approached the door, Charlotte opened it. "Hello, Florence. Please come in."

"Do you mind? Haven't seen you out in the yard and wondered if everything is okay."

"I think I'm going to be just fine," Charlotte said. Florence thought she looked like she was deciding something. "I've intended to have you for tea sooner. Would you like a cup now?"

"My yes, that sounds good." Florence took a few steps and sat at the table where she watched Charlotte fill the teakettle and place tea bags in mugs. "You been sick?" Florence's brown-eyed gaze had a power that would pull the truth from anyone.

"Not sick, Florence. I had a small tumor removed from my breast."

"Cancer?" Florence's mouth dropped open and stayed that way a second.

"Yes, but the doctor thinks he removed all of it. I go for a radiation treatment every day. Fortunately, I discovered the lump myself and it was small." Charlotte placed two steaming mugs on the table.

"Good, good. Well, if you need help around the yard, I guess Kevin and Todd will have to help you. Since Nathan died." Florence's eyes filled, looking magnified by her tears. "I miss him." Her fingers stroked the place mat, sadness descending with the teardrops into the lines of her face. "Got me a boy to mow."

"I'm glad you found someone." Charlotte looked at the soft contour of Florence's hair, the curve of her nose.

"That Trevor fellow seemed nice." Florence dabbed her eyes with a wadded tissue. "You happy Todd's got someone special?" She stirred sugar into her tea.

"We all need someone." Charlotte glanced away.

"Nathan had trouble making friends," Florence said, then sipped some tea. "He talked funny, so kids teased him, but he was smart. He did good in his computer job." She let out a wistful sigh. "He was clumsy—shouldn't have tried scuba diving." Charlotte swallowed, nodded. "I heard Todd yell when he ran out of here, after Nathan's memorial." Florence's eyes circled the kitchen. "Is he okay?" Her body quivered when she clutched the table.

"He's okay. He moved to Alaska . . . has a new job."

"Alaska. With Trevor?"

"Heavens Florence, I don't know."

"I ask too many questions." When she touched her fingers to her lips, the darkened veins in her hands appeared as if in parchment. "Tea tasted good, thanks. I must be going." She leaned hard on the table, pressed her palms down and pushed. When she reached the porch, she said, "Kate tell you about the night Pam Baxter died?"

"No, I forgot to ask her, but she's coming this afternoon, so I'll ask."

"Stop teasing her," Kate scolded Jonas from the front seat of the family van. Amanda let out a wail, and began crying again.

"Stop that, young lady. You're not hurt," Dave said. He turned his head and glared at his children, gritting his teeth. "We're almost there. Now remember Grandma won't feel like playing with you." He hoped Grandpa would.

In fifteen minutes, they arrived in the Keeley driveway. The afternoon sun sat low in the sky. Kevin greeted them near the doorway where he had begun filling a bag with leaves. Jonas dove into the remaining pile, his hair flying into his shiny eyes. "Oh no you don't," Kevin shouted, pretending to trip him with the rake. "Now you have to help me finish putting them in the bag."

"Nah huh, you can't catch me," Jonas shrieked as he ran behind the gigantic maple tree. Amanda's blond curls bounced in amber light as she imitated her big brother, hiding with him and giggling loudly until Kevin encircled them in his arms. Then he gestured their parents inside.

Charlotte started to rise from the couch when Kate and Dave approached her. "Stay put, Mom. Don't get up."

"I'm so glad to see you. I'm doing fine. Being one of the fortunate ones is a balm to my soul."

"Mine too." Kate kissed her cheek. "It's been about a week. How's the radiation making you feel? Are you weak?"

"A bit, but I guess that means my normal cells are using energy to repair the damage done to them."

"You sound so technical."

"I ask the doctor a lot of questions, Kate, just like you taught me. He's not as personable as Dr. Cumberland is, but he seems to know his stuff. He thinks I should be through with the radiation in a month."

Kate felt relief at her mother's spirit. "Want some tea?" She looked at Charlotte. "I'll fix it."

"Sounds good. I had tea with Florence earlier today."

"How's she doing?" Kate said over her shoulder as she moved into the kitchen.

"Misses Nathan."

"I'm sure she does."

Dave had walked outside to see how Kevin was holding up while entertaining his grandchildren. Kate glanced out the kitchen window at the towering maple tree in which she used to play. She was twelve when her parents moved here. She remembered reading in the tree house when her brother would allow her in it. A rope ladder, a newer one, still hung from a branch just below the floor of the structure. Now Jonas loved to climb up to the house, though he needed permission and supervision, often against his wishes. While the water in the teakettle heated, Kate found some china cups on the top shelf of the cabinet, which she washed, knowing how Charlotte would appreciate drinking tea from one.

"Look in the cupboard for a bag of gingersnaps," her mom offered from the living room couch. Kate had poured the tea and was looking for a tray, when Charlotte joined her at the kitchen table. "I can eat here. I'm not an invalid." They sat for a few minutes, glad the men and children hadn't yet discovered them.

"Mom, I talked to Todd last week." Kate watched her mother fluff her hair past her forehead and raise her chin.

"Oh?"

"You haven't mentioned him, so I've been reluctant to myself."

"And what did he have to say?"

"I told him about your surgery. He was concerned, but happy that things went well. He said he wants to come for a visit." Charlotte leaned forward, put her elbows on the table and cupped her chin in her hands. A tiny frown moved through her brows and she pressed her lips together for a second.

"I hope you told him we'd love to see him," she said smoothly, changing her expression to a smile.

"Of course I did, Mom." Kate thought that her mother, if sincere and composed, did seem uncomfortable.

"How is he?" Charlotte asked, after a moment's silence. "We've been so busy this fall and, evidently, he has too. Your dad and I haven't spoken—"

"Yes, I know. He's okay, thinks a trip would be a good change for him."

Charlotte stirred her tea, observing the roses on the china cup. She dipped a gingersnap, ate a bite and looked at Kate with widening eyes. "So, does he still live with Trevor?"

"Uh, I don't know, Mom. We didn't talk long. He didn't mention Trevor." Kate recalled that another man had answered the call, but she let the thought go.

"Guess we'll catch up on his life soon enough," Charlotte said, lifting her cup and taking a sip. "This tea hits the spot, and using the china was a lovely touch."

Kate, smiling, raised her own cup. "To your good health."

When they finished the tea, Charlotte pushed back the wooden chair, stood and took her cup to the sink. Through the window, she looked across the street and noticed Florence sweeping her walk. The sight of her reminded Charlotte that she hadn't asked Kate about Pam Baxter's death. While everyone was outside, she would take the opportunity to do so. She motioned Kate into the living room where they could be comfortable. After the women's brief exchange, the children burst in the door and announced the car was leaving.

When she had cleaned up the dinner mess and rinsed the dishrag, Kate watched the sudsy water gurgle down the drain. "Mommmm," shrieked Jonas. Kate dropped the rag and flew upstairs to the bathroom where she found Jonas leaning over the sink spitting blood. "I lost my tooth."

"Good grief," Kate said, heaving a breath. "Don't scream like that. I thought you were hurt. Go show your dad." While her mother was captive, Amanda begged for a story and after reading one, Kate saw Jonas returned. "Read me *Arthur's Tooth*," Jonas said. So Kate did, reminded by the inscription inside the book that Todd had given it to Jonas last year. Kate helped Amanda brush her teeth, then tucked the children into bed.

Next, she settled into a chair opposite Dave. "Can you believe it?" Kate said for the second time. Dave laid his paper in his lap, and looked at his wife for the first time.

"Believe what? I'm reading."

"Mom knew Mrs. Baxter. You haven't been listening."

"No, I've been reading. Yes, I can believe it. Your Mom knew Mrs. Baxter. So what?"

"It was a perfect time for me to talk about her gay son, but I chickened out."

"Whose gay son?"

Kate gave him a sharp look. "Mrs. Baxter's gay son, remember? I wanted to get Mom's reaction."

"Kate, your mom doesn't care if Mrs. Baxter's son is gay or not. She wanted to know how you felt about being present when she died. Isn't that right? You said she knew her from their garden club."

"Right . . . thought we might talk about Todd."

"Being gay? What will that help? You happened to be working when Mrs. Baxter died. That's all. Florence got the information about her death straight from Mr. Baxter who happened to mention—"

"My name was Kate, a nurse named Kate," she interrupted, moving forward to the edge of the chair.

"What's wrong with you? That *is* your name."

"Her son, Jim, was so enraged, like Todd."

"Not again. I've heard this all before." Dave folded his arms across his chest. "Did you tell your mom Todd wants to visit?"

"Yes I did."

"And?"

"She acted like it was fine with her. She wants to see him."

"That surprises you?"

"I don't . . . I think . . . she was acting. Like me."

"You're acting?"

"Yeah Dave." Her round blue eyes penetrated him. "It's the way they reared me. I'm a different generation, but I feel funny about confronting Todd." She took a deep breath, and touched her back to the chair. If I was honest I'd confront him."

"Confront him because you think he's gay?" Dave looked confused. "Did he wrong you?" His bushy brows went up.

"Wrong me? You don't mince words, do you." Kate studied the carpet a second. "I want to say no, but I feel like he has."

"You have a right to your feelings." Dave paused and rubbed his beard, then said, "But you better be damn sure you want his answer before you ask him if he's gay. He might tell you. How has he hurt you? Does he go against something you learned as a kid?" Kate fiddled with her watch. "How do you feel about gays in general?"

"Knock it off, Dave. Todd's my brother, not just gays in general. I'm not sure what I feel . . . except . . . I know one thing." She shot him a scathing look. "I get irritated when you act superior."

"That's bull. I respect your feelings."

"You better. I can't stand it anymore. Todd is abnormal. No matter how much I try to accept his gayness it doesn't feel right. What if Todd touches Jonas?"

"You mean his penis?"

"Yes. That's what I mean."

"Then say it."

"How would Jonas react? Would he tell us?"

"Why are you getting so worked up? You used to be rational about this. Now you scare me. Why do you think Todd would ever hurt Jonas . . . or Amanda for that matter?"

"I'll tell you why. He's interested in males . . . sexually."

"True, if Todd's gay he feels a sexual attraction to males—not children. I'm attracted to females. Do you worry about me molesting Amanda? Or any other child? Todd is no different. He's a responsible adult, a gay male, not a pedophile. He has Trevor and Trevor has him. It's not just sexual, they love each other."

"Well." Kate let out a breath. "At least they haven't been around the kids much."

"That's not the point. If they are, they're not likely to touch Jonas or Amanda. That's an offensive stereotype. Heterosexual men—and women—usually commit most pedophile crimes, not gays. Don't lump them together."

Kate studied him a minute. "What about abusive priests?"

"Horrendous. They're pedophiles. Yes, some are gay, others aren't."

"What's your answer?" Kate tensed. "Would Jonas tell us if Todd or Trevor did something wrong?"

"I think he would. We've taught him to confide in us. I hope he'd tell us if anyone mistreated him."

Kate bit her lip. "I want to be mature about it. It's just," she shuddered, "I don't know what I feel anymore. I want to accept the fact that some people are gay." Tears welled in her eyes. "But part of me is repulsed, feels it's a perversion." A few sandy hairs fell forward and stuck to her cheek. "God created us male and female for obvious reasons."

Dave went to her, took her chin in his hand, and wiped a wet streak from her cheek with his thumb. His lips brushed the spot sending a warm sensation through Kate's body. "I don't understand it either," Dave said, pulling her out of the chair and enclosing her in his arms, "but I know it's real for people who feel it. It must be excruciating for them. They grow up right along side us and aren't supposed to feel the way they do."

Charlotte wasn't hearing the pastoral prayer during Sunday worship. She heard the muffled coughs, the stir of paper, the fidgets of children. She looked at her hands, at the rainbow of light refracted from the diamond ring on her finger. How could she and Kevin smooth over the fray with Todd? They hadn't talked with him, how would they visit? He's coming home. She glanced at Kevin's bowed head, his closed eyes, felt his thighs next to hers on the pew. She saw her name in the bulletin on the list of persons in need: of healing, comfort, strength or faith. The pastor, Norman Seibert, had visited her and Kevin several weeks after her lumpectomy. We're all in need of these blessings, she thought. Breast cancer was an acceptable problem. What would Norman say about a gay son?

" . . . *the power and the glory forever. Amen.*" As the congregation concluded the prayer, Charlotte noticed the name, Mr. Baxter and family in the bulletin. The preacher moved to the pulpit and Charlotte struggled to focus on the sermon. Close to home, it centered on the relationship between faith and healing. Pastor Seibert said that with our faith, as tiny as a mustard seed, God would heal all our infirmities. The book of Matthew said so. A comforting thought, but not true, Charlotte thought. People with enormous faith suffer and die daily from cancer and other adversities. Mrs. Baxter had been a lovable person, full of life. Could her lack of faith have killed her? All kinds of trouble visit people whether or not they have faith. Charlotte dismissed her pastor's words.

So often affliction was invisible. Charlotte had experienced faith's power in moving mountains; the ones made of doubt, fear, and even grief. The extraordinary truth was that God sustained her when she lacked faith, not when she had it. God didn't cure everything, but became a kind of 'in the midst Presence' she liked to call it. When faith eluded her.

When the collection plate had passed and been received, the pastor called for silent personal prayer. Charlotte prayed. Thank You God for my successful lumpectomy. Please help me understand Todd . . . give me courage to tell Kevin he wants to visit.

Kevin read the bulletin and found the next hymn number. The benediction came and they turned to greet people in their aisle. Several mentioned how well Charlotte looked, but didn't inquire further. The couple passed up the coffee fellowship and walked to their Toyota. As Kevin drove out of the parking lot, Charlotte noticed Harold Baxter getting into his car. A handsome dark haired man sat in the passenger seat. "Hmm, Florence must be right," Charlotte said.

"What are you talking about?" Kevin turned his head toward her.

"Florence told me Pam and Harold Baxter had a grown son. Harold's in that car and I bet the man with him is his son."

"Don't know, I've never seen Baxter at worship before." He didn't give the car a second glance. "Want some brunch at the Dutch Bakery?" Kevin gave her a familiar broad smile.

"Sure, I want to talk with you about something anyway."

"Something? That sounds ominous."

"Several things. Kate told me she was at the hospital when Pam died. It shook her up. It was so unexpected. Pam went in with a kidney infection, had a heart attack and died."

"Was her son there?" Kevin stopped the car at the restaurant.

"No, Kate didn't mention a son."

Kevin took Charlotte's arm as she stepped out of the car and they walked into the café, which bustled with people. After a few minutes wait, a young man escorted them to their table. "I'm having pancakes," Charlotte said. She looked at the windmill strip around the room. "This is where we sat the night we decided to have my lumpectomy."

"We don't want another one. Should we move?" Kevin's eyes twinkled. His mouth became a wide grin.

"No, it worked fine. Maybe this table will work again."

"Work again?"

"With our next dilemma." Kevin raised his eyebrows, then studied the menu. After the server took their order, he didn't speak.

"I . . . I know you don't want to talk about Todd, but Kate said she called him."

"About your surgery."

"Yes . . . anyway, she said he wants to come to visit me . . . us."

Kevin drew a slow breath. "I suppose that would be okay. Except for my outrageous behavior, I'm a civil man. Is Trevor still with him?"

Charlotte thanked the server for the pancakes. "I don't know about Trevor." She sighed and stared at Kevin. "Todd might bring him along."

"Yeah," Kevin said, "he might."

Tuesday morning Kevin squeezed Crest on his toothbrush, and spoke around its bristles. "The contract for the Columbia River Bridge has been negotiated. Our firm will soon be inspecting the construction site and drawing up the blue prints." He swished water in his mouth and wiped off the foam.

"I understood about half of that. Tell me over coffee," Charlotte said. She wrapped a robe around her body patting Kevin's butt as she passed. "Put on your shorts, you're driving me wild. I'll be in the kitchen."

In minutes Kevin walked into the kitchen dressed, with his hair combed and a grin spread across his broad clean–shaven chin. "You smell good," Charlotte murmured as she kissed his smooth lips. "You're proud of your son–in–law aren't you?"

"You bet. Dave Winston is an excellent architect, which is why I hired him to design the bridge. I plan to retire after this project."

"The meeting must have lasted forever last night. You weren't home at ten-thirty when I went to bed."

"Got here at eleven-fifteen and you were asleep. This evening meeting stuff is unusual. Most will be during the day. They're clearing the site before Christmas. I may need to make a few runs out there, but I'm sure you could have a day with Kate and the kids in Portland some day when Dave and I are at the site."

"I think I hear the monkeys calling me from their zoo cages."

"Oh, yeah. Are you feeling up to that trip yet?"

"Wait a minute. Not without you. *We* are taking the grandchildren to the zoo, remember? I have one more week of radiation, then I think I'm up to it."

Kevin bent and slid his arms around Charlotte's torso, lifting her breasts to his face. "I'm glad you are doing so well," he said, brushing his cheek against her bosom."

"Me too. I'm lucky. While we're on the subject of breasts and kids, we should talk about Todd's plans." She drew back to look at Kevin. "According to Kate, he wants to visit in a few weeks. Let's rally our efforts to make it a good time. I think planning something fun would lighten things up."

Kevin studied her face a second, not wanting to disappoint her. "I'll do my best. Invite him to the zoo with us. I'm sure the zoo would be his choice, a day with his parents, nephew, and niece laughing at the funny animals."

"And walking in the rain," Charlotte said.

"No doubt. I need to go. Take care today." Kevin took his coat from the hall closet, and walked out the door wondering about Trevor. Charlotte wondered about Trevor too, when she picked up the phone to call Todd.

# Chapter 8

Arriving from the lab, Todd burst into his house. "I might get a job at Cannon Beach," he shouted over the clang of the door he slammed behind him.

"That would be Oregon?" Trevor yelled from the bedroom.

"Yep. Whale migration," Todd said over his shoulder as he went to the kitchen.

"Could you elaborate a little?" Trevor leaned into the room.

Todd removed a beer from the refrigerator. "Want something?"

"No, I'm polishing off a Coke." Trevor sat down. He kicked a chair out from the table for Todd. "Sit down and tell me what's going on."

"I'm moving up in the world." Todd shook his hair back. "The whales are heading south as usual and they want me to do some research on their habits."

"The whales want you to research them?"

"No, smart ass, the Fish and Game Department."

"Oh, I see. So when are you leaving me?"

"Don't know, maybe in a few weeks. You could land a job, too."

"So you aren't deserting."

"No Trev." Todd, his green eyes intent, looked at Trevor. "What do you think?"

"Is it more money?" Trevor stretched his long legs out to the side of his chair.

"Not much." Todd tipped his head and his beer backward letting its cool refreshment trickle down his throat. "About six percent."

"Sounds interesting. You'd be closer to your family. Is that what you want?"

"I'll work wherever I can."

"Oregon could be a challenge if I'm coming with you."

"You are. They can get used to it. We're making it work for us Trev. I promise I'll do whatever it takes to find work for you too. I've already mentioned it to the boss. Something will turn up."

"Hey, I can take care of myself." Trevor came to his feet. He gulped the last swig of Coke, crushed the can with his hand, then grasped Todd in an embrace. "Congratulations."

"Thanks."

"You're feeling better about yourself, which counts with me. How will this affect your visit?"

"I don't know. Maybe I'll visit them when I go for an interview."

"Interview?"

"Yeah, I don't have the job yet. I still have an interview and there are other applicants. It would be fun to be with Kate's kids at Thanksgiving, but . . . you know . . . I'm not sure it would be the best scenario for everyone. I think we should go sooner."

Trevor sat down. "You sound hesitant about me. I can stay home when you interview, but I hope we can be together for Thanksgiving." He stared at the worn spot in the linoleum.

"The company will fly me there," Todd said. "It will cost you, but we'll have a rented car. I don't mean to sound—" he threw up his hands "—hell, you can go with me whenever I interview. We'll visit Mom and Dad, then the Oregon coast. Maybe Jonas can come with us. He loves the beach."

Trevor's blue eyes looked doubtful. "You're already making waves."

Twelve days later, the biting cold wind whistled through the trees.

Todd zipped his coat under his chin and put on his gloves as he walked his route. He would leave for Oregon on Wednesday. His interview call had finally come last week. Two members of the team were out of town until now, the first week in November. His hopeful new assignment felt like a burst of adrenaline, but Trevor's willingness to stay home during his interview troubled Todd. Did Trev want some time without him? Maybe he'd decide to forget the whole idea of relocating. Todd stepped over a fallen limb. My decision might leave me alone. Trevor might stay in Kodiak and find someone else. The questions gnawed at him.

He paced the trail, his ears rang with the sound of snapping twigs, his head pounded against the rhythmic thud of his feet. Anxiety rippled through his body. He no longer felt dependent on his parents' approval . . . but Trev. He needed Trev. He remembered how he had blubbered like a baby a few weeks before, when he felt abandoned by his family. Now he was all right he convinced himself. Trevor wouldn't have to console him that way again. He felt immense gratitude for Trevor, but also a stinging embarrassment at his own vulnerability. How much could Trev stand?

The drift of Mom's conversation last week when she called was bizarre, he thought. Why would she and Dad be interested in having me join them at the zoo with Jonas and Amanda? Moreover, include Trevor. Todd pushed his hands into his pockets and gripped his keys. Mom chatted as if no tension had existed between us these past months. Though I'm her wayward son, maybe she's happy I want to see her. She acted pleased about the potential job, which gives me an excuse to go. She didn't mention Dad. Nothing makes sense these days.

His stride accelerated at the thought of his dad. He felt his heartbeat and a rise of anger churn in his stomach. He had to prove he could keep Trevor and succeed in a new job. Why did everything make him so angry? Avoiding his disturbing emotions, he rubbed his arms, stomped the dirt from his boots and slowed his gait. When he reached his car, he climbed into it and headed home.

While he drove, Todd took slow, deep breaths until his feelings quieted. It was his turn to fix dinner. He stopped for salmon and bread. By the time Trevor walked into the kitchen at six-thirty, Todd had fish under the broiler and his emotions under control.

During the meal, Todd felt a lump ease down his throat when Trevor declared, "I'm going to the coast with you. What's the point in waiting to spend time with your family, especially the kids who won't be young forever? Besides, your mom invited me, odd as that may seem." He paused, looked at Todd. "What could be more fun than a trip to the zoo?"

"Thanks," Todd laid his fork aside, "that means a lot. Grafting you into my family won't be easy, but I want to start the venture. Do you, Trev?"

"Yes. You're hard to convince." Trevor extracted a fishbone from his tooth and continued to chew his mouthful. "This fish is delicious. The potatoes taste great. What's on them . . . cheddar and onions?"

"Yeah."

"How'd you get them cooked so fast?" He felt an ache of sentiment when he saw Todd's green eyes.

"Boiled them first, something Mom used to do on a hectic night." Todd smiled. "You're like the first real family I've ever had." Todd's face became childlike, exposed. "I guess it was okay when I was a kid, but I can't remember. You don't have to persuade me anymore. I just care more about keeping you, than them."

"Does it have to be me or them?" Trevor felt exasperated.

"I think they're faking it." Todd pushed his chair from the table, moved the dirty plates to the sink.

"Let the dishes go, dammit. Come and sit down. What do you mean they're faking it?"

Todd put his hand on the counter, shook his head. "I don't know. It seems strange that no one talks to me for two months and all of a sudden, you and I are going to the zoo with my parents and my sister's children. I don't fit into their agenda as their son, so how are we going to pull it off as a couple? They'll accept me now that I'm living with a guy?"

"You make me sound despicable." Trevor grimaced. "Am I that bad?"

"To them you're despicable, trust me."

"We're not going to produce any grandchildren, if that's on their agenda."

"The way they feel about Jonas and Amanda, I'm sure they'd expect it." Todd pushed his hands through his hair. "No, the truth is they'd think we're unfit to rear a child." He sounded defeated.

"Kids reared by gays are as healthy as any children and research bears that out." Trevor rose from the table and waved Todd toward the living room. Todd followed, flopping on the couch. Before he joined Todd, Trevor flicked off the inaudible television and a sober mood engulfed him. "I don't understand your parents' expectations or how they see you. I don't think you understand me either . . . how tough it was for me growing up with my aunt and uncle without any parents." His pale blue eyes seemed deeper, and Todd caught his compelling tone.

"Yeah Trev, I understand that you've suffered too, but sometimes I envy you that your folks died in that train crash." Todd's green eyes fixed on Trevor who looked astonished.

"What . . ." Trevor's face flushed. "Thanks Todd. You know . . . therapists . . . would say that losing my parents at that age . . . I was ten . . . is a factor that contributes to my 'emotional arrest' and my," he fluttered his fingers making quotes in the air, "*choice* to be gay. Brother Frank has cut me off his decent people list. I have a few bridges to mend too." He abruptly sank into a chair, this time not next to Todd.

"I didn't mean . . . I'm sure you missed your parents. Coming out doesn't seem worth the agony. Does it?" Todd wished that Trevor's answer would open for them an easy path.

"You keep asking me if we should come out." Trevor studied his large hands, wondering how to respond to the question they'd discussed before. "We'll never know if it's worth the pain till we try. Either way there's plenty of anguish. Let's stop being so afraid of what people think."

"We tried to expose ourselves at Mom and Dad's last summer. That was fun."

"Right, it didn't bring out the best in you or your dad. We still have to find a way."

"Yeah we do. The shrinks stopped categorizing us as sick, way back in the seventies." Todd's voice sounded academic since the fact couldn't dispel their frustration. "I guess we can be glad we don't live in China. Before 2001 they considered homosexuals mentally ill."

"Trouble is, plenty still think we are." Trevor stood up. "Does that *matter*? Does it?" Perception flashed in his eyes. "What we think is what matters. Hell with the experts. How are we going to deal with our lives? I'm talking about our relationship with each other, your mom, dad, and Kate. Frank. Whoever concerns us. I think we better stop feeling sorry for ourselves and do everyone a favor. Stand up for who we are."

Todd groaned. "Right, stand up, easier said than done."

"Are you chicken? Do you care who you are? Do you care if your family knows who you are?"

"I want to care, but I don't know."

"Don't know what? Don't know you have a right to your feelings?" Trevor's pale eyes searched Todd's face. "Look at the people who march to help those living with AIDS, people who fight to support gays' civil rights. Look at the straight people who are making it legal for us to adopt kids. Some people care."

He eyed Todd, his brows pinched together. "You're too sensitive and self absorbed. Stop your whining. Frank's such a redneck that he thinks my muscles and tough guy look disprove I *could* be gay. He thinks I've made a raunchy choice and is embarrassed to have me for a brother. At least that's how he acted when he left. Too many damn myths are circulating. Our families are wrong."

"You think my slim build and weak back make me look like your average fag, a wimp?"

"No. *You* think you're a wimp. I said you're too sensitive and self absorbed. You're reacting to your own opinion again."

"Dad pushed me to try out for soccer and baseball. What did I do? Played piano, read, dreamed and escaped to the beach a lot to get away from him. I got along better with crustaceans."

"So what if you're musical? Your music, reading, dreaming have nothing to do with being a wimp, or being gay. Besides, your parents are the ones who exposed you and Kate to the beach, which is what enticed your interest in biology. It evolved . . . shall we say. Give them some credit for that." Todd glanced up, then away.

"I admit," Trevor said, "I don't know how to approach Kevin and Charlotte on this issue. You can't just drop a bomb and tell them we're lovers." Todd stared at the floor, but Trevor persisted. "But that's what they need to know, that we love each other, so we're lovers. Do they still belong to the church that believes we're sick, perverted, and maybe even criminal?"

"Yeah." Todd sighed, pursed his lips. "They belong to a church that believes we're sick and perverted. Not criminal." He managed a grin. "They believe God will change us to be like them—straight." Todd's voice drifted away.

Then without warning, he jumped up. His green eyes flashed, the veins in his neck and temples stood out; he raised his fist, hit the wall. "Most denominations take that stance today and they call themselves the church. I'm fed up with the church. It infuriates me that the people who are so blabby about God's love for everyone are the ones who most banish us. Am I wrong?" he sputtered, not waiting for a response. "Who cares what the shrinks say about being gay and being sick, if your family and the church reject you?"

Had he heard Todd right? Trevor felt gripped by an insight. Todd's sense of abandonment was at the core of his heartbreak. Todd truly believed healing in his family, acceptance in the church, was not possible. He didn't want to talk about his growing up. It was all too much for him. It's too much for me too, Trevor thought. I can't deal with this stuff. Too scary. I have to end this conversation some way.

After Todd calmed down, Trevor looked at him. "So you *do* care. That's what matters. I told you earlier that I'd go with you to visit your folks. I will. Let's drop this now." He rose from his seat as he glanced at his watch. "Hey, it's eleven-fifteen. I'm going for a shower. He ran his thick fingers through his hair ruffling it, stretched his arms and cradled the back of his head in his palms, a simulation of casualness that he didn't feel.

Todd gave a heavy sigh, shuffled across the rug, and slumped into a chair. With his arms on his knees, his face in his hands, he felt the heat from his forehead and the blood pulsing in his temples. He willed calmness into his body, took some deep breaths. When he looked up, he felt wiped out, he felt the muscles in his face go slack. He anchored his feet, stood and stepped toward Trevor. He put his arms around Trevor's warm chest and he held on, his face buried in the stubble of his partner's thick neck.

# Chapter 9

Two days later, refreshed by sleep and the assurance of Trevor's commitment, Todd awoke before Trevor. It was Wednesday morning. He wrapped himself in his robe and flipped up the heat. With his finger, he traced the frosty design on the kitchen window, as he peered through it into darkness. He showered, shaved, brewed coffee, and then filled a mug and took it to the bedroom. From his top dresser drawer he pulled Jockey briefs, crew socks, a pair of brown dress socks, and a few handkerchiefs. He put them into his suitcase, tossing several T–shirts on top.

Sipping his coffee, he reached past a broken watch and two dried up pens for his nail clippers and sunglasses, tossing them with some Tums into his toilet kit just in case. Next, he took a plaid flannel shirt, a denim jacket, his Levi's and a pair of sweats from the closet. With the interview in mind, he found a beige dress shirt, brown slacks, and the only sports coat he owned. He pulled out a geometric brown and green tie that complimented both. Not until he dropped a shoe did he hear from Trevor.

"That tie will show off your green eyes." Trevor rubbed the sleep from his own. When Todd leaned over the bed, Trevor pulled him down, untied his robe, kissed his neck and face.

"Hey, we have to get to the airport."

"Ah, we have time." Trevor spread his hands over Todd's body and felt him yield to his welcoming touch. The scent of their skin, Todd's after–shave, and the coffee aroma mingled with their expansive pleasure.

When the lovemaking ended, Trevor sat up. "I better get ready." He swung his feet to the floor, pulled up his shorts and began putting his clothes in a duffel bag. "We've got to be at the airport by ten. Don't distract me again."

"Umm," Todd said. "About my eyes, I'm sure they'll be impressed with them." He opened the curtains. "Hey, it's snowing."

"Not a surprise with this temperature. No doubt some ice underneath it too." Trevor sprayed his thick black hair.

"I didn't see it earlier. Who's tagging seals for you while you're gone, Trev?"

"A student who'd love to permanently take my place. He's working part–time, here from Anchorage. I'm going to pore over the newspapers while you're talking with the big shots. Maybe I'll find something."

"Hope so, and thanks for the vote of confidence that I'll get the job."

"Hey, I didn't say that," Trevor teased. "I just like the Oregon coast."

"Whatever. You better get a newspaper or something for the plane because I'm reading Grisham's latest book." Todd dropped a book in a carry on tote.

They ate some oatmeal, and then beneath heavy coats, the men walked to the car. Placing the suitcase and duffel bag inside it, Todd closed the trunk. "I'm glad those chains are there," he said, watching his breath float like tiny clouds in the cold air. He looked at the footprints they left in the snow. "Our studded tires should get us to the plane." They scraped the windows and headed for the Kodiak airport. When they arrived, Trevor pulled into the parking garage where they left their car.

Once the plane was airborne, a flight attendant served them coffee with a bag of peanuts. "This is the life—huh Todd?"

"Yeah, I appreciate having you with me. You're the best thing that's ever happened to me. Do you think we can make our relationship work and still maintain one with our families?"

"I don't know." Trevor looked thoughtful as he warmed his hands around the cup. "You're important to me, but my track record isn't so hot."

Todd frowned. "What do you mean? You gave me the impression you weren't too experienced in your love life."

"I'm not. That could be a problem."

"A problem? You're not making much sense, or is it my dense brain?"

"Your brain." Trevor glanced sideways, his mouth a crooked grin.

"Knock it off, Trevor. If you don't like *that* topic, tell me why you don't like shrinks."

"Tell me when you're going to read Grisham."

"Right now." Todd started digging in his tote for his paperback.

"You want to know if I've seen a shrink, don't you? I'm a scary maniac." Trevor raised his brows and opened his eyes wide. "You better break this up while you still can." Todd ignored him, directing his attention to the first page of his novel. "Hey, do you want to know why I don't like shrinks or not?"

Todd closed the book, blew a breath past his lips. "Yeah Trev, I want to know what you think of shrinks and about your past, but if you don't want to talk about it, that's okay. I'm not playing games with you."

Trevor flushed and looked at his lap, afraid of Todd's opinion for the first time. What would he think of him seeing a psychiatrist?

When his courage returned, Trevor noticed Todd was watching him. "Ever been depressed?" Trevor asked.

"Depressed? I guess so."

"You'd know it—not at first—but afterwards. I knew this fellow in college. We played tennis a lot . . . well, he had . . . I liked him a lot." Trevor leaned closer to Todd. "He came on to me, and we lived together for about a year. One day I took my racket to the court to practice. When I got close, I could see him playing tennis with a good looking sophomore woman. I stayed back a distance and watched them together. He kissed her twice and she flirted a lot. I was stunned because I thought he was gay." Trevor stopped talking, swirled cold coffee in his cup.

"Did you ask him about the woman?"

"Not then, but when I did later he told me it was over between us. I don't know what happened with them."

"I bet she thought he was straight. He didn't know himself, it sounds like." Todd fell silent and waited.

"I withdrew after that experience and my grades dropped. I left school for awhile because I couldn't concentrate. My life was a mess." Trevor leaned forward, pushed up the lap tray and folded his large hands across his knee. Todd looked at his bulk, at his firm jaw. "That was at Oregon State, you know, before I met you. I finally got so despondent that the kind woman who owned the apartment asked me what was wrong. Of course, I didn't tell her, but I started thinking about it. I couldn't figure it out myself, so I found the name of a psychiatrist in the phone book and dialed his number." He eased back into his seat.

"What happened then?" Todd pulled off his coat and laid it on his lap.

"He asked a bunch of questions. What had brought me there, what was important, did I have hobbies or interests. I never mentioned this Karl, but in time, he asked about my love life too. Of course, I thought he was meddling. I told him I had loved Karl and he'd deserted. The doctor appeared non–plused, but then he asked me tons of questions about women. When was I aware that I wasn't attracted to them, or more to the point, when was I sure I liked men?"

"Were you sure then—that you were gay?"

"Absolutely sure. He was just as sure that I could change. He didn't like me for my charming personality." Trevor laughed.

"Liking you wasn't his job."

"He was ignorant about homosexuality. I was feeling wounded and rejected, dealing with grief. He understood that Karl hurt me, but told me it wasn't a healthy relationship."

"Was it?"

"Probably not. Karl wasn't honest with me; that's what made it unhealthy, not because he was a man. He was fooling around with me, but I was naïve, experiencing my first love, my first sexual involvement. I had a sense of identity as a gay man, but he was a bad emotional experience. My misjudgment of Karl made me distrust myself. The shrink thought my problems stemmed from my orientation."

"He wanted you liberated so you'd want women, not a guy like me. How simple can it be?"

"Right."

"What about the depression?"

"I found another shrink who accepted me and helped me deal with it. He didn't offer any answers, but he helped me discover my own."

"Helped you discover your own answers?"

"Yeah, what worked for me."

"So you do like shrinks a little." Todd eyed Trevor.

"A little. The doctor made me see how losing Karl had stirred my anxious memories of losing my parents." He respected my feelings, so I learned to trust them too. He let me feel my own way."

"How did you know what to tell him?"

"I didn't. I rambled and he nodded a lot, so I'd know he was listening, I guess. Sometimes he nodded when he didn't know what to say."

"Or didn't want to say anything."

"Maybe. He was uncomfortable at times though. I could feel his uneasiness, but didn't tell him because we were dealing with my problems, not his." Trevor shifted, looked at Todd and smiled. "Once he almost dozed off."

"Relaxation therapy by example?" Todd laughed. "Not uneasy that day."

"No, just drowsy. I guess psychiatrists are people doing a job like the rest of us." Trevor unbuckled his seatbelt. "I must find the john." Todd scrunched up his knees allowing him to pass, then stood in the aisle himself, stretching his legs until Trevor returned. He felt chagrined by the odd sense that he'd grown a bit taller, that his shoulders felt broader with the knowledge that Trev had troubles too. The pilot told the travelers they would be arriving in Anchorage in fifteen minutes and the current temperature was 20 degrees Fahrenheit.

# Chapter 10

Charlotte bent her head over the kitchen sink as the warm water rinsed the dye from her hair. When she dried and brushed it, a sense of expectancy moved through her. My last day of radiation, she thought. Later in the morning, she left for her appointment. The nurse met her and took her to a room where her radiation oncologist spoke with her. "Following today's treatment, I'm turning you over to your primary physician. I think you will be fine, Mrs. Keeley."

"So I can stop worrying about a return of the cancer?"

"No absolutes in life, Mrs. Keeley," the physician said dryly, straightening his tie, "but, I expect no further problems." When he smiled, a hint of warmth flickered across his face. "I don't expect to see you again. My best wishes for your health." He extended his hand.

Charlotte took it believing he'd done his job. "Thank you for your services, Doctor." When he left the room, she slid out of her coat and waited until someone from radiology called her. She removed her top and laid down for the last high energy x–rays to pass into her breast. It was painless as usual, but she felt a release.

She strode through the waiting room, then spied Amanda sitting in the children's play area surrounded by colored wooden blocks. She squatted and scooped the child into her arms. Kate smiled across the gaily–decorated area then placed her magazine on a table as she rose to greet her mother with a hug. "We wanted to celebrate your final treatment with you. I'm taking you to lunch if that's okay."

"This is your day off. You want to spend it with me?" Charlotte's face blossomed with surprise and moisture came into her eyes. Amanda hugged her grandmother, planted a wet kiss on her cheek, then wiggled for release. Her tower wasn't finished yet. Charlotte lowered herself to the floor, Kate joined her, and the three females sat together for a rare moment. Without hearing a word, Kate knew that her mother's relaxed face meant good news.

"Here. Put that block right here. Now I want a yellow one. It's big. Now we're done, Grandma. We can knock it down. You're not sick anymore?"

"No dear." Charlotte smiled at Amanda. They dropped the

blocks into a box.

"Let's get something to eat, Mom."

"Sounds great to me. I'll follow in my car."

Kate buckled Amanda in her car seat and headed to the Dutch Bakery. When they had ordered their food, Charlotte leaned toward Kate's ear. "Remember you're letting Kevin and me take you and the kids to the zoo this Saturday. I'm up to it now and I could use some fun."

With a glance at Amanda, Kate grinned. "Sure, I remember."

"Todd's coming too . . . bringing his friend."

His friend, Kate thought. "Did he call you?" She watched the server place their plates on the table.

"No, I called him last week.  He said he's coming for a job interview at Cannon Beach."

Startled, Kate concealed her surprise with a whine. "Gee, nobody tells me anything. What kind of job?"

"Researching whales. You know Todd wouldn't take an office job." Her mother laughed, her amused blue eyes looking across the table at Kate.

"No I suppose not." Kate poked her chicken salad, feeling uneasy. "Anyway, he's going to the zoo."

"We invited them to join us."

"Zoo, zoo, zoo," Amanda mimicked.

"Your Uncle Todd is coming to visit and is going to the zoo with Grandpa and Grandma and us." Kate eyed Amanda's sticky hands.

"We gonna see the bears and monkeys? I *like* the animals Grandma." She beamed at Charlotte.

"So do I. Yes, we'll see them and the elephants and giraffes, even a hippopotamus, I think." Charlotte smiled at her granddaughter. The child's cheeks were luminous, her blue eyes sparkling against the tangled curls that fell around her smeared face. Kate dunked a napkin in her water glass and handed it to Amanda. "Please wipe your hands."

"Where's Todd staying?" Kate bit into a roll.

"Uh . . . a motel I guess. He didn't want to impose on us," she said idly. She saw a puzzled frown flicker across Kate's face. "Do you approve, dear? You look perplexed."

"No—I mean yes, it's fine with me, Mom. Todd can stay wherever he wants and it's time the kids saw him. I'm just surprised that he's changing locations." Kate wiped peanut butter and jam off Amanda's face.

"He has to get the job first." Charlotte looked away. She knew what Kate meant about coming back to Oregon, but they'd said enough in front of little ears. She took Amanda's foot in her hand and tied her shoelace, then pushed her own chair back. "I think I'd better be going. Kevin will be waiting to hear from me. Thanks dear for a lovely lunch. I do appreciate your attention."

"And here's to lasting good health." Kate rose and touched her mother cheek to cheek.

"Take care and I'll call you about the zoo. Do come with us."

"I will if Dave is working. Talk to you later."

Charlotte decided to tell Kevin the news in person, so she drove to his engineering firm. She walked into his office smiling. Talking into his speakerphone, Kevin waved her in to sit down, but she didn't. She wandered around the room viewing walls dominated by large photographs of various structures the firm had built. She thought about how this validated Kevin's pride in his work. She knew he enjoyed the structural sight–based portion of his work where he could observe the progress, the completion of buildings, and bridges transformed from paper to reality.

Grouped pictures hung in smaller areas: Jonas and Amanda last Christmas, she and Kevin, Todd and Kate at Todd's graduation from college. In an obscure corner next to an immaculate bookcase, not visible to casual clients, was a photo of Kevin and his older brother, Stephen, on a scouting excursion in Vermont. Charlotte paused with sudden awareness, staring at Stephen's image. In the green eyes, the high forehead, straight blond hair and the lean body, she saw Todd. Yet, this was his uncle as a young man, whom she and Todd had never met. Steve was missing before she had known Kevin. After Kevin had served his time in Korea and left Vermont to enroll at the University of Washington, Charlotte had met him. He had majored in civil engineering, she in English.

She ambled, noticing the ship–shape atmosphere of the office. Venetian blinds hung in three windows, the cream colored walls appeared clean, and a blue and red paisley carpet covered the floor. Three chairs, upholstered in a crisp pinstripe of slate blue and cream fabric, clustered opposite the desk.

"Yes, let me get his name and number." Kevin reached into his drawer for a pad; his bronze arm bent against rolled up white shirtsleeves. Behind him, Charlotte noticed his papers in a neat stack at the edge of the expansive mahogany desk. She observed the perfect desk drawer; pens lined up neatly, paper clips, staples, post-it-notes, and notepads easily visible. She walked to a chair facing him as he frowned and raised his hand, a silent message that he would hang up soon. On one side of his desk, she saw herself smiling back from a birthday photo that she'd given him five years ago. Beside it was a picture of Kevin in his climbing boots in the Grand Canyon at sunset.

Kevin jotted a note, thanked the caller and hung up. He stood, leaned across his desk, touched Charlotte's shoulders. "That smile tells all." His face lit up. "No more radiation, right?" His deep brown eyes held hers reflecting love and relief. Charlotte felt tightness ease in her chest.

"Oh Kevin," she said, fumbling for a tissue in her purse. "I'm . . . I feel like I can breathe again."

He wiped tears from her cheeks with his wrist. "Hey," he protested, seeing the black smudges on his arm. "I'm glad my shirtsleeves are turned, otherwise I'd have mascara all over them. You're right, it's a day to celebrate. Let's have lunch."

"Sorry, Kate beat you to it. We just ate at the Dutch Bakery with Amanda. They surprised me at the hospital."

"Well, great. Did you make zoo plans?"

"Oh, yes." Amanda is excited about seeing the monkeys, bears and elephants."

Charlotte stuffed her tissue back into her purse. "You know, Kate seemed surprised about Todd's ambitious job plans. She hadn't heard about his interview. I thought they'd talked, but not about relocating, I guess."

"Just concerned about your cancer." Kevin glanced toward his intercom. "So we are going to the zoo."

"On Saturday, rain or shine. I told her Trevor was joining us."

"Well, I'm going for some lunch with or without you. Care to join me for coffee and dessert?"

"For a few minutes. Where?"

"Let's walk to the café down the block." Kevin pushed the button on his phone. "I'll be out about forty-five minutes for lunch," he informed his secretary.

Kevin's turkey sandwich and Charlotte's tea arrived quickly. "You know you're a lovely woman." Kevin smiled his broad smile.

"You mean for my sixty-two years, I'm well preserved?"

"No, I mean you're good looking."

"Family resemblance is an interesting study." Charlotte took a sugar packet. "It's stunning how much Todd looks like your brother did as a young man."

"Hmm?"

"The picture of you and Stephen on your office wall. With his green eyes and high forehead, that straight blond hair, I thought I was seeing Todd when I saw it today. How old was Stephen then?"

"Gee, about seventeen I guess . . . our last scouting trip."

"Does Todd remind you of him?"

"Nope, Todd's different." Kevin bit into his sandwich.

"Physically he looks like him."

"Granted, but that's the extent of it."

"You never talk about Stephen. I'd love to know more about what he was like."

"Sometime. He's gone, so what's the point?" He took a bite.

"The point is he was your brother for twenty years. His memory is part of you."

"His disappearance isn't much fun to remember." Kevin looked down.

"Maybe if you talk about it, you can separate the trauma from Stephen. He may get in touch with you some day."

"In touch? Not if he's dead. Aren't we happy about your news today?" Kevin looked at Charlotte and arched his brows. "How'd we get on this topic?"

"Dessert?" a perky woman server interrupted.

Kevin's tension eased into a smile. "Sure, what do you have?" Without persuasion, they ordered hot blackberry pie; the tantalizing aroma and tart taste capped their celebration. Charlotte asked no further questions.

"Thanks for coming by. It's wonderful news." Kevin stood and pulled out Charlotte's chair. When they had walked back to his office, he stopped outside the door. "See you tonight, my lady."

"Good bye, you romantic man." She brushed past him, pulled him inside the office, ran her hands through his hair, feeling its thinness between her fingers. "You look dashing messed up."

"Right." Kevin smiled as he reached in his pocket for his comb.

Kate arrived home before Jonas. When he came through the door with his backpack, Amanda ran to him. "We're going to the zoo with Grandpa and Grandma," she said, tapping her feet in a dance. Jonas tossed his pack on the couch, where leaves and wet sod fell from it.

"Jonas. What have you gotten into?" Kate threw up her hands.

A puzzled Jonas whirled around. "What? Nothing."

"How many times have I told you to stay off the grass on your way home? You have leaves all over your jeans and backpack. Go outside and brush off."

Jonas wilted. "Sorry, Mom. I ate my apple in the park with Micah." Kate glared at her son as he walked on his toes to retrieve his pack, then trudged out the door. He struggled to get the soggy leaves off his back and legs, and then he brushed off his pack and left it on the porch.

When he came in, Kate said, "I know you didn't mean to get stuff on you Jonas, but please be more careful inside the house." She lifted a shaky hand and patted Jonas' hunched shoulders. "I'm sorry—I'm short tempered today. Amanda's right. Gramps and Grams are taking you to the zoo."

"When?"

"Saturday. Your Uncle Todd is coming too, with his . . . friend."

"That'll be fun if Amanda doesn't act like a baby." Jonas narrowed his eyes in a glare at his sister. Amanda stuck out her tongue, wrinkled her nose, and strutted from the room.

"Stop it, or neither of you will go."

"What's the other guy's name?" Jonas said.

"His name's Trevor. Uncle Todd will be in this area because he might be getting a job near the ocean." Kate felt a shred of composure returning to her body.

"I miss him. Uncle Todd's fun, but we don't get to see him much."

"Because he lives in Alaska, which is many miles away."

"Boy, I hope he gets the new job cause then we can see him lots."

"Me too, me too. Amanda hopped into the room with her long top tucked into her underpants. "When's Saturday?"

Kate tugged Amanda's shirt free and before she could answer her, Jonas—with his hands on his hips and his chin in the air—turned to his sister. "In three days, stupid. This is Wednesday, then it's Thursday, then Friday, then Saturday."

"Stop, Jonas, not another word." Vindicated, Amanda ran into her room. "Put your clothes in the hamper and change into clean jeans," Kate told Jonas.

"Can me and Micah play in the park till dinner?"

"May Micah and I."

"Ah, Mom, may Micah—"

"Yes. You must be inside *before* dark."


Leaving Kevin's office, Charlotte drove home. She sank into the pink tulip cushions on the wicker chair, feeling shaky. This was her room of refuge where she relaxed. She kicked aside her shoes and dug her toes into the thick carpet. She pressed her fingers to her temples. This effort exhausts me, she thought. My health, the kids, Kevin—they all matter. She leaned her head back on the cushion for a few minutes closing her eyes, letting her arms drop over the side where her fingers strummed the woven wicker.

When she opened her eyes, she saw small shadowy shapes reflected on the closet door, as sunlight flickered through the eyelet curtains behind her, illuminating the beige walls with a warm glow. She watched the shimmer dance from door to wall. Caught in the ray, her African violet had an iridescent quality, its elegant lavender petals clustered lushly in waxy leaves. A cream colored hide–a–bed with matching tulip pillows and a pastel quilt folded across its back sat against the wall. The piano sat against the wall where Todd's bed used to be.

Charlotte looked at the several wooden shelves, painted white, that held family treasures and collections. A tiny crystal vase that had belonged to Kevin's mother sat next to a clay turtle that Jonas had designed in kindergarten and painted with globs of green and brown paint. She examined a photo of ten–year–old Todd at the piano playing "What Child Is This?" at a Christmas recital. In another, Kate stood proudly in her first nursing uniform. Charlotte looked at the snapshot taken an instant too soon of Amanda holding Kate's hand, just before she released it and Amanda took her first step alone. Near it sat a summer photo of Jonas waving from the tree house with Kevin's smile in the shadows behind him.

Charlotte left her chair, picked up a picture of Todd in his Cub Scout uniform with his second grade troop. She traced his face with her finger, then touched her lips. Jonas favors Kevin, Kate looks like me, and so does Amanda, she thought. Todd—she recalled the photo of Stephen in the office—doesn't resemble his father, but he is the image of Stephen. She set the photo back on the shelf and sat down.

She sank into the couch, remembering the merit badges Todd had earned. How proud she had felt when she put them on his sash: patches for swimming, lifesaving, hiking, and cooking. Dear, sweet Todd. Why does he worry me?

Should I invite him and Trevor to stay here? Charlotte wondered. The thought triggered an unexpected flood of uneasiness, a feeling she didn't understand. What does Trevor mean to Todd? she asked in the quietness. What's he like? Does he love music like Todd? Why won't Kevin talk about Todd and his life with Trevor?

She'd worried a lot. Was it in fact her *last* radiation treatment? Would she face further cancer? Weariness spread through her, a solid, comforting weariness. The detailed features of her family's faces soothed her. A mysterious assurance replenished her: tender love for her children, for Kevin, but in a weird way for herself. The cancer treatment had blessed her.

As the sunlight slid from the room, taking its warmth with it, Charlotte rubbed her arms. She removed her shirt, slacks, and her bra and unfolded the quilt. She stretched out under its mantle knowing that she had changed. I can face the realities of my life, she thought. I feel easier about the future, as if I've received a gift. She breathed deeply, sank wholly into the exhaustion that embraced her. She slept.

Kevin labored the afternoon over figures and scheduling crews for the Columbia River Bridge Project. Next week he would be on sight for a structural check of the foundation. He didn't want his pre—retirement project to cave in. He'd been far more bothered than he'd admitted about Charlotte's cancer. They were so fortunate. He cleared his desk and called Dave. No answer. His watch read five-thirty. No wonder, he thought. I guess I can stop for the day.

Once he had met his promise about the zoo, he'd give his full attention to his job. Even his grandson would have to be on hold for awhile. The truth was he missed Todd and hoped he'd get the job. In the mean time, this Trevor might be good for him. With his chin cupped in his hands, Kevin stared down at the desktop. Come spring, maybe Todd and I can do some hiking, particularly if he moves to Oregon, he thought. Trevor will probably stay with his job in Alaska. When Kevin glanced up, the clock read five forty-five. Shaking the reflections from his head, he pushed his chair back, rose and got his coat from the hook on his office door, turned out the lights and headed to his car.

Charlotte awakened after an hour's nap. In the microwave, she thawed some steaks, an indulgence she didn't often allow herself. Nevertheless, she was cancer free. For the picnic at the zoo, she mixed cookie dough and dropped spoonfuls on the cookie sheet as she licked her fingers. Chocolate chip was still Todd's favorite cookie. When the timer rang, she removed the tray, waited a minute, and then lifted the warm disks from the sheet leaving her thumbprint impression in the edge of one cookie.

"Yum, chocolate chip cookies." Kevin didn't hesitate as he grabbed one and headed toward a coat hanger.

"Take it easy. They're for our picnic."

He returned in Levi's and a plaid blue shirt. "What else are we taking Saturday?" He reached for another cookie.

"I don't know. Chicken? Maybe pasta salad."

"And deviled eggs?"

"Too much cholesterol."

"You're no fun."

"Stop complaining. You're getting steak tonight." She reached into the oven, grabbing a hot cookie sheet. Kevin pinched her. "I'm gonna drop these if you don't stop it."

"It'd be worth it." He kissed her, and then removed the cookies while she prepared dinner.

When they had gone to bed Charlotte took a deep breath and let it go. "Do you ever worry about Todd?"

"Hmm?" Kevin rolled over to face her, but couldn't see her face in the darkness. "What are you asking?"

"Oh, I wonder if he's happy. Think he'll ever get married?"

"We can't run his life. If he gets the job on the coast, he'll be closer and you can keep an eye on him."

"Do you think . . . I'm a little nervous about Trevor. He seems comfortable with him. It's just . . ."

"You worry too much. Trevor seemed an all around nice man. Todd's okay. Go to sleep." Kevin turned and lay on his back.

"I guess I'll feel better after our visit Saturday . . . you know . . . it's been awhile." Charlotte rested her head on Kevin's chest a moment, then moved to her side. He doesn't get it, she thought, and soon she was asleep.

Kevin stared at the light at the edge of the curtain for a long time before he fell asleep.

# Chapter 11

Dave's preoccupation with drafting and computers put thoughts of Kate's brother far away. Having the chance to work on a project as immense as the Columbia River Bridge energized him. The enterprise required his utmost concentration and attention to drafting details. His father–in–law would retire in a few years making this contract of his drafter skills important for future chances with the well–known engineering firm that Kevin Keeley had labored to establish.

He leaned over his drafting board and cursed the puniness of his rented office. The walls were painted white, which helped reflect light, but its' space limitations demanded that the door be closed when he worked. A small window gave a view of the alley between him and a furniture warehouse. Two striped blue and white chairs were available for clients. The softwood floors, blackened and worn, creaked beneath a cheerful area carpet of blue with flecks of red, which he and Kate had selected together. A picture of Kate and the kids in Yellowstone National Park sat near his computer. His drafting tools had their own place on the table.

In the corner of the room hung a white cabinet, which had two shelves and a door. The shelves held coffee, sugar, dried creamer, filters, and four mugs with a few spoons. Beneath them sat a tiny wooden table, which held a coffee maker, plus a few donut crumbs, and a half–eaten bagel.

Dave glanced at his watch, which read seven p.m. He had begun the day twelve hours earlier and planned to stay until eight. He snapped off his drafting light, lifted the glass pot with its remaining stale coffee and headed toward the hall drinking fountain for fresh water. After he filled the carafe and started the coffee, he turned into the hall and took the stairs down one flight to the ground floor. He walked across the street into a cafeteria for a bowl of soup and a fresh bagel.

When he returned he noticed the light on his answering machine was blinking. He filled a mug with coffee, sat at his desk, and pressed the button on his speaker. "Hi Dave, it's me. When will you be home?" That was all. He spooned some vegetable beef soup into his mouth letting it warm him as he savored the aroma of garlic and onions. I know Kate wants to talk. He sighed, and bit into the bagel. This project consumes me while she struggles with the kids. She wants my assurance that it's fine for Jonas and Amanda to be with Todd and Trevor this Saturday. He rolled his chair backward and lifted his feet to his desktop. Steadying the bowl semi–prone, he devoured the potatoes and carrots in their beefy broth. He wondered what would comfort Kate, and seeing his feet, when he had last polished his shoes.

Kate dialed Dave's office again. No answer. When Amanda called, "I want some water," she laid a novel on the end table beside a can of Coke, slid off the couch and started up the stairs.

"Okay, Amanda. Stay in bed. I'll bring it, but then you must go to sleep." She returned with a small glass. Amanda's eyes shone in the dim hall light while she drank the water. Kate lifted golden curls from her forehead, rubbed her daughter's back, and tucked her in. She tiptoed out, went to get her robe and slippers She kicked up the heat, returned to her book and waited for Dave. She read a page, but couldn't concentrate.

At last the door opened with Dave behind it. "I got your message, but I was leaving soon anyway so I didn't call back."

"I know you're tired, Dave. You've had a long day, but could we talk?"

Dave flung his coat across a chair. "Could I stop it?"

"Probably not. Are you hungry?"

"Actually I ate, but it's cold outside. Have any cocoa?"

Kate nodded. "Go change and I'll fix it."

In a few minutes, Dave strolled into the living room in his sweats. Kate had dimmed the floor lamp and she stood waiting with a steaming cup of cocoa. As he slumped to the couch, Dave smiled up at her. "Sit beside me wife." When she handed him the cup, he raised the hot beverage to his lips, assessed Kate's mood. "You're upset. What's going on?"

"I want this family to face reality." Kate sat down. "Dad and Mom are avoiding Todd's gayness. She's pretending and it makes me mad." Dave lowered his cup wiping the whiskers at his mouth with his thumb and finger. He looked at Kate with admiration and curiosity.

"How do you know it's an act?"

"I just do. She's too cool, and Dad's too set in his opinions; he can't have changed."

"Have you changed your feelings?"

"Some, I think." Kate stared at the cocoa in her cup and swirled it. "Every generation comes to terms with new awareness, don't they?" She raised her chin and Dave held her eyes with his. "I felt so edgy when Mom told me Todd and Trevor would be visiting. Having him around the kids seems threatening. I feel doubly guilty because Mom seems so blasé about it. What's wrong with me? I hoped I could overcome my fear. I don't like my own homophobia. So yes, I think my feelings are changing."

"Be easy on yourself. I'm proud of you. Some people are attracted to their own sex and it's nothing new. That doesn't mean it's easy to understand or accept because we're taught to feel it's not okay."

A pained grimace surfaced on Kate's face. "But why have we made it so not okay?"

"I'm not sure. I think we've learned to fear those who are different from us. Loving a person who is the same sex is a scary idea for people." Dave heard the lecture tone in his voice. "I think we may have unexpressed attraction to our own sex. It frightens us. And we're afraid of what others will think."

"Yes, like Mom and Dad." Kate rolled her eyes. "What people think is everything to them, especially Mom."

"Well Kate, I hate to disillusion you, but I think your Dad wants to appear in control too. He wants things to look normal, as he understands it. He'd be more wounded than your Mom would to admit he has a gay son. It's understandable."

Kate pulled her feet under her and nodded her head. She sipped the cocoa. Her sandy hair fell forward framing her heart shaped face, wide at her cheeks, narrow at the chin. Dave noticed her mood had eased. "We all have our own understanding of what's appropriate, our own sense of reality," I guess.

"Exactly. I think your Dad sees homosexuality as immoral, not a natural condition."

"No doubt he does, but he's not alone."

"No. Remember, Jesus didn't talk about being straight, but he challenged the self-righteous often. God clearly created fewer gays, but that doesn't mean they're immoral. Who are we to challenge God's creations?"

"I just know that the hate coming from certain clergy is wrong. Our pastor ignores people by not mentioning homosexuality."

"Doesn't want to turn anyone off, the collection plate, you know."

"Well. Todd always played house with me and my friends. His classmates teased him, calling him a sissy, whatever that meant. He took piano lessons too."

"He did?" Dave looked surprised. "Good for him."

"Yes, he's a good musician, but I remember Dad tried to interest him in baseball, and he wasn't good at it. Why couldn't Dad accept Todd as he was?"

"Beats me, but he paid for the music lessons." Dave shook his head. "The kids teasing him relates more to social training, don't you think—the dolls and trucks stuff? No evidence that behavior or experiences cause sexual preference."

"Umm, it seems permissible for married men to take care of kids, do the cooking and cleaning. People don't seem to mind."

Dave stroked his beard. "People who feel the man should earn the money aren't hot on the idea."

"I guess guys who stay home with kids are caring for the ones they sired." Kate leaned back against a cushion.

Dave grinned. "I expect so. Where are we going with this, Kate?"

"I just want to say that male couples who adopt a child aren't well accepted. Neither are lesbians who have children. We have ideals about how life should be, and they turn out to be illusions."

"When did you learn that?" Dave smiled, but Kate sat silent and thoughtful. "The stigma's real," he said. "I wouldn't want to be gay." He quit talking and studied his lap. "I'm a hypocrite too." He turned and touched Kate's elbow. "You're less angry at me."

"I was irritated that you saw through my vacillation. My emotions need time to catch up with my intentions. You know I'm a fair person, even progressive as a rule. I feel badly that Pam Baxter's son had so much pain. Too bad he didn't feel free with his folks. I hope his father embraces him now. Can you imagine pretending you're not gay when you are?" Kate held her cup in her hands. "I want us to change before it's too late."

"You can't change anyone." Dave wiped his mouth again and set his cup down. "But you can share your feelings with Todd."

"If I can keep up my courage."

"Your heart's big. I don't want it broken."

"My heart's not so big, I just love him. Mom and Dad too. They're products of the old millennium, but Todd isn't. Rules and loyalties run their lives, or at least that's how it seems. We're encountering a new day, but I think Dad believes whatever he learned in Sunday school." Kate sighed.

"That's not all bad, is it?"

"No. Love and loyalty are good. If he's lost a sense of the unfolding mystery of life, I think it's bad. We've learned more about human sexuality. Can we let our beliefs stay the same, when they don't fit or work anymore? Faith in God changes us. Things aren't cast in stone."

"They never were. Your dad didn't develop his attitude about homosexuality in Sunday school either."

Kate laughed. "I suppose not, but gays were considered revolting. In Dad's day you went to scout meetings, period."

"*Scout* meetings? Dave's jaw dropped. "How'd we jump to that?"

"When he was a Scout, Dad didn't wonder if it was moral to admit gay kids to the program." Kate was adamant. "Nobody talked about it. Now it's a big social issue and people who have been leaders get kicked out because they admit they're gay."

Dave cocked his head sideways as he stroked his whiskers. "Yeah, it's wrong, but gays were in scouts then as well as now and you don't know what your dad felt. Have you wondered why he and Todd were never in a troop together?"

"Yes." Kate's expression was puzzled. "Maybe he was protecting Todd, didn't want to banish his own son from a troop."

"Well, we can't solve this tonight and I'm bushed."

"Sorry, I can't stop once I get started."

"You want your parents to see Todd with new eyes, but it won't happen all at once. Before you start your mission, you had better get past this Saturday. Please don't confront Todd and Trevor or your folks while you're with the kids at the zoo." Kate lowered her head, closed her eyes a second and Dave watched her lift her chin, a doubtful look on her face. "You're still uncomfortable about Jonas and Amanda being with them aren't you."

"A little. I know better in my head, but, yes, I feel apprehensive."

"Go, observe, have fun, it'll be good for you." He kissed Kate sensitively, stood and headed down the hall. "It's past my bedtime."

# Chapter 12

In Anchorage, Todd and Trevor boarded the plane that soon departed for Seattle. They settled into reading, one a Grisham novel, the other the newspaper. Their lunch arrived in an hour and Todd, after he'd finished a teriyaki chicken salad, closed his eyes. He slept twenty minutes, waking with his head on Trevor's shoulder. When he opened his eyes, he noticed a man in the window seat next to Trevor staring at him, a sneer on his lips. His eyes were blue–gray and framed by silver wire–rimmed glasses. Todd saw the man's sparse gray hair receding from his forehead. He wore a pinstripe navy suit with an immaculate shirt and tie. He looks about mid–sixties, Todd thought.

After he straightened himself and raised his seat, Todd said, "Hello, I'm Todd Keeley." He offered his hand. "And this is Trevor Johnson."

The man coughed and gave Todd a dubious handshake. "Mitchell's the name." He ran his finger around the back of his collar.

"Business in Seattle?" Trevor plunged in.

"No, business in Anchorage." The man seemed fascinated with his cuffs.

"We're headed for Portland, then the coast." Todd stretched his leg into the aisle.

"I live in Oregon, but I don't get out to the ocean much." Mr. Mitchell looked at his knees. "Well, nice meeting you. Have a good trip." He averted his eyes again to study the clouds that beckoned outside his window. Todd ogled Trevor and smirked with ironic pleasure. He returned to Grisham while Trevor crunched peanuts.

They arrived at Sea–Tac Airport in the late afternoon with an hour to wait before their next flight. Trevor headed for the newsstand for a Portland paper, the sooner to find employment if Todd got the job. He read the want ads hoping something would jump out at him. Todd wandered around looking for a hot dog. He returned to the departure lounge with two hot dogs in one hand, a Coke in the other. He slouched into a bolted down, black leather chair across from Trevor's seat. Trevor folded the paper. "One's mine?"

"Nope, you can get yours where I bought these. I couldn't carry yours too. Go on. Thanks for watching my tote." Tossing his coat over the chair back, Trevor ambled away in the direction that Todd had come.

When Trevor came back with a burger, Todd was biting into his second dog. He wiped his mouth. "Find anything promising in the paper?"

"Nah, nothing. Guess I'll just wait and see what turns up. Your job's not a sure bet." The burger looked small in Trevor's large hand. A woman sitting next to him got up and left with her luggage so Todd moved to her place.

"Sometimes—" Todd eyed Trevor "—I want to give you a big kiss right in public." Trevor gave him an askance look.

"Like now, you mean?"

"Yeah, or in the plane when that bigot sneered at us. When will it be okay, Trev?"

"Right now." Trevor pecked Todd's cheek. "No use getting mushy. I don't like seeing *anyone* in a passionate embrace in public." Trevor swallowed a gulp of Coke.

"Thanks for that weak effort, Trev. I'll try to control my urges." Within fifteen minutes, the men boarded the Portland flight, which landed in an hour.

"It's a pleasure meeting you Mr. Keeley," Jerry Logan said the next morning, offering Todd a chair as he closed his office door. He'd exchanged a firm handshake with his short thick fingers. He wore a fine plaid shirt with the cuffs turned up.

"Thank you and the same to you." Todd noticed Jerry's round, pleasant face framed with wavy brown hair cut over his ears. "I've been anticipating this opportunity to talk with you." Todd took a chair in the simply furnished room.

"Your resume indicates that you've been working in Kodiak researching seals." Larry's round rimless glasses accentuated his brown eyes that showed interest. "This job involves a lot of time on the water, keeping records and data on all aspects of whale migration and mating habits. You'll be with several persons at sea. Not too conducive to family life, if that's important." Todd glanced at a desk picture of Jerry with a woman, a boy, and a girl, who appeared to be in their teens.

"No, I'm single." He noticed the gold band on Jerry's finger. "I love the weather challenge and the unpredictable habits of sea life."

"It's an adventure all right. I was out there myself at your age, until my wife and children started complaining. If you have the time, let me take you to the lab right now."

Todd followed Jerry to his car.

Saturday morning the sun was bright as the partners drove north to Todd's parents' home. "I love the Oregon coast. If I get the job, I'll be out there—" Todd pointed to the ocean "—with the whales."

Trevor's square jaw turned toward Todd a second, then back to the road. "What do you expect today?"

"An ambush." Todd pushed his hand against the dashboard, looking at Trevor's wavy hair in profile. "No, I don't have the vaguest idea. Dad has never expressed the displeasure he showed us last summer."

"He ignored you before that?"

"No, he was quiet. He hasn't known what to do with me since I reached puberty. It's as if all his doubts about me blew up in his mind when he saw you in the flesh. I'm sure Mom chewed him out. The kids will make today okay. He'll be cool in front of them."

Trevor spread large fingers through his dark hair. "You're sure?" He glanced at the dashboard. "Can you?"

Todd released his grip on the dash. "I know I'm uptight. I'd like to give him what-for, but I'll be peaceful."

"Good. If you want my opinion, something besides you and me is bugging your dad."

"You've never said that before."

"Never said it because I didn't think you'd want to hear it."

"Are you saying something's wrong with my dad?"

"I'm saying he's too reactionary. His remark about your behavior with Jonas was off the wall. You wouldn't win an award for your response either, but he provoked it. Take it easy today and you'll do fine. We had better drop this now. Tell me the exit number again."

When Todd and Trevor pulled the car into Kevin Keeley's driveway, Kevin waved while he slid a picnic basket into his car. Kate followed behind with the children who jumped on Todd as he and Trevor opened the car door and stepped out. "I have my Frisbee," Jonas said, pointing to his grandfather's car.

"Are you ready?" Kevin asked Charlotte, who had appeared in the driveway.

"I think we're out of here." She got into the front seat.

Kevin cued Jonas and Amanda who scrambled into the car with Charlotte. Kate smiled at Todd and before getting in with the children, she motioned him to follow them.

"They didn't suggest the kids ride with us," Trevor said.

"No kidding." Todd jumped in behind the wheel and followed his father to the zoo.

Kevin and Charlotte walked with their family from exhibit to exhibit determined they'd make the day go well. Amanda giggled and made contorted faces at the monkeys when Todd lifted her high so she could see them. When the sunny skies turned cloudy, Todd suggested a good place for their picnic before any rains could spoil it. Charlotte spread the food on a table in a grassy spot where they passed it around.

"I've always thought I'd do better at building structures then designing them." Trevor looked at Kevin, hoping that engineering was an apropos topic.

"You have the build for it," Kevin said as he reached for a napkin, and then wiped up baked beans that had fallen from Amanda's spoon onto the table.

"You do chicken right, Mrs. Keeley." Trevor licked his fingers and smiled at Charlotte.

"Thanks Trevor, and my name's Charlotte. More salad?"

Jonas bounced up, leaned across the table, held out his empty plate. "I want some, please." Trevor grinned at Charlotte and nodded for her to serve the boy first. Kate sat still, observing as Dave had suggested.

"I liked the seals," Jonas announced, elbowing Amanda as he sat down. She continued chewing on celery and peanut butter, ignoring her brother.

"I can tell you all about seals." Todd smiled at Jonas, flipping his hair aside the way he always did. Same old Todd, Kate thought.

"Aren't you getting a new job, Uncle Todd?" Jonas looked up, a curious expression in his deep-set eyes. "We could go to the zoo lots if you lived around here."

"Well Jonas, I'm not sure yet about the new job." Todd glanced around the attentive group, his eyes avoiding Trevor. He caught Kate's gaze. "I hope I can do some whale research . . . study. They still have to decide if they want me, but I'd like to move here to work."

"Whales are big." Amanda squirmed and pounded her hands on the slats of the table. "I never saw one, only in pictures."

"No, you haven't, but sometime you will." Todd looked across the table at his niece. "Maybe some day I can show you a big whale up close with a hump, that's a big bump on its back." Amanda clapped her hands and raised them over her head, shaking her golden curls in delight. Trevor, who sat next to her, covered her head with his broad hand and smiled. Charlotte sat serenely sipping a Coke reflecting about this family exchange, thinking that Trevor seemed kind and well mannered.

Kevin passed the plate of chicken again. When he'd swallowed a drink, he set his elbows in front of him and folded his hands. "What are your plans, Trevor? Are you headed this way too?" Now Todd gave Trevor a nervous glance.

"I'd like to find work here," Trevor said, wondering when was the right time to talk to Todd's folks. "I love the Oregon coast. Todd and I get along well."

"You guys are awesome friends." Jonas slid from the bench, ran across the grass to the other side of the table and then jumped on Todd's back.

Todd got up and eyed the sky. Grabbing the Frisbee, he tossed it above him catching it behind his back. "Hey Jonas, catch this." The boy leaped a few yards ahead of Todd and raised his arms toward the flying disc. He laughed, missed it, then picked it up and flung it high into the air to his uncle who zoomed ahead to retrieve it.

"Not bad," Trevor said to Todd. "I didn't know you were good with Frisbees. Maybe you're an athlete after all."

"A girl I knew in the ninth grade taught me." Todd grinned back. Jonas missed two more, then caught a throw from Trevor.

Turning to face the table, Jonas yelled, "Gramps, come on." Kevin lifted his legs free from the bench and ambled to the threesome, with Charlotte observing his reluctance.

She walked with Amanda to a nearby swing and gave her granddaughter a swift push. Then she sat in a swing beside Amanda and began pumping with her legs. "You can do it." Charlotte watched Amanda thrust out her legs, then pull them under herself jerking the chain. She tried again and did better. Kate joined them, an amused smile spreading across her face as she placed her foot on the slide ladder. "Should I go down the slide?"

"You can push us." Charlotte laughed. "These chains are heavy."

In fifteen minutes, sporadic raindrops interrupted their fun. The family hurriedly cleared the table and packed its contents and themselves into the car. Just before she got into the car, Charlotte leaned into Todd's car window and invited him and Trevor to the house.

"I want to ride with Uncle Todd," Jonas called from the backseat of the Keeley car.

Charlotte frowned and glanced at Kate who said, "Then hurry up and get in, you rascal." A relieved expression settled on Todd's face as Jonas climbed into the backseat. Charlotte sat next to Kevin as Kate stepped into the back with Amanda and closed the car door.

"Trevor's nice." Amanda smiled, patting her mother's leg. "Uncle Todd has nice friends."

"Yes, he seems like a fine fellow." Charlotte sounded stilted as she turned in the front seat to look at Kate.

Kevin drove without comment. After awhile he said, "Should I stop for some ice cream to go with those cookies we didn't eat?"

"Chocolate." Amanda prompted Kevin's laugh.

"Yes ma'am."

Kate leaned forward and put her hands on her mother's shoulders. "Mom, you're looking good. Still feeling okay?"

"Yes, and I know that I'm a lucky woman." Charlotte smiled, touched Kate's hand and turned to meet her eyes.

"Even though I'm a nurse," Kate said, "I can't know what you've been through, but I'm happy for you. Keep up your self-exams."

"Like you think I won't."

When they pulled into the driveway, Todd, Trevor, and Jonas stood in decaying leaves surveying the huge, wet maple tree. "Hey Mom, I'm gonna show Uncle Todd my tree house," Jonas hollered as Kate emerged from the car.

"No, not now, it's too slippery."

"I can climb it." Jonas shoved his hands in his pockets, frowning. "I'm not a baby."

"No Jonas, your mom's right," Todd said. "It's too wet now. I'll see it some other day."

"Come on champion, I have ice cream and the house key," Kevin said. Charlotte and Kate served the dessert, which everyone enjoyed, and the children never left the adult circle. Kate knew she had to postpone any frank talk with Todd.

Rubbing a napkin across his mouth, Kevin said, "How did you feel about the job interview, Todd?"

"I'm encouraged. The work sounds very exciting. It's a year old project and they're losing a man for health concerns. I may be doing a variety of jobs."

"Like what?" Kate asked.

"Like tracking gray whales and recording their migration habits. Some of the sightings may take me as far as Cape Flattery off Washington's coast. I'll be out at sea a lot tagging and recording data. Before you ask, the pay is a little better than I'm making now. So, you've caught up on your brother's life." He grinned at Kate who nodded her affirmation. "So, what's going on with you?" Todd turned his attention to Kate.

"Recently I've been working in the cardiac ward at the hospital. I like it. A lot of my job is patient education. You wouldn't believe how many people come in with angina or a heart attack claiming they've never heard of cholesterol." Kate threw up her hands. Todd laughed, catching amused glances from Trevor and Kevin.

"Mom has indoctrinated us in the ways of good nutrition." Todd glanced at his friend, then made a face as he lifted the spoon from his empty ice cream bowl. "Most of the time."

"I tried." Charlotte smirked, raising her brows. "It's low fat."

"She rules around here," Kevin said, "it's true."

"But you're not a dietician, right?" Trevor looked at Kate.

"Nope. I check blood pressure, draw blood, and check for bleeding after catheterization procedures. I spend time convincing patients that the low salt, low fat food that comes on their tray is good for their health. Of course, genetics plays a big role too. All heart diseases aren't related to food and stress, but many are."

"Your brother keeps me on task. We eat lots of fish and chicken." Trevor shot a grin at Todd, who missed it because he was absorbed in watching Kevin twist a napkin, and eye his watch.

Todd slapped his thighs. "Trevor, I think we need to get back to the motel." He rose to his feet. "We'll call tomorrow. We might make a run for the beach." Todd started for his coat.

Kevin dropped his rope–like napkin. "Well . . . when do you expect to hear from the research lab?"

"Hard to say. They're still interviewing. I hope I'll know something by next week."

"Well, I hope you get it, brother." Kate flashed a broad smile.

Jonas emerged from the corner of the living room, his hands full of pieces from a half–finished dinosaur puzzle that Kevin had given him. "Do you want help putting that together?" Kevin said.

"Yes Gramps, will you help me?"

"In a few minutes, Jonas." Kevin came to his feet. The young men stood without a word while Kevin took from the closet a jacket and sweater, which he handed to Trevor. Todd's arms started for an embrace, but Kevin extended his hand. "Good to see you Todd. I hope things go well for you." He took a few steps to where Trevor stood. "Have a safe trip back."

"Just a second, Todd. Where are you staying?" Kate dug in her purse for a scrap of paper and a pen. Todd's eyes questioned Trevor.

"Travel Lodge, but I don't know the number," Trevor said.

"Forget it." Kate wrote her phone number on a torn envelope and handed it to Todd. "Call me tonight when you get back."

"Just as bossy as ever, aren't you." Everyone laughed.

Jonas deserted his puzzle, ran and hugged Todd. "Are you going back to Alaska?"

"In a few days, yes." Jonas raised his head, but his face fell. Amanda approached with outstretched arms, then nuzzled Todd's legs and squealed when Todd lifted her off the floor and hugged her.

"It's great to see you." Charlotte embraced her son. She glanced at Trevor. "Nice to see you again, Trevor."

"You too. Thank you for the picnic and the hospitality." The men edged to the door that Kevin opened. They walked straight to the car and drove off.

"We must finish that dinosaur." Kevin creaked onto the floor with Jonas and began fitting pieces together. Charlotte and Kate moved the bowls into the kitchen.

They washed the dishes in silence and put away picnic leftovers. Absorbed in the awkward stillness, Kate felt uneasy. She laid her hand on Charlotte's shoulder, paused. "Mom, could we do something together, just the two of us?"

"I'd like that."

"Good, I'll call you next week on my day off."

Kate gathered her belongings, the children, and left her parents' house.


Todd drove while Trevor stretched his knees within an inch of the dashboard, listening to the swishing of the windshield wipers. "What do you think, Trev?"

Trevor was silent a moment. "I think the kids like me. Amanda's a pretty girl. She looks a lot like your sister. Jonas is appealing too in a boyish way, not handsome, but engaging."

"Isn't he."

"He looks like your dad. They have those unusual eyes, deep–set." Trevor looked at Todd in a teasing way, seeing his profile in the dark car. "But you don't."

Todd continued driving. "Nope, mine are deep green and set so handsomely in my face."

"Right." Trevor burst into laughter.

"Jonas *is* a winsome kid and frequently gets his way. At least he used to. I can't say for sure now, seeing them so seldom."

"Are you saying he has a mind of his own?" Trevor turned toward Todd. "Like his grandfather, don't you think?"

"I suppose . . . but Jonas' dad is his own man too. You'd like Dave. So much for the kids. What—"

"Do I think of the grown–ups? I would say Kate likes me somewhat, your Mom has reservations, and your Dad forced himself to be polite. Any more questions?"

"Yes. Want to go out on the beach tomorrow?"

"With you, yeah. The weather's getting crummy, and I don't see pushing on the Jonas issue. Another time, just to be safe."

"That's fine with me. Actually, I'm glad you detected the superficiality." Trevor didn't respond. "What are you thinking?"

"Uh, I don't know. Maybe you're too hard on your family. We're all superficial until we feel a sense of trust with someone unfamiliar."

Todd was silent. Trevor studied the lights glimmering in houses as they passed. "I think you turn at the next intersection and the motel is on that drag."

"That was quick."

Relieved that the day at the zoo was over, Kate drove toward their suburban home. "As soon as we're home, it's in the tub. You're first Jonas, then Amanda."

"I hate baths."

"You're taking one . . . tomorrow's Sunday . . . we're going to church."

"I wanna bubble bath," Amanda chirped, and kicked the back of the driver's seat.

"Stop kicking. You can have a bubble bath if you behave all the way home."

"Any cookies left?" Jonas smacked his lips, then Kate heard his shoes drop off his feet to the car floor.

"One each with milk, then bed. No story tonight because it's too late." Kate tuned in a classic radio station and wondered what she'd say to Todd when he called.

When they arrived home, Dave, absorbed with the computer,

gave Kate no assistance in the bath and bed routine. When she'd tucked in the kids and had plopped into a chair, he walked into the living room. "So how did the day go?"

"What do you care?"

"Knock it off, Kate. You know I care. I'm planning a bridge, all right?" He sat down.

"Okay. It went okay. No blowups. The kids loved the zoo and we had a good day until afternoon when, of course, it started raining. I'm impressed with Trevor. He seems like a decent person. He's good with the kids."

"No kidding?"

"No kidding, he seemed at ease."

"You didn't feel squeamish?"

"No, I was dispassionate."

"That'll be the day. How were your folks?"

"Mom did better than Dad."

"What are you saying?"

"I'm saying Dad was stiff, nervous." Kate swallowed hard. "He was cruel."

"Cruel?" Dave turned his chair to face her.

"He refused to hug Todd."

"Why would he hug him?"

"Because Todd made the gesture."

Dave didn't respond for a minute. "I'm sorry."

"I know."

"What about Todd's interview? Does he feel he has a chance?"

"Yeah." Kate let out a breath. "He hopes to hear within a week. Dave, I need to talk with him, but I had no opportunity."

"You will."

"He's got my number . . . he's calling me tonight."

"Kate, you can't expect . . ."

"I know, I know." Two hours later in bed Kate snuggled against Dave. The phone never rang.

Sunday morning Dave poured cereal into his children's bowls. He looked at Jonas and Amanda. "Tell me about the animals."

"I saw an elephant splash in the water. He went way deep and stuck out his nose." Amanda giggled.

"It's a trunk, not a nose, stupid," Jonas piped up.

"Jonas." Dave frowned at his son. "Go ahead."

Jonas reddened and looked down. "Sorry, Amanda."

Dave exchanged a curious glance with Kate, who said, "The zoo has an elephant swimming hole."

"Oh, a swimming hole, that explains it." Dave's teeth parted in a wide laugh. "Finish your breakfast. We're leaving for church."

# Chapter 13

Dave stepped into his boots Monday morning and swallowed a gulp of coffee. "I'm late," he muttered as he grabbed his lunch and rushed out the door.

"See you tonight," Kate called after him.

As Dave approached the construction site, he saw Kevin. Dave stuck his blueprints under his arm, shut the van door, and left his lunch and thermos in the company vehicle. Several dozen men were hammering nails into the forms for the bridge piers. He inhaled the cold air as he walked toward his father–in–law.

"Hello Dave, what do you think?"

"Looks like a start. Why are you here?"

"How about a greeting. Missed you at the zoo."

"Sorry, hi. Too busy with my work."

"Well, I'm here because I'm overseeing this project. My last big build before I retire." Kevin's hair blew in the air as his brown eyes settled on Dave.

"If you ever do . . . I'll believe it when I see it." Dave flashed his white teeth and Kevin eyed the blueprints under his arm.

"Just wanted to get a better picture of this place." Dave thrust the rolled package out in front of him. I've worked on these all weekend."

"Perfect timing. I'll walk you around the site. Put those back in the van and we'll go over them later." Dave obliged, returning with his thermos.

"It's not time for coffee break yet." Kevin laughed. Dave grinned and followed the senior man to the crest of the hill overlooking the Columbia River. He'd seen the location once at twilight, but today the clear sky loomed above them and the surroundings were breathtaking. "Let's meet a few of the crew." They walked past muddy boards and bent nails to where the men worked. "This is Randolph, Mike, and that's Jim," Kevin called and gestured toward the men who nodded and spoke their greetings. "This is Dave Winston, our main architect."

As they wandered around the site and back to the van, Dave smoothed his beard with the back of his hand. "What's Jim's position? He doesn't look like part of the sweaty crew in that sports coat."

"He's responsible for structural inspections."

"What does an inspector do at this point?"

"He makes certain that the land can support the structure's weight, considering soil erosion, all that federal stuff."

"I have lots to learn."

"So, fire your questions, Dave. Let's get in the van out of this cold and take a look at your plans." Kevin shivered and rubbed his hands together, then opened the van's passenger door and climbed in.

"Now I'm having some coffee." Dave unscrewed the thermos top gesturing to Kevin. "Want some?"

"Why not." Kevin smiled and took the filled thermos lid. Dave tipped the thermos up and drank from it. He reached for his blueprints, opening them in his lap.

Kate arrived at the hospital for work, passing the waiting room on her way to cardiology. A man stepped into the hall. "When did they start his surgery?" he asked, a challenge in his tone. Kate, who hadn't started her shift, eyed the man. He looked familiar.

"Who are you here for, sir?"

"My father, Harold Baxter."

"I'll inquire for you."

"Please." The man's thick black hair, clean–shaven face, the smooth arch of his brows, made Kate glance again.

She continued to her office, slipped into her lab coat and checked her patient schedules. She stopped at the patient name, Harold Baxter, admitted overnight suffering from a myocardial infarction. At the nurses' station she inquired about Mr. Baxter, then went to his room. His chart read that his cath had revealed several blockages in his descending aorta, but he wasn't in the bed. Kate discovered that he had been in surgery since eight a.m.

When she reentered the waiting room, Kate could hear the man's fingers tapping against his chair. She noticed his broad shoulders. "Your father's surgery is going well. I talked to an assistant on the team. He's been in surgery since eight." Mr. Baxter's son stopped tapping and turned his brown eyes to Kate. "He probably won't be out for two or three hours," Kate said. "Then, of course, he'll be in recovery until he's stabilized."

A few muscles relaxed in the man's face. "Okay, thank you."

"Do you know where to find coffee and food?" Kate's blue eyes widened, and she raised her brows.

"Isn't it down the hall and then. . ." He raised his hands in question.

"Turn right and take the elevator to the first floor. You'll see the cafeteria straight ahead. The food's good. I eat there a lot." Kate smiled. "I'll see your father when he's back on this floor. My shift just started." She smiled again, wondering why she was explaining herself to Harold Baxter's son.

"Haven't I seen you before?" the man asked, when Kate started to leave.

"Most likely." Kate then hustled off not wishing to explain the circumstances.

The morning flew by while Kate cared for her patients and checked on Harold Baxter's progress. When she finally ate a late lunch alone, she slumped in her chair wanting to sleep. The weekend had strained her and she felt exhausted. She picked a sesame seed from her roll. Some good had transpired. The kids enjoyed Todd and she felt safer about him and Trevor. Such a huge man, Trevor, he's not the gay type. The gay type, she thought. Putting her head in her hands, she wondered how she would change her thinking.

A man is here to visit his ill father. No, a son is here for his father. Do they get along? He seems young, maybe thirty-five. Why hadn't the Baxter family talked? Kate remembered the angry exchange she'd had with the man the night his mother died. Jim, that's his name. Who couldn't handle it, he or his parents or all of them? Were there other kids? She heard a clicking sound in the silence and looked up at the wall clock. Pushing back her chair, she stood and carried a bowl coated with split pea soup to the scullery and returned to the bustling hall.

Entering the women's restroom, she used the toilet, brushed her hair, splashed her face and applied a rosy lipstick. When she stopped by cardiac recovery, she discovered the senior Mr. Baxter, ashen and unconscious. A nurse looked up as Kate entered. "He's slow to come around," the man said, "but he had several transfusions . . . six hours under the knife. I think he'll be okay. One of yours?"

"Yes." Please God let him be okay. Harold's hair was graying in streaks. She couldn't remember the color of his eyes. The resuscitator covered his face, and his hands looked large and colorless. "How long has he been here?"

"A few minutes, just wheeled him in. You know him well?"

Kate shook her head. "No, no, I don't, but his wife died here recently. His son's upstairs waiting to see him." Kate felt foolish so she smiled and concluded. "Thanks for the update. I'll tell Mr. Baxter's son that he's in recovery." She took the stairs asking herself, why do I care. I don't want to be around if Harold Baxter dies, that's why.

As she approached the waiting room, Kate saw Jim Baxter bent over a group of magazines. "Hello," she said. "Had a chance to eat?"

He turned. "Hi, yes, I found some decent food. You were right." This time he smiled. "How's Dad?"

"He's in recovery, but he's still unconscious." Jim shot her a piercing look. "The nurse said he had two transfusions. He's tired, but the surgery went well." Kate stepped closer. Jim stiffened. "As soon as he's on the floor, I will call you." Kate extended her hand, which he took while brushing his forehead with the other. "This is difficult," Kate said. "I'm sorry you've had so much pain."

"You were here when Mom died." His brown eyes held hers, then averted.

"Yes, I remember. Your dad will make it. I'll be back." Kate stepped into the hall, bone tired of cardiac work.

"Smells good," Kate said when she passed through her kitchen that evening. "What are you doing home so early?" She set her purse on the coffee table and kissed Dave's cheek. He set down a *Newsweek.*

"I went over my blueprints with your dad today. He was at the site this morning when I arrived. After lunch we went to the office and he insisted that I take off."

"That explains the meatballs." Following her nose, Kate walked toward the simmering pot on the stove. "Where are the kids?" She returned to the living room. "Tina said you picked Amanda up. Without telling *me.*" She scowled.

"I locked them in the closet."

"Stop it. Never mind I hear them." Kate rolled her eyes and gave an exasperated sigh. "I'm tired of cardiac care. Guess who was admitted last night for heart surgery?"

"Just tell me, love." Dave walked into the kitchen and Kate followed.

"Harold Baxter. The guy whose wife died."

"Who?"

"Pam Baxter's husband. Mom knew her from their garden club."

"Oh, the woman with the angry son."

"Yep, I saw him too."

Dave stirred the pot, licked gravy from a spoon. "Well, what's the story?"

"Harold woke up when my shift ended. He was unconscious for longer than most, but they expect him to be okay."

"Jeez, heart attack so young. He's not sixty is he?"

"About that."

"Was his kid a jerk this time?"

"He was okay. We didn't talk much. He didn't recognize me at first, then his memory returned. He's a handsome man. I didn't pay attention last time."

"Is he still gay?"

"Very funny."

After dinner Kate listened to Jonas read his homework assignment. When she finally put him and Amanda into bed, she cleaned up the kitchen while Dave worked on his blueprints. Later Dave stepped into the bedroom, dripping wet from his shower and looked at Kate who sat in bed reading. "Is that Jim fellow about six feet with broad shoulders, dark hair, brown eyes, and wire–rimmed glasses?" Dave stood naked except for a towel slung around his neck and a grin on his face.

"Yes to all but the glasses. Why?" Kate stared at her husband.

"I think he's the structural inspector that I met this morning. He left about nine when Kevin and I were in the van. Kevin said that Jim's dad was having heart surgery."

When Kate returned from the hospital the next night, she scanned the names in her address book until she found a new entry for Todd. She sank into the couch, dialed his number.

"Hello?"

"Todd?"

"No, this is Trevor, but I can get him."

"Hello Trevor. This is Kate, Todd's sister. How's it going?"

"Hi Kate. Fine, fine. It's cold here compared to Oregon."

"I'm sure it is. Did you have a good flight home?"

"Not bad at all."

"Hey, I'd like to talk to Todd."

"Yep, hold on."

"Hi Kate. I figured you'd call sooner or later."

"Is that so? I figured you'd call from your motel, but you didn't. I have to talk with you Todd."

"Is something wrong with Mom?"

"No, that would be easier."

"Then what's wrong?"

"I've been wondering how you felt when you saw Mom and Dad?"

"How I felt?" Todd paused. "Not too good, but you know Kate, I have my own life. If you guys don't like the way I live, so be it."

Silence.

"We need to talk."

"We can do that if I move. I haven't heard anything yet."

"Let me just ask . . ."

"About Trevor?"

"Uh yes, I just . . ."

"Save your breath Kate. I'm gay and so is Trevor. We love each other. Does that shock you?" Todd twisted the phone cord around his finger.

"Uh, no."

"No?" Todd paused. "If that's true . . . it would be a comfort."

"I figured you must be. Thanks for telling me. This is so difficult by phone. I have been thinking about you a lot since you visited."

"Yeah, well . . . I'm angry."

"This seems stupid, Todd, but a man was at the hospital whose mom died suddenly." Kate stopped, omitting the fact that Jim worked for Kevin. "He was furious. Said he hadn't talked with his mom."

"So, what's your point?"

"My point is that he's gay, but hadn't told his mom. Maybe he thought it would hurt her too much. I don't know. She died and he chewed me out for her death."

"Why?"

"Because I was on duty, I guess. His dad is recovering from a heart attack now. Anyway, that and Mom's cancer made me see that things can change fast. We need to be a family before it's too late."

A long pause.

"Maybe it's already too late, Kate."

"What do you mean?"

"I mean I have to be who I am despite you guys. I want to feel included in this family, to share stuff with Dad, but all I get from him is polite rejection."

Kate winced at the despair in her brother's tone. "Don't forget I'm still your sister. I trust you and I like Trevor. Tell him that for me, will you?"

"Yeah, I will. If you don't mind—" Todd coughed, "—I can't talk about this anymore. Thanks for calling me."

"Sure. Wanted you to know I care about you and I want to stay in touch."

"Yeah, well okay. Bye Kate."

"Bye, Todd." Kate held the receiver before returning it to its cradle. She slipped off her shoes, pulled up her feet and wrapped her arms around her knees. This could go on forever without anyone changing, she thought. Todd doesn't trust me. He thinks I'm spouting empty words. She sank deeper into the couch.

# Chapter 14

They had chosen a corner table with privacy from an ornamental fig tree. Charlotte loved the photos that hung on the walls, the Mediterranean Sea with whitewashed houses in their island settings. Neither she nor Kevin had been to Greece, but wanted to go.

"Something wrong with my face?" Charlotte asked, looking up. Kate was staring, the way she did when she studied you with a critical eye, as if you couldn't feel it. They had finally planned a lunch together. Was it going to undo her, make her feel old and sad? "I need a dye job again, I know. You don't like the grayish line along the part, do you?"

Kate leveled her eyes to meet her mother's insulted ones. "No, I was just thinking, I don't know how your real hair looks."

"Gray."

"Silver or mousy?"

Charlotte made a face. Kate kept her gaze. "Really Mom, why don't you let it grow out? I loved Grandma's silver hair and then it turned white as snow. It was lovely, didn't you think?" Charlotte resisted the impulse to pull out her mirror and study her hair over her Greek salad.

"I suppose I could let it grow out."

"It's not a crime to get older." Kate hoped she sounded kind.

"Just a grief."

"Is that how you feel?"

"Sometimes that's how I feel, Kate. Aging is a time of loss—your parents, your physical stamina, your physical attractiveness." She smoothed the napkin on her lap. "Gains come with age, too, of course. Grandchildren, expressing yourself, taking yourself less seriously. Except this hair thing." She smiled at her own words.

"You've always looked good Mom, and you won't be unfashionable with gray hair. If it isn't silvery, if you look horrible, you can dye it again."

"So you agree it's possible I'll look dreadful. What do I do in the mean time?" Charlotte lifted her teacup to her mouth, glancing over its rim at her daughter.

"Oh silly, you endure the in–between. You're a perfectionist. Be more flexible."

"I'll think about it." Charlotte managed an impish grin. "Now what's new with you?"

"Work is busy. Cardiac care is wearing me out. Remember Harold Baxter?" Charlotte nodded at Kate. "Well, he's healing from a heart attack, had by-pass surgery. He went home yesterday."

"He must be lonesome since his wife died. He's not old. I saw him in church, no, in the parking lot. A younger man was with him who I assume is his son. He must be a comfort for his father."

Kate remembered that she had not mentioned Jim Baxter when she'd told her mother about Pam Baxter's death. "Yes, I met his son. He was at the hospital when his dad had surgery and he seems concerned about his father." Kate inhaled the spicy aroma of lamb in her moussaka. She wanted to discuss Todd, not Jim Baxter.

She noticed her mother's hand when Charlotte picked up a roll; the veins seemed prominent. A few freckles had turned dark. Kate remembered the clothes those hands had sewn for her. She remembered the bird feeders they had helped create for Todd's Cub Scout troop when Charlotte was a den mother. Charlotte's eyes were clear, but Kate noticed the lines around them and the ones around her mouth when she smiled. That stayed when she didn't.

"You are still beautiful, Mom. No double chin and your figure is wonderful compared to lots of women your age. You've even come through this cancer scare. I'm proud that you're my mom."

"Are we back on me?" Charlotte frowned, but reached over and patted Kate's arm, then exchanged smiles with her for the kind words.

"Not for long, I'd like to talk about my brother."

"Okay." Charlotte brushed a crumb from her lap. "What about Todd?" She met Kate's eyes in anticipation.

"What do you make of his relationship with Trevor?"

"Make of it? Trevor seems like a pleasant man who has learned good manners from someone."

"Mom—" Kate paused, swallowed some water, "—I mean, well, what do you think about them being together?"

"I have some reservations about that, why?"

"You know Todd and Trevor are partners. They're gay."

"Oh? What makes you say that?"

"Todd told me that he loves Trevor; they love each other."

"When did he tell you this?"

"I called. I guess I figured it out myself, but Todd volunteered." Kate paused, noticed the awareness in her mother's face.

"Mom, you *do* know, don't you."

"Well. I wasn't born yesterday."

"But when? Does Dad?"

"Awhile ago and your dad's a good question. It's beyond me how Kevin couldn't know. I hint and suggest, but he avoids me. He seems so vulnerable. I haven't out and out said gay. Let's just say he denies it."

"Denies—" Kate started and then abruptly stopped.

"Oh," Charlotte gave a startled jerk and glanced up.

The waiter had approached her chair from behind and stood bent from the waist. "May I bring you something else?"

"Why not." Kate responded first. "Your carrot cake is delicious. Still has gooey cream cheese frosting?"

"Yes," the waiter said in a too–serious tone.

"I'd like a piece with coffee, please." Kate stifled an urge to laugh at his stoic face.

"Make it two, also with coffee," Charlotte said.

When the man had departed, Kate tensed. "Dad denies it? Don't you talk about Todd?"

"Well, yes. We talk about both of you, but we seldom discuss your sex life." The words spewed like a hiss. A smirk slipped across Kate's mouth. She couldn't suppress her amusement and burst into laughter. Charlotte looked at her and irresistibly joined in. Tensions dissolved, bringing tears to their eyes.

"You know Mom, I feel so foolish thinking that I can inform you about the real world." She dabbed her eyes.

"Truth be known, you can. Don't think this gay thing is easy for me. I've struggled to understand it. I can't. Kevin and I have lost something with Todd, and I don't want to lose him completely. I think we have to understand."

"We do, Mom. We need to accept him the way he is. He's hurt. He told me—" Kate fell silent. She put her hand to her forehead and watched her mother make a thumbprint in the condensation on her water glass. "I'm not sure how to say this. Todd said—" Kate took a deep breath "—that he feels Dad rejects him."

Charlotte closed her eyes, nodded her head. "And me?"

"He didn't say you, no. He said—"

"Here comes our dessert," Charlotte said.

"Then let's enjoy it, because that's basically what Todd said. The subject's been a bit taboo, you know. This family needs to make some changes. I've felt that for a long time." Charlotte nodded her head again and accepted a plate of cake.

Kevin tapped his pencil on his desk. "The inspector wants some revisions in the blueprints."

"What kind of revisions?" Dave fumbled in his briefcase.

"Specifically he thinks the main arc should be more gradual."

"That's possible. What's your opinion, Dad?" He half smiled at this rare reference to his father–in–law, but caught Kevin's return grin.

"When it comes to structure, I do what I'm told. So I can't defend you on this."

Dave flushed and glanced down at the drawings he'd spread across Kevin's desk. "Wasn't implying you should defend me. I'm learning as I go."

"Here's his number. You should hear his concerns." Kevin passed a neatly written name and number to Dave.

"I'll call, uh—" he eyed the paper "—Jim, and modify these blueprints and then get back to you." Dave started shoving some notes into his briefcase, then looked up. "By the way, have you talked to Jim since his father's surgery?"

"Yes, I saw him yesterday and he thought his dad was pulling through, had some diet changes in store for him."

Dave decided to come clean and gave Kevin a droll glance. "That would be Kate's department, if Jim's last name is Baxter."

"Well, yes it is." Kevin's face glimmered with realization. "At the hospital? That Mr. Baxter and Jim are related. Charlotte knew his wife through gardening. I'll be darned." Kevin gave Dave a solemn glance. "How do you know Jim's father?"

"Harold? I don't. Kate met him because she was on duty when his wife died."

"I see. Then you tell me how Harold is doing."

Dave looked sheepish. "Same report, I was just checking."

"Well, I'm glad Kate can help. Jim's a fine young man."

"Now I'm out of here," Dave said. The men talked at the door a few more minutes, and then Dave left.

Kevin emptied his pencil sharpener, put pencils and a pad in his desk, yanked a rag from the bottom drawer and dusted the desk until it shone. Then he ran the cloth over his bookcase, placing each book spine the same distance from the edge of the shelf. He dusted his pictures and looked at one of Stephen. He was so young and scared. What had he felt before he deserted?

Kevin recalled the scouting days, the pungent smell of alpine spruce needles, the roaring waterfalls, the drenched mossy rocks. He rubbed his neck, memories flooding back: how their backs had ached from carrying packs, how they had bandaged blisters and fought off mosquitoes. He thought of his own scouting leadership since. Had it been a memorial commitment to his missing brother? Kevin studied Stephen's slender physique, his green eyes. When he closed his own, he saw a bloody face. Todd couldn't—no, no the pain stopped the thought. He fingered the keys in his pocket, closed and locked his office door and headed for his car.

# Chapter 15

Todd paced the living room carpet, back and forth over the threadbare path. Trevor stood at the fireplace his arms spread across the mantle. "We can make it here. I like this area," Todd said smoothly while his fingers fiddled with the letter that held the hurtful news. "Besides, what I'm doing with seals might turn into whale research."

Trevor watched as Todd folded and unfolded the paper. "You're disappointed. I am too. Don't fake your feelings. Another job might come along, but if it doesn't, you're right, Kodiak is a good place for us. You've liked this job haven't you?" His pale eyes shifted to Todd.

"It's a job, I guess." Todd shook the paper again. "It makes me mad. Jerry Logan didn't like my handshake."

"Grow up, Todd. That's not why you weren't chosen."

"Hell, you know everything, right?" Todd shoved the paper in the desk drawer and slammed it. Did you know that in my teens, I . . . I practiced shaking hands with myself to develop a firm grip."

"No, I didn't know, and I don't care. Look at your hands, like them. Use your fingers. Punch the keys and call your mom. Tell her we'll be down for Thanksgiving, that we'll take Jonas to the beach."

"We aren't invited, Trevor. Don't you get it?"

"So you're never going to contact your folks again. Is that it?"

"I don't know."

"I don't know either, Todd. I don't know how long I can stand you and your wounds. Big deal, your folks didn't invite us for dinner. We can have turkey at a restaurant and get Jonas the next day. He's on school break, isn't he? You could call and ask."

"Goddammit, Trevor, I've done everything I can. I've worked since I was sixteen, I did my homework, I practiced the piano, I stayed with scouting, I dated girls." The veins swelled in Todd's neck, his cheeks flushed. "In college . . . I dated women." Todd kicked the ottoman hard, stomped to the door. "Hell with you."

Trevor felt the window rattle when the door slammed shut. What next, he wondered. He sat still for a long time. He clicked on the TV and watched CNN news. Afterwards he got up, went to the kitchen and grabbed a milk carton and some sliced turkey from the refrigerator, searched for mayonnaise, but found none. Spreading mustard on a slice of bread, he added the turkey. He ate the sandwich without tasting it. He worried about Todd. In his mind, he heard again the squeal of tires when Todd had peeled out.

At midnight, Trevor got into bed, after he flicked on the porch light for Todd. A ray stretched across the ceiling where he watched a spider inch its way along. He cradled the back of his neck in his hands. Something has to change or trouble's going to erupt, he thought. He listened to rain splat on the roof, he waited, and he finally slept.

Trevor felt something cold rub against his leg. He jerked awake. "It's me, Trev."

"Huh . . . uh, what time is it?"

"Two in the morning. I'm sorry."

Trevor twisted onto his side. "So am I when you explode like that. I don't know what you want."

"I know."

"What the hell, Todd. Today's Saturday and I'm awake. So are you, so talk. I want something to eat. Want something?"

"I had a burger, but I could stand some hot chocolate. I'll get it."

Trevor nodded. Todd rubbed his cold feet, put on socks and slippers, and his robe. He kicked up the heat. He couldn't find any instant cocoa, so he turned on the gas stove and poured milk and Hershey's cocoa into a pan. He stirred.

Trevor, dressed in sweats, walked into the kitchen with his arms crossed. "You worry me, Todd. Where've you been tonight?"

"I drove to the bluff and walked around, trying to sort things out. I watched the ship lights reflecting off the water. I blew up tonight because I'm so angry."

"Not getting that job is a tough break, but when I suggested that you move on, you said you were a good kid. Maybe so, but it doesn't *matter*. Now you're a good adult. The job has nothing to do with your parents or your handshake. You're living in the past. You grew up in the church, but all you've learned is how to criticize yourself. Guilt, you reek of it. What convinces you that God dislikes you so much?" Trevor watched Todd stir the cocoa, listening, but silent. "Who do you think you are? What have you done? You've got too much baggage, Todd."

Todd looked up, earnest and curiously contrite. "I've always felt like . . . I don't know, like I was climbing a hill to be accepted." He stirred the cocoa. "Somehow . . . if I could reach the top, I thought I would change into . . . okay. I would fit in somewhere." He paused, released the spoon, and pushed against the stove. "But if I ever eased up, I was afraid I'd slip down again." He stood silent. "Maybe the hill doesn't exist." Trevor raised his feet one rung on the stool, listened and waited.

"I wanted to prove myself to my family, but I'm beginning to see there's nothing to prove." Todd took the sugar that Trevor handed him. "I'm me, plain and simple." He stirred the sugar into the cocoa, glanced sideways and saw Trevor's affirming nod. He opened the cupboard and took out two mugs, poured chocolate into each. "Here Trev, thanks for not being mad at me."

"I *am* mad at you. You remind me of my own problems. We have work to do. I think we're on the right track, but staying there is the challenge. It's okay to feel angry . . . we need a creative way to express it."

"Dad makes me mad. I work hard to win his affection. The past rides on me, even if it doesn't matter, and I don't feel too creative."

"I meant it doesn't matter now how you acted in the past. Maybe you can't win his affection. Let your dad take responsibility for his own problems."

"That's enough, Trevor, okay? Let's get some sleep. I'll think about the beach trip." He set his mouth in a firm line.

Later that Saturday morning Todd sat on the edge of the bed feeling with his feet for his slippers. He knew the tiled bathroom floor would feel like ice. It was late, but Trevor didn't stir. Todd brewed some coffee, showered, grabbed his Levi's, sweatshirt and watch from the dresser, and took a shoebox from the drawer, leaving Trevor undisturbed.

In the kitchen he poured his coffee, opened the box and removed a snapshot of a young man in his army uniform. He studied the blond hair, lean body, and the long fingers. Were you musical? Did you like hiking? Next, he found Susanne, a tattered picture of her, the girl who listened to him. He had told her how he wanted to save the seas, like Cousteau. She liked whales, dolphins, seals, and the salty smell of sea air the way he did. She wasn't afraid of science or her own brains, either. Next, Todd touched the parchment music award from his sixth grade piano recital and smiled.

"What are you doing?" Trevor appeared in the room.

Todd looked at his best friend. "You awake?" Trevor yawned and slumped onto the stool, shivered as he pulled his robe around him. He picked up a photo.

"Who's this? Must be a cousin, he looks like you."

"Dad's older brother, Stephen."

"Didn't know he had a brother." Trevor turned the picture and read, "Korea, 1955." His face turned serious, his eyes questioned Todd.

"Missing after two years of service . . . twenty years old."

"Sorry, you've never mentioned him."

"Don't be sorry, I never knew him."

"Not even in stories?"

"Only that he and Dad were in scouting and I think they were stationed together."

"That must have been painful for Kevin."

"Yeah, I've always tried to accept Dad's silence about his brother. Stephen's disappearance has caused him heartaches for a long time. Dad doesn't know if he's dead or alive."

"I had no idea." Trevor turned silent a minute, fingering a photo. "Who's this girl?" Trevor studied a freckled face with dimples. "Cute."

"A girl I knew in ninth grade . . . my Frisbee coach. She studied crabs at the beach with me for a science class . . . she understood me."

Todd put the photos in the box and before he set the lid on top, Trevor saw the bright ribbon with the silver eagle, the Eagle Scout Award, but he didn't mention it or touch it.

He rubbed his eyes and combed his hair with his fingers, then stumbled to the cupboard for a cup. "I need more sleep."

"Yeah, it was a bad night. Give me your cup." Todd filled it with coffee, handed it to Trevor, and then opened the door to a blast of cold air. He carried in the newspaper and held it against Trevor's face.

"Jeez, that's freezing. You read it now. I'm taking a shower when I finish drinking this."

"Hurry up and I'll fix us some eggs." Todd plopped on the couch. He read the front page with half attention, his mind exhausted from conflict. He wanted to confront his father and he wanted to avoid him. He wanted to know more about Stephen. Turning to the religious section, Todd noticed the caption, *Gays and Lesbians Welcome.* A congregation of do–gooders, no doubt, he thought. He read about the church that candidly welcomes persons regardless of their marital status, race, economics, politics, cultural background, or sexual orientation.

"Whoa, how would they know," he said aloud, "ask you at the front door?"

"What?" Trevor yelled from the bathroom.

"Nothing," Todd shouted back.

# Chapter 16

"Down with gays." Dave scowled across his papers at his wife.

"What'd you say?" Kate set her teacup on the coffee table.

"Your friend the inspector wants me to change these blueprints. I called him today."

"Why?" Kate laughed. "I love that in you."

"My blueprint mistakes?"

"No, your humor. Blame the gays. What's wrong with your drawings?"

"Too much arc."

"That explains everything." Kate wrinkled her nose.

Jonas galloped into the room, his hair dripping. "Did you tell Daddy?"

"Not yet. Did you hang up the towel and check the floor?"

"Yessss, Mom."

"Tell me what?" Dave turned Jonas' wet pajama collar right side out.

"Thanksgiving. Uncle Todd and Trevor are coming for Thanksgiving."

"Well, that's good." Dave eyed Kate.

"Go get a towel Son, and finish drying your hair." Dave patted Jonas' wet shoulder.

"Can I watch TV?" Jonas looked at his mother.

"For a half hour." Kate shook her head as Jonas darted off.

"It's okay, isn't it?" She looked at Dave.

"For Jonas to watch TV?"

"No, that I invited Todd here."

"Sure, we talked about it. How'd you decide?"

"He called today. He wants to take Jonas to the beach during break. Dad and Mom won't invite Todd and Trevor for Thanksgiving, so I invited them for dinner. I haven't told Jonas about the beach."

"It's okay with me."

"Are you sure? I want to see how Todd and Trevor interact before I decide about a trip."

"What did you tell Todd?"

"I invited him to come with Trevor for dinner, and said we'd see about the trip."

"Are your folks invited too?"

"For dinner, not the beach."

"So, are they coming?"

"How could they refuse? It's better here than at Mom's house."

"Todd should know about the research position by then."

"He didn't get it, Dave."

"Oh, how's he feel about it?" Dave hadn't touched the blueprints during the conversation and he stretched his arm across the back of the couch.

"He talks smooth . . . I can't tell."

"Job things work out. Something will come along. Which reminds me, your Dad offered me an office in his building that will be vacated after Christmas."

"Great." Kate scooted over and put her head on Dave's shoulder. "No more creaky floors and stairs to climb."

"I can draw with the door open and turn around if I want." Dave grimaced and Kate noticed how white his teeth looked against his beard.

"Right," Kate said in the midst of her laugh. "What did Dad say about Jim Baxter? Was he surprised we had a connection?"

"Yes, amicably. He likes Jim and he's clueless that he's gay, a good sign. And that's how it stays."

"I totally agree." Kate's eyes smiled, her cheeks looked soft. She kicked off her shoes and curled her feet under her. "Mom and I had a good talk at lunch the other day, but you've been so busy I haven't told you. I felt ashamed of myself."

"About what?"

"I haven't appreciated what a classy lady Mom is. I told you she has been acting indifferent about Todd. Well, she isn't acting." Kate's eyes seemed to gaze beyond Dave's face. "Know what I mean?"

"No. Are you saying she's apathetic?"

"No, I'm saying she knows Todd is gay. It's not news to her, but she's never mentioned it."

"She wants peace in the family. That doesn't mean she supports Todd." Dave stroked his beard, his brown eyes reflective. "She's intuitive and observant." He looked at his wife's mystified expression. "Did she say why she didn't tell you sooner?"

"No. Only that she has struggled to get to where she is. She's not fine with it, but she's opened her heart, wants to understand."

"That's a feat because I bet she's also protecting your Dad, who I know isn't fine with Todd."

"No, Mom thinks he denies Todd's gayness."

"It takes time—glad you talked to her."

Kate got up and walked toward the kitchen with her empty cup, then feeling Dave's eyes on her, glanced back. When he stood up and followed her into the kitchen, he found a chair, sat in it, pointed to his lap. Kate sat on his knee, tugging the hairs in his beard. "You're so handsome," she said, pinching his cheeks, "but Jonas is up and I have a cake to frost." Dave brushed his lips against hers and then he watched her waltz to the refrigerator, reach on top for a cake and inside for the icing. He raised his brows in question.

"Jonas' birthday party is tomorrow, handsome, but forgetful."

"I did forget . . . but you work."

"He's taking the cake to school if I get it frosted." Kate whipped out a spoon and knife.

"He's eight tomorrow, so when is Amanda five?" Dave sighed and stuck a toothpick in his mouth.

"April tenth."

"Four has been a good age, hope five is too. Kindergarten here we come."

Kate smiled at Dave's words, then poised her knife in midair. "Little sisters never stop annoying their brothers, but I think each age is good." Eyes on Dave, she trailed her finger over her tongue, licking off the frosting.

# Chapter 17

The pastor sat in an armchair in front of his desk after he had offered Todd a chair opposite it. Todd considered the array of photos and sculptures, needlework, flowerpots and children's art present in the office.

"What brings you here?" The man had an easy manner. The silver streaks in his dark hair shone in the sun that shimmered in the side window. Todd guessed he was about sixty.

Taking a breath he said, "Where do I start? First, you are an Internet connection for me, Reverend Gunderson. I didn't know that churches have web sites until I saw yours in the newspaper."

"It helps us serve people and stay connected. And please call me Larry." His eyes looked warm and little lines radiated out from each corner.

"Okay. As I told you on the phone . . . Larry, the article in the paper intrigued me. I have some issues."

The man nodded, but didn't speak.

"Gays worship here?" Todd looked expectant.

Larry smiled. "Yes—as they do everywhere—but here we make them welcome."

Todd pursed his lips and nodded. He rubbed his palms together and glanced at his lap. Then back at the pastor. "Why?"

"Why not?" Larry furrowed his brow. "All kinds of people worship here."

"Do straight people like being around gays?"

"Some do, some don't. We're all people. Gays and lesbians aren't contagious, you know. It's not a disease."

Todd laughed and leaned back in his chair; his stomach relaxed. "Could you convey that to my family?"

"Tell me about them."

"Well. I have a problem with my father. I'll never be good enough for him. I mean he loves me . . . but . . . uh, he doesn't seem to approve of me." Todd felt his throat tightening and he stopped talking. He studied the wall for a long minute.

"Your behavior, your values, what doesn't he approve?"

"He's doesn't say, it's a feeling. We don't talk much."

"You haven't talked lately you mean?"

"Yeah. The last year or so."

"What has changed over the past year?"

"I live with this man, Trevor. My Dad . . . well my Mom and sister too . . . met him last summer at a memorial." Todd didn't want to divulge his anger with his father's insinuation or talk about his temper. "I don't know what to say."

Larry shifted his leg and rested his ankle across his opposite knee. His hands lay open across the arms of the chair. "You think your dad is uncomfortable with Trevor?"

"Yeah, they all are." Todd tapped his thighs. "We, Trevor and I, saw everyone not long ago and it was tense, kind of awkward."

"In what way?"

"Like, you know, a big black cloud's hanging in the room that nobody mentions."

Larry nodded. "How does Trevor feel about this?"

"My family?" When the pastor nodded, Todd leaned forward. "He wants us to be up–front with them. We feel that Kate . . . she's my sister . . . supports us. That we're gay, I mean. She knows it. Her husband too." He took a breath.

"Accepting a gay child's coming out is agonizing for parents. I think that's what's happening here. I assume you want to stay with Trevor."

"Of course, I love him. But I'm tired of the put–on with my family."

"You know Todd," Larry made eye contact, "accepting yourself is the most important way you help others accept you. Unfortunately, gays and lesbians still carry a social stigma." Larry's eyes smiled. "This isn't news, right. Accepting your own sexuality is the way to be authentic with others."

"I tried to be authentic about being gay, but it blew up in my face. I don't fit into my family's world because I'm gay. They would rather I become straight."

"Possibly or maybe not. Do their wishes alter who you are?"

Todd pressed his fingers into a steeple. "I suppose not." He gave Larry a curious glance.

"You can learn ways to show them that being gay isn't a threat."

Todd heard his father's words. He saw the pasta and plate fragments strewn across his mother's kitchen. "Like not getting so angry at them, I guess."

"Your folks' needs may surprise you. It takes time."

Todd stared at his knees, while he decided what to say next. "Another thing. I've always felt that the church stands against gays."

"Some churches hope to change people's orientation, but did you know that nothing in the Scriptures indicates that Jesus even mentioned homosexuality? He talked about the rich and the poor, the outcasts, and the self–righteous, but not about gays."

"I know we've been around a long time. I guess I don't know the Bible too good." Todd felt his hairs rising on his neck as he studied Larry.

"What most influenced you in your upbringing?" Larry removed his glasses. "Sorry, you owe me no explanations. Obviously the church *has* rejected homosexual persons; we both know it. I only suggest that you examine your past training and move on with what works today. Churches like this one are opening their doors to people of all backgrounds and experiences."

"My folks are concerned with rules and have definite ideas about what's moral . . . being gay doesn't fit with them." Todd brushed his hand over his forehead.

"You want their acceptance."

"Yeah."

"When you appreciate who you are, you'll find it easier to gain their approval. You might give yourself permission to sense where you are in your own faith journey." Todd felt that he was at a dead end in his faith journey, but he wasn't interested in telling Larry, so he just nodded. "Be patient with your father. He likely wants to understand you. He may feel bewildered and afraid. Could have issues of his own."

Todd shrugged. "Yeah, I've considered that."

"You can take responsibility for yourself, but you aren't responsible for your father's feelings."

Aware that the sun had left the room, Todd glanced at his watch. He'd been there for forty-five minutes. He stood and extended his hand. "Thank you, Larry."

"Come and visit us some Sunday," Larry said as he shook Todd's hand. "We'll be here."

"Thanks for your time. You've listened and I think I've heard myself."

"My pleasure, Todd. I've enjoyed meeting you, now take care."

Todd walked to his car and drove until he arrived at the path where he exercised. He turned off the ignition and grasped the steering wheel. Cradling his head in his arms, he felt his hair caress his face. Tears stung his eyes, searing then cooling his cheeks before he wiped them on his jacket sleeves.

When he had walked a few minutes from the car, he felt the ground solid beneath his feet. He visualized the path ahead, and then he paced faster and thought of the distance yet to go.

# Chapter 18

On Thanksgiving Day a saucepan of turkey giblets simmered on Kate's kitchen stove. Cubed bread with diced celery and spice jars lined the counter next to a casserole of yams.

"No more." Kate frowned at Jonas when she saw the white powder that dotted his face. "See where Amanda is for me, will you?" She melted some margarine, sprinkled the yams with brown sugar and when she added the marshmallows, Jonas snatched one more and dashed off. She opened the oven door, stooped to baste the golden breasted turkey before setting the yams beside it.

"Those smell good," Dave said, his head bent over the aroma of cloves and nutmeg coming from the still warm pumpkin pies.

"Would you please move them to the top of the fridge. I'm out of room." Kate turned toward him, and Dave could see the glow of her moist cheeks. She put her hand to them and brushed aside a curl. "You can light the candles in the living room, too. They're going to be here any minute."

Kate's parents arrived first. They were cordial when Todd and Trevor showed up a half-hour later with a yellow potted chrysanthemum. Several hours later everyone felt stuffed with dinner. The table conversation had been pleasant enough, Kate thought. At least she had forewarned Kevin and Charlotte that Todd wouldn't be relocating for a new job. No one mentioned it. Was that why it was easier for Kevin to be courteous? she wondered.

Todd wiped his face and laughed at Amanda. "No more." He took a last olive off Amanda's finger when she, ignoring Kate's reprimand, waved them in his face. Pie would come later. Trevor had taken a stack of dishes to the kitchen. Todd followed Jonas into the living room where they spread out to finish a puzzle.

"You are the dinosaur kid." Todd grinned, picking up a piece of foamed back puzzle. "I've never made a three–dimensional puzzle."

Jonas smiled broadly like his grandfather and stood up, the model reptile's head at his knees. "He's a Tyrannosaurus Rex, it says on the box. Twenty feet high, Uncle Todd. A big puzzle like this is in my school library, but it's a castle, not a dinosaur." Jonas spread his arms and stalked toward Amanda who squealed, then ran and jumped on

Todd's back as he leaned across the rug for a fragment. Kevin watched over the edge of the newspaper. How far would this affection go, he wondered. Trevor cleared the last of the dishes and leftovers from the Thanksgiving feast and joined Kate and Charlotte in the kitchen where they talked over a sink of sudsy water.

"Come on Gramps, we need help." Kevin lowered the paper, looked at Jonas and Todd who were looking up at him.

"He's right Dad." Todd's eyes pleaded. "We want to see how this monster looks finished."

"All right." Kevin laid the paper down and heard his knees creak as he moved to the floor. "Could we maneuver this fellow to the coffee table? I'm not as young as I used to be." Kevin groaned, took a candy dish and magazine from the table. "How about a cookie sheet to slide under it?" Kevin looked thoughtful.

"Mommmm." Jonas skipped to the kitchen. He ran back with the needed tool and they slid the awkward creature onto it and raised it to the table.

"Dad, you two look alike," Todd said to Kevin. "Jonas is a handsome kid and he favors you so much."

"Yes, I guess he does." Kevin glanced at his son and Jonas, then away.

"I seem to resemble Stephen." Todd raised his eyes to see his father. Kevin gazed with a flat expression, but didn't respond. Jonas left the room for the bathroom.

"I found a picture of him, taken in Korea . . . when he first enlisted," Todd said. Tell me more about him sometime."

"Sometime I will, Son."

Son, at least he said *son*, Todd thought. He felt a spasm of longing in his stomach.

"Boy, you guys sure know when to appear engrossed." Trevor ambled into the room wiping water from his hands. "Well, relax, the dishes are almost done."

"See our dinosaur, Trevor." Jonas beamed from the hall. "Let's finish him super fast. I'm putting him on my shelf when he's done."

"Super job, sport. Looks like he needs a longer tail. I'll work on that." Trevor sprawled out on some pillows.

"I'll be back in a minute." Todd jumped up and walked into the kitchen. "Where did Dave go?" he asked Kate.

Kate frowned. "He slipped into his office to work awhile. He'll be out for pie, I'm sure."

"That bridge keeps him busy, huh?"

"Yep, he's working with Dad. They seem to get along." Kate saw a twinge slide across Todd's face, but she'd spoken the truth.

"Um, Trevor and I want to take Jonas with us to the beach. Have you and Dave talked about it?"

"Yes we have. I have, uh, mixed feelings, but Dave thinks it's fine."

"Kate, it would mean everything to me if you would trust me. I'm responsible and I love you and the kids. I would never do anything to hurt you."

"Stop it Todd. I know you wouldn't." She turned away, felt the hairs on her neck stand up and a flush rise to her cheeks. She walked toward the utility room expecting Todd would follow, which he did. Kate took a labored breath, steadied herself against the dryer. "I understand in my head, but that's one thing. You have to give me some time." She watched Todd's face tighten. "Mom and Dad . . . well . . . they aren't okay with your life. Dad won't even talk about it."

"Dad's not involved. Jonas is your son, not his. I'm asking you and Dave."

Then he heard Trevor call, "Hey Todd, get out here and help finish this dinosaur."

"In a minute," Todd called back. His green eyes settled on his sister's face. "Please Kate, give me a chance." He heard his voice quaver, and Kate's expression showed that she had heard it too.

"I am giving you a chance . . . give me some time." Kate held Todd's gaze.

Todd wanted to shake her. He drew a breath. "Okay Kate, I'll back off." He lowered his eyes then flipped back his hair. "Thanks for inviting us today." Kate looked surprised and nodded. Todd walked out of the utility room to the kitchen sink, got a drink, and then strode into the living room where he faced a pre–historic creature.

"Whoa, scary." Todd bent his knees and eyed the dinosaur.

At length, Dave sauntered into the family circle surveying the scene. "Almost finished. Here, give me some pieces so I can say I helped."

"Uncle Todd and Trevor are fun." Jonas smiled expansively at his father. He spread his legs wide like John Wayne, standing with his hands on his waist. "We didn't need you."

"What?" Dave gritted his teeth and jutted his chin, breaking Jonas' pose when he pretended to bite his neck. Amanda trudged into the room, dragging a ragged blanket in her hand, her thumb red and wet when she removed it from her mouth.

"Amanda's up from her nap. Everyone ready for pie?" Kate waved the whipped cream can from the kitchen doorway.

When the relatives had gone home, Jonas went upstairs to brush his teeth and put on his pajamas. While he waited in his bed, he could hear his mother talking to Amanda in the other bedroom. The dinosaur his uncle and dad had carried to his room and put on his shelf looked no larger than a stuffed animal. In the dim light from the hall, it appeared almost affectionate if he didn't look at its jaw. It was only about two feet tall, but Jonas knew that when the T–Rex lived it would have been ten times that big.

When Kate arrived in his room and sat on the side of Jonas' bed, he looked at her. "Uncle Todd told me he didn't get that new job." He tugged on his pajama sleeve. "Now we won't get to see him very much. I'm sad cause we have fun. I love him." Jonas stroked Kate's arm and she saw his dimples and the soft glow in his eyes. She smiled despite the angst in her heart.

"I know you do."

"How come Gramps acts sad when he sees him?"

"Sad?" Kate gasped and stiffened. Kids are so perceptive, she thought.

"He's not fun around Uncle Todd . . . he doesn't laugh." Jonas' eyes pleaded for an explanation.

Kate moved her arms around him, kissed his cheek. "I'm not sure Jonas, but it's late and you need your sleep. Gramps is okay and so is Uncle Todd. I love you Jonas. Good night." She left the room on hollow legs.

When Kate had closed the bedroom door, she leaned against the railing at the top of the stairs for a minute to steady her balance. She made her way down the stairs to the living room and then stopped. Dave jerked past her with a plate of Amanda's half eaten piece of pumpkin pie. "What's the matter with you? I thought you wanted your family to change?"

"Excuse me." Kate shut the guest closet.

"You didn't let Jonas go with them. We decided he could."

"No. You decided he could. Jonas is my son too, and I want him to grow up normally."

"How can he when you behave so irrationally?" Dave threw a pillow against the couch.

"How *dare* you say that." Kate sloshed cold tea in the cup she'd picked up. "What if they influence him? Jonas could end up gay."

"End up gay? Whew," Dave blew the sound past his lips. "You amaze me sometimes." He raised his hand to his forehead. "He can't catch homosexuality like a cold, for God's sake."

"I've heard that older guys recruit boys . . . what about that?" Kate felt her temples pulsate."

"Do you believe that rubbish? Please tell me you don't."

"Just let me be. I need time."

"Well, how much time do you need? We're not getting any younger."

No response.

"You spent most of the day in your office, not visiting with the family."

"Well, your brother thanked me for my support."

Kate felt some nameless thing suck out of her. She walked past the kitchen into the utility room and shut the door, took a towel from the laundry basket and buried her face in it. She heard Jonas' words: "I love him."

The next day Todd walked along the beach beneath clouds that hung like wet blankets threatening to drench him. He kicked the pebbles ahead with his boot, heard the surf crash in his ears, like the fury in his heart. Kate doesn't trust me, forget Dad, he thought. It isn't right, and it never will be. I'd have to trade Trev for my family. His throat felt choked with a bitter taste, an ache he couldn't swallow. He raised the collar of his jacket, shoved his hands farther into his pockets. Stench assaulted his nostrils. He stared at sand flies that hovered in black puffs over a decayed seagull. Against the colorless sky, the dank smell of seaweed and decay, the bird in its sandy grave held a cleansing power for him, a natural death. Clean and fit in the scheme of things.

He'd go home with Trev; he'd stay away until he felt welcomed, loved for himself. If that day didn't come, at least he'd be who he is. His own voice, though unspoken, seemed stronger, louder against the roar within and around him. The mist in his hair, on his face, salty in his mouth, felt weirdly comforting. Todd headed back to the motel and Trev, while the gulls swooped above him, their squalls echoing his heart's rallying cry.

# Chapter 19

Dave walked into Keeley Engineering, closed the door behind him and dropped his blueprints on the desk. Kevin looked up.

"My son in law, Dave Winston," Kevin said turning to Jim Baxter, who had arrived a minute earlier.

"Pleased to meet you, Dave."

"Same here." Dave grasped the inspector's outstretched hand. "Kevin pointed you out at the site, but its good to meet you. My wife Kate talked with you at the hospital."

"Your wife?" Jim looked puzzled.

"She's a nurse in the cardiac ward."

"Oh my." Jim brushed his forehead and glanced down. "Then you know I made a scene the night I first met her when my mother died." He looked up again.

"Forget that." Dave shot Jim a wary eye. "How's your father doing?"

"He's walking, cutting down on fats . . . he'll be okay."

"That's good," Dave said.

"Let's see those blueprint revisions." Jim dragged a stool up to the drawing table. Dave spread out his work and Jim studied the prints awhile. "This arc is going up," he said, his thumbs raised. "These prints are perfect." Jim stuck a pencil behind his ear and shook Dave's hand. "Congratulations." Kevin praised Dave with a slap on the back.

"Whew, I'm glad you approve." Dave grinned, flashing his teeth at the men. "Maybe I'll have time to talk with my wife again."

"Hey, you'll get Christmas off," Jim said. "What else can you expect? People in my field have the same problem, always traveling around inspecting this and that. Wives get jealous of construction sites. Me, I'm lucky to have a male partner, although he whines sometimes too, but I still love him." An intentional announcement, Dave thought. Kevin's eyes darted from Jim to Dave, and then he stepped back, rubbed his chin and nodded blankly at Jim.

"Next time I'll see a new span across this old river." Jim pulled the pencil from his ear and stuck it in his shirt pocket.

"Don't we wish," Kevin said.

"I'm outta here. Nice meeting you." Jim opened the office door and walked out.

Kevin snatched up some papers off his desk "How revolting."

"Revolting?" Dave stared sharply at him.

"Revolting. What else can I say about queers? He had me fooled."

"Get used to it, they're everywhere, closer than you think."

"I know, too damn close." Kevin felt his throat tighten.

Dave gathered his papers and stood in the doorway. "You've shared your opinion regarding gays. How do you feel about bigots?"

Kevin's nostrils flared, but before he could speak, Dave was striding out the door.

Two tomato and tuna salads sat on Kate's kitchen table. Her mother leaned against the counter. "I'll fill the teakettle." She opened the faucet as she snapped on the stove.

"Raspberry or Constant Comment?" Kate held two teabags for her mother's selection.

"I'll try raspberry." Charlotte studied Kate for a second.

"What are you thinking, Mom? You've got that look."

"I'm thinking that I'm pleased you're my daughter. Kevin is too, but you may not hear it from him. And it's wonderful of you to make me lunch on your day off."

"That's good, but give me specifics on why you're pleased. Wait until I get Amanda." Kate laughed, although she wasn't joking. She could use a few strokes. Charlotte poured boiling water into their cups and stirred, releasing the berry fragrance. Then she opened the cupboard.

"What's missing?" Kate appeared holding Amanda's hand.

"You have any honey? It just suggested itself to me."

"Next shelf." Charlotte looked and retrieved an amber jar.

Charlotte cut Amanda's sandwich in half. "I'm proud of this charming little granddaughter for starters." Charlotte smiled at Kate. "I'm pleased with how you've reared her. We have fun at the grocery store and playing with Spike, don't we, Amanda?" Charlotte patted Amanda's arm, slid into a chair, and pulled it to the table, lifted her fork and pierced a tomato.

"Thanks Mom." Kate felt a twinge of disappointment. What had she expected?

"We'll talk more when Amanda naps. Anyway, it's good to spend time with you when your days off are busy and rare."

Kate sipped her tea. "It's true, people get stressed out and overeat during the holidays and end up in the hospital. Beds will be full until January."

"Oops," Charlotte grabbed for Amanda's overturned glass, but milk already had dribbled into her lap, and Amanda burst into tears.

"It's okay. That was an accident. Would you like a cookie since you ate all of your lunch?"

"Uh–huh." Amanda looked at her wet jeans.

Kate brought two gingersnaps and a glass of milk to the table. She wiped Amanda's face and hands, noticed the sweet smell of her hair. She felt Charlotte's eyes on her.

"You're doing an excellent job. Kids need approval, acceptance just like you're giving."

"That's Mister Rogers' legacy. Or did I learn it from you?" Mom is going somewhere with this, Kate thought. What's on her mind?

"Maybe both." Charlotte smiled and turned toward Amanda. "Let's find your dry clothes."

"Grandma, I wanna do the little teapot."

"Stand up." Amanda jumped up, arms in place. "I'm a little teapot, short and stout," Charlotte began. After three renditions, she ushered Amanda off for dry underwear, her blanket, and a nap.

"Is she finally in bed?" Kate whispered fifteen minutes later when her mother staggered into the kitchen.

"Yes. She insisted, so I *sat* to read *The Cat in the Hat*."

"How about *that*." Kate laughed. " Want some light cheesecake?"

"Why not." Charlotte made fresh tea and set the cups on the table. When she sat down, she lowered her eyes to inspect her fingernails. "I'm worried about Kevin." She lifted the teapot and poured without looking up. Kate handed her mother a slice of cheesecake and a fork.

"What's the matter?"

"He's, I don't know, quieter than usual, seems preoccupied."

"You have a clue why, don't you?" Kate raised her eyebrows.

"Yes, I do. It's Todd. He's troubled about him."

"I know."

"That's why I'm proud of you."

"Proud of me for what?"

"You've bridged the gap and included his . . . Trevor in family gatherings. Kevin wouldn't have wanted them at our house."

"Mom, that's too harsh. Dad will come around." Kate felt deceitful. "He'll come to grips with Todd." She lowered her eyes, sighed. "Don't be proud of me. I keep changing my mind." Charlotte was expressionless, the way she could be when she was listening. Her blue eyes stayed on Kate's face.

"After you left on Thanksgiving, Dave and I had kind of a blow up. In the back of my mind, I'm uncomfortable about letting Jonas go off with Todd and Trevor. I tell myself I trust Todd, but . . ."

Charlotte hadn't moved and now she shook her head, her lips a thin line. "We don't know Trevor either, we don't." She poised her fork over the cheesecake.

"Dave got mad . . . well . . . you and Dad taught us that it's wrong, perverted to be gay or lesbian. So I feel . . . caught." Tears came to her eyes, and Kate covered her face. "Part of me feels it's Todd's *problem* and part of me feels guilty for being prejudiced," she said into her hands.

"You're right, we raised you with the understanding that sexual love should be between a man and a woman." Charlotte saw the curls on top of Kate's head. "I've spent anguished hours in getting to where I am. I've read some, but mostly I love Todd. He entered the world with all the tendencies that have affected his life. God created him with his biological variation. It's nothing new, only for us."

Kate raised her head, looked at her mother dumbfounded. "You told me that you knew Todd was gay. Why haven't you talked about this before?"

"I don't know." Charlotte trailed her finger over the rim of her teacup. "I suppose Kevin has influenced me. This is excruciating for your father . . . the reason why is what baffles me. I mean . . . I know it's difficult . . . we don't know Trevor, but it's more than that. Todd's a grown man who can make his own decisions."

"Will Dad talk to you?"

"Not much."

Kate held her napkin in a fist at her chin, then wiped her eyes. "This changes everything. At least I can talk with you about my feelings. I've kept quiet too and the silence is tearing us apart."

Charlotte sipped her tea. "I'm doing the best I can to support Kevin and I want you to share your feelings, Todd too. But I'm not destroying my relationship with Kevin." Charlotte cut a bite of cheesecake and looked at Kate. "Why was Dave mad at you?"

"First, explain why you always support Dad, even when you disagree with him. You can't be a peacemaker at all cost. You need to gain a voice."

"My mother taught me to support, I learned to support." Charlotte looked away. "Kevin is a fine, loving man. He's been sensitive during my recuperation from surgery. And he likes to be in control."

"He shouldn't control you and your opinions. I'm not like you, which is why I get in trouble with my mouth. Dave's the opposite of Dad too. He's as broadminded as Dad is—intolerant."

"We deal with adversities in different ways, Kate."

"I know." Kate took a breath. "I told Todd he couldn't take Jonas to the beach. He accepted it, but I know he felt hurt. So then, he told Dave. That's why Dave was mad . . . fed up with my vacillation. Dave's fine with the prospect of Jonas being with Todd and so was I. But Mom, I guess I got scared. You're right, we don't know anything about Trevor."

# Chapter 20

Todd walked into the bathroom and handed the phone to Trevor. "It's for you." Trevor raised it to his ear with his free hand while he guided the razor through his whiskers with the other. Todd grabbed his jacket and left the house, headed toward the trail. Getting out of the car, he shuddered, rubbed his arms, and inhaled quick breaths of icy morning air. The sun glistened off the dew, which laced the grass and hung in little tufts from the spruce needles. Saturdays didn't come around often enough. Todd started his paces, cognizant of the sheer beauty that enveloped him. He wondered if he could find a way to see his father's perspective. He didn't have a son, hadn't lost his parents or lived with the uncertainty of a missing brother.

Trevor had asked him why he hadn't challenged his dad. They'd had another bout over it. Because I end up too upset, Todd thought. Trev had to get used to it. Compatibility won't happen. I'm out, I've told Kate and the rest is up to them. Besides, Trevor knows I can't make my father change. If he doesn't like me gay, tough. My job's gotten more interesting anyway, since Mac gave me more work on the computer. Keeping the whale migration data is fun and gives me experience and less time with seals. I can do hands on work with whales later. Todd and I will relish the distance from my family and enjoy our own life. He walked briskly into the morning.

When he returned, Todd put his coat in the closet, poured a cup of coffee. "It's cold out there."

"It's winter in Alaska." Trevor sat in the midst of scattered newspaper pages, eyebrows raised. "Guess who invited us for Christmas?"

"Can't imagine." Todd eyed Trevor, and sank into a chair.

"My Aunt Anna was on the phone." Trevor slapped his knees, ran his hands through his hair. "I didn't recognize her voice, but she identified herself."

"You're kidding. What'd she say?"

"Scott, my uncle, is retiring in June, they're both well and they want us to come for Christmas."

"Us?"

"Yes, Todd. I told you that when I wrote her in October I made it clear I lived with a male partner. One of these days I'm gonna crack your protective shield." He raised his arm and made a fist.

"So what'd you tell her?"

"I said I'd check with my better half and let them know and thank you very much. You want to go?" Trevor cupped the back of his neck in his hands, smiled.

Todd sprawled his legs and leaned back. "Yeah I do—Idaho—that's the best offer we'll get. I wouldn't mind pumping Anna about your childhood either. She's your mom's sister, right?" He tipped his mug to his lips.

"Yep, I moved in with them when I was ten, so she didn't know me too well before then."

"But you saw her a lot didn't you?"

"Not much. Anna and Mom got together at Christmas, sometimes during a summer trip, but we lived in Ohio when I was small . . . before the train wreck." Trevor put his elbows on his knees, leaned forward. "Anna and Scott didn't have any kids, and I think they liked it that way."

"So how'd it go when you first started living with them?"

"Frank and I were a handful. He's three years older and was an independent rascal."

"Think he'll be there for Christmas?"

"Frank? I doubt it. No one's seen him—well, what do I know. I haven't seen him and Anna didn't mention him."

"Well. I'm still going to quiz her. I may discover a lot about you and she might even like me."

"Like you?" Trevor jumped up with a fistful of newspaper. "Give me a break," he said and swatted Todd's head. "Don't expect a miracle."

Todd slowly grinned. "Okay, okay, guess it's my turn to fix breakfast." He stepped across the papers and headed toward the kitchen.

# Chapter 21

Jonas' feet pounded the sand as he ran along the beach with Spike chasing at his heels. He opened his gritty hand, flung the driftwood and watched it soar toward the waves. "Go get it, Spike." The dog raced into the foam.

Kevin followed the zigzagged path of wet sand clumps that had flipped from Jonas' tennis shoes. The wind had a bite, but it wasn't raining or snowing. He saw the boy's hair flying in the gusts, his unzipped red jacket billowing. The sea was part of Kevin, his heart burned with memories of his own boyhood. The child who looked so much like him brought him a burst of joy.

Jonas stopped, spun around and cupped his hands around his mouth. "Hurry, Gramps." Spike bounced against him, dropped the driftwood at Jonas' feet, and shook water everywhere, his long fur flying straight from his body. "*Good boy, Spike.*" The golden retriever had joined Kevin and Charlotte when the grandkids were babies. Jonas couldn't remember a time without Spike.

Kevin caught up with the twosome, bent for a piece of kelp. He tugged on it until he pulled it free from its sand encasement. "Watch this, Jonas." He took an end of the seaweed in each hand, arched it over his head and jumped across it when it reached his feet.

"Gramps, you're *silly*." When Jonas laughed, his dimples sank into his cheeks. A few jumps later Kevin was convinced that Jonas wasn't impressed with his antics. He dropped the provisional rope. He picked up the retrieved driftwood and hurled it out for Spike, who frolicked again into the surf.

"Gramps, where are the starfish?" Jonas' deep brown eyes questioned, then watched Spike as he splashed through the water.

An image of Todd as a boy rushed into Kevin's memory. They'd discovered together that starfish could grow up to four new legs. "The tide's high and there's not much beach now," Kevin said to Jonas, catching his balance as Spike almost knocked him over with the wood prize. "Starfish like tide pools and we'll find some when the tide goes out. Let's go back to the cabin and I bet we can get some hot cocoa."

"Come on Gramps, can't we stay more long?"

"Longer? Let's walk to where the river comes across and then we're heading back." Jonas threw a wide smile over his shoulder as he dashed ahead, Spike barking at his side.

The gray sky didn't deter their pleasure, and Kevin pointed out the glowing colored lights in homes along the bluff. When they reached the river, Kevin noticed that no logs crossed its banks and he couldn't budge any he saw on shore. The gushing water lured Jonas to its pebbled bank and he slipped into the water when the edge gave way. "Gramps, help!" Before Jonas' words were out, Kevin had caught his hand and yanked him to shore.

"You have to watch out, young man. That river could pull you right into the ocean."

Jonas looked down at his dripping jeans and shivered. "I didn't mean to fall."

"I know you didn't, Jonas." Kevin squatted and wrapped his grandson in his arms. "I just want you safe. Water is powerful and you have to be careful." When Kevin stood, he took Jonas' hand and started back toward the cabin. They walked in quiet cadence to the sound of squishy tennis shoes, and the roaring surf.

At the cabin, a fire and the smell of warm sugar and vanilla welcomed them. Jonas snatched a golden sugar cookie off the paper sack where it cooled. "Hey, did you go swimming?" Charlotte knelt, removed Jonas' coat, and hugged his cold body.

"Nah, I fell in the river . . . but Gramps pulled me out fast." Jonas flashed a smile. Kevin swallowed hearing the tone in his voice.

"Where're your dry clothes?" Kevin hung his coat on a hook and started toward a bedroom.

Jonas sat on a wooden chair, tugged at his wet shoelaces. When they were untied, he pulled the shoes from his feet and peeled off his socks. "Come in, I found your stuff, Jonas," Kevin called. Jonas left and soon returned to the kitchen in a green sweatshirt, dry jeans, and slippers.

"Where did you get those lights?" Jonas' eyes brightened when he noticed the blue and white tree lights that outlined the kitchen doorjamb.

"I put them up when you were out." Charlotte handed Jonas another cookie and a hot mug.

"They're pretty." Jonas relished the festive room then looked in his mug. "Thanks Grams, but how'd you know we wanted cocoa?" His mouth turned into a crooked smile.

"Grandmas know a few things." Charlotte smiled at Kevin who grinned back, leaned against the counter and kept his gaze on her face. When Jonas reached for another cookie, Charlotte said, "I better get you a sandwich before you fill up on cookies. We can decorate them later."

"Before Amanda gets here?" Jonas scrunched his mouth and his eyes turned into slats.

"Yes, if you'd rather." Charlotte flashed an amused grin at Kevin. "We can do some after lunch and save a few for Amanda. I think they'll be here by four." Charlotte opened the refrigerator and took out a jar of mayonnaise and some pickles.

Kevin trailed out the door with Jonas behind him. They returned with armloads of presto logs, which they dumped on the fireplace hearth. "Your Dad and I are going to cut down a tree tomorrow too, and you can help us."

"I wish Uncle Todd and Trevor were here." Jonas looked at his grandfather, but Kevin averted his eyes and brushed sawdust from his jacket.

"You know they're having Christmas with Trevor's aunt and uncle in Idaho," Charlotte said from the kitchen.

Jonas scuffed his slipper through the sawdust on the tile. "Yeah, I know. Why don't they want to be with us? I miss them."

"They had other plans." Charlotte gave Kevin a helpless glance.

"Why is Trevor at his aunt's house? What about his mom and dad?"

Charlotte's eyes darted to Kevin. "Good question, Jonas." She spread mayonnaise on bread with slices of turkey. Kevin was silent. Charlotte put the sandwich on a plate. "Todd never mentioned them. I don't know about Trevor's parents or where they live."

"You should ask him." Jonas stared at the floor and walked from the hearth to the table, where he dropped into a chair and set his face in a frown. He looked at his grandfather. "Uncle Todd didn't come because you're mean to him."

Dave pulled out of the McDonald's parking lot. "Nothing like junk food hamburgers and fries." He glanced at Kate who was facing the backseat wiping ketchup from Amanda's face.

"Once in awhile it can't hurt." Kate adjusted herself and snapped her seatbelt. Now it's on to the beach cabin. I'm glad you're able to have some time away. I've missed you. After the holidays, we'll move you into your new office."

Dave sped onto the freeway. "Assuming your father still wants me."

"Why wouldn't he want you?" Kate looked askance at her husband.

"I ended our last conversation by calling him a bigot and walking out of his office."

"You called him a bigot?" Kate stared at Dave, then spun her head to observe Amanda in her car seat. "Go ahead, she's asleep."

"Well, I told you that the inspector approved my blueprints. Then he announced he had a male partner. Kevin wasn't too impressed."

"You called Dad a bigot in front of Jim Baxter?"

"No, Jim had left. Your dad made a snide remark about gays that made me furious and no, I didn't actually call him a bigot. I asked him how he felt about them." Dave gave Kate a side–glance. "Then I walked out."

"What'd he say?"

"He said queers were revolting. It set me off. I'm tired of the hate, the jokes directed at gays. It flashed in my mind how upset you were that night at the hospital when Jim's mother died. Gays shouldn't have to hide who they are from their families."

"No they shouldn't." Kate let out a long sigh.

Dave looked at her. "Don't worry about your dad and me. Obviously, we're getting together at the beach. This will blow over, but I'm glad Todd made other plans for the holiday, and that you called him and found out he had. It makes it easier for everyone. At least you and your father can relax."

Kate frowned and didn't speak for a minute. "If you will get off your self–righteous kick, I might relax. I called Todd to let him know we wished him a good Christmas even if we wouldn't see him.  My emotions have to catch up with my intentions. It's been difficult, but it will get easier for me."

Dave stroked his beard. "I was rough on you about Jonas, but I hate seeing you in constant turmoil. I know you can accept Todd and your own feelings, even if your father can't. Maybe it's growing pains you're feel—" Dave bit his tongue "—oops, I forgot I'm not your counselor."

Kate loosened her seatbelt, turned sideways, and rested her chin on the seat while she looked at Amanda. She listened to the whirring car tires, Amanda's deep breathing, and noticed her beautiful face. She wrapped a blanket around her. "Someone's relaxed back here."

Then she flipped around, punched Dave's arm and grinned at him. "Thanks for admitting you can be a little pushy. My concern is how my folks will affect Jonas. We can give Todd and Trevor freedom with him, but we can't control Dad's comments. He could make Jonas' time with Todd a bad experience."

"No he won't. Kids see through people and Jonas will appreciate Todd for himself. Your dad won't badmouth Todd to Jonas, anyway. Even if he did, Jonas would learn what prejudice is about, be open and loving. What more can we wish for him?"

Kate sighed. "My emotions are powerful. I'm not rational about this."

"What's rational? Your dad's not mean spirited. Let's give everyone a chance."

"You think Todd's gay life will influence Jonas?"

"No, I don't. Jonas could be gay due to inherited tendencies, but not because of his affection with Todd. Plenty of studies indicate there's a chemical basis for homosexuality; even the brain looks different in gay people."

"So I've heard."

"Doesn't mean they can change other people. Think about it, given our society's attitude—who would want to be gay?"

"We're not comfortable with diversity. Think we'll ever stop discriminating against people in the minority?"

"Some day." Dave gave Kate a loving look. "You're okay, wife." He felt her soft touch as she brushed his beard with the back of her hand. "By the way, did you remember the fruitcake?"

"What?" Kate sounded amused.

"You said to remind you to bring the fruitcake for your dad."

"Aren't you a tad late? I remembered it." Kate caressed his thigh with her fingers, leaned her head against the seat and closed her eyes. Dave watched a few raindrops splash the windshield and spread out in patterns. The sky turned darker as the clouds thickened and he moved up the heat lever. The droplets turned slushy, making slurping sounds against the wipers. Kate's eyes popped open. "I'm dreaming of a slushy Christmas."

"We rented a cabin with a fireplace. Take a nap."

The next morning Kate dressed Amanda as they sat on the lower bunk bed in the pinewood bedroom of the cabin. She bundled her into a snowsuit and rubber boots. Then she joined her mother who was finishing a cup of coffee. "The cabin looked so inviting last night with the flickering candles and your chicken and dumplings were delicious." Kate smiled at Charlotte.

"Nice place isn't it." Charlotte looked wistful. "Jonas is disappointed Todd isn't here. Thought you'd want to know."

"He's fond of him. We'll have a good Christmas, don't worry."

"I'll cook some cranberries while you're out walking," Charlotte said, setting her cup down and moving to the cupboard. Amanda tugged Kate until she put on her coat, knit cap, and went out the door to a winter wonderland.

"It looks like sugar on the trees," Amanda said as she clomped along with Kate who had grasped her hand to break her stumbles. The powdery white stuff dusted the needles, although the sun had melted the snow near the cabin. Out here, it still looks like fairyland, Kate thought. She saw scattered waffle–like footprints that a light snow flurry hadn't erased.

"I see them, I see them." Amanda cheered as she skipped toward three figures among the trees. Kevin, Dave, and Jonas, who had ventured out hours earlier, now approached her. The men carried a tree across their shoulders, while Jonas kept pace with wide strides.

"Welcome committee's here." Kevin grinned at Dave when they stopped in front of Kate and Amanda. He freed one hand from the fir boughs and patted Amanda's head, smiling at Kate.

Amanda danced around. "Christmas tree, Christmas tree."

Jonas held out a bundle of cones. "These are for a wreath."

"I wanna cone too Mommy." Amanda tugged Kate's hand. Jonas' face grew serious. "I can find you guys tons of 'em . . . all you do is look under the trees."

Jonas sat on the braided rug that evening struggling with his wreath. "I can't get this string to hold these together," he muttered and shoved the prickly cones with the back of his hand. "Uncle Todd would help me."

"Wait a minute, Son." Dave called into the kitchen. "Do you have a large bowl we can use, Kate?"

"I'll see." She bent over a cupboard from which she grabbed a wooden bowl and handed it to Dave.

"Let's put the cones in here," Dave suggested, "and maybe Grams can find us some ribbon and we'll make bows and mix them with the cones. We don't need a wreath outside. We can see the decorations better if they're inside." Dave flashed his white teeth at Jonas. "Okay?"

"O . . . *kay.*"

"That big bowl should work well." Kevin eyed the project as he entered the room, his arms full of tangled tree lights.

"Where's the ribbon, Grams?" Jonas had escaped to a bedroom closet where he was rummaging through a cardboard box.

"Hold it, unwrapped gifts are in there." Charlotte hurried in, found red and green ribbons that satisfied Jonas. In a few minutes, Amanda joined them, watching her father and brother tie bows and place them among the fir cones. A short while later when Kate helped her with a sponge bath, Amanda complied and soon was asleep.

A pungent whiff of fir stopped Kate when she returned to where the tree stood straight, its needles still wet. "I like it." She put her hands on her hips. "Tomorrow we'll decorate it—oh, look at your bowl of cones and bows." Jonas held the creation up for her approval, his deep eyes affectionate. "Now it's time for bed young man."

"Will we see the starfish tomorrow, Gramps?"

Kevin looked at Jonas. "We'll look tomorrow—Christmas Eve." He reached for the plug at the end of the tree lights, which he had arranged in neat rows across the kitchen table. He plugged it into the wall snapping off the ceiling light. "Presto."

"Awesome." Jonas ran and grabbed Kevin's waist. "I love you Gramps."

"Me too. Now off to bed."

Dave followed Kate to the bedroom and after they tucked Jonas into the bunk bed and left the room, he kissed her on the nape of her neck. Kate nuzzled her cheek into Dave's beard. "I hate to mention the subject, but I guess your dad's not too sore at me," Dave whispered outside the bedroom door.

"I hope not. I wonder how Todd's doing with Trevor's relatives."

"Don't know, but your dad's more relaxed without him around."

"Tell me about it. He's in for a long overdue chat with me."

"Take it easy, it's Christmas." Dave kissed Kate's cheek.

"I'll be wise. By the way, you've been good with the kids," she murmured.

"Thanks. Maybe we could turn in soon, so I can show you how good I am with you." He nibbled her ear.

"Uh, remember these thin walls aren't soundproof."

# Chapter 22

"You better pull over until it lets up." Todd sat forward, struggled to see out the front windshield. "How can you drive in this? It's coming down sideways."

"With trepidation." Trevor kept his eyes ahead with his hands on the wheel and didn't look at Todd. "It sure seems dark for four o'clock." A car light shone through the whiteness. "I think I'll stop when I find a wider place in the road. We need space so no one skids into us."

Ahead, the men noticed a building with lights, maybe a grocery. Trevor steered into the parking area and stopped the engine. "I'm going inside a minute." Todd watched Trevor disappear into an entrance that he could barely see through the blizzard and then he walked behind the car to check the tire chains. He saw a tall figure crouched behind the back wheel of a blue Chevy. "Need some help, mister?" Todd leaned over so the man could hear him.

"These blasted chains . . . I forgot my lug wrench . . . you have one?" He stuck his head out from under the fender, grunted and smiled.

"Yeah, we do. We stopped because we can't see the road." Todd grabbed a wrench from his trunk, squatted and handed it to the fellow. He felt snow slide down his collar when he straightened.

"Thanks." When the man adjusted a knit cap over his ears, Todd noticed his bushy eyebrows covered with snowflakes, and his dirty, frayed jeans and jacket. He looked about his own age.

"What's up?" Trevor returned to the lot, two cups of coffee in his hands. He handed one to Todd, nodding toward the back of the stranger.

"He needed a wrench." Todd took the coffee, leaned against the fender.

The man emerged and slid on packed snow to the opposite tire. "Nothing like a decent tool," he said.

Trevor brushed snow from his coat, and looked at the man. "My name's Trevor, and yours?" He stooped for a good look.

"Frank here." The man raised his head.

"My God. I thought you sounded familiar. It's been a long time. I'm your brother."

Smells of meat and potatoes wafted through the house when Todd and Trevor arrived. Frank pulled in behind them a few minutes later. Dinner was ready within the hour and everyone sat down at the creaky wood table. "So you met up on your way here?" Trevor's uncle chuckled and his beady brown eyes almost disappeared into his round face. His mustache crinkled around his small mouth, as he wiped gravy from it and patted the edge of the dining table. "We're glad you made it, you and Frank." After a clumsy pause, "We're pleased to have you as our guest, Todd."

"Yes, our pleasure." Anna smiled as she reached her short arms past Todd and put more mashed potatoes on the table "It's been a blizzard outside all afternoon. I always worry when people are driving in the stuff." Anna, no more than five feet tall, plump, dressed in a soft fabric dress that reached to her ankles, was more maternal looking than Todd had expected. "You might as well leave those chains on your cars, since I don't expect a thaw in the next few days," she said and sat down.

Frank smiled and reached for the bowl piled with potatoes. He had taken a shower and dressed in clean jeans and a burgundy pullover. Todd looked up to see Anna looking at him. Her features were delicate with soft makeup, her hair silver, short, and softly framing her square face. Anna's eyes next turned to Trevor. "So, tell us how you met," she glanced at her plate a second, "well, first tell us how you ran into Frank."

"We might have literally run into him had we not stopped," Trevor said. Everyone laughed. "The road was treacherous, no visibility."

"That's right," Frank said. " I stupidly left my tire iron at my work site. This storm was unexpected and I didn't listen to the weather reports."

"Construction site?" his aunt said.

"Right, about two hours from here. Anyway, I was sliding all over the road, but I thought I could make it without chains. When I stopped to put them on, this guy," he pointed to Todd, "walked up and offered me a lug wrench. Next thing I knew. my brother was introducing himself and shaking my hand." When Frank turned, his hair, secured with a green rubber band, fell black and thick in a ponytail at the base of his neck.

Trevor observed Frank with startled awareness. Could this be the same Frank who, when he was eighteen, had left so abruptly? "You're a damn fag," Frank had said. "I don't need to be hanging around you." Was Frank making some holiday effort at civility? Was he married? He glanced at his left hand. No ring.

"We may be a bit surprised you invited us back after we've taxed your endurance so long. Right Trevor?" Frank looked at Trevor.

" —What?"

"We were a pain in the butt, right?"

"Uh, yeah, I'm sure we were." Trevor wiped his clammy hands on the napkin in his lap. "I think I feel a little gratitude now though, how about you?"

"Ah, never too late for that." Frank smiled at Anna.

Scott cleared his throat and wadded his napkin beside his plate, gave his chair a push backwards. "Enough of this. We're glad you turned out okay, if you know what I mean." He chortled. The brothers exchanged a puzzled glance, didn't know what he meant, but laughed anyway.

"We'll do the dishes, Anna," Trevor offered. "Do you mind if I call you Anna and drop the Aunt?"

"Of course you can call me Anna." She stood, stepped back, placing her hand on her chin. "You know, you've grown taller and filled out since I've seen you. When was that anyway?"

"I visited you once after I graduated from college. It's been about five years, I'm ashamed to say."

Well, we were in Europe for a year when Scott worked for IBM." Anna gathered leftovers and placed them on the counter. "And this past summer I spent time with my mother who's in a nursing home in Wisconsin. She's—" Anna stopped to study the uneaten Swiss steak "—ninety six next May. She's frail, but still knows me."

"Amazing. You're the picture of health." Trevor stepped past her with a stack of plates.

"You're too kind."

Todd opened the cupboard under the sink, found the garbage can and began scraping dishes. Anna made a face. "I don't have a dishwasher, you guys. This old place never did, but I have apple pie for dessert." Her gray eyes twinkled.

"Fair enough." Todd laughed.

"Now, you never told me how you two met." Anna wiped her hands on her apron.

"In a mutual effort to save our environment, that is, study seals." Trevor swam his hand through the sudsy dishwater. We met in Oregon. Our work is about studying the habits and behaviors of seals. I tag them and researchers track and observe their behaviors. Last September we moved to Kodiak where we found a job with the Alaska Fish and Game Department.

When Trevor and Todd were almost finished washing and drying the dishes, Frank stuck his head into the kitchen. "Seals is it. I knew you'd end up in the great outdoors. Do you still play tennis?" He looked at Trevor, his bushy brows raised.

"When I can find someone who wants to play. Todd walks for

exercise. Get your hands in this water and it'll clean your nails, Frank. You never were eager to help around the house, were you?"

Frank pushed Trevor aside. "Okay I'll help. I've matured some." He plunged his hands into the sudsy water, wetting his sleeves.

"You married? Trevor dried his hands and stepped aside. "I don't see a ring."

"Nope, but I've got a gal." Frank pushed up his sleeves.

"Good for you. Where is she?"

"She's with her folks in Mexico right now, visiting for Christmas. I couldn't go because of work."

"So when's the wedding?" Trevor elbowed Frank.

"S-l-o-w down." Frank rolled his eyes. She's the sister of a fellow on the building crew. I met her six months ago . . . her name's Maria."

"Lives here in Idaho?"

"Yep." Frank finished the discussion of his personal life. "You don't have a ring either."

Anna and Todd glanced at each other. Trevor looked at Frank. "Nope, I'm not married." Trevor stacked the plates. "What are you building?"

"A huge apartment, one hundred fifty units, south of this area."

Todd had left the kitchen, wandered into the living room, passed the armchairs with lace doilies and then he continued down the hall toward his guestroom. On the way, he passed an attractive room with a maple desk and a vinyl recliner. A grand piano, still gorgeous, was crammed into a corner. He stopped, went in and touched the smooth keys, noticed Christmas sheet music on it. Better wait until later he decided and left the room.

The next room had a queen bed in it, which he and Trevor would share. Their opened suitcases lay on top. Next to the bed was an attractive old dresser, painted white, and on it a clay pot of red poinsettias. He pulled out the top drawer, ajar and empty. He laid his underwear and socks in it. A wooden chair with a floral print seat completed the furnishings.

He took out his toiletries and placed them on the dresser. When he opened the closet, he found it cleared and stocked with hangers, which he used to hang his few shirts, an extra pair of slacks. His

Levi's fit on the shelf. I can't believe how easy this has been, he thought. Here, it's okay to be me. I'm welcome in a stranger's house. He wondered about Frank. What did he know?

"What's up Todd?" Trevor loomed in the doorjamb.

"Just making myself at home, since Anna and Scott are so gracious. Look at this room."

Trevor nodded. "Scott, well I think he goes along with whatever, but yes, Anna is gracious, always has been." Trevor lifted his clothes from the suitcase, set them on the bed, and then shut the case with a bang as he swung it to the floor near the chair. He brushed Todd's face with the back of his hand. "Let's get back with everyone. Scott was getting out the slide projector when I walked past the den." Trevor groaned with a sympathetic eye on Todd.

"Good, I won't have to quiz Anna about you. I'll see it all in living color." Todd flipped back his hair with a dramatic wrist to his forehead.

"I know. I'm sure Frank is just as thrilled. Let's go."

Frank sat sprawled in an upholstered chair, his hands outlined by the doilies covering each armrest. Todd and Trevor sat down on the dark couch. Scott fumbled with trays, and pointed the lens of the projector at the wall where the screen stood. When Anna appeared in the dining area untying her floral print apron, she smiled. "Tell you what, we'll bore you with a few slides, then I promise you dessert." Frank gave his eyes a quick roll at Trevor as they rose to set up the screen and the show began.

"Not this far back." Trevor and Frank moaned together. On the screen an attractive slender woman, whose hair fell to her shoulders black and curly, pushed a dark haired child in a backyard swing.

"Your mom, I bet," Todd said, "and is that you?"

"Yep," Frank said, "that's Trev, four years old. Ain't he cute?"

"Cuter than you were," Trevor shot back.

"Your mom's the one who's cute. She looks like you, Anna," Todd said turning to her.

"Well aren't you the welcome guest." Anna smiled at Todd. He saw the warmth in her gray eyes before she lowered them and smoothed her dress with her hand.

Slides of family vacations, Idaho Christmases in the same living room, illuminated the screen. How young the boys looked. One came on the screen, a family trip, the boys' faces peering out of a tent, a river winding in the background, but no one could remember the location. The next picture showed Frank seated in his fancy red sports car, followed by one of him leaning against it, a dripping sponge in his hand and a water bucket near by. His cut–off shorts and T–shirt revealed his lean limbs and bulky body, but he lacked the muscle mass that Trevor had. A shot of Trevor in his high school football uniform made him appear gigantic. More slides came and went.

At length a large man with pale blue eyes appeared on the screen. The same black-haired woman stood next to him, her head even with his shoulders. "No wonder you guys are tall," Todd commented as he glanced at the brothers. Trevor felt a spasm of pain the moment he saw the image of his dad, so strong and alive looking. He leaned forward and felt his aunt's tender eyes on his face.

"He'd be proud to see how you grew up Trevor, how much you favor him. So would your mom. Twenty-one years have passed and I still wonder why."

"We'll never know why, Anna. That crash was a tragedy that can't be explained." Scott looked at the men. "The investigators never determined why those trains collided." He snapped off the projector, slapped his knee. "Well honey, where's that pie?"

When the family turned off the lights and went to their rooms, Todd stretched out with his arms behind his head and glanced at Trevor who lay next to him. "What did your father do for a living, Trev?"

"He taught PE and coached high school football."

"So that explains why you're athletic. Would he be as proud of you as Anna thinks?"

"Why wouldn't he be?"

"No reason . . . well, I guess I do have a complaint. I'm jealous as hell."

"I don't know if he'd be proud or not, if you mean my sexual orientation. I was ten when Dad died so it was a non issue."

"Yeah. I wish I was as comfortable with my folks."

"Your father isn't dead."

"True."

"Hope you sleep well, Todd. Tomorrow's Christmas Eve, so I want you to enjoy it and put your longings on hold." Trevor rolled to his side to check Todd's response, a simple sigh in the darkened room.

"One more thing . . ." Todd raised up on his elbow. "Is Frank acting the way you remember him?"

"Nope. I'm waiting for the other shoe to drop."

Trevor awakened the next day to the smell of bacon frying. He rolled across the empty bed and hoisted his jeans up his thighs, grabbing a pullover as he went for the hall. He found Anna turning the crisp slices onto a paper towel and she smiled when he appeared. "You're up. How many eggs do you want? How about some coffee?"

Trevor felt the cool floor tiles against his toes and ran his hand through his hair. "Coffee sounds great, one egg is plenty." Then he glanced at the kitchen table. "Is that your homemade raspberry jam? You made such good jam."

"Still do, we picked those last July from our backyard. Is Todd up?"

"He's in the shower, I think, unless that's Scott."

"My no, he left an hour ago with my grocery list for Christmas dinner."

The front door banged when Frank came in with a few bags. "Hey, I'm ready to chow down. Close your eyes while I pass with these presents."

"Right." Trevor made a face with a glimpse at Frank. "That reminds me, I have some in my trunk too."

After breakfast, Todd elected to stay at the house and help Anna wrap gifts while Trevor and Frank took a walk to catch up on each other's life. Frank strode in step with Trevor along the acreage that their aunt and uncle had owned for thirty-five years. The sun had softened the snow so that it appeared molded to the chain–link fence and clung like milky glue along the gutters of the house. They could hear the crunching sounds made by their boots as they walked. "Are you surprised how well Scott and Anna look?" Frank said.

"I wouldn't say surprised," Trevor said, examining the undisturbed blanket of white before him, "but they do look great."

Frank scooped up a handful of snow and began smoothing it into a ball. "They were good to us, weren't they. A lot of memories in those slides."

"Yes." Trevor eyed the snowball. "You're not planning to shove that down my neck, are you?"

"Not unless you provoke me."

"If I had justification, I would. You've been damn agreeable since we met last night."

"Any reason I shouldn't be?" Frank half smiled as he tossed the snowball over the fence.

"No reason."

"How do you and Todd get along? He seems like an okay fellow."

Here it comes, Trevor thought. "Fine, we get along fine. I know you don't like it, but we are together, so I appreciate your tolerance."

"Hey, no, I . . . I was a real jerk when I took off to find my manhood."

"You find it?"

Frank glanced sideways at Trevor. "I think so. Maria's helped me a lot. Nothing like a wom—"

Trevor looked up. "That's okay." An amused grin spread on his face as he turned to Frank. "Just someone to love works." Frank nodded his head. They walked in silence.

"I don't think I ever accepted Mom and Dad's death until about a year ago," Frank said, concentrating on his feet as the road curved. "I was thirteen, just reaching puberty and wham. I felt guilty that you and I lived. Ever felt that way, like it was your fault?"

"Yeah. I still miss them too. Uncle Scott provided the necessities, longer for me than you, but he never seemed like a father to me. I missed all the sports stuff. Anna and I hit it off, and she helped me grieve for Mom. She lost her only sister." Trevor looked at Frank. "Sorry it was so hard for you."

"I thought I was too old at thirteen to let anyone console me, too macho. Both at once, too much." Frank stared at the tips of grass sticking through the snow mounds along another fence. "Anyway, how are Todd's folks with you two?"

"Not good. Todd has a sister, Kate, who's making an effort. She and her husband have two kids who Todd adores. You'd think that we expected them to adjust to us. In a sense we do."

"I would think so."

"Mostly we want them to accept us as individuals."

"You should move to Vermont where you could get a legal union." Frank kicked a broken limb aside. "No, strike that, I guess it would solve nothing."

"Vermont's his dad's home state."

"How ironic."

Trevor slid his hands into his pockets, wondering what had changed Frank. He flipped some snow up with his toe. "Frank, the way I remember it, you weren't too keen on having a fag for a brother. What gives?"

Frank slowed, looked at Trevor, then each stopped. "I've changed my mind about gays," Frank said, pulling his hair out of his collar. "Happened to meet a fellow who kept his life a secret, at least from his mother. Then she died. He told me how mad he was at himself for not having the guts to tell her he was gay. He resents his dad because his dad knew he was gay, but he didn't inform his wife. Having a gay son seemed too shameful for either to accept. That was my friend's conclusion, anyway."

"How'd you meet him?"

"He inspects construction sites, used to work around here, and he came out to the apartment complex I'm building."

"I see." Trevor noticed Frank's eyes and the snowflakes that clung to his thick eyebrows as a flurry began.

"We had already talked about a lot of stuff." Frank knocked snow from his boot. "He didn't broadcast his intimate life. He was a friend first; later I learned about his hurt. We had lunch together one day and he told me."

"He trusted you." Trevor looked at Frank, then away.

"I guess he trusted me. Strange isn't it. I didn't have many friends, still don't, being the loner I am. Well, he's really been alone." Frank pursed his lips when he looked at Trevor. "Being gay must be lonesome . . . tough for you too."

"Not as tough as it is for Todd. For some reason, Anna and Scott accepted me as I grew up. They knew I was gay. Todd needs his family's approval because they won't acknowledge him." Trevor started ambling ahead. No more about Todd, he thought. Frank fell in step beside him. "So Frank, do you keep up with your friend?"

"No, I don't know how he and his dad get along now." Frank stopped. "Jeez, Trevor, could we lighten up? It's Christmas Eve. We'd better head back since it's snowing and I've got all your presents to wrap."

"Right." Trevor gasped when Frank punched him in his ribs, then laughed and whacked Frank back, pivoted and sprinted toward the house.

# Chapter 23

Charlotte stood at the kitchen counter in the cabin feeling the cold gusts of wind that howled through the cracks in the windows and under the doorjamb. Inside it was comfortable with the fragrant scent of cinnamon and apple. She rolled out the pie dough and looked up as Kate approached. "Except for the kids' presents, all the gifts are ready," Kate said.

"Bring 'em out and I'll help you wrap them as soon as I finish this crust." Charlotte brushed her forearm across her check, her fingers gooey with flour and shortening.

"Where'd he go?" Kate asked whirling around realizing Dave had disappeared from the room. She heard a thump on the cabin door, opened it to a huge cardboard box with her husband behind it.

"I need to assemble this thing before Amanda shows up." Dave laid the box on the braided rug. "It was jammed into the trunk, but it finally budged."

"I forgot about the trike. I'll help you with it, if you'll help me wrap their gifts. We can do them in the bedroom later if necessary." Kate cut open the box while Dave returned to the car for his tools. "Whoa, it comes with hot–pink handlebar streamers." Kate laughed as she pulled the pieces out. "She'll love this."

Charlotte smiled through the lighted doorway. "I love Christmas. Have you had it awhile?"

"Yes, I forgot what it looked like."

When he returned, Dave made a face and rolled his eyes.

**153**

"Fuchsia pink," he said, mimicking Amanda's voice, "my favorite color."

In an hour they had assembled the trike, covered it with an old bedspread. "Put it in our room," Charlotte suggested. "Amanda won't be in there, I hope." After pushing the trike into her room, Charlotte returned to the kitchen where she found Kevin, Amanda, and Jonas yanking shells, rocks, and sand from their pockets.

"Look what I found, Grandma," Amanda squealed, her hands full of ordinary pebbles. Jonas showed an almost perfect sand dollar. "I'm putting this on my shelf with my dinosaurs." He grimaced at Amanda. "You better not touch it."

"Did you see any starfish?" Charlotte's eyes widened.

"A few . . . they're awesome. Gramps told me they can grow new legs, but I can't bring them back. Know why? Cause they'll die and it hurts nature." Charlotte felt a tug of affection and saw Kevin grin. Jonas peeled off his coat and surveyed the counters. "Yum, apple pie. Any cookies left, Grams?"

"How about a tuna sandwich first," Kate said, walking to the refrigerator. "You better put that in a safe place right now, Jonas." He carefully laid the sand dollar on a wooden shelf, which stuck out from the kitchen wall.

The afternoon passed with a flurry of activity: food preparation, gift wrapping, fire log stacking; with festive sounds: whispering children, crinkling paper, chopping knives, a crackling fire; with aromas: cinnamon, hot apples, bayberry scented candles.

After supper, the excited children emerged from their baths sweet and clean. Kate ushered them into the small living space, where tree lights and fire flames cast a luster on gifts and the faces of Kevin, Dave, and Charlotte who sat talking.

"Are we gonna tell the story about baby Jesus?" Amanda's blue eyes were as luminous as her golden hair in the soft light.

"Who wants to tell it?" Kevin's eyes looked like deep–set gems in his face; the lights played on his hair, highlighting the silver–auburn strands.

"Mary was real tired," Amanda said. "They couldn't find a room for her to sleep. Joseph kept trying to find a place cause he loved her lots." Amanda folded her hands in her flannel lap. "She was having a baby."

"Someone gave them a barn to sleep in and Mary had Jesus in it," Jonas said. Kevin nodded. Kate observed Dave opposite her. His eyes were bright, but his face obscured by the low light seemed lost in his beard. When Kevin turned quiet, Dave leaned forward, palms up. "Why was this baby so important?"

"You know why, Daddy . . . Jesus loves us." Amanda patted her lap.

Dave smiled warmly at her. "Yes, Amanda."

"I don't get it." Jonas frowned, raised his knees, and put his chin between them. "How can Jesus be God's son?"

"We're all God's sons and daughters. It's okay if we don't get it. God is with us anyway because that's how love works. God loves us like a good parent does. It's quite mysterious." Dave fell silent, leaned back, laid his arm around Amanda's shoulder. He looked over at Kevin who was staring into the fire.

"What's that?" Amanda looked up at Dave.

"Mysterious?" Dave rubbed his beard. "It's like a puzzle, something you can't explain. You have many pieces of a real picture, but you don't know what it is. If you keep turning the pieces, you can fit them together until you see the picture."

"You could look at the box."

Dave smiled. "But if the box didn't have a picture, you'd have to wait till you put the pieces together."

"What if some pieces are missing?" Jonas said.

"You still know what the picture is about even if some pieces are missing. Love is like that. It's real, even if we don't see the whole picture."

"Oh." Amanda wiggled her toes towards the fire, as if satisfied.

"Dad," Jonas said, "I think mystery is awesome like dinosaurs."

"Right, Jonas."

Seated next to Kevin, Charlotte felt the loss of his attention, absorbed in the fire and she wondered about his thoughts. She rose and bent to Kate's ear. Kate got up, flipped on the kitchen light. "Grandma's going to make you some popcorn, then it's time for bed. I'll get your stockings so you can hang them. Christmas is almost here."

When the children had hung the stockings and eaten the

popcorn, Dave and Kate tucked them into the bunk beds. Kate took a sack from her closet and returned to the adult circle. "Let me fill them," Dave said as he followed her into the living area. "I look the most like Santa Claus."

"Yes, all you need is some flour to whiten your beard. Let me get you some," Kate teased, "but wait until they're asleep."

Kevin stood at the window with his hands cupped around his eyes. "More snow has fallen, but nothing's coming down now. I think I'll take a short walk."

"Mind if I join you while Santa and Grandma tend the fire and do their magic?" Kate looked at her dad then at Dave who frowned in question.

"Fine, get your coat." Kevin kicked off his tennis shoes and reached for his boots.

"Be right back," Kate said.

Father and daughter started into the stillness, walking side by side. They passed a cabin, its windows bright with colored Christmas tree lights. A window of a second cabin glowed with a burning white candle. Kevin felt the cold air nip his face as he listened to the snow crunch. He stopped at the bluff overlooking the beach. He brushed snow off the peeling bark of a Madrone tree that hung over the edge and Kate leaned against it. Kevin gestured toward the high tide, swelling into visible whitecaps against the night sky. "Let's watch a minute," he said.

They were silent when Kate looked at her father. "I remember the times you took Todd and me to the beach, and something of the sea has always stayed with me."

"Yes, it's a kind of a legacy." Kevin shook snow from his gloves. He felt Kate's fingers touch his arm.

"We haven't mentioned Todd lately, but I feel he chose marine biology because of you and Mom. He'd never be happy with a desk job."

Kevin didn't speak for a moment, made a design in the snow with his boot. "Suppose not. I guess we did something right."

"He's hurting." The pounding surf muffled Kate's voice. Kevin didn't hear her. "Do you like Trevor?" she said louder.

Kevin heard the question. He felt stunned at Kate's directness, shifted his weight, and became pensive. "Trevor seems like a fine man, but I don't like his attachment to Todd."

"Todd loves him. He said Trevor is more important to him than our opinions about him."

*Why won't she stop?* Kevin wondered. He stood silent: to search for words, to watch a wave crest and crash. "Todd's choice repulses me." He folded his arms. "I'm not . . . comfortable . . . talking about this with you, Kate. I see sexual . . . deviation . . . risky behavior."

Kate looked out at the whitecaps. "Todd loves Trevor in ways that have nothing to do with sex, just as you love Mom. He loves the person Trevor is, the companionship and the trust they share."

"You're entitled to your views." Kevin set his hand on the tree trunk, gave it a tap, and pushed himself around in a half circle, as if he had resolved his understanding of homosexuality. "Let's go back."

"Okay, Dad." Kate's easy compliance stirred Kevin's sense of his own complexity; the perseverance he used for protection and control, his gentleness mixed with anguish. They followed their footprints back to the cabin. As he passed the candle aflame in the window, Kevin felt Kate's hand slip into the crook of his arm. He couldn't convey what he felt, an inexplicable comfort in her touch.

# Chapter 24

The brothers stomped snow from their boots and entered the house, hearing keyboard music. "Ah, Maria's favorite song," Frank said as he unzipped his coat to the tune of 'Greensleeves.' "She wants it sung at the wedding."

"Aha." Trevor slapped Frank's back. "You *are* serious about her."

Frank smiled. "Who's playing?" The men walked into the room where Todd sat moving through the music. Trevor touched his neck.

Todd stopped playing. "Your hands are freezing, Trev."

"Keep playing, it's beautiful. I had no idea you could play this well. Trevor leaned over Todd's shoulder and read the song title. "Why does Maria want a Christmas song at her wedding? 'What Child Is This?' is the name of it." He looked at Frank.

"It's based on 'Greensleeves.' Maria wants the love song." Frank rolled his eyes toward Todd.

"Music isn't my thing, okay?" Trevor felt thankful that Todd had spared him further embarrassment.

Todd looked contented and confident. "I'll play a verse, then you two sing, the Christmas words, please." Todd's fingers danced across the keys. He played the notes as if he'd practiced them for weeks, which he had as a boy. Frank started singing and Todd joined in while Trevor attempted to hum along. He held back and observed, felt baffled by the scene—Todd emerging with his talent, Frank revealing his sensitive nature, and he catching up with his own sense of loss and finding courage to trust. Trevor heard footsteps in the hallway, interrupting his reverie.

"You sound great, Todd," Scott said poking his head into the room. "Nobody plays this thing much anymore, though your aunt once played often."

"Speaking of Anna—" Trevor seized his opportunity, "—does she need some help in the kitchen? I smell mincemeat."

"Sure thing. I bought enough food to feed an army. Tonight it's whatever Anna fixes and tomorrow baked ham with scalloped potatoes."

"Idaho spuds," Trevor said. "It's good to be here."

Trevor ambled into the kitchen. "What can I do, Anna?" he asked rolling up his sleeves. "I cook better than I sing."

Anna stood on her toes taking cans of cranberries from the cupboard, her back towards Trevor. "I'm about to make some Jell–O molds for tomorrow," she said when she faced him. "Why don't you fill the teakettle with hot water, then you can chop the celery and apples. I remember you were a great help in the kitchen." She softened her voice. "But not Frank." Trevor squeezed her shoulders and she added, "But you know, he's changed. I think Maria has affected him."

"So do I." He studied his aunt's face a moment. "I've changed too." Trevor grew serious. "Frank and I were just kids when Mom and Dad died and it hurt. You were wonderful to us, but I don't think we fully appreciated you until now."

Anna waved a dismissal. "It broke my heart." She started rubbing a spot on her apron. "I didn't know how we'd all make it, but we did." She tilted her chin up.

Trevor kissed her forehead. "Thanks, if I never told you."

"We've always loved you boys, you know that." Anna hugged her nephew.

"Thanks for your kindness to Todd too. He appreciates it more than you can imagine."

"I'm glad you found someone special. Does he have folks nearby?"

"What's all this chit–chat? I sent Trevor in to help you with the cooking." Scott had wandered into the kitchen and Trevor watched his eyes disappear when he laughed. Scott filled the coffeepot and started a fresh brew. "Smells good in here, Anna, that's for sure."

"Oh my goodness, I forgot the pie . . ." She hustled to the oven and pulled out bubbling mincemeat.

"I've missed your pies," Trevor said. Then to Scott, "I *am* going to help. Just catching up." He picked up the kettle, filled it with water and turned on the stove. Are the apples in the pantry?"

"Yes, on the bottom shelf," Anna said.

Trevor returned with the fruit, which he laid by the sink. "To answer your question," he said to Anna, "Todd's sister and parents live in Oregon. Kate has a couple kids, a boy and a girl."

"And they like you?"

Trevor closed his eyes. "The kids do."

"I see."

"Todd's having a terrible struggle with his family over his orientation. I think we'd have stayed in Kodiak this Christmas if it weren't for you."

"Give 'em time. Where'd Todd learn to play the piano? I've been listening."

"As a kid, but I haven't heard him play much. We don't have a piano and he should have one."

"He plays well."

"That's for sure," Scott echoed as he emerged from the cellar with a sack of potatoes. "Want these peeled and sliced now?"

"Yes, aren't you all so helpful," Anna said, patting her hips.

Frank stepped into the kitchen and opened the cupboard. "Anyone want a cup of coffee besides me?" Anna eyed Trevor and they turned and together said, "Yes."

"Here's the musician." Anna applauded when Todd joined the circle. Frank raised a mug and Todd smiled and took it.

"Let's hear you play, Anna," Todd said.

"My fingers are rusty, but I've practiced a few carols when Scott wasn't around. Maybe tonight."

"By the way," Frank looked at Anna, "I need some wrapping paper for gifts."

"Of course, I have paper, but sit down. I'll get some cheese and fruit, which should hold us for the afternoon. It's too late for lunch, since I'm making pasta in a few hours."

In the evening Todd and Anna played and sang. The brothers and their uncle talked about construction, marine biology, and computers. Scott shared his computer knowledge, then found his photo album of his trip to Europe. He was three fourths through it, explaining each picture, when Anna walked in with a tray of fruitcake and fudge. Todd followed with red wine. He left the room, returning with the poinsettia, which he'd found in the guestroom, placing it on a lamp table.

"Thanks, Todd. We'll enjoy it since we have no Christmas tree." Anna offered the sweets.

"So where're your folks tonight?" Scott asked as he swirled the wine and tipped the goblet to his lips.

"Would you believe they're at the beach?" Todd half laughed. "My parents rented a cabin and my sister and her husband are joining them. Their kids have never seen a winter storm."

"Sorry you're missing that." Scott wiped his mouth. "It sounds like it would beat Idaho."

"Yeah it might . . ." Todd gave Trevor a *help me out* look.

"Todd didn't have a choice," Trevor said. "I insisted he meet you."

"We're pleased you came. You're welcome any time."

Anna smiled and said, "Yes, Todd, our pleasure." Trevor gave Todd a smug glance.

"Thanks, I'm enjoying it very much." Todd eased back in his chair, felt a stab of longing. Would his father ever accept him?

When Todd awoke, he saw streaks of daylight illuminating the blinds in the guestroom. He rolled over and saw that Trevor was asleep. He got up and lifted one of the slats of the blinds, saw a clear sky, though it was not light. Most of the snow had melted and he saw no evidence of more flurries.

He put on his robe and slippers and went to the kitchen. No one else was up, so he started some coffee. He lifted the morning paper from the porch. It's Christmas, no family around and I'm feeling good, he thought. He read the first section and when he smelled the coffee, he got up for a cup. Scott walked into the room as Todd returned from the kitchen.

"Merry Christmas, Todd. Mind if I join you?"

"Of course not and same to you. Let me pour you a cup of coffee, since I've made myself at home."

"Glad you did." Scott took the mug before he sat down. "Looks like it's going to be a clear day."

Todd nodded and took a chair. "It'll be easier driving home than it was getting here."

"Yep, the roads will be fine, I'm sure. Coffee's good." Scott studied Todd a minute. "I know it's none of my business, but how do your parents feel about you and Trevor?"

"Uh—" Todd felt as if someone had punched his stomach.

"Sorry, that's my finesse. What I mean is, you two seem good for each other and I know that being gay is not easy in our society." Scott sipped his coffee.

"My parents are . . . upset . . . about us, but we're working on it." Todd pressed his lips together, hoped this would satisfy Scott. "What . . . how did you and Anna get . . . so accepting?"

"Hard to say. We just figure each person's unique. Sort of a live and let live attitude. Personally, I don't know what the fray's all about." Todd knew Scott's words couldn't help him with his parents, so he swallowed the lump in his throat and didn't respond.

"Don't you ever sleep in?" Trevor asked from the hallway.

"Merry Christmas," Scott said, his eyes crinkling as he glanced at Trevor.

"Hey." Todd gestured toward the presents. "I got up early to shake my presents. That's what I always do Christmas morning."

"I don't remember you shaking presents. Did you do that last year?"

Before Todd could respond, Frank's voice boomed above the slapping sound his slippers made on the hardwood floor. "I remember you shook everything." His eyes fixed on Trevor as he entered the living room.

"Because you put rocks in my packages." Trevor laughed. "I'm trying to get through these two days without a fight, so watch it. Now that you've shuffled in, we're all here except Anna. Let's make breakfast for her."

"Good," said a quiet voice from the hall. "I'll take a long shower."

Todd, Trevor, and Frank took over the kitchen, prepared a Christmas Day breakfast, complete with fresh orange juice, hash browns, bacon and eggs. They opened presents. In the afternoon, they ate ham, potatoes, Anna's home–canned green beans, and mincemeat pie. Later Trevor followed Anna into where the piano sat. Todd and Scott washed and dried the dishes.

"Sorry about your folks," Scott said, setting a dish in the rack. "It's tough when they're upset."

"Upset?" Todd's eyes went to Scott's. "It's more like they have abandoned me. They can't bring themselves to say it." He looked away.

"The truth is, some parents can't ever accept a gay child. I hope yours ultimately can." Todd didn't speak. It sounded final, like a stab of reality.

"We'll be here."

"Thanks." Todd's voice cracked. They finished the dishes, joined Trevor and Anna with whom they enjoyed the rest of the day. Later Todd and Trevor packed their suitcases and set them in the corner of the bedroom for their morning departure.

Amanda circled the cabin living room on her trike, echoing the horn."Beep, beep."

"Slow down." Dave straddled the handlebars as he leaned over them with an eye to eye reprimand. "But I'm glad you like it." He brushed her nose with his beard.

"Okay Daddy." Amanda giggled.

While the women prepared Christmas dinner, Kevin and Jonas erected a model dinosaur on flattened cardboard, which lay on the children's bedroom floor. Kate stood one hand on her hips, the other on the doorjamb. "How are we going to get that home intact? We are traveling by car, remember."

Kevin winked at her, shifted his hips. "We'll put it in this box again. It can ride just fine. Toss me that pillow, will you? My posterior's killing me." She aimed the pillow that landed on Kevin's head messing his hair, but Kate noticed he didn't smooth it. His eyes laughed, and he returned to the serious bone study. Jonas sharpened his reading skills by stumbling through the directions with help from pictures, and Kate left the room unnoticed, returning later to announce dinner.

"The ham tastes delicious, but what's this raisin sauce?" Kevin studied his plate.

"A hostess served it at a nurses' dinner and I wanted to try it." Kate waited. "Well?"

"I guess I have to taste it."

"It won't hurt you to try something different Dad, you're such a diehard."

"What's a diehard?" Jonas sucked a spoonful of Jell–O, glanced up at Kevin. Kate covered her smirk with her napkin and waited for Kevin's answer.

"Uh, that's a person who likes things the way they are—who

fights change." He spooned sauce over his ham, took a bite. "Not bad."

"See Gramps, you're not one of those guys. You tried something new." Jonas' dimpled smile showed approval as they all laughed, all except Kevin. Despite this, Kate noticed the little changes that Kevin had made; he had relaxed.

"I'm eager to see the bridge take shape. Aren't you, Dad?" Dave said.

"Yes, I'll be pleased to see the project completed. Perhaps Charlotte and I can do some traveling when it's finished."

"Now I'm all ears. Where do you want to go?" Charlotte set a cup down on the table, glanced at Kate before studying Kevin.

"Maybe Europe, I'm not sure." Kevin smeared apple butter on a roll.

Kate set her elbows on the table and cupped her face in her hands. "That'll be the day, when you travel, you're such a homebody." However, her thumbs went up when she turned to Charlotte.

# Chapter 25

The day after Christmas, Scott and Anna stood beside the car with Trevor and Todd. Scott laid his arm across Trevor's shoulder. "Bring Todd back again."

"I will." Trevor turned toward Todd and Anna who were embracing.

When Todd released Anna, he smiled. "You're a wonderful hostess. I hope you and Scott will come to Kodiak. We don't have a large place, but we can make room for you."

"We might."

"Thanks for putting up with us," Trevor said, taking the suitcase and opening the car trunk. As he shut it, Frank appeared and punched his arm.

"Call us when the wedding plans are firm." Trevor jabbed him back.

"Be my best man?" Frank eyed Trevor, a crooked grin on his face.

"Will I have to wear a tux?"

"That's up to Maria."

"Why not. Thanks, Frank." Trevor turned and opened the car door. Todd slid in behind the wheel.

Once they reached the freeway, Todd settled back and followed it for two hours, lost in his own thoughts. Trevor read while the morning sun shone on his paperback. Presently he closed it and gave a sigh. "So what did you think of my relatives?"

Todd pondered for a long time. "It's a funny thing, I mean . . . I felt like I was in a place where it was okay to be me."

"Uh–huh."

"I've never been in their home before, but . . ." His emotions flooded by surprise. "Scott is a character. First he seemed rather simple, a jovial fellow, but lacking depth." Todd glanced at Trevor, making sure he was with him. "How can Dad and Scott, so close in age, have such divergent views?" Trevor didn't answer. "Anna is sweet, well, so is Mom, but protocol is such a big deal with her. She's more accepting than Dad is, but I think she goes along with him because she feels she should."

"Could be."

"Anna's her own person." Todd held the steering wheel, tightening his fingers around it as if for support. He felt his hair brush his cheeks. "I was wrong about your uncle." He wondered if he wanted to tell Trev that Scott had asked how his parents felt about them. "Thanks for insisting it was you who roped me into this visit, when the truth is I didn't feel welcome with my own family."

"What are lovers for?" Trevor noticed too late that Todd's face had twisted with agony. "This visit was a mixed bag for you, Todd. Let's talk about something else."

"A blessing and a curse. It's hard to experience first hand what I've missed. I've yearned for Dad's approval, but he may never—" He stopped.

"I know." Trevor wasn't certain what to do, so he reached to the backseat for a box, which Anna had given them, opened it and took a square of candy between his fingers. "Want some fudge?"

Todd opened his mouth and took a bite of Trevor's fudge, using the moment to gain his composure. He tasted the smooth chocolate. "Start looking for a place for lunch where we can also get gas, then you can take the wheel."

"How does Chinese sound?"

"Okay with me," Todd said flipping back his hair.

People chattered over the blaring announcements while the icy snow fell steadily outside the dark glass windows of the Sea–Tac Airport. "The Seattle–Anchorage flight is delayed one hour," a voice announced from the departure gate. Todd and Trevor groaned in unison. "Well, we're stuck here," Trevor said. He gave a side–glance to a man who sat staring out at the tarmac. Todd fixed his eyes on the runway lights, which captured the hail in an eerie glow as it bounced off the fixtures.

"Ice on the wings is what I heard," the man said to Trevor.

The familiar voice caught Todd's attention and when he turned, he took a good look at Larry Gunderson. "Larry, do you remember me?" Todd walked closer.

Larry leaned forward. "Yes I do, hello. Going home too, I presume."

Trevor looked puzzled, but Todd said, "This is Larry Gunderson, the pastor I told you about. Larry, this is my partner, Trevor Johnson."

"My pleasure," Larry said shaking Trevor's hand.

"Uh, the weather's gotten colder, but I didn't see any ice on the car windshield," Trevor said.

"Well, apparently a storm is headed our way."

"Is that so?" Trevor removed his coat and ran his hand through his tangled hair. "We haven't heard any weather reports, just been driving and eating."

"We spent Christmas with Trevor's family. How about you?"

"Same here. I have a brother in the north end," Larry said, removing his glasses.

"Do you have a family?" Trevor said.

"Oh, yes. My wife insisted on staying here for a few more days to visit with our daughter and her husband who came with their two–month–old baby girl. She's beautiful, and we hadn't seen her before. They drove to my brother's home from Montana, and since the weather's worsening, I think their decision to stay is wise. My wife will fly back to Kodiak at the end of the week, but I have a wedding and a funeral in the next couple days."

"Occupational hazard, huh?" Trevor grinned. "Well, congratulations. Is this your first grandchild?"

"That's right."

"The holidays are a great time for surprises," Trevor said. "I had an unexpected chance to get reacquainted with my brother. Will you men excuse me while I find something to drink? Can I get you anything?"

"Hot coffee sounds good to me, black." Larry looked toward Todd. "How about you?"

"Coffee's fine." Trevor left his luggage and walked off.

"How's it going, Todd?" Larry motioned to a seat across from him that Todd declined, not wanting to shout. "Okay, about the same. I had a good time at Trevor's place."

"His folks live in Seattle?"

"Uh, no, we were with his aunt and uncle in Idaho. Very accommodating."

Larry stood, turned to face Todd, and cupped his hand over his ear. "Hard to hear in this place. Glad you had a pleasant holiday." Todd eased up when Trevor approached with a tray, and he got a whiff of coffee. The younger men sat across from Larry and made small talk until all three boarded the plane for home.

"That flight wasn't bad, but I can't get this sucker started," Todd moaned as he tried revving up the car engine in the near freezing Kodiak garage. Todd pushed on the throttle. "Ah, now it purrs." He idled for a minute and headed away from the airport to their house.

When they entered their home, Todd tossed his watch on the dresser. "One in the morning. No wonder I'm bushed. No food here either, so we may as well crash." After flicking on the furnace, he peeled off his jeans, splashed his face, brushed his teeth, and got into bed.

"I'm hitting the shower first. I'll try not to wake you," Trevor called from the bathroom.

When he awoke early, Todd slipped out to exercise. He watched his breath turn into clouds as he exhaled into the freezing air. He stretched his legs, his torso, and arms. He felt something expansive inside, but he couldn't name it. His feet paced the rigid turf.

Invigorated, he returned to his car, remembering they needed food. He stopped at the grocery and picked up milk, eggs, and bread, plus some salmon for dinner.

"It's cold out there, right Todd?" Judd greeted him. "You're going to be busy studying those whales."

Todd handed the clerk a ten–dollar bill. "Yeah, it's back to work tomorrow." Todd managed a baffled smile. He left the grocery and drove home.

When Todd opened the door to his house, Trevor said, "The boss man left you a message."

"Yeah? You're up already."

"Knock if off or I won't tell you what Mac said."

"What gives?" Todd smelled fresh coffee, poured himself a cup, and broke into the bread loaf.

"It seems some whales swam into the harbor this past week, and they've been checking them out. Mac wants to talk with you. Left a message the day after Christmas."

"So that's what old Judd meant."

"Judd?"

"At the store he mentioned the whales. Didn't know what he was talking about."

Todd clicked on the voice mail. "If you're there Todd, I need you down here. Got a couple whales we haven't seen before. One beached, and we're running some studies on her. Get down here when you can. We could use Trevor too. Hope you had a good Christmas."

"Guess I should give him a ring, but first I'm having some eggs, want any?"

"Okay. You going to the lab?"

"Yeah, aren't you? Sounds like Mac wants us both."

"You'll make me look bad if I don't show up."

"Suit yourself, Trev."

After breakfast they drove Trevor's jeep to the lab and immediately Mac escorted them to the beached whale. "We hauled her out two days ago, but she came back yesterday. Her vital signs are good and she may make it if she'll stay put when we take her out again."

"She's a killer all right and a beaut. How'd she get away from her pod? It makes me wonder about noise pollution," Todd said peering at the whale's white markings.

"She's long isn't she?" Trevor walked along the mammal's side.

"Check the chart. I remember something like thirty feet . . . that's a gut full of salmon." Mac hiked his waders up and laughed. "Reports south of here indicate more beached orca."

"Maybe they're getting too close coming in for my seals, which seem to be getting scarcer," Trevor said, grinning.

"Ah, don't know about that," Mac said, and then turned his bulk around and started toward the lab. Trevor heard the soil crunch beneath their boots as he and Todd followed him.

# Chapter 26

Friday afternoon Dave stopped the car in his driveway. "I'm glad to be home."

"And eager to move your office?" Kate said.

"Yes, I'm heading there as soon as we clear out the car. I've got some packing to do."

"I'll help you with it."

"Nah, stay here with the kids and tomorrow Kevin and I will transport stuff to the new office. School starts again on Monday?"

"Yes, but I don't work till Tuesday." Kate opened Amanda's seatbelt. "Hope all the beds aren't full, but they will be following a holiday." Kate sighed as she carried luggage through the front door.

"Can I call Micah? I want to know what he got for Christmas." Jonas flopped down by the phone.

"Well it's four. Just talk today and you can see him tomorrow."

Jonas picked up the phone. Amanda jumped on her trike to circle the driveway while Kate and Dave unloaded the car.

Later Dave shut the door behind him and laid his office mail on the table. "Kids in bed already?"

"Yes, they were tuckered out. Get your packing done?"

"Most of it. We need to scour a bit." He looked at her. "It's good to have you to myself for a change. That cabin was tight quarters. Sit down so we can talk." Dave motioned Kate to a chair, which she took.

"What?" She scanned his face.

"Oh, just wondered how you felt about the beach."

"I thought things went fine. The kids had fun and Mom and Dad enjoyed them. They behaved well don't you think?"

"Mom and Dad or the kids?"

"All of us, now that you mention it."

"No complaints," Dave said.

"Dad talked about Todd, like I told you. No miracle cures, but I didn't expect any."

"Good Kate, because people don't change that fast." He gave Kate a strange look. "My own perspective has shifted."

"What are you talking about?" Kate leaned forward.

"We have a wonderful relationship with your folks. Your Dad's helping me establish my business and he enjoys the kids, especially Jonas."

"You've noticed that too."

"When dinos are involved."

"I'm glad to see the child in Dad. So what's your point?"

"Well, I hate to push too hard right now. I think your dad will come around."

"Push too hard? You mean alienate Dad, put your job in jeopardy?"

"Not exactly," Dave glanced away. Then back. "Yes. I don't want any friction between us. We can't fix Kevin and Todd's relationship. They have to do that."

"We can help, Dave, you know we can. Your job's important, but—"

"Kate, it will get better. Let's go easy."

"Go easy? By playing hide–and–seek with Todd? He's ticked with me for balking when he wanted to take Jonas to the beach. You were too. Now you're backing off with Dad. Can't we find more compelling reasons than our kids and your job to excuse our reluctance to embrace my brother?" Kate jumped up, flung a pillow in her chair. "I'm going to bed!"

Dave arrived the next morning at his father–in–law's firm with a load of office supplies. Kevin met him and helped carry in the desk, chair, and drawing board. "Congratulations are in order, Dave. Charlotte and I want to take you and Kate to dinner to celebrate your success. How about next week?"

"Sounds good. I'll check with my social secretary. Kate's cleaning the old office right now." Dave turned back toward the company van. "I better see how the mopping up is going. She deserves a dinner out," he called over his shoulder.

Kate had vacuumed the rug, cleaned out the cupboard, and washed the windowsills. When she had locked the door and was half–way down the hall, she bumped into Dave. "Where are you headed?" he said.

"The rug needs shampooing. You left coffee stains everywhere." She still felt irritated with Dave.

"I'll get a shampooer."

"That's where I'm going," Kate said, brushing her forehead.

"Show me what you've done." Dave turned Kate around and they walked down the hall into the room. "Looks great," he said. "Don't do any more. I'll clean the rug, then you can take it home tomorrow since I can't use it in my new office."

"Fine." Kate brushed a dry tear from her eye. "Good bye, first office."

"I won't miss you at all." Dave made a face.

They walked to their vehicles. "I'll catch up on the laundry and get myself psyched for work tomorrow. See you at home." Kate stopped at Tina's Care for Tots and loaded Amanda and her inseparable trike into the car. She bought some groceries, then went home.

The holidays indeed brought many people into the cardiac unit. Tuesday morning Kate checked a list of patients. She felt weary of care giving, tired of sick people. Nevertheless, she familiarized herself with their conditions and bolstering herself, she entered a new patient's room.

"Pie's not on your diet, Mr. Nelson. Where did you get that?" Before the man could explain the apple pastry, a huge woman marched through the patient room door with two cups of coffee.

"He's starving, so I brought it for him," she said. She set the coffee by the bed, forcing her width into a chair. "I'm his wife, Emily Nelson."

"I'm his nurse, Kate Winston. We need to talk." She waited while Mr. Nelson laid his fork against the remaining bites. The chart put his age at sixty. His hair was short, black with white streaks; his jaw was set in an unyielding mode. He didn't look more than fifteen pounds overweight. He studied Kate with a haggard face that looked prepared for a lecture. "Just a second," Kate changed her mind, "I want to get some printed materials. You have it now, so finish your pie and coffee. I'll be back." She swished out of the room.

"You're here because of severe blockages in your arteries, and have survived a four graph by–pass." Kate pulled a chair up to the bed. "You're a fortunate man. This hospital provides information to help you change your eating and exercise habits so you'll have a good chance for a healthier future." Mrs. Nelson leaned forward, more an adjustment of posture than a display of interest. "Genetics plays a big role in heart disease, but a healthy life style can help. It's tough, but you can take small steps." Kate smiled at them. "What are your favorite foods, Mr. Nelson?"

He hesitated, then said, "Pizza, spaghetti, ice cream, and pie."

"Okay, that's fair. Do you know which ingredients in pizza are good and which are bad for your heart?"

"I do," Emily said. "Cheese is bad because it's loaded with fat, but the dough is okay."

"True. What's good for you on a pizza?" Kate looked at Mr. Nelson who appeared reluctant rather than uninformed. He set down his cup. "Vegetables like mushrooms, tomatoes, and peppers can't hurt."

"Yes." Kate smiled. "So, don't cut out pizza, just use less cheese, or use low fat, and lots of veggies. The pasta in spaghetti is fine too. What kind of meat do you buy?" She waited for Mrs. Nelson's eye contact.

"Hamburger, what else?"

"Have you noticed that the labels show the different fat contents of hamburger?"

"Nope." Emily shrugged.

"This pamphlet discusses the various fats in beef and it can make a difference if you choose the lower fat meats. Milk too." Kate opened the tri–fold pamphlet.

"He drinks whole milk." Mrs. Nelson looked at Mr. Nelson.

"You can start by trying two percent. You had it for breakfast this morning."

"I could tell." Mr. Nelson glared, then gave a tiny grin. Kate finished the discussion by extolling nonfat yogurt and graham cracker piecrusts. She explained high and low–density cholesterol and pushed the importance of walking.

When she returned to the nurses' station, Kate met Samantha, the head nurse, who stood without her white coat ready to leave the building. Kate had shared her woes about Todd before Christmas with this matter–of–fact woman. She admired Samantha, her dignity, the way she carried herself.

Samantha raised her head as Kate walked in. "How were your holidays? We've gone non stop since then and I have wondered how things played out." She twisted a stray hair around her finger and anchored it in the thick, black and silver French roll that accentuated her sharp nose and high cheekbones.

"Not much different. Todd spent time with his partner's relatives, as I mentioned he would. Dave is immersed in work and I've put my own feelings on hold."

"I wish I had that talent." Samantha laughed. "You look exhausted." Her blue eyes held Kate's. "Just remember I'm your friend."

"Thanks. I'm weary with this job, need a change. I've spent the past half–hour convincing Mr. Nelson that he has a role in his own health care. His wife is a real challenge too."

"He'll follow your advice and live to a ripe old age. The cranky ones do."

Kevin returned from his office with two extra file cabinets, which he wrestled into the garage. As he walked out of it, he saw Florence waving at him and calling. "Please Kevin, could you help me get into my house? I went for the mail, but the door's locked. Can't remember nothin' these days. Left my keys in the kitchen." Kevin strode across the street with Florence, wondering what he could do.

"Think my bathroom window's open." Kevin peered at the tiny window, then circled the house checking for other possibilities.

"I'll get my ladder. Stay here." Kevin brought the ladder to the sill and pushed in the window. It would take a small person to get inside and open the door. "Come back to our house. I think Amanda can help us, but we'll have to wait until Kate is home from work to bring her here."

Florence followed Kevin inside his kitchen, sat down and leaned back on the kitchen chair. She peered at him, massaged her wrinkled fingers. "How's Todd? A shame he had to move so far away. Alaska, Charlotte told me."

"Yes, he's in Kodiak."

"Trevor too?"

Kevin stiffened. "Doesn't matter."

"I miss my son so much. He didn't have many friends. I was glad Todd found somebody. Gays get treated mean. Just like my Nathan. They want to be liked for who they are."

Kevin stared at Florence. "You saying Todd's gay?"

"I thought he . . ."

"I don't care what you thought, Florence. It's none of your business." Florence's head fell forward; she twisted the button on her sweater. They heard a step on the porch and Kevin looked up to see Charlotte at the door, returned from shopping.

"Hello," Charlotte said. "What's wrong?" Her eyes darted past Kevin's irritated face to Florence.

"Locked myself out. I'm such a pest." Florence fidgeted with the yarn loops in her sweater. Charlotte regarded Kevin before she set her packages on the counter.

"I'm sure we can help you out," Charlotte said.

The kitchen door popped open. "Here we are." Kate stuck her head inside. Kevin dashed out the door, grasped Amanda's hand and proceeded to Florence's bathroom window, where he released Amanda onto the counter. She bounced to the floor and ran to open the back door. Charlotte steadied Florence's gait with her arm when they crossed the street.

"Thank you sweetheart." Florence touched her fingers to Amanda's cheek. "Appreciate it," she said with a quick glance at

Kevin. Then she shuffled inside.

Kate checked her schedule the next morning, straightened her jacket, and walked into Mr. Nelson's room. "I see you're eating your oatmeal." She watched as her patient spooned the last bite from his bowl. "Keep it up."

"I guess I have to if I want to live, but don't think I prefer this to sausage and eggs. When do I get out of here?"

"As soon as your doctor gives us the okay which we expect will be today. Is your wife ready to deal with you at home?" Kate made a playful grimace to which Mr. Nelson responded with a snort.

"She damn well better be. I waited on her hand and foot when she had her gall bladder removed."

"So you're taking turns, are you?" Kate put the blood pressure cuff on his arm. "Your blood pressure is good," she praised as she read it. "You've put your heartfelt effort into eating the hospital food." Kate paused for his reaction.

"Yeah, I have, ha–ha."

"I know it's a big change. Mrs. Nelson will need your help in learning to cook in a different way. Do you like to cook?"

"That's women's work."

Kate rolled her eyes. "I thought you might think so. Try oatmeal, it's easy. I'll see you when the doctor's orders come." She touched Mr. Nelson's arm and left. She readied the packet to send home with the Nelsons and made her rounds to her remaining patients.

Her senior patient, Mrs. Beaumont, had hung on through the holidays. An aide had fed her breakfast and dinner each day while her son often visited her at lunchtime. In the past four days, as recorded on her chart, she had refused food. Kate approached her bedside with a quiet step when she saw her son. "I don't want her to suffer pain, but please allow her to go without heroics." His eyes sought Kate's. "She woke up earlier and all she said was, 'I'm ready to go Andy.'"

Kate had expected Mrs. Beaumont's death. She sat down and faced Andy Beaumont. "Yes, we'll let her go with dignity. It makes it easier for us with her living will. I'm sorry she's so weak now."

"How long do you think . . ."

"A day or two." She went to Mrs. Beaumont's side, took her blood pressure, filled her water pitcher, and smoothed the sheet around her feeble body. She looked at the woman's face, her eyes closed, her skin sunken and drawn, her thin, white hair matted on her scalp. Kate turned around, gazed at her son, at his red hair now graying at his temples, at the freckles that spread across the nose shaped like his mother's nose. She held his brown eyes with hers. "Death is sad even when you expect it, Andy. It's a celebration of life too. If I can help you in any way, I will."

"You already have."

Exhausted when she entered her house that night, Kate checked her messages. She learned that in the afternoon her mother had called 911 because Florence had fallen and she was unconscious when the hospital admitted her.

Friday was as hurried at the hospital as the whole week had been. Kate hustled from one patient to the next. She had no time for a break until two in the afternoon when she walked to a nearby café for a breath of fresh air and a garden burger. A woman seated at the table next to her kept glancing at her. Kate returned a smile, which brought the woman to her feet and she walked to Kate's table. "Excuse me for staring, but I think I know you, or at least I know your mother." The woman extended her hand, which Kate shook. "My name's Debbie James. My mother, Florence, lives across the street from your parents. I saw you at Nathan's memorial."

"Of course, please sit down, I'm Kate." She regretted that she'd not yet visited Florence. "How's she doing?"

Debbie stepped back to her table, retrieved her order and slid into a chair opposite Kate. "Not well." She looked at Kate. "She slipped into a coma during the night."

"Sorry to hear that. Things have been hectic in cardiac. I haven't seen Florence yet. Mom called me last night about her fall. Tell me about it."

"She apparently tripped on the threshold between the kitchen and back porch, a route she takes often." Debbie grimaced. Hit her head. She has a bump on her forehead. No one saw her fall, but thank goodness, your mother saw her lying on the porch. She has a bruise on her right shoulder and a few abrasions on her right arm. The doctors are running some tests." Kate nodded.

"She's been slowing down." Debbie sighed. "Mom's knees are arthritic and her legs aren't steady." She took a bite of salad, motioning to Kate. "Please eat. I didn't mean to keep you from your lunch."

Kate guessed that Debbie was in her mid–fifties. Her hair swirled softly around her chin. Her large hazel eyes and prominent cheekbones accentuated her angular face. "I remember meeting you once," Kate said after chewing a bite of her burger, "when I was in college. Your mother moved here about sixteen years ago. You were already married."

"Now divorced. Mom moved across from your folks after we lost my father."

"Yes. Now your brother."

"Nathan was nine years younger than me and he and mother were close. Somehow he replaced my dad for her." She caught Kate's puzzled expression. "In many ways he took care of Mother. They took care of each other."

"She's in intensive care, I assume."

"Yes. Her doctor said they'd keep her there until she is conscious."

"I'll see her today."

"You can't do much, but just listening to me helps."

"Well, thanks for introducing yourself, Debbie."

"Thank you for your concern about Mom. I'm staying in her house for a few days, until she's conscious, so I might see Charlotte." Debbie slid a dollar under the salad plate, rose and smiled. "Mom speaks well of your mother."

"Thanks. Florence is a good neighbor." Kate noticed Debbie's coral suit, how tall she seemed as she walked away.

Kate made time to see Florence. When she stepped into the room, Debbie rose from her chair and greeted her. "It's so kind of you to come." She stretched her arm around Kate in a hug. "I was about to leave, there's no change, but her vital signs are good. Her doctor thinks she suffered a stroke, which caused her fall."

"Get some rest, and we'll hope for the best," Kate said. Debbie nodded and walked from the room while Kate stayed with the unconscious woman, feeling her own weariness.

Charlotte carried in the grocery bags, after coming home from Kevin's office, where he was working late. She'd spent the afternoon having lunch with friends from her book club. She took a head of lettuce to the sink and reached to lower the window blind when she noticed lights in Florence's house. She dropped the lettuce, dialed Kate's number, and sat at the kitchen table. "Hello dear, this is Mom. I'm wondering if you know anything about Florence tonight. I see her house lights and can't believe she could be home already."

"No, she's not. She's in a coma, but I ran into her daughter, Debbie, today and she may be at her Mom's house now. Why don't you call her. She appreciated our interest and praised you up and down."

"For calling 911? Aren't I wonderful." Charlotte felt a twinge of guilt when she thought how annoyed she felt with Florence at times. "Tell me more . . . what happened?"

"The doctor thinks she had a stroke, but her vital signs are stable."

"Maybe I will call Debbie. What did you think of her?"

"I don't remember her much, but she is quite different from her mother. Poised and confident and bright."

"Oh, you know Florence has a problem with grammar, but she's no fool. I'll visit her tomorrow. Good night . . . and thanks for checking in on her." No fool, Charlotte thought as she hung up. Florence felt for others, penetrated hearts unintentionally. For a moment, Charlotte remembered Florence's not so innocent questions, her personal self–revelations, and the gifts of flowers from her yard. Then she stepped to the sink, cleaned the lettuce, and put away her groceries. She marinated chicken, placed it in the refrigerator, and dialed her neighbor's home.

"A coma?" Kevin frowned while he peppered his chicken and listened to Charlotte relate the day's events.

"Debbie will be here for a few days. What's absorbed you at the office?"

"I've spent a few hours clearing out my files. Some I haven't used in fifteen years. I want to make a clean break when I retire, not leave a paper trail."

"You keep your files immaculate." Charlotte looked up.

"Maybe. The bottom line is Dave needs a filing cabinet for his stuff, so my archaic papers have to go."

"Well, Jonas could have helped. He loves anything that's extinct."

"Yeah. I enjoy studying the blueprints, too." Kevin folded his napkin. "Dave's a talented guy." He took a deep breath, exhaled and sat back in his chair. "I'm proud of how Kate and Dave have parented their kids."

"Yes." Charlotte eyed Kevin.

"He's truly like a son . . ." Kevin folded his arms, and then pushed himself from the table. "Where's the paper? Guess I forgot to bring it in."

"I haven't seen it." Charlotte was startled when Kevin stood. She felt a rush of anger. "Remember when we were deciding about my breast surgery? Remove the lump or the whole breast?"

"Of course I remember."

"You wished you had a crystal ball. That's what I wish I had now."

"A crystal ball?"

"A way to tell what you're thinking."

"So you'd know my mind?"

"So I'd know why you change the subject whenever it approaches Todd."

"Todd? We weren't talking about him."

"No. You said Dave was like a son, then stopped."

"Well . . . he is, but that doesn't . . . mean . . . anything. If that's all, I'm getting the paper."

"No, that's not all."

"It's all from me." Kevin picked up the plates and put them in the sink where Charlotte was rinsing silverware. She didn't look up.

# Chapter 27

"This steak melts on my tongue . . . almost," Dave said flashing a smile at Kate.

"I know I'm mean when it comes to meat meals." Kate eyed her parents who sat opposite her and Dave in the restaurant. "He doesn't get it often."

"Well, this is your celebratory steakhouse dinner," Kevin said. "You're a man with a future and I'm impressed with the looks of the bridge you designed."

"Spread it a bit thinner, Dad, or I won't be able to stand him."

"We're proud of you too, and those kids."

"Thanks, but I live with him and his head is big enough."

The expression on Charlotte's face, the way her eyes sparked and widened with understanding made Kate laugh aloud. "They eat it up, don't they Mom."

"Oh yes," Charlotte said. "We all do."

Kate noticed Kevin and Dave, who had ignored them and were engaged in work related conversation. She leaned over the table. "What did your doctor say this morning, Mom?"

"Good report. I'm still cancer free."

"Wonderful. Have you talked to Todd? I think he'd want to know the good news."

"That's what Florence said."

"Florence? She was in a coma when I left work at noon . . . she still is, isn't she?"

"No, she woke up at twelve–thirty. I visited with her about three."

"I can't believe it. Nobody tells me anything. How is she, what'd she say?"

"Debbie was there when she opened her eyes. The doctor thinks she suffered a mild stroke, just as you said. She's feeling some numbness, but had no trouble talking. She amazes me, always has."

"How did she know about your bout with cancer or your appointment today?"

Charlotte suspended her teacup. "Telepathy." She gave Kate an amused look. "I told her of course, when I had the surgery."

"What about today?"

"Debbie said it was wonderful that Florence woke up and since my cancer seems to be cured, I just spontaneously shared my own good news."

"How did Todd come up?"

Charlotte glanced at Kevin who continued talking with Dave, and then she leaned toward her daughter. "It was the oddest thing." Charlotte pressed her fingers into her forehead. "When I told Florence my cancer was gone, she asked me if I had told Todd yet. I said no, but I would soon."

"Why would she mention him?"

"She lost her son."

"I *know*."

"Florence wasn't herself today." Charlotte paused. "Her advice is that I should appreciate Todd while I have him because Lord knows how long I will. She embarrassed Debbie when she held my hand. After she had our attention, she said, 'you know, it don't matter one whit that your son is gay, just love him.'"

"Oh my gosh."

"She's known it all along. Today I understood how much she's grieved Nathan."

"You two better eat more and talk less," Kevin said, his attention turned to the women, "because Dave and I are thinking about dessert." Charlotte twirled her fork through a mound of pasta and put it into her mouth. She sipped her tea while Kate chewed chicken in the silent moment.

# Chapter 28

Todd was captivated with computers, testing, and noise pollution research. He had helped move the beached orca into deeper waters. The churning surf, the salty taste of the sea, exhilarated him. Today was no exception. He caught his balance as the boat rocked through the waves and behind it in toe, a rescued whale slammed the water with its tail. Maybe he's as glad for life as I am, Todd thought. He swept aside stiff strands of hair that whipped his face.

"He's trying to get free from the rope," Mac called from the galley.

"Or clapping for his life. What creatures they are." Todd drew a deep breath.

"Stick with me and we'll keep them awesome for your grandkids," Mac yelled. "Or someone's."

"Maybe mine someday." Following the brawny man into the galley, Todd spread his legs for balance in the shaking vessel, hearing the rumbling thunder of the motor in his ears. "I couldn't push a pencil all day, no fresh air. Research is okay as long as I get out like this too. How will we know if our friend finds his pod?"

"We won't," Mac said, "unless he beaches again. Then whoever finds him should see his tag and report it."

On a Sunday morning in mid February, Todd rose early. A sheathing of ice covered the windows when he turned up the furnace. He brewed coffee and ate two pieces of toast. He left Trevor asleep when he drove to the trail. As he pounded along, he yearned to break out, take a risk. Life's more, he thought, than rules and good behavior. He was restless even after he finished his routine and headed home.

He shut the door behind him. "I think I'm going to shower and go hear Larry."

"Whatever. Don't forget they let gays in that place." Trevor held up the newspaper, which Todd snapped in his face as he passed.

He returned dressed in clean Levi's. "I feel like I'm missing something—haven't been in a church in twelve years, except for weddings and Grandma's memorial." He zipped his coat.

Trevor lowered the newspaper exposing his pale blue eyes. "Am I holding you back?"

"I didn't say you were, buddy. Later."

Todd drove to the church, entered the narthex where a man said, "Good morning," and offered him a bulletin, which Todd took and then found a seat three rows from the rear. A woman dressed in blue slacks, a sweater, and a blazer sat near the pulpit. Next to her sat Larry Gunderson, wearing a black robe with a white stole embroidered in brightly colored symbols unfamiliar to Todd.

A few minutes later the woman stood. "We need one more person to cook for the homeless woman's shelter. If you can help, please see me after worship." Todd stared at his bulletin wondering who in Kodiak was homeless.

A tall man rose. "Everyone is invited to the potluck tonight to welcome new members." The choir huddled in a side loft and Todd counted twenty persons. Larry greeted the congregation and invited them to extend their welcome to their fellow participants. Todd watched as the two men in front of him shook hands with the persons on each side of them. Next they turned together and welcomed him and Todd grasped their hands. No other attention came to him for which he felt relief. He listened while the choir sang and when Larry preached. The hymns were unfamiliar, so he didn't sing aloud, but read the words, enjoying the organ music. Then he left.

Entering his house, Todd stepped over the papers strewn across the floor. "Hello, virtuous one," Trevor said from the kitchen.

"Stow it, Trev."

"Sorry, I didn't mean . . ."

"Yeah, well just think before you speak."

Trevor quieted for a minute. "How about a cup of coffee?"

"Fine."

"How was it?"

"Okay, nothing unusual."

"What did Larry say?"

"Good to see you, Todd."

"See any gays?"

"Why are you being such a jerk?"

Trevor set down the mugs. "Because I am one, I guess. I hate to see you get hurt by the church again."

"That's immature, don't you think? Maybe as a kid, I got the wrong impression or my parents did. If it's okay with you, I want to give God a chance as an adult."

"Whatever. I admit I have my own prejudices. Anna and Scott never took me to church, but I knew they loved me. I remember going a few times at Christmas and Easter with my folks when I was a kid, but not since their death. I grew up real fast."

"Yeah. Do you have problems with trains now? Would you ride one?"

"I have. I knew it was an accident. People die every day in car accidents. We still drive cars."

"Yeah."

"All right, listen to Larry preach any time you want." Trevor looked solemn. "I believe in God too."

"Yeah, well . . . you got orphaned and I got ostracized. Maybe we blame God." Trevor listened, tapping his fingers on his chair. "But, we're not kids anymore." Todd pressed his palms together. "God won't break if we speak our truth. We can make our own decisions. Please don't bug me about it."

"Okay." Trevor lay on the floor and started doing push-ups. "I'm glad you've stopped giving your parents all the credit—and blame—for who you are."

"Yeah, it's a start."

# Chapter 29

When Florence came home from the hospital, Charlotte volunteered twice a week helping Debbie care for her. Now the last days of February had arrived. Today, Kate took her mother's turn at the older woman's house. She stood by the linen closet holding the sheets in her hands, watching as Florence, sprawled in her chair, attempted to get up. Florence wiggled her bottom back and forth, tried to pull forward, her hands on the bars of her walker. She pinched her lips together and squinted making Kate wince although Kate respected her effort.

"Are you okay, Florence? Need a boost?"

"Nope, it's hell gettin' old, but if I can move by myself, I'm gonna."

"I'm making your bed." Kate breezed past Florence's struggle.

"I can help, if I can get to you."

"You're stubborn, you are." Kate smiled over her shoulder. She stalled, checked the medications in the bathroom, and then snapped a sheet in the air. She heard the walker clicking in rhythm with a shuffling slipper and a bare foot dragging behind. A triumphant light spread across Florence's face as she passed the threshold and allowed Kate to ease her into a chair.

"Smells fresh," Florence said, plunging her nose in the sheet that lay on the arm of her chair. "When's Todd coming to visit again . . . haven't seen him for a spell."

"When did you last see him?"

"Well, let me think, he and his love, I guess—oh, I remember—they went to the zoo with you. Amanda told me, saw you come home that day." Despite the throb in her fingers, Florence stuffed a pillow into a pillowcase. Kate finished making the bed, listening as Florence talked on. "Your parents okay with . . . what is his name?"

"Trevor." Kate turned down the sheets.

"It's not my business, but Todd's gay isn't he?" Kate looked at Florence, but didn't answer. "Thought he was that way. It don't bother me none. My son Nathan was different too. Does Todd bother Charlotte?"

"You'll have to ask her, Florence." Kate fluffed the pillow. "Let's get you in bed now. You've been up awhile."

Florence didn't resist when Kate wrapped her arms around her back and lifted her. Hanging toward the side, she shuffled against Kate into the bathroom and then back to bed. When Kate tucked the covers around her, Florence's eyes softened. "I talk too much."

Kate touched Florence's gnarled knuckles, which rose like miniature mountains in the sheets. "It's all right, Florence." She smoothed white wisps on her balding head. "It really is."

A few weeks later Kate put her mug down and blew crumbs off the kitchen table. Pushing a plate of blueberry muffins aside, she opened a birthday card, and wrote:

> *Happy Birthday Todd, I hope you do something fun to celebrate. Sorry I haven't checked in with you recently. Dave has wrapped himself in his work. I can't believe it's the middle of March, but maybe in June we can visit Kodiak. Jonas likes softball. Amanda will be five next month. Say hi to Trevor. Love, Kate.*

She addressed the envelope, licked a stamp, then frowned.

She felt a peculiar bond with her mother in their truce about discussing Todd and Trevor. They stood in perverse loyalty to Kevin and Dave. Kate rubbed her neck, wondering if Charlotte had remembered Todd's birthday. She had left Kate's kitchen fifteen minutes ago for a dentist appointment. Neither had mentioned him. They had discussed Charlotte's attention to Florence during her slow return to health, Kevin's need to work, and the progress of the bridge.

Kate put the greeting in her purse, zipped a coat around Amanda, and took her to the car. She mailed the card, bought groceries, and returned to spend the afternoon of her day–off cleaning the house. Her mind churned, while the vacuum whirred. The smell of Clorox reminded her that she needed a change at work, but didn't know what. Was she bored with the routine or heart patients? Todd and Trevor had kept away, Dad and Dave worked on the bridge. Was she the sole person who couldn't dismiss Todd's life? Did her father's prejudices rule this family? Had Dave's ambition clouded his heart? When she placed a purple hyacinth on the dining table, Kate's nostrils tightened with the heady scent that mingled with the smell of lemon polish. Taking a deep breath, she vowed that in June she'd take the kids to Kodiak.

A thrill raced down his spine when Dave witnessed the workers along a partial span of bridge. "It looks like it may happen." He turned to Kevin.

"What did you expect? Otherwise I'd fire you." Kevin thumped Dave's back. "You've got the talent, Son." They shielded their eyes from the sun and studied the bridge.

Dave welcomed the praise, but wanted independence from his father–in–law. Late in March, Kevin still came to work daily. Dave could see his pleasure in being on site, viewing the progress. Kevin had no obvious hobbies, as Charlotte did. She read and discussed the classics with her friends, sewed clothes for Amanda, and recently kept busy helping Florence while she recovered from her stroke. Kevin loved his role as grandfather, but Jonas and Amanda would grow up. He didn't discuss Todd; this avoidance made Dave uneasy. Dave hoped Kevin would retire soon, but he wondered what he would do with his time.

Dave took the beater from Amanda's hand. "Look at you," he said, wiping frosting from her fingers and face. "We'll change your T–shirt too." He loosened the warm chocolate cake from the pan onto a cooling rack. He scanned the counter, tossed the cake box in the trash and the dirty bowls in the dishwasher. "Go get a clean top," he said. Amanda hustled to her bedroom, where she grabbed a shirt from her bureau; she pulled it over her head, returning to the kitchen as Kate entered.

"We did fine." Dave smiled.

Kate raised her eyebrows. "I'm sure you did, or do you protest too much?" She put a plastic bag filled with noisemakers, balloons, party cups, and candles on top of the refrigerator. "I made a mess Mommy, so I got my clean shirt."

"I see." Kate smiled with an eye on Dave. "Tomorrow we'll have your friends here for your birthday party. The cake looks yummy."

"I helped too." Amanda put her hands on her hips, circled her feet.

"You did a good job." Kate kneeled and hugged Amanda who then darted from the kitchen. "Thanks Dave. I appreciate your help, too. You're always good with the kids."

"Except for the past few months?" Dave rubbed his beard.

"Maybe." The phone rang and Kate picked it up. "Hello? Yeah, Mom, we're ready. Are you sure you're up to that? All right, we'll come by in the afternoon." Setting down the phone, Kate eyed Dave who made a face, but nodded. "She wants to have us for dessert for Amanda's birthday."

"Well, I have some office work . . ."

"Please, she wants us to come on Sunday. Let's be a family together for just an hour or so." Kate turned on those words and walked to the desk. "By the way, Amanda received a birthday card from Uncle Todd today." She handed the envelope to Dave.

"What do you know. I wonder why he—"

"Because he's family, Dave."

"We haven't touched base with him lately is all I meant."

"His birthday was in March and I sent him a card. He just responded back."

"That's good. I won't be so sensitive about Todd when your dad retires."

"Todd can wait till Dad retires. Is that it?"

# Chapter 30

The next week Kate handed a post surgery packet to a patient after checking the doctor's release signature. That morning she had wrestled Amanda's trike from the van and left the children with Kevin, who stayed home from work. She had jumped at her parents' offer to take the kids during part of their spring break. A huge gift of time, "and a break from Kevin at the office," Dave had commented.

When Kate entered the last patient's room, Samantha, the head nurse approached her. "I need to see you, Kate." She felt the woman's hand on her arm moving her toward the hallway. Kate felt her stomach drop at the grave tone in her colleague's voice. "Your son is in the pediatric ICU. He fell from a tree in your parents yard." Kate closed her eyes. *Intensive Care?* "He's unconscious and has lost a lot of blood from a gash in his temple."

"Oh dear God." Kate looked away. "Thanks, I'm going right now." She turned, then stopped. "Who called?"

"Your father . . . he's shaken and wanted me to tell you. He came with Jonas in the aid car."

"I want to see Jonas, then I'll call Dave."

"Should I come with you?"

Kate took a deep breath. "I'm okay."

She walked into the room where Jonas lay still, his head wrapped in bandages, blood dripping into his arm. The I.V. was familiar, but not on Jonas. His mouth was a line, his chin pale. In a chair at the wall, she saw her father, who sat statue–like, his head in his hands. Kevin didn't look up when she entered the room. She touched Jonas' hand, uncovered his arm where the needle entered. Without speaking, she left the room and found a nurse. The woman grasped her hand. "I'm sorry."

Kate searched her eyes. "Tell me everything. How serious are his injuries? Where did he hit?"

"Come in here." The nurse led Kate into an office. "Sit down. Jonas arrived here about ten minutes ago. His condition is critical. He's lost a lot of blood. He hit something hard and we think he punctured his carotid."

Kate fingered her own temple. "I wish I'd been there."

"Mr. Keeley did well. He put pressure on the gash. He insisted on riding in the aid car, he kept talking to him, but Jonas never regained consciousness."

"He was a medical corpsman."

"Your father seems devastated with guilt, terror in fact."

"Will Jonas . . . does he . . . what's his blood pressure now?"

"Not good. We have blood running, but he still hasn't stabilized." The nurse placed her hand on Kate's arm. "We don't know. We're doing everything we can. Dr. Lowe is on his way. He should be here in ten minutes, and then you can ask him questions." The woman who spoke to Kate offered her hand. "I'm Wanda."

"Thanks." Kate lifted herself from the chair with effort. "I need to call my husband."

"Of course. Use this one." Wanda pointed to a phone on her desk, and left the room.

It rang repeatedly. When she returned to Jonas' bedside, Kate saw Dave bent over their son.

"How'd you hear?" Her eyes met his.

"Your mom." Dave buried his head in Kate's neck, and they clung to each other.

"I had just finished nailing the two–by–fours," Kevin spoke his first words, "on the maple. Jonas was handing me the boards. We'd finished the ladder. I—" his voice broke into a sob. "I was putting my tools in the garage. Amanda came screaming . . . she said Jonas had fallen." He shook his head. "I'll tell you later."

"Where is Amanda?" Kate said.

"With Charlotte."

"But she's with Florence today."

"It's okay." Dave caught her eye. "Amanda has priority over Florence."

Kate glanced at Kevin. She had never seen him so distraught. She felt protective and strong observing him. "Have you eaten anything, Dad?"

Kevin looked startled. "No."

"Then let's get something. We can take care of ourselves, even if we can't do anything for Jonas right now."

"I'll stay here, you go," Dave said.

Kate took a long look at Jonas. She went to her father and slid her arm through his, pulled him up. She thought she would vomit. When they reached the cafeteria, she sipped tea, and Kevin picked at a Danish roll. His face looked ancient, drawn and frightened. His mouth was set in a grim line. "I'm sorry. I was gone only a minute. He must have run up the tree."

"He's always moved like a monkey," Kate said. "Nobody blames you." But she did.

"I told Jonas he couldn't climb to the tree house until I nailed up some new boards. Today was sunny, a good day to do it." Kevin pushed his chair back, spread his legs, and bent over them. "Kate," he removed his glasses, held his head, "—I feel terrible."

"Tell me what happened." Kate glanced at her watch. She wanted to be with Jonas and Dave, but she had to know.

"I was putting the hammer away in the garage. Amanda ran in crying. She said Jonas fell out of the tree and he wouldn't move." Kate kept her eyes on Kevin's face. "I flew to him. He must have hit his head on the handlebars."

"Handlebars?"

"Amanda's trike was right where he fell."

Kate's hands flew to her cheeks. A coil of fear twisted through her. Was Dad getting old, were the kids safe with him? Amanda's *trike* was under the tree? Her thoughts were selfish, irrational. She lowered her hands to the table when she felt her dad looking at her. He had stopped talking.

"I'm listening."

"Blood was all over his face, and I . . . I couldn't find the gash at first. I took off my sweatshirt and wiped his face. I sent Amanda for a clean towel. She got it Kate, she did. Then I saw a cut about an inch long on his temple . . . deep. The blood was pouring. I kept pressure on it." Kevin stared at his fingers, folding and unfolding them. "Eight stitches." He rubbed his mouth, but didn't look at Kate.

"He came in an aid car," Kate said.

"Yes, I didn't want to move him, so I ran for the cell phone and called 911. Then I called Charlotte and she arrived first and took

Amanda," Kevin said to his lap.

"How high was he . . . when he fell?"

Kevin looked at her. "Kate, I didn't . . ."

Kate nodded. "Yeah, stupid question."

"Let's get back to them," Kevin said, pushing the Danish aside. Dave stood as they entered the room, offered his chair to Kate. "The doctor wants to give him another transfusion. He has that rare AB negative blood type. Does it matter, Kate?"

"Did I miss Dr. Lowe? What did he say?"

"No. He didn't come in yet, but the nurse talked to him."

"I think Jonas can use O positive blood," Kate said. Declining the chair, she left the room looking for Wanda. The woman stepped from a door with a unit of blood. "We're giving Jonas another transfusion, but I'm checking him first."

"Is he getting AB negative blood?" Kate looked at Wanda.

"No, but he can receive O positive just fine." Wanda entered the room in front of Kate. The men stood, joined Kate at the doorway while Wanda took Jonas' blood pressure and read his vital signs. "His blood pressure is more stable, but his pulse is weak." Wanda smiled at the anxious family. "We're treating this like a concussion."

Kate slumped against Dave, who held her. Words were futile. She closed her eyes remembering Jonas' birth, his firsts: smile, tooth, and steps. She saw his wiry little body, his red cheeks, and his shinny dark eyes. His dinosaurs had given way to softball. She forced herself to look at Jonas, at his face, his bandaged head, his cheeks, pale and barely visible beneath the wrapping, at his still mouth and body. "The longer he hangs on, the better his chances," Wanda said, securing the needle and starting the transfusion.

"Not much comfort," Kate said when Wanda had left the room.

"We can't forget Amanda," Dave said, massaging Kate's neck. She felt the tightness ease in her shoulders, felt tears seep.

"I'll leave you two alone and come back later." Kevin stood and left them.

"He's got to make it." Kate stared at Jonas. Dave touched her chin and looked at her. He stroked his thumb across her cheek, handed her a tissue. Then he lifted the covers from Jonas' feet. Kate looked at his toes.

"Just checking." Dave gently lay the covers back. "Do you want to go see Amanda or should I? One of us will stay here."

Kate sank into a chair. She twisted her watch. "When will the doctor get here?"

"It's been a half-hour since he was called and he's already ordered a second unit of blood," Dave said.

Wanda stuck her head in, then continued to check the transfusion. "Hang in there. Dr. Lowe is in close contact with the staff and will see you as soon as possible."

"Did you eat when you went to the cafeteria, Nurse Kate?" Dave raised his brows.

"You know I couldn't."

"I'll get us something and be right back. If Dr. Lowe shows, you won't miss him."

"Okay." Kate stood at the doorway and watched Dave go through the double doors until he was out of sight. The clock in the nurses' station read twelve forty-five. She gazed at bustling staff, heard the clang and clack of gurney wheels and operators paging doctors. She inhaled the disinfectant smell, usually common, but not today. Then she saw a dear face, her mother approached in the hall.

"Hello dear," Charlotte said. She didn't look at Jonas immediately. "I got here as soon as I could. Tina at day care took Amanda."

"Is she all right?"

"Scared, but all right. We'll watch her and make sure she gets lots of attention, but I had to come." Charlotte laid her coat across the chair, glanced at Jonas and stopped talking. *He looks . . . dead*, she thought. She stared at the bag and red tube. "A blood transfusion?"

"Uh–huh, number two."

"What does that mean?"

Dave returned shortly with sandwiches and coffee. "It's decaf," he said to Kate's scowl. Minutes later, a man tapped on the doorjamb. "Dr. Lowe. You're Jonas' parents?"

"Yes, yes." The couple stood together. The white haired man shook their hands, then pulled a chair closer, motioning them to sit down. He looked at Charlotte. "My mother, Charlotte Keeley," Kate said.

"Glad to meet you." The doctor shook her hand. He leaned forward folding his hands. "I'm sorry for the wait, but I've kept contact with my staff. Jonas has sustained a serious blow to the head. He has lost a considerable amount of blood. I think the transfusions are beginning to stabilize him, his blood pressure is now rising, but he's not out of danger. We'll continue to monitor him."

"Why is he still unconscious?" Kate leaned toward him.

"We aren't sure, except for the trauma to his body. Let me examine him now and I'll answer any questions I can." He didn't request that they leave, which reassured Kate. She disliked arrogant doctors when she worked with them. This man's humility she trusted. Who was he? she wondered.

Dr. Lowe examined Jonas with steady, gentle hands. He asked questions about Jonas' history. Had he had seizures, diabetes? "I think your son will respond. While the bleeding is troublesome, it has limited any internal edema, that is, fluid retention." Kate nodded. "The unconsciousness doesn't necessarily indicate brain damage."

With that, Dr. Lowe smiled. "I'll make my rounds at nine tomorrow and will give you a report. His blue eyes were kind beneath thick, brown brows. "Don't despair. Hippocrates, the father of medicine, said 'No head injury is too severe to despair of, nor too trivial to ignore.' That was in the fourth century BC. Trust life. I'm rooting for Jonas. Trust him to be well." When the doctor shook his hand, Dave observed that Dr. Lowe was younger than his white hair suggested.

The doctor left Kate staring at her half eaten sandwich while Dave dumped their coffee in the sink. Dr. Lowe had turned Jonas on his side, but he looked as still as before, except that Kate could see he was breathing okay and hadn't needed a respirator.

"I'll stay here," Charlotte said, tugging at her blouse sleeve, "if you want to see Amanda."

Seeing Kate shrug, Dave said, "Why don't I drop by the day care, see Amanda, then come back here. Kate can stay as long as she wants." Kate sighed and managed a weak smile. Dave hugged her, grabbed his coat. "I'll take her a treat," he said over his shoulder.

"All right," Kate said mechanically.

"Don't you need to get out of here?" Charlotte asked, her hand in her hair.

For a second Kate focused on a stray lock curled around Charlotte's finger. "You'll never show the gray, will you Mom."

"The gray?" Charlotte was thinking, *unconsciousness doesn't necessarily indicate brain damage.* She felt a sting of tears, swallowed, and embraced Kate.

At dusk, Charlotte twisted shut the kitchen blinds. She took a warm roll from the oven, handed it to Kate who sat at the table. "Just sit, I'll get you a refill." Charlotte poured more hot tea into Kate's mug, then kneaded her shoulders. Amanda hadn't left her mother's lap. She chewed on animal cookies, content as long as Kate held her.

"How's the response been?" Kate eyed her mother, pointed her finger at the back of Amanda's head.

"We've done well I'd say, considering everything. More subdued than usual. We had spaghetti when I got home. You can all stay here tonight, since we're close to the hospital."

"When's Jonas coming home from the hospital?"

Kate took a deep breath, closed her eyes. "As soon as he's better. The doctor wants him there, so he can take care of him."

Amanda's hands flew to her head. "Jonas cut his head . . . bad. His face was all bloody. Grandpa told him to wait, but he didn't mind. He didn't listen, so he got hurt."

Charlotte stopped her. "Yes Amanda, it must have been scary for you."

The sassiness left Amanda's face. "Cause Jonas didn't talk to me."

"Grandpa says you helped him," Kate said. "Now the doctor is helping Jonas get better. When he feels okay, you can go see him."

"Let's go have a bubble bath," Charlotte said as Kate, fighting tears, eased Amanda down.

"Mommy, you come too." Amanda tugged at her arm.

"You go with Grandma and I'll come in and wash your hair." With reluctance, Amanda slid off Kate's lap. As Charlotte left, Kate mouthed her thanks. She went into her mother's bathroom and rinsed her face, then borrowed her robe. She took the bedroom phone and called intensive care asking for Dave. Nothing had changed. Jonas was unconscious.

"Your dad invited me to stay tonight," Dave said.

"Yes, Amanda's already in Grandma's tub." Kate stepped into Charlotte's slippers and walked into the bathroom, which smelled like strawberries. She smiled at the child who sat in a tub of bubbles, smiling back, her wet curls dripping down her pink cheeks. Kate knelt and squirted the shampoo, gathering Amanda's silken hair in her fingers. The ordinary task brought her extraordinary comfort.

# Chapter 31

Todd wasn't sure what attracted him to the church, but he found a seat in the back of the sanctuary. Larry seemed amiable, but he didn't badger him about coming. He welcomed him when he attended, but didn't act as if it he'd done something horrible if he missed. Todd liked how people talked, how they used language that included him. He was one of those who lived an alternative lifestyle. Todd looked around and recognized a few faces. The people in the choir hadn't changed. Their voices sounded good with the organist. He fidgeted with his hands when Larry prayed about mending a bridge to someone who had offended. Dad. Could he ever stand next to him with equal footing, a son, but also a mature man? He dropped a five–dollar bill in the offering plate when it came past him.

He felt weird when the congregation sang the hymn, "Bring Many Names." The words sounded strange, yet they held a captivating hope for him. He sang the lyrics. *Strong mother God, planning all the wonders of creation.* God as a strong mother? A feminine God. *Warm father God, hugging every child.* A God who hugs kids like a good father. *Young, growing God, crying out for justice.* Who insists on justice. *Great living God, never fully known– everlasting home.* He didn't know what was happening, but when he finished singing, Todd felt a deep shift of weight within. I'll sort my feelings alone, no help from Larry or Trevor, he thought.

The air felt good against his face, cooling him, as he passed through the sanctuary door. He took a deep breath. The shrubs, which surrounded the church, looked lush dotted with dewdrops. He started the car, drove past the houses, along the bluff, wondering if Kate meant what she'd said. Would she bring Jonas and Amanda to Kodiak? The temperature was in the forties today, but by June, it would be warmer. Those kids were so important to him. He stopped the car at the bluff, opened the window, and inhaled the salty air. His eyes took in the surf below, his feelings changing like the rolling waves.

He shut the car door and headed out on foot along the bluff. He hummed the tune of the hymn. Instead of pacing, Todd ambled along, appreciated that Trev was a gift, the love in his life. *Strong Mother God, warm Father God.* He missed his father. What made Dad happy, afraid? He shook his head; he didn't know. His suede loafers, snug around his toes, darkened as he stepped through clumps of grass beaded with mist. He heard a seagull cry as it swooped past him. *Crying out for justice, stronger than despair.* He shuddered, felt a load lift from his body. A sense of well being overwhelmed him. Todd turned back, his steps quickened by an inner energy that was good. Enough.

Trevor stepped out of the shower glad for the heat lamp of the Motel 6. He dried, flung the towel over the rod, stepped into his Jockey shorts. After he shaved he combed and sprayed his thick hair. He hung his suit coat in the doorway and pulled his tie and shirt from the closet. He checked his watch. In ten minutes, he'd be ready for pictures.

Kate had called Thursday morning and that night Todd decided to fly home. Reaching for his suit pants that lay on the bed, Trevor's thoughts raced back to Jonas. The kid remained unconscious. He needed all the support he could get. He couldn't join Todd tonight because he was Frank's best man and felt committed. Besides, Todd needed time alone with his family. After Todd scrambled to get off for the weekend, they'd flown together to Seattle. Then Todd had flown to Portland, he to Idaho.

Trevor cocked his head at the dimly lighted mirror as he buttoned his shirt and tied the blue tie that matched his eyes. He slid his arms into the charcoal suit coat, which emphasized his thick, dark hair. Frank will be married in a few hours, he thought. Grinning at his reflection, he felt thankful he didn't have to wear a tux. He locked the door, wondered how busy this burg was on a Friday night, and gave an address to the hotel clerk who called a cab.

Todd declined the soft drink and stared at the wing of the plane outside the window. It was cold at this altitude and he noticed the window itself, the icy etchings in the rounded corners. He propped his elbow in the space between his seat and the sill, placing the dinky pillow under it. He pushed his hair back with his palm. How long, he mulled, can a person be out without permanent damage? This wasn't fair to Kate and Dave, certainly to Jonas, who was just a kid, for God's sake. Could he please be awake when he arrived?

Jonas was the darling in the family, at least to his grandfather. Was it because he favored him in appearance? Those deep–set brown eyes, and the straight dark hair, short and neat, not long like his. Was Jonas like a son, a real boy who made Kevin feel pride? Already into softball, Kate had written in his birthday card. Dad had played catch with me too, when I was a kid, Todd thought, enrolled me in Little League, but when I showed no interest in sports, he backed off. Did he wish he hadn't? Did he think a boy wasn't okay if he wasn't an athlete?

The plane swerved knocking Todd's elbow off its perch and the seatbelt sign lit up and chimed. His fingers checked the fastened buckle as he leaned the back of his head against the seat. Sometime when I was in my teens, Dad backed off or did I? I worked my damnedest completing my scouting activities, earning my eagle. Todd tightened his grip on the seat arms. *That's* when Dad withdrew, he remembered now. The phony, what did he want? He wanted his reputation; he didn't want his precious position tarnished. A Boy Scout leader with a *gay son.*

A deep anguish erupted in Todd. He remembered how the troop kids had called him a faggot; remembered the way he looked at them, how he felt about a few of the guys, but never admitted his feelings. No one had caught him, no one could be sure if he was or wasn't. He hadn't yet tried dating girls. He earned his eagle award, then got the hell out of scouts. When Dad decided I wasn't right sexually, Todd thought, he decided I wasn't right at all. Yet, neither of them had said a word. Why do the wounds feel so fresh now? he wondered. Because I feel sick about Jonas, sick, worried, and scared.

At the airport, Todd hailed a taxi giving the driver a motel address near the hospital. He felt dreary and alone as he entered the room. No answer when he dialed Kate. When he heard what must have been the tenth ring, Todd hung up. He smelled the Chinese food wafting from a restaurant nearby, so he walked to it and ordered a meal. He'd hoped Kate would invite him to stay with her. He could babysit with Amanda, shop or do laundry. He felt so bad. This must be tough for Kate. After eating, he returned to the sparse room, brushed his teeth and called the hospital where Kate worked. Jonas would be there.

When Todd arrived in the ICU waiting room, it was vacant and quiet except for a TV turned to half volume. He approached the double doors, entered and took a deep breath. The nurse's station looked deserted too. He waited after he noticed a woman writing at a desk. Her face was broad and kind, tired looking with traces of makeup left on her eyelashes and lips. A few strands of her strawberry hair had escaped the hair clip and hung at the side of her cheeks. She glanced up. Her light–brown eyes smiled receptively. "May I help you?"

"Yes. I'm here to see Jonas Winston." Todd noticed the name, Wanda, on her lapel. She hesitated a second. "I'm his uncle, my name's Todd, his mother's my sister."

Wanda's face brightened. "Oh, glad you came. Nobody's visiting now, so this is a good time for you to see Jonas. You know he's unconscious."

"Yes." Todd swallowed. "Still?"

"Unfortunately, progress is very gradual, but we are expecting him to awaken. It's important, it helps if you will hold that thought too. I'll show you his room."

Somehow, Todd felt reverent as he followed the woman into the room, which the bed light dimly lit. When Wanda left, he stood near the bed, his eyes on Jonas. Dear God, he looked awful. Todd studied his face, exposed except for the small gauze dressing on his temple, which hid one eye. Todd noticed the red carnations on the bed tray, pushed away from the bed. When his eyes adjusted, he saw a sink in the corner. He went to it, squirted the antiseptic soap on his hands, scrubbed, then dried and rubbed them together until they were warm. He hesitantly touched Jonas' cheek with his fingertips and felt an urgent surge in his stomach. "I'll throw Frisbees with you again, Jonas. I'll take you to the beach, help you with your homework. I'll convince your mom to let me. I'll do anything." He grasped the raised railing on the bed, closed his eyes. God, just let him wake up.

When Todd opened his eyes, he stared at the bag of sucrose, which silently dripped through the tube into Jonas' arm. He leaned over the boy, determined. "Bet you'd prefer pizza or spaghetti, huh Jonas? We want you back, sport. We're not letting you go. Wake up kid."

He walked around the bed and eased into a chair. On a shelf high on the wall opposite Jonas, he saw a softball, within Jonas' line of vision if—when—he opened his eyes. He couldn't make out what the item next to it was so he got up, examined it, discovering a model dinosaur. He fingered the blanket that covered Jonas, felt a thick lump near the kid's still hand. Todd lifted the cover exposing a catcher's mitt. He swallowed hard, replaced the cover, and dropped into the chair, pulling a handkerchief from his Khakis.

He heard voices, footsteps in the hall. "I don't want to do this again. I think someone should always be with him in case—" The voice was Kate's and she stopped talking when she walked into the room and saw Todd. Their eyes locked for a second. "How long have you been here?" Kate asked, now surrounded by Kevin, Charlotte, and Dave who had followed her into the room.

"Here? About ten minutes," Todd said, moving his wrist to see his watch. "I've been in town about an hour and a half." He stood, took Kate in his arms. She hugged him back, pressing her head into his sweater. "I'm terribly sor . . ."

"I knew you would be. Thanks for coming." Todd extended his hand to Kevin who grasped it, and his mother hugged him as fully as Kate had.

"We appreciate your visit." Dave put his arm across his shoulder.

"Is this too many visitors?"

"It's okay for short periods." Kate sat down in the chair closest to Jonas. Next to her, Todd noticed Jonas' fingers, uncovered. Hadn't he covered his arm? Had Jonas moved his hand? Todd wondered, but didn't speak.

"Tonight Kevin took us out for dinner," Charlotte said. "Ordinarily one of us is here with Jonas, except in the middle of the night."

Kate twisted sideways to look at her brother "All my training about taking care of yourself. It's a lot harder when the patient is your child." Her smile was bleak.

Kevin walked to the other side of the bed with Charlotte who said, "Come on, dearest boy, wake up, we're all here." She leaned over, kissed Jonas' cheek, and Kate put a tissue to her nose. Todd thought Jonas' fingers trembled. He glanced up at Kevin whose eyes had seen it too and now held his.

Dave missed it, shuffled his feet, and gestured to Todd with his hand. "Would you like a cup of coffee while the women stay?" He included Kevin with a gesture and the three men left the room.

When they had bought their coffee and found a table, Todd scanned Dave's face. "Tell me the prognosis." He glanced at Kevin who didn't respond and then back to Dave.

"Well, it's over forty–eight hours now. If things haven't changed in two days, we've been told," Dave cleared his throat, "he could have brain damage."

"I have to say something." Todd placed his elbows on the table as he fingered a sugar packet. "Has Jonas responded with physical movement at all?"

"Nothing but a twitch, now and then." Dave eyed him. "Why?"

"Because," Todd glanced at Kevin who now was watching him, "before you guys came in, I felt a bump under the blanket, so I checked it out and saw the mitt, then I covered Jonas' arm back." Dave listened; they both stared at him. "I noticed that his hand was uncovered just now, and when Charlotte kissed him, it shook a bit." *Dammit, why doesn't Dad speak up? He saw it too.*

Dave folded his hands, lowered his head. "I want to believe you, if only . . ."

"I thought his hand moved too," Kevin said. "I wasn't sure and I didn't want to start any false hopes."

"You too. Tonight, just now?" Dave lit up.

"Yes," Kevin said, and Todd nodded.

"Then what the hell are we doing here?" Dave jumped up and

angled his way through the tables to the elevator. Todd and Kevin followed. When the door opened on the ICU floor, Kate almost crashed into him as Dave stepped out.

"Jonas moved his arm, he moved his arm," Kate shrieked.

"Hot damn! Why are you out in the hall?"

"To find you," Kate cried back punching him in the ribs.

Kevin felt his chest rise. He followed them into the room, took a deep breath, saw his wife's face, an angel, he thought. She knew how guilty he felt, how helpless. She had supported him. Bent over Jonas' blood pressure cuff, Wanda looked up. Her eyes smiled and circled the room, including everyone. Kevin felt a weight lift as he watched Charlotte's body relax against her chair. He noticed the earnestness in Todd's face.

Wanda wrote some figures in Jonas' chart and felt the family's eyes focused on her. "This is good news. Jonas' blood pressure is close to normal," she said. "I didn't see him move his arm, but I believe you and it's a hopeful sign that more will come." Wanda felt the electricity in the room, and couldn't bear to add that movements are sometimes involuntary and spasmodic. She moved Jonas to his side, straightened his linens, bent over his head. "Way to go champ. Your family is here and very proud of you. Keep it up. Your Grandpa can't wait to pitch you some curves." Wanda picked up the mitt and tossed it to Kevin. "You can give it back to him tomorrow. My shift is over, and I want his bed cleared when I leave. He moved his right hand, so it must have helped."

Todd gazed at Wanda as she left, her hair mussed, her walk weary, and her face peaceful. No wonder Kate liked nursing. So many people counted on you, loved you for what you did. He watched Kevin lift Charlotte's coat from the chair, and hold it for her. "I think we're ready to go home, aren't we?" Kevin said.

A tired smile spread across Charlotte's face. "Yes." Then to Todd, "How long are you in town?"

"Just the weekend. I wanted to see Jonas and add my moral support." He watched Kevin as he pushed chairs aside, zipped his jacket.

Observing her father, Kate said, "Maybe we can get together for lunch, Todd. We have to eat, and we're here every day anyway."

"Yeah, I'll call you, or see you here tomorrow." Todd inspected his shoes and backed toward the doorway. "I'm so glad Jonas wiggled a little."

"Me too." Kate gave Todd a sideways hug.

Kevin walked to the door, and shook Todd's hand. "Good seeing you, Todd." His mother hugged him. Then they were gone. Todd waited a minute, then made his exit, hailed a taxi, and stepped out of it in front of his motel. Good seeing you too, Mr. Keeley, Todd thought one more time, before he fell asleep.

Jonas' parents watched their son's face, illuminated by the soft light over the hospital bed. "I gather we're not sleeping at your folks tonight." Dave rubbed his chin.

"No, I told Mom I thought we would go home tonight. She's getting Amanda from Tina and we need to stop and take Amanda home. Okay?"

"Of course." Dave placed his hand on Kate's knee. She touched the dark hairs around his knuckles, looked into his tired eyes.

"Do you think the mitt helped?"

"I think everything helps . . . thoughts, prayers, words, touching, and yes, even physical things like mitts. I'm glad your dad brought that mitt. He seemed pleased with Wanda's response, comforted. Maybe Jonas does know it's next to him. Is that the mitt he leaves at Gramps house?"

Kate nodded. Dave took her hand, pulled her against him as they went to Jonas' side. He kissed his son, and then Kate took Jonas' face in her hands, kissed his cheek and stroked his arms. "We'll see you tomorrow, sweetheart. We love you."

Dave drove to the Keeley home where he gathered a sleeping Amanda in his arms. He gently placed her in Kate's lap. Kate pulled the seatbelt around both of them, cradling Amanda until they arrived home, where they fell exhausted into bed.

When Charlotte awoke Saturday morning, she crept out of bed while Kevin snored. She called the hospital which gave her fresh hope. Jonas had stirred in the night, moved his legs. It seemed early to call Kate, so she brewed some coffee. She made toast, took it with her coffee into her sewing room and sat down in the wicker chair.

Thoughts of last night troubled her. She and Kevin were exhausted from stress as were Kate and Dave, but Kevin was barely civil to Todd. He treated Todd like an outsider, an intruder. She couldn't ignore his behavior anymore. Todd was her son too.

She looked at a snapshot of Kate. She's right, Charlotte thought. I do support Kevin even when I disagree with him. I want to preserve our relationship at all costs. I'm afraid of a fight, of losing Todd and Kevin. What intimacy would I lose by finding out what's bothering Kevin?

The morning light peeked into the room when Charlotte opened the curtains. She could see the bumper of Debbie's Mazda across the street and remembered Florence. She pictured her balding head as she tended her flowers, the earth she flicked from her nails when she rubbed her knotted fingers. The woman's words exploded into Charlotte's mind like a command. "It don't matter one whit that your son is gay, just love him." She must confront Kevin. As soon as Jonas moved out of critical care, she would.

# Chapter 32

Todd arrived before dawn at the hospital. "Your nephew caused some cheering around here last night," a tall nurse told him when Todd had identified himself at the ICU station. "He moved his legs and his blood pressure is steady. His pulse is stronger too."

"Whew, what a relief. What are his chances for complete recovery?" Todd flipped his hair back.

"It's encouraging, but save your questions for Dr. Lowe. He comes around about ten on Saturdays. The night nurse notified Jonas' parents, since they had requested a call if anything changed. Your sister and mother called this morning, but you're the first one here."

"Suppose they're exhausted from the stress," Todd said, tapping the counter.

"It's tough. We allow twenty–four hour visiting in ICU for intimate family. People call at three in the morning because they can't sleep and need to talk."

Todd weighed that a moment. "Yeah, it's a worry."

"Did you come from a distance?" the man asked, pulling a pen from his white coat.

"Alaska. I'm here for a couple days." Todd looked at the nurse's red hair, the freckles on his face and hands.

The man wrote something in a chart while Todd studied his hair. When he felt Todd's stare, he glanced up. "You okay? You're welcome to go to Jonas' room now."

"Yeah, fine. Thanks, I will." Todd stepped into the hall and walked into Jonas' room. He bent over Jonas, touched his cheek, which felt soft, but looked nothing like its usual rosy color. Todd sank into a chair, feeling heavy, as if a harness surrounded his chest. He saw the mitt and softball on the shelf. Would Jonas pitch and catch balls again? Would Jonas be the athlete he never was? A new bag of sucrose was dripping into the boy's arm. Todd watched each droplet fall as gradually as the morning light crept beyond the edges of the drapes.

Jonas' hand stirred. Todd jumped from his chair and spoke in Jonas' ear. "Good, Jonas, wake up. This is Uncle Todd. I want you to be okay. You can do it, I know you can." He stroked Jonas' cheek, rubbed his free arm. "Your softball is waiting for you." He got the mitt and placed it near his nephew's hand. "Here's your mitt. Gramps brought it for you."

Then Todd dropped into the chair, wiped his eyes. He had loved the tree house too, had escaped there to read. Often he would watch the clouds change shape on a sunny day or just hide from his sister and her silly friends. Freckle–faced Susanne was the girl he'd liked. Fun, yet serious, she'd made him think. Todd had laughed at her when she told him she didn't care if he knew she was smart. She had encouraged him in marine biology, a girl full of life and love. Then dating took her away. He'd had no romantic interest in her; rather he'd fantasized about the boys at the pool. He'd never made any passes, but he would have if he weren't so scared.

Todd glanced up when the tall nurse walked in. "My name's Jeremy if you need something."

"Thanks, Jeremy. Jonas moved his hand."

"Great, keep talking to him." Jeremy opened the drapes and then placed a cuff around Jonas' arm. "Hmm, I suppose this mitt can't hurt either." He chuckled, giving it a thump. "You'd be amazed what people can remember when they regain consciousness."

Todd stood up. "I'll talk to him." He bent over Jonas. "I'm going for some breakfast, Jonas, but I'll be back to see you later. Keep wiggling." Todd looked at Jeremy. "He's through with the blood transfusions, isn't he?"

"According to his chart, his blood supply is okay. This is my first day with him. I work weekends. I have a nephew too, so I can imagine how you're feeling."

Todd doubted whether Jeremy had a clue how he felt, but he said, "Yeah, thanks." He took the elevator to the lower floor, found the cafeteria and ordered orange juice, coffee, and scrambled eggs with toast.

Jonas had enough blood. That was good. He'd never donated blood before, knew he couldn't, although Jonas' same rare type coursed in his veins. It didn't matter to the blood banks whether donors were promiscuous or not, only that they were straight. They didn't want a gay person's blood. Todd understood that. He didn't want to give AIDS to anyone, so he didn't donate, but he didn't have the dread disease. Neither he nor Trevor was HIV positive. He trusted Trev. What else could he do? It didn't make sense to him that heterosexuals could donate and he could not, given the tremendous need.

Todd ate his breakfast, bought a paper and returned to the ICU waiting room to read it. He skimmed one article, then another. Laying the newspaper across his lap, he looked around the room noting the comfortable chairs, magazines, and peaceful mountain scenes on the walls, a phone and a TV in opposite corners. Except for him, it was a vacant, silent place. Where are they? Where's the doctor? His watch read ten o'clock.

He walked back into Jonas' room, stood beside him, his hand on the side railing. He glanced at the tube in his arm. "Hi Jonas, I see you've finished half of your breakfast." He lifted the covers, found the mitt, smiled and patted it. "No school today, Jonas. How's your sister? I haven't seen her for a long time."

He heard a gasp as Kate stepped into the room. "You surprised me. How is he?"

"He moved his hand this morning, so I've been, uh, talking to him."

"Thanks Todd. The nurse said he moved his legs in the night. Waiting is awful." Kate laid her hand on Jonas' forehead, kissed his cheek. "Don't you think his color is better today?"

Todd didn't. "I don't know, I haven't seen him as often as you have. How is Amanda doing?"

"Okay. Kids are amazing. I told her the doctors were helping Jonas get better and she seems to accept that she can't see him. Dave's with her now for some quality time."

"How's Dad taking this? I understand from what you said that he was there when Jonas fell."

Kate looked at Todd. "He blames himself that Jonas got up the tree without his supervision."

"Yeah, I can imagine. I was nine when Dad and I built the tree house. Jonas wanted me to go up with him when it was slippery. It's a compelling tree for kids."

"I remember how you loved it, Todd. So did I. Jonas couldn't wait to be old enough to go alone, and now that spring is here—"

"He's going to be okay."

"But Todd, he'll be brain damaged if he doesn't wake up soon."

"Not necessarily," said a voice in the doorway.

"Dr. Lowe, I'm glad to see you." Kate brightened. "This is my brother, Todd."

"Pleased to meet you," Dr. Lowe said and went to Jonas. "I've been briefed on Jonas' activity during the night. His blood pressure is good, his pulse is stronger, and his color is improved."

"See." Kate spun around to face Todd. "I knew it."

"These signs are important, Kate." Dr. Lowe smiled at her exuberance. "If your son has the spunk you do, I expect his full recovery."

"You are new here, aren't you?"

"That's right, two weeks ago I arrived from New Jersey."

"Welcome," Kate said.

"I understand you are on staff here in cardiology."

"Yes I am." Kate gave a surprised smile to Dr. Lowe. "Nursing staff, that is."

Kate glanced toward the hall as Jeremy walked past with a frantic woman. "I need to go now," Dr. Lowe said. "I'll return this afternoon. Keep talking to Jonas."

"That woman must have an emergency," Todd said, as Dr. Lowe left them.

"It makes me shudder." Kate winced. She looked at the sucrose bag that hung all but empty.

"The nurse will bring one soon, I'm sure," Todd said. "Could I help out with Amanda today?" Maybe take her for ice cream or just sit with her?"

"Look, he turned his head," Kate almost shouted, not hearing Todd's question. Todd looked at Jonas, who now faced the window.

"Good Jonas, wake up. We're here." Kate kissed him and touched his matted hair.

"I'm so glad he's moving." Todd smiled at his sister.

"What's the commotion?" Jeremy asked as he entered the room.

"He moved his head." Kate sounded ecstatic.

"Hurrah." Jeremy smiled at them as he replaced the sucrose bag. "He's better off than the kid I just left."

"What happened?" Todd asked.

Jeremy moved from Jonas' hearing into the hall and Todd followed. "The boy was thrown from a car when it hit a telephone pole. The cousin who was driving was hurt too, but not gravely. The tyke has suffered massive internal injuries." Jeremy moved back into the room, shaking his head. "He's three."

"How do you stick with it?" Todd looked at Jeremy.

"That's how," the nurse said pointing to Jonas who that moment moved his fingers. Kate also witnessed it.

"His eyelashes fluttered too . . . did you see them?" Kate twirled around. "Stay here, Todd, I'm going to call Dave."

"Here's a phone," Jeremy said, but Kate was already down the hall.

"She wants privacy," Todd said.

Jeremy nodded, then went to Jonas. "Hang in there, young man." He rolled him over, replaced his sheet, turned him again and smoothed the covers. "Your family loves you, Jonas. They're counting on you to get well. Me too." He squeezed the boy's feet.

"Did you see his eyes move?" Todd asked.

"No, but that doesn't mean they didn't. Don't discourage Kate's hope. I swear it helps our patient. Any movement is significant. I'll be checking again." Jeremy walked out.

What a sensitive man, Todd thought. Left alone with his nephew, he leaned over his ear. "Jonas, when you are well, I promise I'll spend more time with you. You're important to me. You've taught me about myself." He sat silently for awhile.

"Did he do anything else?" Kate stood in the threshold.

"Nothing else, but keep up your patience. Is Dave coming?"

"Yes, when he finishes the laundry, he's taking Amanda to a playmate's house."

"Oh," Todd said. Kate didn't need his help with Amanda. "How does Dave like his office?"

"Fine. He'll be on his own soon."

"Yeah, the bridge is Dad's last big effort before retirement, I guess. He and Dave seem close. He appears proud of Dave."

Kate looked at her brother a second. "Yes he is." Todd moved two chairs and they sat down. Kate took a deep breath. "I don't have the energy to talk about Dad now."

"Okay."

"Todd, I know I haven't called you. Is Trevor all right?"

"He's fine. Last night he was best man at his brother's wedding."

"So he has a brother. Where?"

"Idaho is where he was married. I don't know where they're going to live. Trevor hadn't seen him in fifteen years until last Christmas."

Todd stopped talking when he heard voices in the hall. His father came into the room with Charlotte behind him. "Hello Todd. You're still here, I see."

"Hi," Todd said. Yes, I'm *still* here.

Kevin picked up the softball and tossed it gently into the air while Charlotte smacked Todd on the cheek. "We're so glad for the progress," she said. "Dave called us. Any other changes?" Everyone turned toward Jonas who didn't respond.

"He moved his head and his hands. He almost opened his eyes." Kate gave Jonas an earnest stare. "Didn't you, Son. Wiggle your fingers for Gramps and Grams."

Jonas lay still. His family surrounded him as Kevin wrapped Jonas' hand around the ball and held it there. Without a word, they watched Jonas' fingers quiver again. Todd swallowed, felt a mix of joy and yearning.

When Dave joined the circle, Todd felt apprehensive, uncertain how he would interact with everyone. In a surge of emotion, he said, "I'm going out for some fresh air." He left the ICU, walked out into the spring weather. He had to walk, run, or something. Why couldn't Kevin love him as he did Jonas? He felt it; he saw it. Trevor is right, he thought. I've wanted approval all my life. He paced the sidewalk, crushed the cherry blossoms beneath his feet. He passed a bank and a bakery, finally stopping at a deli that had a telephone.

"How'd the wedding go, Trev?" he said into the receiver.

"Hey, Todd, without a hitch. Maria's a beauty. What's happening with Jonas?"

"A little progress. He's starting to wake up I think, but it's slow."

"You okay?"

"Yeah," Todd said, pushing his hair back. "I'm out of here by tomorrow night unless something drastic happens. Jonas is coming around."

"Glad to hear it. I miss you. At the wedding, Scott and Anna said hello. See you soon."

Todd found a table inside the deli, ordered a bowl of chili. Even Trev has fixed his relationship with Frank, he moaned, swallowing a spoonful of chili. When Todd finished his meal, he walked for forty minutes, a mulch of misery. Arriving at his motel, he went inside, lay on the bed and stared at the ceiling fixture. Here I go again feeling sorry for myself, Todd thought. Jonas struggles for consciousness while I mope in a motel. I'm so damn good at running away. He got up, splashed his face, zipped his jacket and left the motel on foot. The cool afternoon air cleared his mind and in a half–hour, arriving at the ICU room, he found Kate sitting with Jonas.

"Where've you been?" Kate's face had a quizzical expression. "You missed the excitement. Jonas opened his eyes. We all saw him."

"Great, that's great, Kate."

"Dr. Lowe came by," Kate said. "He's encouraged by the progress, but says Jonas has a ways to go. Dad and Mom went to get Amanda. I thought we were having lunch together, but it got so late, I gave up on you."

"I needed some air, so I took a walk. Sorry." Todd shoved his hands in his pockets.

"I brought you a Coke," Dave said, entering the room. "Oh, hi Todd. Glad you're back." He sat, looked at Jonas, then at Todd. "Kate tell you?"

"Yes, wonderful news."

"It takes the edge off our apprehension," Dave said, his brown eyes on Todd. "I want to say this too. I know I've been a class A jerk toward you . . . not calling."

"Thanks, but I could have called too. I feel like a lousy fifth wheel in this family."

"Could you take your discussion elsewhere?" Kate frowned, pointing toward Jonas.

"Let's get you a drink." Dave wiped his beard and the men left. At the empty waiting room, Todd stopped. "Sit down, I don't want anything."

"Fine." Dave took a chair, so did Todd. "Your dad is a bigger jerk than me," Dave said. "I admit I let him influence me and I'm sorry. You're as important in this family as anyone else is. If you feel like a fifth wheel, you'll have to work it out, because you're not."

# Chapter 33

Late Saturday afternoon Kevin's eyes scanned his home office admiring the photos of buildings, his favorite architectural designs. He moved the papers on his desk, plopped his elbows. As he massaged his forehead, he stared at the ancient collage of childhood snapshots beneath the glass. He studied a picture of Stephen and him, four and two, in a rowboat with their father, one of his grandparents standing with Stephen and him in their Vermont yard. He loved these boyhood pictures: flying down a snowy hill on their sled; young men in their army fatigues. Kevin looked at a picture of his nine–year–old son on his lap in the tree house. Todd was a spitting image of Steve at the same age, he thought. Why did he have to show up at the hospital now when I have enough guilt? Jonas, you have to make it. Kevin held his head. What's the matter with me? Am I too old to watch Kate's kids? Why didn't Jonas wait for me?

Charlotte closed the kitchen door behind Dave when he came to get Amanda. She felt drained, glad for the reprieve, yet grateful for Amanda, with her teapot rhyme, her books, and her gift of diversion from the worrisome wait. She put the teakettle on the burner, took a casserole from the refrigerator and placed it in the oven. When the kettle whistled, she made herself a cup of tea, sat for ten minutes, her feet up on the kitchen chair. Then she opened the den door, stuck her head in the room. "I wondered where you were."

"Here I am," Kevin said vaguely.

"I've made some tea. Do you want a cup?"

"No, I'll wait for dinner."

"Are you going with me to the hospital tonight? I hope to visit with Todd."

"Why don't you go without me." Kevin glanced at his wife. His dark eyes looked hollow, she thought, but she felt depleted of patience.

"What's wrong with you, Kevin? Todd cared enough to show up for Jonas, can't we have the decency to welcome him. Things are turning around for our grandson, but we have a son too."

"I'm glad Jonas is getting well, but that doesn't mean things are changing with Todd."

"Fine, if that's how you feel. We are due for a talk, but not tonight. There's some leftover casserole in the oven. I'll be at the hospital." Before Kevin could speak, Charlotte shut the door, grabbed her purse and coat, and headed for the hospital.

Kevin dished up chicken and pasta, ate it, rinsed his bowl and placed it in the dishwasher. When he turned on the porch light for Charlotte, he picked up the newspaper. After reading it for a half–hour, he heard a knock on the front door. He opened it and saw Todd standing on the step, one hand over his eyes shielding them from the light bulb. "Hello Todd. What happened?"

"Nothing. I didn't see Jonas tonight. You were there when he opened his eyes, right?" Todd flipped back his hair, golden in the porch light.

"Yes, yes." Kevin moved out of the doorway. "Come in. You must have caught a bus."

"Yes, I did."

"Do you want something?"

Todd shut the door, walked to a chair. "As a matter-of-fact, yes." Kevin felt threatened as he moved toward the couch and sat opposite Todd.

"This isn't easy for me," Todd said, "but I think . . . it's time we had an understanding." His green eyes penetrated Kevin's being.

Kevin crossed his arms and Todd saw his jaw tighten. "What kind of understanding?"

"I'm a grown man, Dad. Please accept that. I'm gay. A grown gay man and it's not going to change."

"I accept you," Kevin said, his lips tight. "Don't ask me to accept your gay choice."

"Choice? You're telling me my sexuality is a choice." Todd kept his gaze steady. "Then you chose to be straight. When did you do that? You don't accept me. You accept an image you have of me in your head. It isn't me." Todd's face tensed, his eyes darkened. "It never will be."

"Gay sex is plain immoral, Son."

"Son? Don't you dare call me son if that's how you feel."

"The Scriptures say homosexuality is wrong."

"The Scriptures oppress women and sanction slavery. Jesus said nothing about homosexuality. Nothing."

"Let's try to get along."

"Try to get along. Right. It doesn't work. What I need—" Todd's voice broke, "—is your love."

Kevin felt helpless at Todd's intensity. "I think we're anxious about Jonas. This isn't the time for us—"

"This time is as good as any, Dad." Todd's green eyes implored. "Yes, God help us, Jonas is involved because I know how much you love him. I love him too. He's why I'm here." Todd struggled for control. Kevin didn't speak. "Don't worry, it's not contagious. Jonas won't turn queer." *Mistake,* he thought. Todd drew a breath and searched the walls for words. "What I mean is being gay is natural for me, not for you." He looked at his father. "I think you loved me when I was Jonas' age," Todd took a breath and studied his knees, "but when you found out I was gay, you couldn't stand it. What would your church friends say? A Boy Scout leader whose son lusts for males?"

"Stop it." Kevin averted his eyes.

Todd fought back tears, turned silent for a moment. Then in a controlled tone said, "So you pretended I didn't exist, *pretend* I don't exist. I think you see me as a sex act instead of a person. My feelings for Trevor are more than sex. They're about loving someone who loves me. About sharing our lives."

Kevin blew a breath past his lips when he saw Charlotte enter the kitchen. "When did you get home?"

"Right now. Obviously I walked in where I'm not wanted." She moved a dining room chair into the middle of the living room and sat down. "Hello Todd," she said concealing her surprise at seeing him. "We've all been dealing with plenty of stress, but I have good news." She looked at Kevin and Todd. "Jonas opened his eyes tonight for several minutes and lifted his arm." Charlotte noticed Todd's eyes, fervent with feeling, but not because of Jonas.

"Was Dave there?" Kevin said.

"No, just Kate and I. Dr. Lowe left a few minutes ago, and is encouraged with Jonas' progress."

"Can he talk?" Todd flipped back his hair and looked at his mother.

"Hasn't talked yet, but the doctor thinks that he should soon."

The tension had dissipated some, Charlotte sensed. "Let's celebrate. I have frozen yogurt," she said, dismissing her own irritation with the men.

Kevin rubbed his arms, stood up. "I'll help you."

"Yeah, sounds good. I'll eat some for Jonas," Todd said.

Dave rushed to answer the phone after tucking Amanda in bed. "Hello?"

"Oh Dave." Kate sobbed.

"What?"

"I'm so happy. Jonas opened his eyes and looked at me. Dr. Lowe thinks he's going to be all right."

"What a relief. Are you coming home?"

"In a few minutes."

"You must be exhausted. Thanks for calling and drive carefully." Dave cradled his head in his arms on the counter, feeling a weary joy flow through him. Jonas, you're back. Come completely back to us. I want to see you, he thought. He dialed the hospital room. "Wait a minute, I'm coming."

"What about Amanda?"

"I'll get your Mom."

"Okay."

When he heard Charlotte's voice, Dave said, "Can you babysit with Amanda while I run to the hospital?"

She eyed Todd. "Todd's here, would it be okay if he came?" Todd nodded his willingness.

"Does he have wheels?"

"No, but I'll drop him off, if you'll take him to the motel later."

"Fine. See you soon."

"You just volunteered to stay with Amanda." Charlotte smiled at Todd. Her expression to Kevin was defiant.

"Yeah, I guessed that Dave wanted to see Jonas," Todd said.

While Charlotte and Todd exited through the back door, Kevin clicked a spoon against his bowl stirring his melted yogurt. He put the dirty dishes in the sink. Had Jonas seen his softball or felt his mitt, he wondered. Bring anything that would make him remember, the doctor had told them. Kevin retreated to the den where he examined the picture of his brother again, who looked back with his green eyes. Kevin studied the high forehead and blond hair. Essentially, I've lost Steve. Have I lost Todd too, by some failure of fatherhood? He felt a wave of nausea at the memory of his exchange with Todd.

Jonas' accident had stirred the guilty plague he'd carried since Stephen's disappearance, memories he'd abandoned for nearly fifty years. He'd told Charlotte years ago about Steve's disappearance. She knew they served together in Okinawa, but he hadn't elaborated and she hadn't pried. He'd told his parents only that Steve was missing. He wondered now, will the thought forever haunt me that if I'd been present I could have stopped the violence?

Kevin closed his eyes, his mind filling with images of Todd in bed with Trevor; he felt sick and frightened. Todd's accusation weighed on him. Do I see my son in terms of a sexual act? Do I define him as immoral by definition, based on his sexual orientation alone?

Kevin stood, closed the room door behind him, and sat down again, his mind on Jonas. You rascal, he thought. You've come back to us. He reached into his pocket, then the tears came, soaking his handkerchief, bringing a release he hadn't felt since he saw Jonas, stone still under the maple tree.

Dave opened his kitchen door. "Thanks for helping me out, Todd. I'm like a kid, very excited. Don't worry, Amanda's asleep."

"I'm thrilled too," Charlotte said, "I understand why you want to see Jonas tonight." She noticed Todd looked earnest, as confident as she could remember him. Well. Everyone needs to feel needed.

When she returned home, Charlotte let the garage door bang her presence. She found Kevin in his chair, showered and in his pajamas. He looked calmer than when she'd left. Standing behind him, she put her arms around his neck. "Are you relieved?"

He raised his head, nuzzled it against her breasts. "I can't tell you how much." Charlotte kissed his bald spot.

# Chapter 34

Wanda reported for duty early Sunday, her turn for a weekend shift. She read with care Jonas' chart before entering his room. "Hey, Jonas, I hear you opened your eyes last night. Will you talk to us today?" She wrapped the blood pressure cuff around his arm and recorded a normal pressure. As she hung a full sucrose bag on the stand, the empty bag slipped from her hand and sent her clipboard crashing to the floor.

"What was that?" Jonas' eyes popped open.

"I dropped something that made a noise. My name's Wanda." She touched Jonas, whose eyes had closed again. "You fell from a tree and are in the hospital. We're taking care of you until you feel better." Wanda's voice was melodic with joy, but he didn't respond. She picked up the used bag, tossed it in the trash and left the room. She stopped Jeremy in the hall. "Jonas thinks I'm too rowdy."

"Huh?"

"My clipboard fell and he said, 'What was that?' "

"Way to go, Wanda."

"I'm calling his mom."

"Now? It's six o' clock Sunday morning." Then he grinned. "Yes, call, they'll be ecstatic."

"You're learning." Wanda patted his arm. "I'm sorry your three year old died."

"I feel sad for his parents and glad for some good news." Wanda shook her head and continued to her office.

"Jonas talked this morning. The nurse called me. I couldn't wait to tell you," Kate sang into the receiver.

"I'm so happy dear," Kevin said as he sat up in bed. Charlotte rolled her head toward him. "Kate," Kevin said looking at Charlotte. "Jonas spoke."

"Let me talk to her." Charlotte took the phone. "What did he say, Kate?"

"Wanda dropped something and he said, 'What was that?' "

"Good for him. We'll see you later. Glad you called." Charlotte snuggled against Kevin. "I'll make some coffee while you sleep."

"Okay. What good news."

Kate leaped into her jeans. "I think I'll eat a bagel and go right to the hospital, since I'm too excited to sleep anymore."

"Sounds good." Dave stretched and rolled over. "I'll feed Amanda and you can call me from the hospital."

When Kate passed the guestroom, Todd stirred. "Something wrong?"

"No, something's right. Jonas spoke a whole sentence this morning. I'm going to see him. How'd you sleep?"

"Fine. Thanks for the bed."

"Glad to have you. Sorry we were so late. You'll have to pay for your motel room too. Want to come with me?"

"Do I get a quick shower first to wake me up?"

"Okay, I'll toast you a bagel. Use the main bathroom because Dave's sleeping. The towels are in the bathroom cupboard. I think you'll find a new toothbrush too, but hurry. I want to leave before Amanda wakes up."

Together they greeted Wanda who walked with them to Jonas' room. "We are elated," Wanda said. "Jonas' question was rational and it indicates he can hear." Wanda gave them her warm smile and left them alone.

Todd took the mitt from the shelf, stuck his fingers into it, and then laid it near Jonas' hand. Kate blinked. "Do you think he'll be all right, you know, that everything will work okay?"

"I hope so." Todd tossed his hair back. "It's best to keep that idea, right, Jonas?" He walked to the railing. Jonas' face looked pinker, Todd thought, the fresh bandage smaller. As Todd observed, Jonas opened his brown eyes.

"Uncle Todd."

"Hi Jonas." Todd's eyes flew to Kate who stepped to his side, where their faces hovered over the boy. Jonas didn't speak again and his eyes closed.

"I'm leaving today on a three o'clock flight." Todd motioned Kate to the hall. "When Jonas is well, will you visit me in Kodiak?"

Kate felt the intensity in his casual question. "I'm learning new things about you, but I think you're basically the same Todd I knew growing up." She brushed her cheek against his. "Only better."

"Whew, don't I wish." Todd exhaled. "I told Dad how I felt last night, but it was horrible. We may never have a break through." Pain rippled through him, evident on his face, but Kate didn't quiz Todd when he turned away. In a moment, he sat down inside the room. Kate locked her gaze with his earnest eyes. "I'd planned a trip to Alaska before Jonas fell. We'll come."

"You will? Thanks."

"No need, you're my brother."

After starting the coffee, Charlotte showered in the second bathroom, where she wouldn't disturb Kevin. She watched the water splash in tiny streams over her satiny breasts, as she circled her soapy fingers feeling for lumps. She smiled at the thought of hearing Jonas talk, laugh, and play again. How can Kevin and Todd be reconciled? She shook last night's ugly scene from her mind. No lumps. Squirting the shampoo into her hair, she worked it into foam, lifted her head to let the water run down and soothe her back. When she finished, she toweled dry and plugged in the hair dryer, which she held over her short curly hair until the warm air dried it full and shiny. *Blond*, she thought, as she caught her image in the mirror. Her clothes were in the upstairs bedroom, so she wrapped her blue velour robe around her, sat down with a cup of coffee and dialed Kate's home.

"Hi Dave, do you know where Todd is staying?"

"Last night he stayed with the Winstons. He's already left, why?"

"Oh. I wanted to tell him about Jonas."

"I don't mean he left for Kodiak . . . he knows about Jonas. I think he must be at the hospital with Kate. Both were gone when I got up."

"Okay." She wanted time with Kevin, so she didn't offer to babysit with Amanda. "Thanks, Dave."

"Are you heading for the hospital?" Kevin asked Charlotte when she entered the kitchen. She looked at her husband, dressed in Levi's, the morning sun high–lighting his bare chest. The budding maple tree, like a backdrop, stood solid outside the window.

"I think I will. Dave says Kate and Todd are already there. You coming?"

"It might be better if I stayed home."

"Why Kevin?" She looked at his bare chest, thinking of his vulnerability.

"I could stay with Amanda. After last night, I'm not sure how

Todd and I will manage in the same room."

Charlotte pursed her lips. "Let it go, Kevin."

"Let it go?" Kevin's fingers tightened around his mug.

"Charlotte touched her temples. "I don't have the energy to discuss this until Jonas is home and out of danger, but *please* be civil to Todd for Kate and Dave's sake."

"Todd gets so angry," Kevin said, sloshing his coffee on the table.

"Something is eating you, buster. Right now Jonas needs all of us pulling together."

"Okay, I'll go." Kevin put his palms on his knees and came to his feet. Charlotte bit her tongue, as Kevin left the room. "I'll make us some toast and juice."

"Whatever." Kevin went to the master bathroom, shut the door, rinsed and lathered his face, took his razor and began shaving. He had to get a grip. An illusive anxiety loosened inside him with the thought that Jonas would be all right. I'm irrational, he thought. Just because I happened to be the adult around when Jonas fell. He squeezed his eyes shut a second. He hadn't faced a personal crisis for a long time. Jonas wasn't the whole issue. He had to come to terms with Todd. He'd felt repulsed at the idea of Trevor with Todd, but he'd dismissed it. No more, he thought. I can face Todd, handle at least a few hours until he goes back home, back to work. That's all I have to do. Kevin dried his face, pulled a blue sweater over his head, and made a precise part as he combed his hair. He hoped he would feel better when he saw his grandson.

"How's the patient?" Kevin sounded confident when he stopped in front of the nursing station. Wanda looked up, her light–brown eyes rested and smiling, her hair drawn back with a barrette.

"Hello Grandpa. He's making progress, yes indeed."

Charlotte followed behind Kevin. Hearing their voices, Kate met them in the hallway. "He's talking. I called you, but you'd already left the house." Charlotte saw the animation in Kate's face and her own impatience with Kevin melted as they stood beside Jonas' bed. Dave sat opposite them, his face softened with joy.

Charlotte looked at Jonas and turned to Kate, pure pleasure in her voice. "His color is so good."

Kate laughed. "A big item with women."

Todd stood up, decided to embrace his parents together. Surprised, Kevin returned an unexpected hug. "He talked about the mitt, Dad."

"Oh?"

"He said, 'Gramps brought my mitt.' "

Kevin felt a lump rise in his throat. He bent over the bed and said, "Jonas, Gramps loves you."

Todd wiped his palm across his lips, feeling his neck hairs prickle. Jonas opened his eyes. Kate saw a shadow cross the bed as Dr. Lowe walked into the room. They all turned toward him then back to the bed when they heard a small voice. "Are you a doctor?"

"Yes I am. How are you feeling, Jonas?"

"Head hurts."

"You fell from a tree and hit your head. Do you remember?"

"Huh?" Jonas' brown eyes looked perplexed, but curious.

"That's okay. I think we're going to move you to a new room." Dr. Lowe began examining Jonas as his grandparents and Todd moved into the hall.

Kate pressed her face into Dave's chest in a silent moment. "Where's Amanda?" She pulled back and looked at Dave.

"You won't guess. Tina's a jewel. She called to see if she could take Amanda to Sunday school with her son."

"You didn't have time to dress her did you?"

"Nope, jeans and tennis shoes. God won't mind."

"No." They stood at the end of Jonas' bed and watched Dr. Lowe examine Jonas, this time from head to toe.

"Why am I here?" they heard their son ask.

"You climbed a tree and fell out—" Dr. Lowe hesitated, looked at Kate, who showed four fingers "—four days ago. You fell last Thursday and this is Sunday." The doctor waved Kate closer.

Jonas' face lit into a dimpled smile. "Mom, when do I get to go home?" Kate's eyes questioned Dr. Lowe. Dave joined her, locking his eyes on the physician.

"I'll decide later, Jonas." The doctor's blue eyes smiled under thick dark brows. "We'll move you to another room today, and when you feel strong enough you can get up for awhile."

In the hall, Todd waited with Kevin and Charlotte until Kate and

Dave waved them into the room. Jonas was sleeping again. Dr. Lowe left with a nod to the group. Todd saw the tension slide from Kate's high cheekbones when she smiled. "Dr. Lowe is making arrangements to move Jonas out of ICU today," Kate said.

When her parents had embraced and released her, Todd kissed Kate's cheek and put his arms around her back. "I can't tell you how happy I am about Jonas. I hate to leave now, but I need to get to the airport."

"You are wonderful." Kate smiled and Dave nodded at his brother–in–law. Charlotte moved toward Todd with what looked like an apologetic flicker in her eyes. "You've helped us bring Jonas back," she whispered in his ear.

"Nice to see you again, Todd," Kevin said putting an arm across Todd's shoulder.

"Yeah . . . well I have a quick errand to run before I leave."

"Let's get something in the coffee shop," Dave said, his eyes scanning everyone. "We'll be downstairs," he called to Todd who had stepped toward the huge double doors.

After finding the hospital gift shop and searching through its shelves, Todd made a purchase. He walked to the coffee shop, found Kate and handed a bag to her. "Please give this to Jonas and tell him I'll be back to play with him. I need to go now." Kate smiled at Todd as he turned and walked away. She reached into the sack and pulled out a blue Frisbee.

Todd walked to the motel, packed his bag and called a cab. When he arrived at the airport, he had time to spare. Finding a corner seat in the bustling lounge, Todd closed his eyes, his mind filling with images of Trevor. He envisioned his pale blue eyes, his thick black hair, and the muscles that rippled in his arms. Thinking of being in Trevor's arms stirred Todd. Yet, he had needed this experience away. He'd learned about himself, his feelings, his growing independence, and his manhood. Trevor had allowed him his space. His father and he had work to do on their relationship. Todd bowed his head, his eyes still closed, tented his fingers to his lips. The barrier that loomed between them was scarcely dented, but he and his Dad had connected on the dreaded subject. Yearning for acceptance, Todd also ached with a searing desire to comprehend his father.

His eyes opened when he heard heavy raindrops plunk against the lounge windows. He glanced across the row of seats where he watched a teenager drop into a chair, his face troubled. How complex people are, Todd thought, remembering how he felt different from other boys in high school and how that knowledge disturbed and frightened him. He struggled still with his own homophobia, his feelings of shame in breaking social mores. Is it a similar fear, those same mores that keep Dad from accepting diversity in human beings? Can he allow for differences? Would he understand that despite being gay, I'm homophobic too?

Todd felt his neck tense, his stomach churn. Why should I go home and leave this unfinished business with Dad? He folded his arms in front of him and read his watch. Fifteen minutes until he boarded. He rose and walked to a bank of telephones. He had to talk this out. Todd pressed the digits of his father's number half–hoping he'd still be at the hospital. What good would a call do; he knows where I stand. After a few rings Todd hung up and walked back to his chair. When he heard his flight announced, he took his carry on and walked onto the aircraft.

As the plane left the runway, Todd took a deep breath, let out a sigh for a decision made. He'd hung up wisely. No more pleading would change his father. Let it go. He chose a 7–Up, which the flight attendant handed him. Pouring the bubbling liquid into a plastic cup, Todd sipped it thoughtfully. Jonas would toss Frisbees with him again. He knew it. Kate would bring the kids to Kodiak. He set the cup on the tray and absorbed the scene out the window, where fluffy clouds floated across blue skies above the storm. He caught glimpses of buildings, green plots and turquoise dots marking outdoor pools. Then he leaned his blond head back on the seat, closed his eyes and folded his slim fingers against his sweatshirt. He felt a ray of sunshine warm on his forehead. Thankful for Jonas' recovery, he felt grateful for Trevor too, whose face flashed into his mind. Todd felt touched for a moment by the grace of God. This awareness carried him until he arrived in Seattle where he made an immediate connection to Anchorage.

# Chapter 35

"You need your indoor voice when we go inside the hospital." Dave was squatting to level his eyes on Amanda's face.

"Okay," Amanda said, as she skipped through cherry blossoms that drifted in the hospital parking lot. "Jonas will like this," she said in a louder voice when her father stood. She stretched her arm straight, watched the red balloon dance at the end of the taut ribbon tied around her wrist. Dave smiled down at her. Amanda's blue eyes, pink cheeks, which had lost their baby fat, her blond curls, filled him with pleasure.

"He'll love it."

Kate scanned her patient charts, making mental notes of the changes that had occurred in her absence. She straightened her desk area, sniffed the red carnations that someone had placed on the counter, and read a card addressed to her, inscribed with co–workers' signatures. Everyone celebrated Jonas' progress. She moved lightly on her feet, glad for the day.

"I'll fill in for you so you can take a morning break to see Jonas." Samantha was breezing past the desk. Then she backed–up. "How is he this morning?"

Kate looked at the head nurse, her friend. "I saw him early without his bandage. Wanda gave him a mirror so he could see his face. He thought he looked fine and I'm glad that his scar isn't too ugly. Isn't that vain?"

"Not for a mother. I bet that was the last thing on your mind, these past few days."

"True, I'm finally breathing easier, thinking about the everyday stuff again."

"Cut yourself some slack, Kate. Take a half–hour with Jonas."

"Thanks, I'll finish my rounds and take a long break."

Later Kate laid her coat over an office chair, and stepped down the corridor toward pediatrics. Delight filled her when she found Jonas sitting up in bed drinking orange juice. Amanda stood next to him in a dress, with her hair combed. She pulled on a ribbon making a balloon dance above Dave's chair where he sat in his charcoal suit pants.

"Hi Mom. Where were you?" Jonas' cheeks dimpled when he smiled and spoke.

"I've been working in my part of the hospital. You are doing so well." She put her arms around him planting a kiss on his cheek, then with the back of her hand brushed a tear from her own.

"I thought you were bringing Amanda this afternoon." Kate fixed her blue eyes on Dave. Amanda laughed and hugged Kate's waist.

"She couldn't wait and neither could I after I picked her up at Tina's. The balloon was her idea. Time well spent," he said fingering his beard.

A small bandage dressed Jonas' temple and his skin looked clear and rosy. "When can I go home?"

"As soon as the doctor tells us."

A few minutes later Dr. Lowe approached the Winston family. "At last I get to meet you, miss." He bowed and shook Amanda's hand while she beamed back.

"Amanda, this is Dr. Lowe, Jonas' doctor," Dave said.

"Hi, Dr. Lowe," Amanda said with respect as Kate and Dave exchanged glances.

"I like that red balloon," Dr. Lowe said. "Did you bring it for Jonas?"

"Uh–huh."

"Let's go into the hall while the doctor checks Jonas," Kate said. Dave remained in the room while Kate escorted Amanda out. "You look beautiful in your yellow dress."

"Daddy said I should wear it because it's a special day. My play clothes are in the car cause I'm going back to Tina's house."

Entering the hall Dr. Lowe saw Kate. "Things are looking excellent, Mrs. Winston. I spoke with your husband and he'll share my comments with you." He smiled and touched Amanda's head, then left as swiftly as he had arrived.

"What did he say?" Kate caught Dave's arm as he came into the hall.

"Maybe two or three more days." Dave's brown eyes twinkled teasingly.

"He can come home?" Kate grabbed and held Dave to read his face.

"That's right." Dave picked her up and Kate's feet felt light against the carpet when he put her down. He squeezed Amanda, leading them both into the room where Jonas sat holding the blue Frisbee. "I'm going home, right Dad?"

"In a few days, yes."

"I can't wait."

"Neither can I," Kate said. "I need to get back on the job. See you kids later." She waved and left the room.

After she'd tucked Amanda into bed, Kate sat down beside Dave and leaned her head against his shoulder. "Maybe there's a lesson in what we've experienced."

"With Jonas?"

"Yes. He helped me make a decision. His unconsciousness and Todd's visit made me see what matters, what matters to me."

Dave brushed his whiskers against her neck as he turned his head and studied her face. "And what matters?"

"Family. I promised Todd that I would bring the kids and visit him in Kodiak."

Dave fingered his beard, his eyes on her. "With or without me?"

"That's your choice. You're welcome, but I didn't speak for you."

Dave's face looked unreadable for a second. He touched his knee. "I apologized to Todd for being a jerk, so I'll have to decide if I meant it. I guess your Dad's feelings shouldn't affect me so much. After all, it's just a job."

Kate's blue eyes smiled. "I know. You can take your skills elsewhere if necessary, but I don't think Dad knows what he wants."

Kevin rose earlier than usual Monday and sat reading a magazine when Charlotte offered him a cup of coffee. "Can we talk?" she said.

Kevin gave her an annoyed glance. "Sorry you walked in on us."

"I didn't have to walk in on you." Charlotte moved a chair to face him. "Your problems with Todd have been apparent for a long time. You've been civil, that's all."

"I've felt stressed . . . guilty about Jonas' accident." Kevin rolled the magazine, avoiding her eyes.

"If it was that simple, I'd let you alone, but you are hurting me too. Todd has done nothing to us. We don't discuss his being gay, but it isn't breaking news is it?"

Kevin stared at the hairs on his knuckles for a long time. He raised his dark eyes to meet hers. "No, it's not breaking news."

"You think it will go away?" Charlotte's voice softened with her gaze.

"Please. He repulses me, Charlotte. I can't think of anything he could have done that would repulse me more."

Charlotte looked at Kevin as he sat rigid and broken. She reached across the space that separated them, touched his arm. "What exactly has Todd done that repulses you?"

Kevin's face lifted, his eyes widened and he didn't hide his anguish. His throat felt dry when he rasped, "He has chosen to sleep with a man."

"Maybe he chose Trevor because he loves him." Charlotte kept her eyes on Kevin's face.

"You mean lusts for him?" Kevin sounded angry, but in his eyes, Charlotte detected fear.

"No." She leaned back into her chair. "I mean loves. Cares for, respects."

Kevin closed his eyes, fought to keep his voice level. "You think it's a normal way to live—healthy?"

Charlotte touched her forehead, took a deep breath. "I'm sure some gays, like some straights, don't live a healthy life, but many do. Yes, I think it's healthy for Todd." She leaned toward Kevin. "Is it healthy when we cut him out of our lives?" Kevin propped his elbow on the arm of the chair, put his head in his palm, but he didn't answer. They sat in silence.

At length Charlotte said, "Do you think I haven't felt repulsion, a sense of failure and helplessness too? Well. One day I decided it's not our fault that Todd is gay. He just is. Todd is the one who has suffered."

"Yes." Kevin came to his feet. "Because of his own choice. He could make another choice."

Charlotte looked up as he stood over her. "Did it occur to you that Todd is simply being who he is?"

"He made the choice, Charlotte."

Charlotte felt her pulse in her temples. "You're heterosexual—

straight—did you make that choice?"

"No, I didn't. I'm a normal male."

"What's normal?" Charlotte took a breath, and rubbed her neck. Kevin looked away. "Why do you say Todd has suffered?"

"He's suffered because he's gay in a society that fears homosexuality. Too many people believe being heterosexual is the only normal sexual expression. We ignore that brain chemistry indicates—"

"That's baloney." A loud ringing intruded. Kevin stormed out of the room when Charlotte reached for the phone.

"Jonas gets to come home in a few days," Kate said.

The news edged its way past Charlotte's turmoil. She took a breath. "Wonderful Kate, that's exciting."

"Maybe this Friday for Easter."

"Did he talk to you this morning?" Charlotte hoped she sounded composed.

"Yep, ate his own breakfast and sat up the whole time. Dave brought Amanda in to see him. Mom, his scar isn't bad at all."

"I'm so glad. We're running a little slow this morning, but I'll come by." They ended the conversation. Charlotte gathered her nerves, pulled her robe together, and walked into her room to dress.

Kate pored over her patient charts, resumed her duties after seeing Jonas. She wished she had some other job. She disliked being unprepared and felt responsible for her nursing. She saw her patients and when she had returned to her desk in an hour, she checked her messages. "Mind if I join you for lunch?" Mother. Kate considered her agenda before she returned the call.

"If you mean in the cafeteria for forty-five minutes that's fine," she told Charlotte. "As I mentioned earlier, I spent a long time with Jonas while Samantha stood in for me. I better take my regular lunch break."

"That's fine. I'll stop in to see Jonas first, then meet you. What time?"

"A late lunch is best, say one?"

"Thanks dear." Charlotte hung up while Kate sat down and bent over the chart she held in her hand, not seeing it. Something's wrong, she thought.

"Some problem?" Kate bobbed her head back up to find Samantha watching her.

"No, no problem. My mother wants to have lunch with me."

"Oh. How was your brother's visit? He visited Jonas over the weekend you told me."

"Yes, he left yesterday."

"How'd it go?"

Kate hesitated. Samantha's crisp, persistent manner annoyed her today. "It was . . ."

"Never mind." Samantha waved her hand. "Just remember I'm your friend if you want to talk."

"With this how could I forget." Kate plunged her nose into the gardenia plant that Samantha had given her. "I have a few things to sort out first, but thanks."

"Anytime." Samantha left Kate alone.

Finishing his lunch, Jonas licked the last dribble of sherbet from the spoon, and pushed his tray aside with a glance at his grandfather. "Why didn't you come with Grams? She came to see me too."

Kevin looked at the boy's deep brown eyes, his tousled hair. He hadn't spoken again with Charlotte since their argument. "She had some things to do today, so I just came alone." Kevin managed to sound casual. Jonas picked up the mitt that lay beside him, smacked his hand into it with his eyes on his grandfather.

"Are you going to play catch with me, Gramps?"

"When the doctor says you can."

"I get to go home in a few days."

"When did you hear that?" Kevin felt surprised.

"Didn't you know? Grams did."

"Well that's great, isn't it."

"I can't wait. Do you think I can—" Jonas dropped the mitt and took hold of Kevin's hand, "—can go up to the tree house again?"

Kevin rubbed Jonas' hand between his. "Do you remember anything about your fall?"

Jonas pulled his hand away, and picked at the covers on his lap. "No, Gramps. I remember climbing up." He raised his eyes. "I'm sorry I didn't wait for you."

"I'm glad you're okay. We'll decide about the tree house later."

After visiting Jonas, Charlotte walked to the cafeteria. She found a table, sat so that she could see Kate when she arrived, but she had a few minutes to wait. Now that she had called her, Charlotte questioned burdening Kate with her own anger. She smiled at her daughter when she approached.

"Hi Mom. I'm so happy that I have a routine today. As busy as I am, it still feels good to be back to routines."

"I'm sure it does. Jonas will be home soon, which will be an adjustment for everyone. I visited him. He seems enthusiastic and looks good."

"I agree. Let's get our salads." Kate and Charlotte angled their way to the food counter. When they sat down, Kate picked up her fork and eyed Charlotte.

"So, besides Jonas, what's on your mind, Mom?"

"Oh, I wanted a few minutes with you."

Kate lowered her eyes and her mouth made a determined line. "Dad's on your mind, isn't he."

"Your father? Yes, but I've decided to spare you that subject."

Kate lifted lettuce to her mouth and sighed. "I appreciate that. The strain between him and Todd was obvious. We all have our burdens and I've felt overloaded, so good luck with Dad." Kate smiled a dismissal, then saw Charlotte nod her understanding. "Sam brought me an exquisite gardenia this morning and the staff sent a bouquet of red carnations with a card."

"How kind. No one wants to see a child injured." Charlotte sipped her tea. "You've always liked your co–workers, haven't you."

Kate smiled. "They're super, but I'm dissatisfied with heart patients. I think I'd like a change."

"Like what?"

"I think I'd like pediatrics. I'm tired of preaching about nutrition, and think working with children would be fun."

"Are nurses needed there?"

"I hope so. I'll find out and let you know." Kate took a bite of her roll. When they finished eating, she pushed her chair back and rose to her feet. "Sorry, my time's up, Mom. Thanks for your support. Take it easy." Charlotte wiped her fingers on her napkin, feeling good about her decision to spare Kate.

Together the women moved through the cafeteria door, parted in the hall. On an impulse, Charlotte took the elevator to pediatrics. She peeked into the room and saw Jonas' closed eyes, so didn't enter. As she rounded the corner at the elevator, Kevin brushed her arm.

"Could we talk?"

Charlotte bristled. "About what?"

"I'd hoped we could talk calmly about Todd. We could have lunch."

Charlotte bit her lip. "I've had lunch." She thought Kevin's face looked frayed and pale. "I need some distance first, maybe later." Charlotte smiled, but not with her eyes.

"Okay." Kevin pursed his lips. "I think I'll take a walk, so I'll see you at home."

Charlotte stepped past him into the elevator, but he didn't follow. When she parked in front of their garage, her eye caught the budding green leaves, which curled out from the maple branches. She slid from the front seat, ambled through the grass beneath the giant umbrella of branches, and remembered. More than twenty years ago Kevin and Todd had spent hours building the tree house, which looked like an appendage nestled near the trunk of the tree. She remembered the various bird feeders she had constructed with Todd and hung from its limbs. The maple had been a safe, nurturing place for Kate too, had taught her solitude, a love of biology, patience with growing things. Charlotte pictured the children's rosy cheeks in the crisp fall air as each year they had raked and bagged the golden–brown leaves.

She rubbed her neck, squinted against the afternoon sun, and thought of Jonas' narrow escape. He'll climb it again, she told herself. Will he have an opportunity to share it with Todd as if he'd discovered it himself? She grasped the new ladder boards, shook them to test their sturdiness, and then abruptly went to her front door. She entered and closed it behind her, wondering if anyone had inquired about Trevor during Todd's weekend visit. She slipped into her jeans and a sweatshirt, found her tennis shoes and went to the garage. She picked up a tray of yellow and red primroses, which she had purchased a few days before.

Kevin returned home in the late afternoon, greeted Charlotte then went into his office and closed the door. At the sink, Charlotte scrubbed dirt from beneath her nails while she admired the flowers she had potted and placed in the window box. She left the house to pick up dinner.

Kevin was quiet, sullen behind the newspaper when Charlotte walked in, but paced to the kitchen when he smelled the Chinese food. "Good stuff," he said spreading plum sauce across his moo shu pork.

"How was your walk?" Charlotte squeezed a teabag against her cup.

Kevin stilled his fork and looked across the table at her. "Not enjoyable. I spent it soul searching."

"That's no fun."

"No, but maybe necessary now and then." Kevin's eyes seemed sad. He cut a bite of almond chicken. "What have you been doing?"

"I planted some primroses." She smiled and waved her hand toward the windowsill. "Behind you."

Kevin turned around. "Spring."

"They add color. Do you want to talk about Todd?" Charlotte tilted her teacup so she could read his face.

"If it's okay with you. After dinner's fine. When I saw Jonas, he said he'd be coming home in a few days. Is that true?"

"That's what Dr. Lowe said. I'm so relieved. It's like our lives have been on hold this past week." She lifted a fork of rice.

"Seems like a month." He ate in silence for a few minutes. "I've gone over it in my mind a million times, and I can't believe that Jonas could have climbed the blasted tree so fast." Kevin wiped his mouth, dumped the empty containers in the garbage.

"He'd have raced up no matter what. Forget it now, he's all right." Charlotte stacked her plate on his.

"Thank God." Kevin took the dishes to the sink. "Let's wash these by hand. It won't take a minute."

Kevin squirted detergent under the faucet and put the plates in the sink. "Todd—I take him too personally." Shaking his head Kevin washed and rinsed a plate.

"How do you mean?" Charlotte reached for a towel.

"I guess I feel disappointed in him as a son. I feel like it's my personal failure that he can't find a woman." Charlotte cringed, but listened. "He knows we love each other, Charlotte." Kevin held the dishrag still. "I did everything I knew to be a good father."

"You were, you *are*." Charlotte stopped drying. "You think you failed as a parent?"

"Something like that."

Charlotte took a breath, set the plates on a shelf. "It's Todd's life, Kevin. Are you sure he's miserable without a woman?"

Kevin didn't answer. He wiped off the counter and headed into the living room with Charlotte behind him. He sank into his recliner and she sat opposite him.  At length, Kevin said, "I think he's troubled, yes."

"How do you know he's troubled?"

A perplexed expression flickered in Kevin's eyes and he pursed his lips. "Okay, I don't know. Every man needs a woman, that's all." He lowered his eyes. "Someone to love—" he swallowed the word, then looked at her, "—like I love you." Charlotte searched his face, saw hurt and confusion.

"And Todd doesn't have someone to love."

"No." Kevin bent his head, rested his arms on his thighs, and clasped his hands.

"He has Trevor. He's someone to love."

"I asked you if you think that's healthy." Kevin stiffened.

"I said, yes. Todd's healthy. His relationship with Trevor expresses who he is."

Kevin looked at her. "You think so."

"Yes.  It's reality, Kevin. I don't know why or how it works. You don't accept the brain chemistry stuff, but like it or not, ten percent of the population is gay. All ages and races, religions, nationalities, women and men working in many occupations."

Kevin shifted his body, his eyes perplexed. "Don't you find it a damn problem that *our* son is gay?"

"No, not anymore." Charlotte felt her patience drain. "I'm his mother, not his judge. I can't support your position forever. If being gay is Todd's problem, then rejecting him is yours."

"My problem?" Kevin looked stunned.

She observed the creases around his eyes, the wrinkles on his forehead. "You've lost your brother. Please don't lose your son."

A wave of agony washed over Kevin's face. He studied his hands for a long time. "Do I expect too much from Todd because he reminds me so much of Stephen?" Kevin closed his eyes. "I don't want to lose him."

"I know. I wanted to hear you say it."

# Chapter 36

When the flight from Anchorage landed, Todd stood on the Tarmac at the Kodiak Airport where he gazed for a minute at the shimmering stars. He walked to the garage, and drove his car home. When he reached his driveway, the porch light welcomed him. He unlocked the door, behind which Trevor sat stretched out in blue sweats, his hair shiny and wet. He jumped up and spread his arms as Todd closed the door.

"Hey, maybe we should part more often," Todd said as he embraced Trevor.

"Sit down and tell me about Jonas."

"He's out of the ICU. He's talking, but best of all Kate told me she'd bring him and Amanda to visit in June."

"Whoa, a successful trip, I'd say. We'll need the time to clean up the bedroom for them." Trevor rolled his eyes in the direction of the small room that overflowed with their accumulated belongings. "Anyway, you think Jonas came through unscathed, he's okay mentally?"

"You mean brain damage." Todd ran a hand through his hair. "He seemed okay. Jeez, I've tried not to think about it."

"How was your Dad?"

"Strained, as usual. We had a little talk, but it didn't go too well."

"As in?"

Todd folded his arms. "He thinks he can separate me from my sexuality. He told me that he accepts me but not my gay choice."

"You repulse him."

"That's me." Todd tightened his jaw. "All of them—my sister, her kids, Dave—they made his approval list, but not me. I don't want to be an architect, but it cuts deep when Dave—" Todd bent and fumbled with the lock on his suitcase, recovering his composure. Trevor was quiet. "The rest of the family, even Mom, treated me well. Dad may never accept us and our relationship."

"Can you live with that?"

"Yes, I think so. I know he thinks I'm abnormal and repugnant. Odd, isn't it. Kate must irritate Dad with her obvious support." Trevor nodded. "Of course, Dave changed his mind about me when he got the drafting job with Kevin, but this weekend he apologized. I'm jealous that you've improved things with Frank, but hey, I'm coming along." Todd smiled a satisfied smile. "How scary. I must be growing up. Enough about me, how was the wedding?"

"Simple and eloquent. Maria's a striking woman, at least when she's in a white satin sheath, with her black curls piled on top of her head. Frank looked fine too. He's handsome in a black suit with his dark hair, which, by the way, he had cut even with the top of his ears."

"No ponytail, huh?"

"No ponytail. You might try it." Trevor made a cutting movement with his fingers.

"I thought you liked my hair." Todd wove blond strands through his fingers, a serious expression on his face. "I'm ready for some shuteye, but maybe I'll let you take the scissors to this mop tomorrow night."

"Surely you jest." Trevor's pale eyes danced as a grin spread across his angular face.

"No, a fellow can change, you know. If he must."

The next day came too soon. Todd awakened in time for a bagel and a cup of coffee before he left for work. When he arrived at the lab, Mac approached him. "How would you like to join the research on stellar sea lions? Their population keeps dwindling and we aren't sure why, but the evidence points to the lack of food resources."

"Yeah, too many people fishing for pollock."

"Some research disproves that link with the decline. We've already expanded no–trawl buffer zones around rocky beaches and eliminated pollock harvesting from the Aleutian Island waters south of the Bering Sea."

"That really ticks off the fishermen—their bread and butter—but we've a job to do here too." Todd looked at Mac.

Mac hiked up his trousers. "Touchy, though, because pollock is in such demand in the lower forty–eight, low–priced."

Todd studied Mac's untrimmed beard. "Tell me more about the job."

"The study should show what percentage of sea lions are disappearing from natural predators or foul play with rifles. It would involve aerial surveys of their haulouts. I know you're not a pilot, but you'll be with a team. Some research will involve cruising as well."

"Sounds interesting boss, as long as you pay me. Full time?"

"Nah, about twenty hours a week, so you can continue your whale work. Congress has appropriated forty million. I'll pay you. So you'll start next week?"

"Yeah, I'm game."

"Good. By the way, how is your nephew doing?" The lines around his eyes softened as Mac placed his palm on his bearded chin.

"He's going to be all right. He might be home by now."

"I'm glad to hear it. Kids get hurt so often, it's a wonder any of us grow up."

"Yeah."

That night Trevor stood back to examine the evidence of his barbering skills. "I see your ears." He eyed the blond hairs that had fallen from Todd's shoulders into the pile on the kitchen floor.

"Yeah, I feel a breeze. Give me the phone so I can call Kate."

"Reporting haircut to sister?"

"No, getting report on Jonas."

"Say hi from me and tell her about your new job with the sea lions."

Todd took the phone and in a few minutes, he said, "He's going home in a couple days."

Two days later Todd parked in the church lot and when he and Trevor stepped into the office, he asked the secretary if Mr. Gunderson was available. Larry Gunderson rose from his desk, stepped into the hall and called to Todd and Trevor. "Yes I am, good to have you drop in."

"We should have made an appointment, but we were in the area.

You remember Trev?" Todd looked at Larry then toward Trevor.

"Yes, I do. We met at the airport. How are you?"

Trevor smiled. "I'm here. A step for me, since I'm wary of counsel."

Larry laughed and shook Trevor's hand. "How'd I get such a bad name? I have no answers, but I'm willing to listen. Sit down. I was about to get a Coke. Like one?"

They said they would and Larry disappeared in the hall to a kitchenette where he found the drinks and returned. "How goes the battle?" he asked, handing a Coke to each man. He pulled a chair from behind his desk and sat down. "Unfortunately I have only a half hour, then I need to make a hospital call."

Todd tipped the cold can to his lips, drank, and leveled his gaze on Larry, who sat in his tennis shoes and jeans. "Thanks to my nephew, I think I can survive my childhood."

"Your nephew?" Larry pulled up his sock.

"Yeah, Jonas, he's eight and he fell from a tree, was unconscious for a few days. Scared us all, but he came around and seems to be headed toward good as new."

"Well that's fortunate," Larry said. "And you?"

Todd ran his palms along his thighs and leaned forward. "When I saw how scared my father was, I had a glimpse of his humanness." Trevor turned his head to look at Todd.

"You saw your father as a human being." Larry hadn't intended sarcasm.

"Of course he's human. What I meant is—he has trouble expressing his feelings." Todd quit talking and looked down.
Larry's brows creased, he removed his glasses. Todd twisted his watchband, and after a silence he looked at Larry. "I was afraid that Jonas might die, just a kid. Being with him, I felt a sharp sense that I was an adult, not a child anymore. Jonas' fight for consciousness moved me. Does that make sense?"

"Yes." Larry swung his glasses between his fingers. "A lot of sense. You are taking responsibility for how you feel as an adult. That's been a fight for you."

"Real progress, if I may say something." Trevor's eyes went to Larry. Todd shifted, noticed Trevor as if he had forgotten his presence. Larry waited.

"You can say whatever you want as long as you support my story," Todd said, a grin creeping across his mouth.

"I support you. Glad you're moving on." They laughed.

"Your humor is a plus for you. You'd be surprised how many can't laugh." Larry returned his glasses to the bridge of his nose, came to his feet. "I'm sorry to cut this short, but I must excuse myself. Keep expressing your feelings."

The men stood at once. "Thanks, good to see you."

"Drop in again, it's always a pleasure."

"Next time we'll call."

# Chapter 37

Jonas sat on his own bed Friday afternoon, surveyed his room. He was home where everything looked the same. He checked his Tyrannosaurus Rex model and picked up each piece of his dinosaur collection. Amanda hadn't ruined anything. He socked his hand into his catcher's mitt. "Mom said I have to stay in here today," he said to Amanda when she poked her head into the room. "So I can play on Easter."

"Read me a story." Amanda bounced out and back with two books, crawled up on the mattress with Jonas.

"This is too hard for me." Jonas put down *Corduroy*, the teddy bear story. "I can read *Amelia Bedelia*. I like this book cause Uncle Todd gave it to me."

Kevin felt restless, his mind was scattered, his emotions stirred up. It was Easter. His attention flitted from the white lilies clustered at the altar, to the white robe of the pastor, and then to the words the man spoke. Next, he noticed a pew several rows ahead in which Harold Baxter sat with his son, Jim. He imagined Todd and Jim in bed together. Why do I do this? Jim's work with inspections is top notch, he admitted. Jim had never mentioned his lover, Kevin thought, until I introduced him to Dave. Kevin shifted his hips in the pew, glanced down at his bulletin. Todd's gay. Does it matter?

Charlotte might be right. I can't do anything about my brother, but I can do something about my relationship with Todd.

He heard the rustling of pages turning and knew the sermon had ended. Charlotte had found the right page and she handed him the hymnal. So he sang the Easter hymn, his attention on the congregation's attire: some in dresses, many in slacks, few suits, no hats and gloves. His mother had worn gloves in Vermont. The men wore slacks or jeans, casual shirts, a few with ties. Change, he thought, fifty years of change. Could he? "Alleluia," the congregation sang and sat down. The benediction followed the offering and everyone left the sanctuary.

When Kevin turned his key in the door, the phone was ringing. He answered it in the kitchen. "Dad, Jonas is worse," Dave said. "Dr. Lowe thinks he has a . . . hematoma. We're at the hospital."

"Is Kate with you?"

"Yes, with Jonas. He's having a CT scan."

"What happened?"

"When Jonas woke up, he seemed confused, had slurred speech."

"Today?"

"Eight this morning. We rushed him to the hospital. Pressure on the brain from leakage of blood, Dr. Lowe told us. They have to relieve the pressure. The CT scan should locate the hematoma."

"We're on our way."

"Meet us in Intensive Care."

"Right." Kevin slumped to a chair.

"Was that Kate?" Charlotte glided into the room with two baskets brimming with candy and eggs. Stopped. "What's wrong?"

"Jonas. Get your purse. We're going to the hospital." Charlotte's hand flew to her head as she spun around.

They approached Dave and Kate who stood facing Dr. Lowe in the waiting room. The doctor nodded and stepped aside, including them in the circle. The family's eyes went to each other, then back to Dr. Lowe. "As I was saying, Jonas has developed what we call a subacute subdural hematoma. Sometimes this happens after a head injury. The cause usually is a slow leakage of blood between the membranes covering the brain. It can occur up to ten days or so after an injury. This situation is serious if the pressure isn't relieved."

"How serious?" Kevin said.

"Could result in brain damage or even death."

"Where's Jonas now?"

"Surgery prep. I'll drill a small hole in his skull to drain the hematoma."

Kevin took a deep breath and Charlotte shuddered. Kate's freckles were evident; her blue eyes round with shock.

"Nothing showed up on his CT scan last week," the doctor said. "The procedure takes about a half–hour. I'll get back to you as soon as I'm finished. Courage."

Kate sank into a chair next to her mother. She felt a wave of nausea. Anxiety. Then she was numb. She looked toward Charlotte who, frayed and pale, was rubbing her hands, but Kate didn't see her mother. Charlotte stopped wringing her hands when she saw Kate's vacant stare. She touched her daughter's arm. Kate's eyes flickered toward her jean–clad thighs; she didn't speak and didn't draw back. The men stood across the room looking out a window that overlooked a garden.

After what seemed an eternity, Kate and Charlotte saw Dr. Lowe in scrubs, approaching them. "A success," he said. "We relieved some pressure. Jonas will be in recovery until he can move his head, which we now have held secure. We're keeping him awake. He's not out of the woods yet, so hang on. You may as well take a break. You can see him in an hour. He's in excellent care."

Dave spoke first. "What can we expect?"

"We watch him, keep him in critical care. I can tell you more when I see him in an hour."

"Appreciate your time on a holiday," Dave said without feeling.

"Of course." Dr. Lowe pulled off his green cap, brushed his palm across Dave's forearm. "I'll be in touch."

# Chapter 38

Jim Baxter pored over a work order on his desk. He spoke into the receiver. "I have a job lined up in Idaho in the next few weeks. I hoped I could make the last bridge inspection for you prior to that." He waited for Kevin's response.

A wave of disgust passed through Kevin. Into the receiver he said, "That should work." He tapped his fingers against his desk. "What's your project?"

"An apartment complex in Idaho. Well, I must run, talk to you later."

*What's my problem?* Kevin wondered, hanging up the phone and glancing out his home office window at the open garage door. Charlotte had left earlier for her book club and to visit Jonas. He had remained conscious, but the doctor wanted him kept quiet, wanted to watch for signs of seizures. Kevin couldn't bear to stand by and wait. Talk of seizures made him queasy. Jonas hadn't had one, but he might. Even two years from now, the doctor had said.

Today I'll keep moving. Jonas won't die, Kevin thought. I can clean out the garage. He probably won't have any brain damage either. From the window, Kevin could see the papers and boxes he would recycle. Jonas will function fine once he gets through this.

When he turned from the window, the pictures on the wall summoned him. Here I am with the Eagle Scouts; if one had told me he was gay, I'd have ousted him from the troop. It was scouting policy, still is, he thought. I pretended I hadn't heard the taunting words a few hurled at Todd. Earning his life saving badge was painstaking for Todd. He was no athlete, isn't now. He worked so hard. For my approval? What have I learned in my sixty–five years? I *am* a bigot.

Kevin opened his office door and walked to the room where he'd seen his sweatshirt. He found it thrown across the bright cushion on Charlotte's wicker chair. He loved the woman who loved this room. He was hurting her. He noticed the dormant piano. He remembered how Todd plunked those keys until they sounded good. Kevin thought of the tree house venture and the scouting excursions. I changed when Todd reached puberty. Lost pride in him. Did he know? I didn't admit Todd's development. Had he done anything to shame me? Kevin closed his eyes. What if Jonas dies? Todd may be all I have. He lifted the ragged sweatshirt from the chair, put it on. He pinched a shriveled lavender petal from the African violet and headed to the garage.

Using his pocketknife, he slit and flattened cardboard boxes for the recycle bin. The knife was sleek, pearl coated, yellowed with age. It had belonged to his father, Martin Keeley. As Martin had dusted and displayed in tidy semblance the tools and hardware in his shop, so Kevin had preserved the knife.

His father had worked his own business six days a week, but he refused to labor on Sundays. Martin's faith involved absolutes and rules. He was a disciplined man who had no patience for imperfections, his or others. Kevin cherished the evidence he had that his father had loved him. He had worked with him on his days off from grocery clerking. Just work. His dad never talked much. That's why he had kept the knife. "I want you to have this, Son," Martin had said when he handed it to Kevin. That was it.

Kevin was eighteen at the time, Stephen twenty. Stephen had left for Korea. When Kevin graduated, he took a job. Afterward he went to Korea too. The National Parks had hired him for the summer when he finished high school. He repaired trails, sometimes assisted in visitor information centers, but best of all he enjoyed the nation's beautiful parks. The public's desire and need to be in these grand surroundings had captivated him. Increasingly he became an activist, at first with his voice speaking to tourists and later with his wallet supporting wildlife and natural resource preservation. The same things Todd cherishes, he thought ironically. Several months later, the family had faced Stephen's disappearance and three years later Martin Keeley died.

Kevin closed the knife and slipped its smooth surface through his fingers into his Levi's pocket. He took a screwdriver, pried the lid from two old paint cans, looked at the leathery surface and tossed them in the trash. Crammed in the corner of the shelf, he saw a brown object covered with cobwebs. Kevin retrieved it and stood still. He held a catcher's mitt for a child. He wiped the sticky threads from leather that had aged, but showed little wear. Todd. You were about my dreams, my goals, Kevin thought. In trying to make you into someone you weren't, I missed connecting with the person you are. He put three fingers into the mitt. Now? It's about my wounded pride and judgment. My alienated son, he thought. Maybe a dead grandson. He wiggled his fingers out and laid the mitt down.

On the shelf, he found a birdfeeder, encrusted with clumps of seeds and dung. Scouting. Just a boy when Todd made this with his troop. The split wooden base had a piece of broken plastic that caught Kevin's fingernail. He retrieved the blade and trimmed his nail. Did I see the difference in you all along? Kevin examined a cracked clay pot, then laid it aside. I can't fix the family tie. I'm too stubborn. What can I give Todd? Not a keepsake knife. Has Todd lost his father too? Kevin threw the feeder in the garbage pile.

He raised his head when he heard a clicking sound outside the garage. Florence bent over her walker as she pushed it ahead of her, one foot dragging behind. "Wait, let me help you."

"I'm okay, gettin' my mail."

"I see that." Kevin glanced at several envelopes in the wire basket attached to her walker.

"Gettin' rid of stuff?" Florence clicked closer and began inspecting the garbage pile. "That birdfeeder was hangin' in your big maple when I moved here. Todd was proud of it."

"Yes he was." Kevin ran his fingers through his hair.

"Have a good Easter?"

"Uh, no. Jonas had a setback."

"Isn't he home?"

"No, he's in the hospital."

"Oh, too bad. Tell him hi for me."

"Yes, thanks." Kevin watched Florence's gnarled fingers squeeze the aluminum bars; the wheels of the walker swiveled as she turned around. "I'll help you back."

"Would you? S'posed to stay inside, but I had to smell the flowers." She stumbled against Kevin. With one arm, he supported her back, maneuvering the walker beside them with the other. He stopped at her porch, handed her the mail.

"Thanks. . . don't be mad." Her eyes pleaded in her wrinkled face.

Kevin looked puzzled. "Mad?"

"At Todd. He needs your love."

They heard the engine of Debbie's Mazda. She parked in the driveway and stepped out of the car. "Mother, why are you outside?"

"Needed some air. Goin' in right now."

"Thanks Kevin," Debbie said, opening the door through which she and her mother disappeared into the kitchen.

When Charlotte returned, she drove into a clean garage. The old pick–up truck that Kevin used for hauling was gone. She felt a wave of pleasure that Kevin had made good use of his time instead of brooding. He hadn't said much the past two days. She'd backed off, didn't insist he see Jonas today. Guilt had erupted—Jonas' condition, Todd—Steve?

The truck rumbled into the driveway, and she watched Kevin emerge. She looked at his mussed hair, dirty sweatshirt and felt a yearning she didn't understand. "I see you had a burst of energy," Charlotte said when Kevin walked through the kitchen door. "Garage looks great."

"The clutter had piled up and you know I can't stand that." Kevin sat on a kitchen chair, untied his boots, and peeled off his sweatshirt. "Jonas the same?"

"About the same. They're being cautious, keeping a close eye on him."

"Good. Anyone call Todd?"

Charlotte took a breath, couldn't hide her surprise. "Not me."

"Just wondered." Kevin got up and went to take a shower. When he finished, he sat in his office before dinner, running his fingers through his wet hair. He flipped the pages in his personal directory. He didn't have Todd's Kodiak number. He called Kate. Dave told him Kate was at the hospital.

"No change in Jonas?" Kevin heard the strain in his own voice.

"He talked a few times today. Sounded all right—you know what I mean."

"Yeah, I do. Could you give me Todd's phone number?" Kevin wrote the number on a scrap of paper. "Thanks. You take care." He hung up. Trevor answered on the third ring.

"This is Kevin Keeley. May I please speak to Todd?"

"Uh, Mr. Keeley, I'm sorry he's not here." *What's wrong?* he thought. "Could I take a message or have him call you?"

Kevin swallowed. "Tell him Jonas was taken back to the hospital on Sunday, has a hematoma. The doctor drained it and he's responding."

"How scary." Trevor lowered his long–legged self into a chair. "What do you expect—"

"That's all I have."

"Well, thanks for calling. Todd will want to know."

During dinner, Kevin looked at Charlotte. "I've been thinking." He laid his fork across the plate of chicken and pasta. "I've decided it's time for me to hang it up."

Charlotte locked her blue eyes with his. "Retire for good, you mean?"

"We could spend more time with the grandkids, travel a bit. I'm getting older you know."

"And more relaxed. I hope you do retire." When Charlotte smiled the lines around her eyes crinkled. "You haven't combed your hair all day. I like you this way."

Kevin trailed his fingers over his scalp. "Not much to comb. It's not easy realizing the bridge will be finished with or without me, but I didn't miss the job these last two days."

"You sure the fumes at the dump haven't affected you?" Charlotte laughed.

"I'm sure." Kevin's face broke into a broad smile; the one Charlotte had missed seeing. He forked up a bite of pasta. "How did your day go?"

Charlotte knew he wanted to hear about Jonas. "Kate didn't work this afternoon. We sat with Jonas, read to him. Then he talked about the book. Appropriate talk."

Kevin shook his head. "Good. He isn't sitting up yet, is he?"

"Not yet. He lay flat, but Dr. Lowe says the emotional attention is critical. This morning I discussed Austen's *Pride and Prejudice* with my book club. So, I'd say we've all had a productive day."

Jonas turned his head. His face burst into a smile when he saw his mom walk into his hospital room Thursday morning with his blue Frisbee in her hand. Wednesday, he'd transferred to the main floor of pediatrics. His head was elevated on a pillow and next to him stood Dr. Lowe. "Hello Kate. Jonas continues to do well with no relapses," Dr. Lowe said. Before Kate could assimilate the doctor's news and Jonas' smile, she had to catch her breath, for the joy that had caught in her throat.

"I feel overwhelmed." She kissed Jonas, then followed the doctor to the hall. "Part of me expected to lose him. You sure he's out of danger?"

"I think this hematoma developed as a result of his head injury, but no further problems have shown up. That's good news. We'll do another CT scan tomorrow. Next week we'll discuss sending him home." When Dr. Lowe disappeared into the next patient room, Kate hurried back to Jonas.

His smile had left his face. "Nothing to do." Jonas' voice sounded pensive. Kate smoothed the bedding around her son. He bowed the Frisbee with his fingers. "I wanna play with my friends."

"I know. You've been a brave boy. You're feeling tired of the hospital because you're getting well."

Wanda breezed into the room—her broad face, strawberry hair drawn up in a barrette, her kind smile—and said, "Hi Jonas. Glad to see you, Kate." Wanda's light–brown eyes smiled at Jonas, who gave her a reluctant grin. "We're going to get you up and home as soon as possible," she said, wrapping the blood pressure cuff around Jonas' arm. "This time we want you to stay well." She tweaked his cheek when she released the cuff.

"Yes." Kate moved to the door with Wanda.

"The news of his hematoma shocked me," Wanda said. "He's a miracle kid."

# Chapter 39

Friday morning Charlotte offered Kevin a cup of coffee. "Coming with me?" she said. "Jonas has his CT scan today."

"Think I will. Let's go this morning, then I'll putter at the office for awhile. Dave must think I've already retired."

When his grandparents arrived, Jonas was walking in the hall with the nurse. To Kevin's alarmed expression, Wanda said, "I'm with him just as a precaution. He's doing well." *Seizures*, Kevin thought.

"Hi Gramps." Jonas left Wanda's side and hugged him. "Did you bring the softball?"

"No softball this time." Kevin laughed, his dread driven off by Jonas' happy face.

"We could play catch on the bed." Jonas' dimples coaxed, his eyes pleaded.

"We could, but we aren't. I'll play with you when Dr. Lowe says you can."

"Promise?" Jonas expanded his chest, crossed his arms over the buttons of his pajamas.

"Promise."

Wanda raised her arms up and out. "He's all yours. You can circle the ward again, then go back to his room." Charlotte went to Jonas' side; with Kevin on the other, they paraded Jonas down the hall in a final victory lap.

Kate arrived at the hospital after lunch to be with Jonas during his CT scan. "Will it hurt?" Jonas looked at his mother.

"No, it won't hurt. You had one earlier, before you came home. You'll lie on a table called a gurney."

"That table that slides into a tube that looks like a big donut?"

"Right, it takes pictures of your head and the person doing the test can talk to you. I will be watching you, too. Remember you must lie very still. Think you can do that?"

"Sure Mom, I can do it again."

Saturday morning the sunshine streamed through the corner window where Kevin bustled in his office. He stripped each personal photo from the walls and his bookcase and set them in a box: his wife, Todd, Kate and the kids, Steve. He stuck his other valuables in a box. In a way, Jonas had helped him make the decision to clean out the engineering office. Jonas' health had sprung back. A new day, hope restored. Jonas' eagerness for play had moved Kevin, imbued in him a determination he didn't understand, a yearning for family, for healing.

The news that Jonas' CT scan was normal came to him Friday afternoon, and nothing could have kept him from the hospital. In route he'd stopped and bought a softball. Before heading to Jonas' room, he'd found Wanda. "Okay if I give this to Jonas?" he'd asked.

"Sure, if he's old enough to refrain from tossing it across the room."

"He won't," Kevin had told her.

He carried the wrapped photos and the box to his car. Before he locked the office door, he sat in his executive chair and stretched his legs across the bare desk. He scanned the empty walls. Years of loss. Not knowing what happened to Steve was worse than death. A bitter grief. A horrible secret. He felt a chunk of resistance crumble inside him like a cracking nutshell, exposing him to a vulnerable place he'd not explored.

Charlotte pulled the Toyota into the driveway after visiting Jonas. He had looked wonderful when she saw him at the hospital. She had repeatedly dropped the new softball into the mitt, which he gripped three feet from her.

She walked into the house, took cutters from a kitchen drawer, then wandered into the garden where she cut several pink Cotillion roses, fragrant like sun–ripened raspberries. She couldn't resist the heady aroma of the coral Royal Wedding blooms either and clipped a few more stems. Inside she arranged the blooms in a vase, which she placed on the dining table. Celebration. Jonas returned.

She spread waxed paper, laid a few roses on it, and then she carried them across the street. Her knock had to wait a minute. Florence looked rested today. She had improved in handling her walker. "How pretty. Sit with me." Charlotte couldn't refuse. Her eyes scanned the cluttered kitchen. Debbie hadn't come yet this Saturday morning.

"Can I find a vase for you, Florence?"

"Over the fridge. How's Jonas?"

"Better, much better. Should come home next week." Charlotte turned on the faucet and ran water into a glass container.

"I'm glad. Todd coming to see him?" Florence had settled into a padded wooden chair. She fixed her brown eyes on Charlotte.

"I don't know. It's a long trip." Charlotte set each rose in the vase.

"Your boy won't be young forever. Shouldn't keep Todd away from him. Kids need relatives." Florence eyed the roses. "You can put those roses right here on the table."

Charlotte set the vase in the center of the table and sat down. Florence smiled. "Don't matter that Todd's different. My boy was different too. Didn't like loud noises or bright lights. He didn't like parties either. Couldn't keep jobs cause he couldn't pay attention."

"I thought he was a computer programmer."

"Yes. He did good too. Had a nice man who hired him. Gave him a quiet office. He couldn't stand to hear other computers makin' noise. Some workers laughed. Kids called him names, treated Nathan sorta like an outcast. Like Todd."

"Like Todd?" Charlotte's eyes pierced Florence.

"Gays get called names, I mean. 'Mental,' they called Nathan. Hurt me. People blamed his father and me. He had a different kind of brain. Nothin' we did but love him."

Charlotte drew a deep breath. The soft brown of Florence's eyes resembled a deer. "Sometimes the mind doesn't work right, just like the body. I know it hurt you. We don't know enough about brain diseases, but every day doctors learn more. When we understand the diseases better, people won't be afraid, and the stigma will go away."

"Uh, well." Florence grasped the vase with her hands, pulling the coral and pink roses toward her nose. "Smells good." She gazed at Charlotte.

"What did you say will go away, stig . . .?"

"Stigma. Feeling ashamed of a disease or a person."

"Like some people feel about gays."

"Yes."

"You ashamed of Todd?"

"No, I guess not." Charlotte glanced at the table.

"Don't be. Least you have a son. He's special. Would be even if he didn't have that eagle thing in scouts or his fancy job with the seals. He's a sweet man. Love helps."

Charlotte's throat tightened. "I'll remember that, Florence. Love helps." Charlotte pushed back her chair, rose and left the house. When she returned to her kitchen, she saw Debbie's Mazda pull into Florence's driveway. She was glad that Florence was not alone.

At noon Kevin stirred from his reflections, balanced the box of office supplies on his hip, and locked his office door. At his kitchen door he knocked to no answer, opened it, and then pushed it shut with his foot. "Cleaned it out," he shouted, setting his load on the counter. "I'm home."

Charlotte turned off the vacuum. "I didn't hear you." She eyed the mixture of photos, rulers, pencils, drafting instruments, then saw the wide grin on Kevin's face.

"This stuff goes in the den," he said. "Dave's welcome to it, but I doubt he needs anything. Let's go see Jonas this afternoon and have dinner at the Dutch Bakery afterward."

"Okay with me. I played catch with him this morning . . . sort of."

"Nothing broke, I hope."

"No." Charlotte reached into a plastic bag and took out four slices of rye bread.

"He'll need to catch up with school work."

"At home, I hope."

On the other hand, he has to get back to normal at some point."

"I know, but fall is soon enough. Turkey sandwich?"

"Sounds great." Kevin picked up the box and walked into his office. Todd hadn't returned his call about Jonas. He couldn't blame him. Kate will call him, he decided, if she thinks he needs to know.

Kevin joined Charlotte at the kitchen table where he sank his teeth into turkey and bread, tasting a burst of tart cranberry. Charlotte got up when the phone rang. When she hung up, she sat down at the table. "That was Debbie—Florence died."

"When?" Kevin set his sandwich down.

"About noon."

"That was an hour ago."

"I know. I was with her at ten and she seemed okay."

Kevin went to the hospital to visit Jonas in the afternoon.

Charlotte stayed home, broiled a chicken breast, which at dinnertime she took with a few rolls, oranges, and grapes to Debbie. "Thanks for coming," Debbie said and opened the door wide. Charlotte sat in the same chair she'd sat in hours earlier. The roses had opened a bit. "Mom enjoyed them," Debbie said, staring at the petals.

Charlotte folded her hands. "I'm sorry."

"She went fast and sure. The doctor came, but I knew she was gone. Heart attack he thinks."

"We didn't see his car. Too busy dealing with our own trauma, I guess." A puzzled flash crossed Debbie's face. "Kevin's decided to retire and this morning he cleaned out his office. Pictures, desk, and all."

"I see."

"Debbie, can I call anyone for you or help with service plans?"

"I think I'll call Mom's pastor. Can't remember his name."

"Norman Seibert."

"She has a few cousins that will want to know, but the rest of her kin are dead. Mom wanted cremation." Debbie's voice cracked as Charlotte listened. "I made those arrangements already. Always said she'd rather go back to the soil and help grow a poppy. I'll sneak into the park and scatter her ashes among the rhododendrons where she loved to walk. One of her gardening friends knows that's what she wanted." Debbie looked at her lap. "Maybe she'll go with me."

"I'd be glad to go if you like."

"Thanks for the offer. I may call you. I'll call her cousins myself. Good to keep busy, but I'd appreciate it if you would call a few people from the church."

"Sure." A silence fell between them. "Florence was a wonderful person . . . sensitive and caring."

"She was, needed to be for my brother. He had his problems, some autistic characteristics, but he functioned fine in a limited environment."

"Worked with computers?"

"Technical problem solver. He had an office door he could close, couldn't stand the loud servers, the noise of the fan, things like that. Autism covers a spectrum of traits and each person is unique."

"We talked about Nathan this morning. Your mom . . . well she taught me about love. Kevin and I have had a terrible time accepting our son's orientation. You know he's gay."

"Yes. Was Mom too blunt?"

"Um, yes and no. One more social stigma. We've been too concerned with our social standing. Kevin especially has had a hard struggle, but this is no time for me to ramble. Florence brought us up short is what I'm saying."

"Your grandson is still in the hospital, Mom said."

"Next week he should come home. We'll gather and be a family, with Todd in our thoughts—a tribute to Florence. She loved Kevin and Todd alike."

"Thanks for your kindness." Debbie glanced at the chicken and bread Charlotte had placed on the counter.

Charlotte rose. "Sure. I'll be in touch." She embraced Debbie, then walked away.

Monday morning Kate walked into Jonas' corridor and looked into his room. He was sleeping. She found Wanda at the nurses' station. "Everything okay?"

"Yes, yes. Jonas' progress is steady. Dr. Lowe will be discussing his discharge with you."

Kate smiled at Wanda. "It'll be good to have him home." She smoothed her hair and touched Wanda's arm. "Are nurses in demand in pediatrics?"

"I suppose, why?"

"I'm feeling burned out in cardiology, ready for a change. Kids are invigorating. I'd love to help other parents as you have nursing Jonas. Kate dropped her hand and glanced away. "I have no words, Wanda."

"I know what you mean. So glad he's made it." Wanda was silent a moment. "We have heartbreaking cases as well."

"I know. I want to try pediatrics anyway."

"Go for it, Kate."

At five in the evening, Dave closed the engineering firm. He drove home and joined Kate at the dinner table. "Good news," she said. "Dr. Lowe thinks Jonas can come home by Thursday or Friday if nothing changes."

"Super. What about school?"

"No school. I can't bear the thought of rough and tumble now."

"It seems wise." Dave looked at Amanda who sat next to him. "Did you hear that, Amanda? Your brother will be home in a few days."

"Will he have to go to the hospital again?" Amanda's eyes looked perplexed.

Dave glanced at Kate. "We certainly hope not."

"He better not," Amanda said. She finished eating and ran off to play. Dave and Kate ate in silence a minute. "You better call Todd and tell him the Kodiak trip is off."

"I know. I'll tell him that I'll bring the kids in August."

"Me too."

"Good. Think Dad called Todd when you gave him the number? He may not have the news on Jonas."

"I don't know, but it's not your problem. You have good news, so tell him that."

Wednesday afternoon Jonas sat straight on the papered examination table watching Dr. Lowe's hands. He thought the doctor's hair looked as white as his coat. Jonas smelled his pine-scented shaving lotion when the doctor bent toward him. A feeling of importance flickered through him when Dr. Lowe touched his scar.

"You are a lucky kid," Dr Lowe said. "This red spot will get lighter and in awhile you won't even see it. I can't see the other one because your hair covers it." Dr. Lowe raised his eyes above Jonas' head to Kate. "Full indoor activities." He looked at Jonas. "Summer's almost here, but you can do school work at home till school is out. You're a smart boy and you'll catch up." Dr. Lowe patted his shoulder and Jonas felt good.

"Can I climb the tree too?" His eyes widened.

"Not yet. In late July or August you can try the tree if you have your parents' permission." Dr. Lowe saw Kate's face turn anxious. "An adult should go with you," he said, his eyes locked on Jonas. "I'll see you in a few weeks. You can walk and play quietly outside, but no strenuous, no rough play, until I see you again. Any questions?"

"No," Jonas said, and Kate gave a half-hearted grin as the physician lifted Jonas from the table. With his back to Jonas, Dr.

Lowe touched Kate's hand. "He'll be fine. I'll sign his discharge papers for tomorrow morning."

Kate took Thursday off to take Jonas home from the hospital. When she arrived, Jonas threw his arms around the nurse. "You're a nice lady." Wanda smiled and handed him his sweater. He stood in his jeans and a red T–shirt that made his cheeks look red.

"You were a good patient, young man." Wanda turned to Amanda who stood quietly at her mother's side. "You've been a good sport too. I thought you'd like this." Wanda handed her a yellow balloon and gave a blue one to Jonas.

"I like balloons." Amanda held it to her chest and Kate echoed her appreciation with her eyes.

As soon as Kate secured the seatbelts and drove out of the parking lot, Jonas asked, "Can Micah come to see me when we get home?"

"Not today, you need some time to get used to being home."

"Can we have an ice cream cone?"

"A good idea." Kate felt pleased with the easy transition. She stopped for cones and when they had settled into the house, Jonas busied himself with some books while Amanda batted her yellow balloon around the house.

Dave left the office early Friday afternoon to stay with Jonas while Kate and her parents attended Florence's memorial. The sanctuary overflowed with flowers from friends: rhododendron, geraniums in clay pots, and lacy lilac, which impregnated every breath with its sweet scent. Charlotte caught her own breath at the simple beauty, so like the woman it celebrated.

Saturday morning Jonas poured syrup on his pancakes. "Can Micah come over to play?" Kate glanced at Dave who nodded.

"Tell you what," Kate said. "Micah can come if you play inside with a quiet toy."

"My Lego blocks?"

"Good choice."

At noon, Jonas and Micah ate a sandwich. To Kate's relief, rain had poured all morning, so she heard no grumbling about staying inside. When they finished eating, the boys went back to Jonas' room to finish a Lego building. Micah's eye caught a blue object under Jonas' bed. He started for it, but Jonas grabbed it first. Micah stood with his hands on his hips, his freckled–face intent with curiosity. "Where'd you get that Frisbee?"

"My uncle gave it to me when I was in the hospital." Jonas tucked his fingers under the edge of the disc, eyeing Micah with caution. "Uncle Todd likes playing with me."

"Maybe he'll play with us this summer. When you can run again."

"Uh, no he can't Micah, he doesn't live close." Jonas twisted his shoe into the carpet.

"Where's he live?"

"Alaska. He works with sea animals like seals and whales."

"He can't play Frisbee much if he lives far away." Micah took a step forward and reached for the Frisbee. "Let me see it."

Jonas hunched forward protecting the disc. "No. You can play with it some other day."

"Let me have it," Micah shouted.

"What's all the noise?" Kate reached the threshold just as Micah pushed Jonas and grabbed the Frisbee.

"Give me that, please," Kate said. "I'll keep it until Jonas can play. Maybe it's time for a rest. You can come again another day, Micah."

"We're going to see my uncle in the summer," Jonas said as Micah stomped out the back door. Jonas straightened his shoulders. "That's right, huh Mom."

"Maybe."

On Sunday, when he and Charlotte visited, Kevin noticed the scar at Jonas' temple had lightened and his memory flashed to the boy's bloody face when he lay unconscious. An image of another bloody face intruded, which Kevin shook from his mind. He hugged Jonas and placed a strawberry dessert on the kitchen table. Amanda held up the hem of her pink dress and tapped her white Mary Jane pattens in a little dance. He swished her up, glad for the reminder of little girls in dresses, knowing that before dinner Amanda would discard the frills for her jeans and tennis shoes.

They gathered around the dinner table for chicken, mashed potatoes and Charlotte's fresh strawberry shortcake. "Does Uncle Todd know I came home?" Jonas said watching his mother.

"Not yet, but he should, don't you think?" Kate smiled at Jonas, avoiding a look at Kevin. "After dinner we'll call him."

# Chapter 40

The days of mid June were exhilarating for Todd. Today he'd flown over Prince William Sound several times, where he and the pilot observed the stellar sea lions. When he returned home, he went to the kitchen where Trevor prepared dinner. "I bet we saw two hundred sea lions today."

"You saw that many from the air?" Trevor carried a pot of clam chowder to the kitchen counter.

"Yeah, with binoculars. The reddish–brown ones were easy to detect with their blunt faces and bear–like heads." Todd yanked his bootlaces, kicked off his boots.

"Sounds like a lot considering their population is diminishing." Trevor handed him two bowls, and motioned to the table. Todd set the empty bowls on the table while the soup cooled in the pot.

"That's true. The pilot told me stellars are down by eighty percent in the past thirty years. Of course, Montague Island is a breeding ground.

"I'm sticking with seals," Trevor said, stumbling over Todd's boots.

"Ah, those pups are cute. Prince William Sound from the air is a whole different perspective."

"So you think you're going to like the study?"

"Yeah. We'll be studying their diet before and after the decline, then compare it with the diet of ones in South Eastern Alaska. Seems there's no evidence of decline in that area in the past three decades."

"How long will this study take?"

"About a year, four month segments. Should be interesting." Todd pushed his sweatshirt sleeves to his elbows and looked at the desk. "Any news?" He threw back his head.

"You don't have hair in your face now, so you can't flip it back." Trevor laughed. "You never called your dad back did you?"

"No, I figure Jonas must be okay or Kate would let me know. I have nothing to say to Dad."

"You're hoping Kate will call about a visit in a few weeks, aren't you? We didn't clean the room for nothing."

Todd propped his elbows on the table, folded his hands under his chin. "Hoping is the right word. I try not to expect too much, especially now. Then I can't be too disappointed, right. If Jonas isn't entirely well, Kate might not come." He leaned aside as Trevor poured hot chowder into his bowl.

"She might not be able to bring them, but she said she would; let's go with that."

"Yeah, you're right." Todd slurped a spoonful of the creamy chowder. "Delicious. I guess she'll tell me one way or the other. I think I've matured a bit. I love my job, but still have trouble accepting my relationship with Dad—my non relationship. I wish he'd retire. Maybe he'd relax and change his rules."

"Change his rules?" Trevor sprinkled oyster crackers into his bowl. "Don't expect it."

"Yeah." Todd made a face and swatted the air. "I'm dreaming again. He'll probably never feel comfortable with me."

"Never is a myth . . . he's dealing with his feelings, his own perspective. If he doesn't want to change, that's his right. What do you care? You're an adult. If he changes one day, that's his business. You can't spend your life waiting for him to see you in a different way." Trevor sounded exasperated.

"No." Todd pushed his bowl aside. "I know the lecture Trev. I can't change anyone but me."

"Smart man. I think Kate will show up with the kids, so please let the rest go. You're wearing me out."

They ate in silence. Todd put his spoon into his empty bowl, stood and walked to the counter. He opened the faucet and stared at the water that filled the sink. Trevor was right. They needed a break from family affairs. Loneliness engulfed him. Did he think he could fill the void if he talked enough? He needed approval that he couldn't give himself. He took a deep breath. Not true. He was one person who could give himself approval. Why must he remind himself again? And again.

Trevor finished his chowder in the moments that Todd reflected. When he put his bowl in the dishwater, he noticed the tense set of Todd's mouth. He laid his arm across his rigid back. "Things will work out, Todd."

Todd turned off the water, paused. These are ghosts, old insecurities, and anxieties he didn't need or want. Trevor's right. Kate said she'd come, so she will. He plunged his hands into the water, his eyes on Trevor. "I know. We better clean our sleeping bags since the kids will have to sleep in them."

"First we have to find them."

"Either on the shelf in the garage or in the back closet cubby hole. I'll find them right after I wash these bowls."

When Todd returned from the garage without the sleeping bags, Trevor handed him the phone. "Some kid wants to talk to you."

"Hello?"

"Uncle Todd, it's me, Jonas."

"Hey kid, what's up?"

"Mom said I could call you. I came home from the hospital and we had a big dinner today. Gramps and Grams are here. I wish you were too."

"Well, thanks Jonas, so do I. Are you doing what the doctor said?"

"Can't play. A little, but I can't run and jump and stuff. I can't go to school. Can't toss my Frisbee because I can't run."

"Just wait. Later you'll play Frisbee."

"Mom wants to talk to you."

"Okay, Jonas. Glad you're home." Todd waited a minute.

"Hi Todd," Kate said, moving with the phone into the bedroom.

"Hi Kate. What's the story?"

"Jonas had it right. Homework until school is out, no rough play, then by the end of summer—he may be able to climb the tree again. Scares the day lights out of me. You busy with your research?"

"Uh, yes. Think I'm going to like it."

"That's great, Todd. Trevor okay?"

"Yeah, he's fine."

"About our trip to Kodiak. I don't . . . um, think we can come now. Jonas developed a hematoma that sent him back to the hospital. They drained it and he has responded well. Sorry I didn't let you know."

"I heard."

"You did?"

"Dad told Trevor."

"Dad called you?"

"Yeah."

"Good. He didn't say a word to me. We still plan to visit, maybe in July. I haven't told Jonas yet, so please keep it quiet."

"I will. Thanks for the call."

"Something else. Florence died last week. A heart attack."

"Oh. A good woman."

"Yes, she was. Talk to you later."

The first week in July, Jonas sat on Dr. Lowe's patient table where the doctor examined him for the first time since he'd left the hospital. While the boy dressed, the doctor spoke to Kate in his office. "Everything looks and sounds normal. I think a trip to Kodiak in the middle of the month will be fine. Jonas may play more vigorously now for short periods of time."

Kate eyed the man. "How vigorous and short?"

"Toss the Frisbee with him, play catch. Be aware. Half–hour at the beginning so he doesn't get fatigued. Report anything unusual. I don't anticipate any problems. Then he can resume rougher play with his peers. Bring him back in September before school starts."

"Thanks, Dr. Lowe."

Later in the week Samantha listened as Kate clarified her feelings. "I don't know if I'll like it, but I have an interview Tuesday for a job in pediatrics. Kind of a gratitude thing. You know what I mean?"

"Sure." Samantha's sharp nose pointed at Kate. "I hate to lose you, but I think I understand." Her blue eyes met Kate's. "You've never had heart trouble and neither has Dave. You'd like to make a difference in an area that you've experienced. So you're applying for a position in pediatrics where you can help injured and sick kids."

"Bingo." Kate fingered her cup, inspected the coffee grounds. "You're the best, Sam. Thanks for listening."

"What's happening with your brother?"

"Funny you'd ask. Dr. Lowe gave the go ahead, so we're taking the kids to Kodiak to see Todd later this month."

"I'm glad. I've seen how procrastination affects people."

Samantha slipped her thumbs in her coat pockets, jutted her chin. "You're doing the right thing." She gave Kate a wry grin.

"Your support is part of the reason I'm going to Kodiak."

"One thing I don't get." Samantha made a face.

"What's that?"

"How can you start a new job if you're on vacation?"

"I'm not available till after my vacation."

"I see." The women rose and together walked back to the nurses' station where Kate circled her vacation days on the office calendar.

It was Kate's day off, and she'd promised Jonas a visit to his grandparents. "Get in the car so we can go see Gramps," she said. Amanda and Jonas scrambled into the car. When Kate pulled into her parents' driveway, Jonas stepped out, ran to the maple, and gazed up at the tree house.

"Sure wish I could climb up there."

Kate came to his side, took his face in her hands. "Jonas, you must promise me that you will not climb the tree today."

His deep brown eyes steadied on hers. "I wanna but I won't." He kicked the tufts of grass at his feet. "You said I could show the tree house to Uncle Todd. Do I get to?"

"Yes, when he can come. You can climb it with Gramps, before you see Uncle Todd, but not today." She saw Kevin walking toward them.

"Okay." Jonas shoved his hands in his pockets. Kevin's eyes never left Jonas while he played outside.

Kate wandered through the roses with her mother. "I received a letter from Jonas' teacher today advising me that she passed him to the third grade."

"Good for him," Charlotte said.

"Yes. In addition, Mom, we're going to Kodiak in ten days. I promised Todd I'd visit. Want to join us? We're going to fly and rent a car. Stay two nights. You could get a motel and spend the days with us."

"Is Jonas well enough?"

"Yes, the doctor cleared it. Dave and I intend that he know Todd, since Jonas talks about him all the time."

"Well, dear." Charlotte crossed her arms and pressed her shoe into the dirt. "I would love to come, but I couldn't get Kevin to join me."

"Ask him. If he says no, come alone. Dad doesn't rule."

"I don't think that's a good idea. Todd doesn't expect us does he?"

"Suppose not." Kate shrugged. "Will we ever be a family again?"

"I don't know." Charlotte uprooted a dandelion.

"By the way, I think I'm getting the job in pediatrics."

"Wonderful." Charlotte dropped the weed, feeling relief at a change of topic.

# Chapter 41

When he heard Trevor's footsteps in the kitchen, Todd grunted from his hunched position. "Do we have a teapot around here? I can't see a blasted thing in this bottom cupboard."

"Are you planning a tea party?"

"No, you jerk." Todd's voice echoed from within the cupboard. "Kate left a message that Mom is coming with them. She likes tea and we—" Todd backed out of the cupboard, stood and turned toward Trevor "—don't have a decent pot."

"So buy one. Get a couple teacups too."

"Yeah, I guess so. I thought I had the chipped pot she gave me in college."

"Come on, your mom's a classy lady, she deserves a decent teapot. The question is where will we put her?"

"She'll get a motel. I'm sure she'll enjoy the peace and quiet after traveling with those two kids." Kate said transportation wouldn't be a problem because they'll have a rented car.

"Congratulations to the Keeley family. How remarkable that your mom decided to leave Kevin and come. We'll have a great visit."

"Yeah, that's my plan. In the meantime, we have groceries to buy and a house to clean. They'll be here Saturday."

"Make a list. I think I'll go to the old loop road and get some exercise. I'll stop at the store on my way back."

"Right. I might be out doing my paces when you get home, but I'll put a couple potatoes in the oven and lay out some steaks to defrost."

Trevor left with the grocery list and drove his jeep out where he could park and walk an old logging road. He started out over a muddy path that soon dried out and wound through thick spruce. The sun felt warm against his skin. He knew the upcoming visit with Todd's family could be a turning point for Todd. Their expected visit at his home made a tremendous impact on his outlook. His father's approval seemed less important to him since his sister and mom were coming.

Trevor heard low voices approaching. The filtered sun formed light streaks across the road. At a distance, he saw two silhouetted figures walking toward him. When they were several yards away, he saw that one man was a stranger, but he'd seen the other man somewhere. The man studied him. "Well—if it isn't the fag." As alarm registered, a swift blow hit his mouth and Trevor tasted blood. Again, his head jerked back with the weight of a fist at his eye. Trevor reared back and drew a breath, plunged his knuckles at the offender who ducked and missed his fist.

Trevor's eye throbbed and in the mirror looked like a bluish slit in puffy, purple flesh. He held the cool wet washcloth over it. His lip had stopped bleeding, but he tasted sticky blood that oozed from the gash inside.

He checked the baked potatoes. Todd had forgotten the steaks so he opened the freezer and removed one, placing it in the microwave to defrost. He grabbed a handful of ice cubes, folded the washcloth around them and lay down on the couch holding the compress over his eye.

In a few minutes the front door swung open and he heard familiar footsteps. Todd stood over him. "You don't look so good. How's the other guy?"

"Guys."

"No way. Thought you hit a tree. What happened?" Todd sat at Trevor's feet.

"Two friends after a fag, I guess."

"You know 'em?"

"Seen one around and he must have seen us. We're so threatening." He attempted a laugh but the sound he uttered was "ow."

"Any teeth chipped?"

"No, but I don't want a steak. I took one out for you. Didn't make it to the store."

While Kate straightened a few items in her desk, which she hadn't transferred to pediatrics, Samantha poked her head into her office. "I'm going to miss you."

"Me too. Now I'm thinking more about Kodiak than the next hospital adventure. Mom decided to go with us."

Samantha eyed her. "She did?"

"First she said no, but Dave took a call from her last night. She changed her mind and now she wants to go, so I called Todd. We'll make it fun." Kate tilted her head back with a laugh that swept her blond curls off her cheeks.

"Good." Samantha blinked a smile. "Have a wonderful time."

By day's end Kate had written her reports and prepared her patients for her absence. The way people quizzed her whereabouts when she was absent always amazed her. She didn't explain she wouldn't return to cardiology. The week had flown and it was Thursday already. She'd wash the kids' clothes tonight and get their things together.

Todd called after dinner. "Hi Kate. Can't wait for your visit, but I thought I'd better warn you that two guys beat up Trev today."

"Oh no."

"He's okay, but has a shiner so he'll have a swollen face when you get here. Don't worry, just letting you and Dave know, so you can deal with Mom beforehand."

"He's all right except the black eye?"

"It's a doozie, has a cut lip too, but he's fine."

"I hate fights. Were you involved too?"

"Wasn't a fight, Kate. Trev was alone and two guys punched him because he's gay."

At dusk Saturday, the trees cast shadows across their patch of grass while Todd swept spruce needles from the wooden steps. He spun around when he heard a horn. Through the window of a bronze SUV, he saw Dave's bearded face. As soon as the car stopped, Jonas and Amanda bounded toward him. They circled his legs, held up their arms, so he bent over and returned their affection as they hugged his neck. Trevor came out of the front door and together they greeted Dave, Kate, and Charlotte. Kevin stepped from the back seat.

"Dad—" Todd's mind went blank.

"Hello, Son. Thought it was time I saw your place." Kevin adjusted his sweater and extended his hand.

"Yeah, yeah, come in. Can I help you with your bags?"

"No need, we have a motel lined up." Kevin smiled toward Trevor, whose puffy lip seemed curled into a snarl. He noticed Trevor's bluish–yellow, swollen eye.

Dave stepped forward and touched Todd's arm. "This is our motel, so you can help me with my bags." Dave laughed off the awkwardness. Stepping past Kevin, Todd hid his indignation and reached for Dave's suitcase.

Kate took the children into the room that Todd showed her. When they returned to the living room, Jonas and Amanda were in pajamas. "Your house is small," Jonas said plopping on the couch next to Todd.

"Smaller than your house, yes, but we're only two. We don't have many visitors." Todd looked at the smiling boy. "You kids hungry?"

"Yeah."

"They've had dinner." Kate laughed.

"Oreo cookies and milk can't hurt." Todd headed toward the kitchen.

"The flight was uneventful, I assume." Trevor looked at Kevin.

"Good weather," Kevin said. He examined Trevor's face, a decent black eye, but no worse. The beating was the reason he'd come to Kodiak—to relinquish his right to remain silent.

The children had followed Todd into the kitchen where they ate the snack and soon afterwards got into the fresh sleeping bags. "This is just like camping," Jonas said.

The adults discussed the colder weather in Kodiak, seals, whales, and sea lions. Charlotte asked about Todd's research, but Trevor answered most of her questions. Constrained or silent, Todd and Kevin didn't aid the flow of conversation. Close to eleven, Charlotte yawned and Kevin asked Dave for the car keys. Before they left for their motel, Charlotte said she'd call in the morning.

When he heard the car engine, Todd jumped to his feet. "What the hell is this, some kind of joke?" His face reddened, his eyes drilled into Kate.

"We didn't know. He showed up with her at the airport. We thought he was dropping her off, but he had a ticket." Dave spoke for Kate.

"He's treated me like garbage. Now he thinks he can land at my house unannounced? You could have called me, dammit."

Kate glanced at Dave, then toward the children's room. Her eyes appeared rounder, her freckles visible against her pale face. "It'll be all right, Todd." She wished he would calm down.

Todd backed up to his stuffed chair and dropped into it. He forced his voice down. "Why did Dad come? Tell me that."

"No clue." Kate sat forward. "He didn't say why he changed his mind, nothing."

"You could have asked Mom, found privacy in the lady's room or somewhere." Todd's eyes were slits of green beneath his knitted brows.

"I did ask her. Dad told her this morning that if he could get a plane seat, he'd come with her. She assumed it would be okay as long as they stayed in a motel. She doesn't know what changed his mind."

Trevor regarded Todd, watched him struggle for control and sink into the chair. Then he caught Kate's eye, a plea for dismissal. He came to his feet and with slow strides walked to the front door and snapped the lock shut. He turned with deliberation, his words an answer to Kate. "You must be ready for bed, Kate, after your long day." He glanced again at Todd. "We'll learn more tomorrow. Let's get some sleep, Todd."

"Think I'll sit here awhile." His sister and Dave said good night and left to join the children.

"Wait for an explanation, Todd. Your Dad will tell you. I'm going to bed."

Todd let out a curse, glad to be alone. Why now, what's changed?

Why do I act like this, get so upset? Just when I had accepted the way things are, he shows. The questions came in waves. Dad's attention is what I've wanted, but I don't need another confrontation. Is he here to chaperone his precious Jonas? Inspect Trevor? He clicked off the lamp, sat in the stillness letting the darkness engulf him. Todd inhaled and exhaled until he felt a fragment of control. I'll be mature, I'll manage my anger, but I won't take any garbage. A promise in the dark.

The next morning when Todd reached for Trevor, he felt the skewed pillow and sheets that Trevor had abandoned. He heard the children's voices, which led him to the kitchen where he found Trevor and Kate mixing pancake batter. The Sunday comics surrounded Jonas on the front room floor. Amanda stood in her pajamas, hair tousled. "Did we wake you up, Uncle Todd?"

"Nope. I bet you just got up too."

"Uh–huh. You look funny in your pajamas." Amanda giggled, raised her arms and Todd picked her up and hugged her.

"Well, so do you, curly." He set her down. "Smells good in here."

"They're almost ready." Kate waved the spatula in Todd's face. You want some coffee, right?"

"Yes, please give him some," Trevor said. "He's usually not this pleasant before coffee." He grinned at Kate and laughed.

"Not true, most days I'm the first one up." Todd held his own as he took the mug.

"Okay," Trevor threw up his arms, "I confess. As a rule Todd's up first, but I do make the best pancakes."

After breakfast, Kate straightened up the children's mess. She felt uneasy about her father's last minute decision to visit Todd. Yet, nothing had seemed amiss in his behavior. On the contrary, he had amused the children during the flight and the drive from the airport. If anything, he showed an inexplicable ease until last night—he was too quiet. Mother hadn't discussed her discomfort, but her frequent nail examination and her heroic pains at conversation had exposed her nervousness. Kate decided that Charlotte was as bewildered by her husband as the rest of them.

When she rolled the sleeping bags, Kate saw an object soar past the window. Through the glass, she saw Todd and Trevor with

Amanda and Jonas outside. The yard was a postage stamp, but she noticed the blue disc swish again and she smiled. She watched them play until the phone rang. Answering it, she heard a pleasant hello from her father. "Is Todd around?" he asked.

Todd growled a response when she announced the caller. Then Kate took his place in the damp grass. Amanda threw the Frisbee backward or straight up whenever she had it, but Jonas showed his skill. Somehow, Trevor kept them both engrossed with the game.

Dave stepped into the kitchen for a second cup of coffee when he'd finished his shower. Hunched on the kitchen stool, Todd gripped the phone. "I don't know if I want any more talks with you, Dad." Dave poured his coffee quickly and returned to the living room. He could discern a few words, but pretended he wasn't eavesdropping.

In a few minutes Todd hung up and came around the corner of the kitchen into the room where Dave sat. "Dad wants to talk to me at his motel."

Dave looked at Todd. "It can't get much worse than it is with your dad. Maybe he wants—" Dave saw the dark green of Todd's eyes, and decided against offering any solace, "—I don't know."

Before Todd could respond, Jonas burst in the door with Amanda, Kate, and Trevor in tow. "I'm getting good, Uncle Todd." Jonas' cheeks dimpled into a smile.

"I know you are." Todd smiled at Jonas, pushing his hand against Trevor's shoulder as he ushered his partner from the room. They stopped outside on the back porch. "That was Dad. He wants to see me alone, so I'm going to their motel. Will you handle things here for me? Maybe take them to the lab or the park."

"What's wrong?" Trevor searched his face.

"Beats me, but this is it, Trevor. God help me."

"Keep your cool. If your mom's present it can't get too ugly."

When Todd tapped on the door, his father opened it wide. He offered Todd one of the two chairs furnished with the unit, while he took the other. Todd's mother had made coffee and Todd saw some dried apricots in the ice bucket lid on the table. He felt his anger ease into a curious tension. Charlotte greeted him, then propped pillows behind her and sat at the end of the bed, her face tense.

"Like a cup of coffee?" Kevin ran his finger around the neck of his sweatshirt.

"Okay." Todd reached for the carafe before his father had a chance and poured coffee into a mug. He raised the pot and looked at his parents. "You?" They both nodded and before he handed a cup to each, Todd tore a sugar packet and sprinkled its contents into his mother's mug.

Kevin spread his legs wide and set the beverage on the table with a thud he hadn't intended. He pulled the chair out from the wall. "I need to get some things off my chest and I want you both to hear it." He pursed his lips as he leaned forward and rubbed his thumb and forefingers across the lines of his forehead.

Todd glanced at his mother, saw in her expression an indication she didn't know what was coming either. Kevin took a drink of coffee, then cleared his throat. "I thought I wanted to spare you pain, but in the past six months I—I've been hiding from myself." Kevin noticed Todd's short hair, his thin lips, and green eyes. "You look like—remind me so much of—my brother. I've crammed my agony inside me thinking it would disappear. It won't."

Todd felt his throat grow dry. He eyed his father. Charlotte sat nearer the edge of the bed. "I've never talked about this." Kevin's voice thickened. "Steve wasn't missing in action. He fled. He was involved in a murder."

"Murder?" Charlotte's lips parted in a whisper. Todd stared at Kevin, who lowered his head and spread his fingers across his brow. "I told you that he was missing. He was. That's what mattered then." Kevin shook his head and met their eyes. "Steve and two guys beat and kicked a man until he was unconscious. He died two days later." Todd's knuckles tightened around the edge of the table as Charlotte's hand muffled a gasp.

"I slept through the whole incident even though the assault happened not more than a hundred yards from my barracks. Thirty yards in front of ours was another barracks and someone happened to look out and see the attack. The three of them had knocked the corpsman to the street and were stomping him. It took a few minutes for the guys to grab broomsticks and get to the scene. When about twenty men with pool cues and some broomsticks approached them, the men—including Steve—disappeared into the night. When the M.P.'s arrived," Kevin looked at Charlotte, "the military police, they found the man unconscious and bleeding over most of his body."

"In the morning, my boss told me that the man was in critical condition. Since I was a medic, he told me to report to the hospital as one of his special duty nurses. When I arrived about eight and first saw him I felt sick. I would have vomited if I had had any privacy. I knew the kid. Hank's hair was matted with blood. His eyes were swollen shut and his face so ripped apart, I barely recognized him."

Kevin caught his breath, paused when he saw Charlotte recoil, noticed she still held her hand over her mouth. "I know this is hard to hear, but let me finish. Since they had directed all their efforts toward keeping Hank alive, they had not cleaned him up. The doctor gave me instructions and I started to clean his badly damaged body. He was literally one big abrasion, his whole body encrusted with gravel, dirt, and dried blood. When I got to his mouth I found large chunks of the inside of his cheeks and most of his teeth were missing or loose."

"While I was cleaning him, he stopped breathing. I climbed on his bed and started artificial respiration. In those days, we didn't perform mouth to mouth. A very prissy Army nurse in freshly starched whites started screaming at me to get off the bed with my filthy shoes. At that moment two doctors walked in the room, heard her ranting at me and yelled at her to 'get the hell out of this room, as a matter-of-fact, get the hell off this ward.' One of them relieved me, while the other one went to grab the crash cart. After ten to fifteen minutes, with several more doctors who had joined them, they got Hank breathing again." Kevin stopped, took a breath. "He lived for two more days. Died without ever regaining consciousness."

Todd flinched as he moved his hand across his clammy lips. "Dad—"

"Why did Steve do it?" Charlotte's shock compelled her to her feet.

Kevin fell silent. Charlotte felt the mattress against her legs and sat back down. Todd's stomach turned queasy at the disclosure he feared his father might make. He drew in a breath. "You don't have to tell us if you don't want to."

Kevin's eyes locked with Todd's. "Yes, yes, I do have to tell you. Steve hated gays. Enough to kill." Charlotte let out a sob, and covered her cheeks.

"I've taken this long to realize what I've done. You remind me of Steve in appearance and temperament. Hank in . . . in . . . I was afraid of Steve's hatred. I believed that if Hank had been straight he'd be alive. Steve wouldn't have killed and needed to run. All these years not knowing." Kevin stopped. His eyes didn't leave Todd's face, though Todd gave no response. "What I've harbored against you, my own flesh, has been the worst kind of bigotry."

Todd blinked, averted his eyes. Could he believe these words? When he heard his father blow his nose, he looked at him. Forty–some years later, Todd thought, he realizes the source of his pain.

Kevin put his handkerchief in his pocket, raised his head, and met Todd's eyes. "I never told my parents what happened. It was the fifties. Mom and Dad couldn't have accepted the truth; their son murdered a man because he was gay. I thought it pointless, cruel to tell them. You're right, Todd. Everything you said about me is true. I feared what others would think, feared my own thoughts. When I realized you were gay, I denied it. In some dark way, I feared for you too, feared someone would harm you. At least that's how I felt." He looked at his hands. "Mainly I was homophobic." His eyes then held Todd's, which were green pools of discernment. "And I was protecting Steve, hoping he'd show up someday."

Kevin shifted his gaze to his wife, perched at the edge of the bed, still stunned by Kevin's story and its long silence. "My big mistake," Kevin said, "was my silence, the unspoken grief, guilt. Why hadn't I been there to intervene?" He shuddered, shifted his hips in the chair, and looked at the carpet. "I don't know where Steve went or where he's been all these years. Europe I assume, under false identity." Charlotte and Todd looked at each other. "I couldn't expose my uneasiness with homosexuality. How could I tell you and not do that?"

Todd felt weighted by Kevin's confession. It was too much. He'd given little thought to his father's wounds, only his own. Could Dad change his attitude so quickly? Now will I learn about Steve's short life? Did they catch the others? Todd stared into those deep eyes, at the creases around them and the wrinkles at Kevin's brow and mouth. He couldn't bear to hear more, not now. He could wait for the answers. After a long silence, he placed his hand on his father's shoulder. "Thanks for telling me."

Charlotte's face had softened with compassion and her cheeks were as moist as her eyes. "Did they catch the others?"

"Yes, the other two. I'll tell you later."

Charlotte rose from the bed and stretched her arms between Kevin and Todd; her fingers massaged their necks. "I love you guys. Just be safe, Todd. I worry about AIDS."

"Yeah." Todd turned, burrowed his head under Charlotte's arm. "AIDS is scary, but we're clean." He brushed his lips against his mother's arm and blinked wet lashes. Then he straightened his shoulders and took an apricot from the ice bucket lid. "Think I better get back to the house. Want to see the lab where we do our research? I might take the kids later if Trevor hasn't."

Charlotte bit into an apricot too and glanced at Kevin who appeared depleted. His head bent forward, and he didn't respond. She looked at Todd. "Could we meet you after lunch, and go this afternoon?"

"Yeah, call me. You have my number."

"We do." Kevin rallied his energy. "Thanks for coming." He glanced at his hands. "I'm worn out."

"Heavy stuff, Dad." The kindness wasn't lost on Kevin as he lifted his eyes, a gleam of gratitude. Todd wanted to embrace him, but instead laid his hand on his father's arm. "I'm sorry you carried such a burden so long." He turned toward the door. "See you later."

Kevin and Charlotte sat without speaking for a minute. At last, Kevin drew a breath and sighed. "That wasn't as wrenching as I had dreaded, but I'm exhausted. He dropped onto the bed next to Charlotte who leaned into him.

"Thanks for sharing your guts with us, for including your son."

"Our son." Moving back on one elbow, he brushed a blond hair off her curved cheekbone. "It's strange. Todd didn't need my approval. He figured out who he is despite me. I regret—"

"No regrets." Charlotte pressed two fingers against his lips.

In the pit of his stomach Todd felt the knots relax as he followed the road back home. His fingers encompassed the sun–warmed steering wheel, which felt hot against his skin. He felt the breeze lift his hair. The sun affected the trees; they seemed greener, the flecks of light through their leaves danced as shadows transformed into new shapes. I stayed in the driver's seat when I listened to Dad and I didn't confront him, he thought, blowing his breath past his lips. Dad, more vulnerable than I've ever seen him, exposed his indefensible self without questioning me.

Why had his father suffered so long? Why hadn't the public reminders made him talk? Like the beating death of the gay student, Matthew Shepard? What did Kevin think then? Had he changed his heart or was this an act of catharsis for past grief? Todd felt tenderness stirring him, an incentive to end the malaise in their relationship. Something extraordinary had happened. He had heard what he had longed to hear and he felt shaky.

When he pulled the car into the driveway, Todd saw Jonas run past the window, then out the front door to his car. "What took you so long, Uncle Todd?"

"Gramps and Grams wanted to visit with me because I'm such a wonderful son. Where's your Frisbee, sport?" Todd's question sent Jonas racing to find it.

When Trevor saw Todd had returned, he went to him, his eyebrows creased into a frown. "What's going on?"

"In short, Dad told me that his brother killed a gay man . . . I'll explain later." Todd's voice was discernable to Trevor, but not to Jonas who approached. Todd ducked as the Frisbee whirled at his face. He hurled it back and Jonas caught it sending it back again in a beautiful curve.

Todd missed the Frisbee and bent to retrieve it. "Why is this thing so slick?"

"Dad sprayed it with furniture polish." Jonas jumped up and laughed.

Jonas' laughter roused Dave, who sauntered toward them rubbing his chin. "We didn't have any silicon." He gave Todd a shrewd grin.

"Watch me catch a high one. See my thumb's up on top," Jonas shouted as he caught the Frisbee. "I can spin it on my finger too."

"I can play too." Amanda ran between them. Todd tossed the Frisbee to her and she caught it.

"Good for you."

Kate walked to where Jonas stood, smiled into his shiny eyes. The health that had reddened his cheeks had also returned her joy. She wondered what occurred at the motel, but Todd seemed in full control. "Jonas, it's time for quiet play."

Todd glanced at his sister. "Trevor and I'll pick up some sandwiches while you rest." Trevor ambled to the car, slid into the driver's seat so Todd could concentrate on talking and they drove off.

Kate took out a puzzle and some books. She gave Jonas and Amanda a glass of juice and read to them while Dave retreated with his briefcase. Later, Dave stuck his head into the bedroom. "Your dad called. They're ready to go to the lab anytime." As he spoke, Todd entered the front door with lunch.

After lunch, Dave and the kids rode with Todd and Trevor. Kevin followed in the rental with Kate, who sat in its back seat observing her mother, who was quiet as they drove. Yet, her father chatted about the passing scenery, rolling down the window and pointing beyond the grassy knolls to the spruce forests through which he saw glimpses of the sea. Todd and Trevor drove around the bluff giving the family a tour of their research lab. They showed footage of seals and sea lions, which delighted the kids.

Twilight shadows had stretched across the grass before Todd and Trevor dragged themselves indoors with Jonas and Amanda. After they discarded the Frisbee, the children crawled into their sleeping bags. Kate closed the bedroom door when she felt convinced they were asleep.

The adults recounted the rugged beauty that is Alaska, and their pleasure in seeing Jonas well. Dave looked at Todd. "While you were outside entertaining our kids, Dad told Kate and me about Stephen. I assume you've talked with Trevor." He saw on Todd's face an anguished wave of affirmation. Dave turned to Kevin. "Were the others caught?"

Kevin folded his hands and stared at the carpet. "You may as well hear it all." He looked up aware that all eyes were on him. "When the M.P.'s, the military police, saw the quantity of blood spilled on the pavement, they went from barracks to barracks for a surprise inspection, checking each man's shoes for traces of blood. By morning, they had one soldier in custody and by the end of the day, he identified Steve and another man who had participated. Those two were charged with murder and convicted, although one on a lesser charge because he supplied the information to convict the other."

"Horrible experience for you." Trevor touched his swollen eye.

"What really hurt was that one of the medics attached to our company was involved. He was a slight, short man from the Deep South, always smiling and full of jokes. His grandmother sent him a care package at least once a month that he would bring to the sick bay to open. He always shared that treasure–trove of goodies with me until the last crumb. Especially the bourbon balls." Kevin stopped talking, his face contorted. "He was arrested first and charged with the murder. Steve and another man were with him. We learned later at the trial that they jumped Hank solely because he was gay."

"Not racial," Kate said.

Kevin shook his head. "No. Three whites killed a white. Homophobic I'd say."

"How did they know Hank was gay?" Trevor glanced at Todd, stretching his arms to relieve tension.

"One guy said Hank looked at him too long in the shower. Maybe someone saw Hank on liberty. Could have been anything." Kevin closed his eyes and was silent.

"Doesn't matter, it happened. Hard to share such experiences. I don't think Todd has told you that my brother and I lost our parents in a train wreck. Mom's sister, Anna, had to identify their bodies and she still can barely talk about it."

Kevin's eyes moved to Charlotte and back to Trevor. "No, Todd didn't tell us. You were young?"

"Ten, but my aunt took us in. We survived and so have you."

"Want something to drink, anyone?" Todd moved to his feet. Kate jumped up too and went for the kitchen. When she returned she had a tray of soft drinks, which she offered everyone.

Opening his, Kevin took a long drink and paused. "I want you to know one thing." The room quieted. "This sexual orientation stuff is a problem for me. I don't understand it, but I'm willing to work at changing my outlook."

"Bravo, Dad." Kate clapped, hoping to lighten things up. Todd combed his fingers through his hair. He left unsaid what he was thinking—that gays had made historical contributions to society, their presence was nothing new. Since the *stuff* was a problem for his dad, Todd appreciated that he had moved beyond his comfort zone and he smiled his genuine gratitude.

Trev helped too. "Thanks for your efforts. My brother Frank knows a man whose mother died before he had told her he was gay. Sad. Jim Baxter's his name. I think he might have worked for you as an inspector." Across the room, Dave watched Kate's face fall. Then he felt Kevin's eyes on him and waited for his response.

"Indeed he did work for me. I remember the day when Dave suggested I was a bigot." Kevin creased his brows. "Because I expressed my bigotry regarding Jim. Of course I'm a new man now." He paused, and then the slightest grin crept across his jaw. Dave burst into laughter, his wariness abated and everyone else joined in.

Kevin eyed Todd. "No more soul baring. Jonas shows a real skill with the Frisbee. You taught him well." Todd returned a half–smile.

Kate witnessed the softening in her father's face. "You helped a lot pitching the softball to him," she said. "Bringing his mitt to the hospital might be what woke him up." Kevin drew an expansive breath and smiled at the carpet.

Kate felt Charlotte stir, sensed appreciation in her face. She watched her mother's shoulders relax against the back of the chair. They knew that Kevin had shown his courage today. They all had.

When they had returned to their motel and were lying in bed, Charlotte laid her head on Kevin's chest. In the lamplight, she trailed her finger across his torso. "I love you."

His jaw widened into a smile. "Changing is arduous for me, but at least I've started talking about the possibility. All these years I felt I knew the final word on homosexuality. I guess God is still speaking."

"Do you think Steve intentionally killed Hank?"

"No. He must have lost control."

"When did you last see him?" Charlotte wrapped her body around Kevin.

Kevin lay motionless, felt the warm comfort of Charlotte's flesh. "A few nights after the attack Steve called me at the barracks. He said he was in deep trouble and needed money fast. I told him he was stupid and better turn himself in. 'I need help, not a lecture,' he said. So I met him and gave him two hundred twelve bucks I was able to scrape together. Somehow he used the cash to get away."

"He left Okinawa?"

"Don't know how or where. I never heard from him again." They lay silent a few minutes. "Think the kids will be patient while I grow up?"

"They better. Growing up takes a lifetime." A hush enveloped them.

The next morning Charlotte and Kevin packed for the family's afternoon flight. They arrived at Todd's house for breakfast. Kate and Trevor prepared French toast with warm maple syrup while Todd exercised. After Todd had returned, showered, and changed, his father tapped on his bedroom door. "I cleaned out the garage not long ago," Kevin said, "found something of yours." He held the catcher's mitt out to his son.

"I remember this, never used it much, did I."

"No, but you know someone who might like it."

Todd nodded. "Thanks. Let's eat breakfast."

# Chapter 42

A few months later Todd stepped from his lab into the sunshine. He walked, flexing his arms until his muscles felt limber. He'd kept busy researching and recording data on the stellar sea lions, with no time left for much else. A week ago he and a team member had rescued a pup entangled in a net, and returned it to its nursing mother.

The wind that whipped his hair and face felt forceful but pleasant. The bay waters lashed the shore. His father had e-mailed that morning about his official retirement. His engineering firm had scheduled a dinner in his honor next week. Todd pulled the invitation from his pocket, smiled at its informality. Kevin had felt compelled to mention that the inspector, Jim Baxter, was included in the guest list. Neither he nor Trevor could get away, but it was good to be invited. He felt no urgency to go to his father's retirement party, but gratification that he is welcomed. He promised Kate and his mother that he and Trevor would come for Thanksgiving. By then, Amanda would have kindergarten stories to tell and with the luck of a dry day, Jonas could show him the tree house.

He edged upward along the bluff, inhaled the taste of salty air while his eyes followed an eagle that soared from a gray snag in the rocky cliff. It dipped toward its prey in the surf below. He kept his focus on the bird. In a minute, he saw a fleshy salmon dangling in the eagle's talons.

Todd circled back toward the lab, feeling sustained within. His chest expanded with each breath, filling him with a sense of his own significance, insight into his father's history. Old ideas, obstacles that once blocked their affection, were giving way to new beginnings. A healing sensation blew through him like a creative insistent wind, baptizing him with freshness wholly unknown.

Charlotte clicked the camera shutter, once, twice, as Jonas climbed the maple tree with Kevin behind him, hands ready, feet steady. From the tree house they smiled and waved at the lens. Click. Amanda shouted from the sidewalk as she honked the horn on her trike. "Look at me Grandma, look at me." Charlotte spun around and clicked the shutter in Amanda's blue eyes, which shone from her not so plump face; her arms and legs had lengthened too, marking her growth into girlhood.

Charlotte sauntered to the mailbox, felt the warmth of the September sun against her skin. She opened a lab report from her doctor, studied the page that read her mammogram was normal. Her blood tests likewise were cancer free. Though expected, she savored the news, just as she cherished in Kevin each effort to accept Todd. She knew change required work after the intent of the heart was set. Kevin had struggled for years, as she had, in making a place for Todd as he is. She remembered Todd and Trevor's promise to come for Thanksgiving, though they hadn't attended Kevin's retirement dinner. An easy rapport in which the children didn't feel obligated felt comfortable. She skimmed her fingers through her hair as she stepped up onto her walk. A car pulled up behind her in the driveway.

"Hello, golden girl," Kate said from behind the steering wheel.

"Charlotte fluffed her hair again. "Yes. Blond till I can't use my hands or get to my hairdresser." She smiled over her shoulder.

"Has he been behaving?"

"Kevin or Jonas?" Charlotte laughed and opened the door of the now parked car. "I think they're planning an expansion."

"Without consulting Dave?" Kate's eyes followed Charlotte's to the tree house.

"Hi Mom." Jonas waved at Kate's upturned face.

Kate slipped her arm around her mother's shoulders. She eyed the envelope in her hands. "What's the clinic report?"

"Everything looks great. Come inside before you go home."

"I will. I have something to tell you." Kate watched Charlotte turn on the stove from habit. "I had an e-mail from Todd last night. He's socializing in Kodiak. Said he sometimes plays the piano at informal gatherings."

"Really. He attends a club?" Charlotte set the filled teakettle on the stove.

"A church. He likes the pastor, the people welcome him, and he feels comfortable."

"Interesting."

"He and Trevor are checking out the real estate too. They need more room. I think they're ready to buy a house."

"Who's ready to buy a house?" Kevin said, as he walked in with Jonas. He pulled out a chair at the kitchen table and sat down.

"Todd and Trevor might." Charlotte looked at Kevin for a moment before her eyes sparked. "I have the best idea. Come with me." They followed her into the sewing room. "This has sat here silent long enough. If Todd and Trevor find a place with enough room, let's ship it to him as a house warming gift."

Kevin laughed. "Slow down, Charlotte. We'll make that decision when the time comes, but I doubt Todd still plays the piano."

"Wrong. Kate tells me he plays at a church in Kodiak sometimes, just for fun." A whistling sound filled the air. "Time for tea."

Charlotte walked to the kitchen. Through the window, she could see Florence's now rented house. Weeds had crept into the flowerbeds where she no longer puttered. Debbie came twice a month, but it wasn't enough. It takes vigilance, Charlotte thought, and Florence's words rooted deeper into her mind. "*Love helps.*" She brewed the tea and poured milk into glasses for the children. Kevin and Kate returned to the kitchen with Jonas just as Amanda rushed through the door. They sat in chairs around the kitchen table. "So Todd still plays." Kevin smiled at his wife. "Good."